# ROBINSON CRUSOE

*Illustrated by* EDWARD A. WILSON

POOR CRUSOE

The Life & Strange
Surprising Adventures of
ROBINSON
CRUSOE
OF YORK, MARINER
by Daniel Defoe
With an Introduction by
J. CUTHBERT HADDEN
and Illustrations by
EDWARD A. WILSON
• • •
THE HERITAGE PRESS
New York

# The Making of "Robinson Crusoe"

### BY J. CUTHBERT HADDEN

I n connection with the famous wars of the Spanish Succession, several English merchants had entered into a scheme for a privateering expedition to the South Seas. One of the vessels, the *St. George,* was commanded by William Dampier, who had already distinguished himself in various naval enterprises of that lively, cutthroat age. Filled with magnificent designs of capturing gold-laden ships, Dampier sailed from the Downs in the April of 1703, and a few weeks later was joined, somewhere on the Irish coast, by a vessel called the *Cinque Ports,* of which Alexander Selkirk had somehow or other been appointed "sailing-master." An exciting story could be told of the fortunes—and misfortunes—of the buccaneering crews; but the only point worth noting here is that "honest Alexander Selkirk," as one old chronicler calls him, fell out with his captain, and an "irreconcilable difference" was the sequel. By this time the *Cinque Ports* had been well riddled with shot, the result of more than one "engagement" on the high seas; and Selkirk, putting the "difference" and the danger of getting drowned together, determined to leave the vessel on the first opportunity. The opportunity came, somewhere about the end of August or the beginning of September, 1704, when anchor was cast off Juan Fernandez. Apparently Selkirk made no secret of his intention to desert the ship, for his effects were landed just as if he had been a passenger bound for the island. In telling the story afterward, he remarked that he went ashore under the full conviction that the prospective change of life would be "more eligible than being exposed to further dangers" with a captain who had "used him so ill." But he had miscalculated the strength of his resolution. The moment he saw the vessel putting off, "his heart yearned within him and melted at parting with his comrades and all human society at once." In short, his courage utterly failed. He made signs of entreaty to be taken on board again; but the captain had construed his conduct as mutiny, and exile was to be the punishment of his defection. The *Cinque Ports* vanished from the sight of her old sailing-master, and in a few weeks her captain and crew, to avoid a watery grave, had surrendered themselves prisoners to the Spaniards. Meantime Selkirk was making the best of his solitude.

Such, in brief, is the incident to which the world owes the existence of *Robinson Crusoe.* It is truth, there had already been an exile on Juan Fernandez. Dampier had made a call at the island in 1681, when, by some unexplained accident, one of his seamen, a Mosquito Indian, was left behind. This predecessor of the real Crusoe remained in company with the goats until 1684, living pretty much the life that Selkirk afterward lived. But the Indian failed to find his Defoe, and his exile, in consequence, went for nothing. What Selkirk in reality did with and for himself during the four years and four months of his imprisonment may be taken for granted. The story, if he had himself written it out, could hardly have been prosaic; but Defoe having employed his "lively fancy" on it, there is no need to deal with the naked details, supposing these were available, which they are not. One or two points, however, may be noted, and for these we must look to the account given by Crusoe's deliverer. It is a curious circumstance that, as Dampier was indirectly the cause of Selkirk's exile, so he was also the means of his rescue. Dampier had not been very successful in the exploits with which Selkirk was at first connected; but the succession wars still continued, and in 1708 he managed to prevail on some Bristol merchants to fit out a couple of vessels for the usual cruising business in the South Seas. The command of one of the vessels, the *Duke,* was given to a certain Woodes Rogers, and this "master mariner," fortunately, had the forethought to keep a journal of the voyage. It is the earliest account we have of Selkirk's exile, and is therefore worthy of special attention.

It seems that when he was left on the island he had only some clothes and bedding, a firelock, some powder, bullets, and tobacco, a hatchet, a knife, a kettle, a Bible, and his mathematical instruments and books. He diverted, and provided for, himself as well as he could, but for the first eight months had "much ado to bear up against melancholy." He built two huts with trees, covered them with long grass, and lined them with the skins of goats. In the smaller hut he cooked his food; in the larger he slept and employed himself in reading, singing psalms, and praying, "so that he said he was a better Christian while in his solitude than ever he was before, or than he was afraid he should ever be again." At first he never ate till hunger compelled him, nor did he go to bed till he was quite tired out with watching. For his food he relied chiefly on the goats, of which he killed about five hundred, from first to last. He told Rogers that he caught as many more, which he marked on the ear and liberated; and it is interesting to note that Commodore Anson found several animals thus marked when he touched at the island some years later. After his powder gave out, Selkirk took his game by speed of foot. Rogers had a bulldog, which he sent with several of his nimblest runners to assist him in capturing the goats; but he "distanced and tired both the dog and men, catched the goats, and brought 'em to us on his back." His feet were so hard with this racing through the woods that for a long time after his rescue he could not wear boots. For clothing he made himself a coat and cap of goatskins, which he stitched together with a nail. He had his last shirt on his back when found. Rogers says that when he first came on board he had "so much forgot his language, for want of use, that we could scarce understand him, for he seemed to speak his words by halves." Nay, more curious still, "we offered him a dram, but he would not touch it, having drank nothing but water since his being there, and 't was some time before he could relish our victuals."

Selkirk's experiences on the way back to civilization were very much what they had been on the way to solitude. He took a leading part in the undisguised robbery which was the object of Rogers' expedition; and when at length he landed in London, in 1711, he was able to boast of some eight hundred pounds as his share of the spoil. His story seems to have made the proverbial nine days' wonder. Steele, who met him and drew from him an account of his experiences, which he published in *The Englishman,* speaks of him as being quite "familiar to men of curiosity." His aspects and gestures, according to Addison's friend, showed that he had been "much separated from company"; there was "a strong but cheerful seriousness in his look, and a certain disregard to the ordinary things about

him, as if he had been sunk in thought." Steele says he did not regard his return to company with unmixed delight, and quotes him as remarking that, though he was now worth eight hundred pounds, he would never be so happy as when he was not worth a farthing. Perhaps the "men of curiosity" were to blame in asking him to tell his story too frequently. Steele had found him very friendly and communicable; but some one else who tried him, not long after, reported him to be "an unsociable, odd kind of man," far from being so free as Steele would have led one to believe.

In course of time Selkirk, naturally enough, made his way to his native town, Largo, in Scotland. He seems to have given his people no warning of his arrival in England; at any rate, when he appeared in Largo kirk, one Sunday forenoon in 1712, nobody knew him. To be sure, he was clad in "gold-laced clothes," but that would only excite the greater attention. At length the mother's keen instincts detected her bairn, and with a cry of recognition she rushed to Sandy's arms! Then, it is said, the Selkirk pew was cleared out, and the family went home.

What happened to Selkirk after this is not very clear. Largo, sluggish and sleepy as it must then have been, could hardly be so dull as Juan Fernandez; yet there is some reason for believing that Selkirk found it too lively for his taste. He erected a sort of cave dwelling in his father's back garden, and when he was not "meditating" there, he was in the woods or walking moodily by the shore. People evidently fought shy of him, as of some uncanny creature who had been in league with Satan's invisible world. The parish minister of the town, writing in 1798, refers to an old Largo man who remembered having, when a boy, slept with him for one night after his return. He could not be persuaded to do it a second time, being "terrified at the uncommon whiteness of his linen and the hairiness of his body." Imagination truly *does* go a long way! To the unmarried females of Largo, Selkirk had, however, a romantic side; and one fine day it was discovered that the eccentric exile had eloped with one Sophia Bruce, who had succumbed to the charm of the white linen and the interests of the island story. Why there should have been an elopement it would have been difficult to make out, had it not afterward appeared that the union was of that sailor type not likely to be sanctioned by the rigid rules of Largo kirk. The pair were traced to London, where Sophia was presently found alone, Selkirk having gone back to sea. Before he thus dared the "perrills" of the deep, he made a will in her favor—this was in January, 1717—in which he describes her as his "loving friend, Sophia Bruce, of the Pall Mall, London, spinster," and bequeaths her a house at Largo, which had come to him from his father. But the sailor's affections are notoriously unstable, and poor Sophia, being out of sight, was soon out of mind. Before

1720 Selkirk had yielded to the blandishments of a certain widow named Frances Candis, and the old will was revoked. At this time the worthy seaman, as we learn from the will, was "mate of His Majesty's ship *Weymouth*." That is practically the last we hear of him, for he died on board the vessel before December of the following year.

Thus ends the authentic history of Alexander Selkirk. He left no children, but representatives of the family from which he sprang are still to be found in his native town. Mr. David Gillies, whose mother was a great-grandniece of Selkirk, has commemorated him in a statue which, since its unveiling by the Countess of Aberdeen in 1885, has made the leading feature of Largo for every visitor to the place. If you ask a native where any one lives, the position will almost certainly be indicated from a reference to "the statue." Nor is there any difficulty in identifying the statue, for the sculptor has dressed his Crusoe in the very garb with which necessity first and Defoe afterward adorned him. And there are other interesting memorials of Defoe's hero to be seen in Largo besides the statue. That elopement of which we have heard led to a good many personal effects being left behind, and such of them as were associated with Selkirk's island existence have naturally been guarded as interesting heirlooms by all his descendants. There is the gun, there is the chest, and there is the drinking-cup. The chest, a clumsy-looking affair made of cedarwood, bears the exile's initials on the lid, with certain other rude carvings—the practical result, no doubt, of hours of ennui on the island. The drinking-cup was made by Selkirk himself out of a cocoanut-shell. Such are some of the Selkirk relics still to be seen in Scotland. And Juan Fernandez has its memorial, too. Two thousand feet above the sea-level, on the height which Selkirk called his "Lookout," a handsome tablet commemorates him in the following inscription:

*In memory of* ALEXANDER SELKIRK, *mariner, a native of Largo, in the county of Fife, Scotland, who lived on this island in complete solitude for four years and four months. He was landed from the* Cinque Ports *galley, 96 tons, 18 guns, A. D. 1704, and was taken off in the* Duke, *privateer, 12th February, 1709. He died Lieutenant of H. M. S.* Weymouth, *A. D. 1721, aged 47. This tablet is erected near Selkirk's lookout, by Commodore Powell and the officers of H. M. S.* Topaze, *A. D. 1868.*

Thus, while Defoe himself remains undistinguished by statue or mark of public favor of any kind, the humble hero whose fame he created is memorialized in two widely separated corners of the globe.

Whether Defoe ever met Selkirk is a question that has been much discussed. There is an absurd story to the effect that Selkirk put together a rough account of his adventures, and gave the manuscript to Defoe to "improve the style." According to this legend, Defoe, discovering the elements of a stirring tale in the sailor's notes, set his "lively fancy" to work, and when *Robinson Crusoe* was completed, "returned Selkirk his papers, telling him his history would not sell." Isaac James, in his rambling account of Selkirk's adventures, published at Bristol in 1800, professes to believe this very circumstantial tale, and quotes a Shrewsbury clergyman who in 1777 told him he had "heard upon good authority that when Defoe was on his death-bed nothing seemed to lie with such weight upon his mind as this unjust transaction with Selkirk." Dr. Beattie, the author of *The Minstrel,* felt perfectly certain that Defoe got his materials direct from Selkirk, but was willing to believe that Defoe shared the profits of his great romance with "the poor seaman." The whole thing is a myth. *Robinson Crusoe* was not published until 1719, at which time, as we have seen, Selkirk's story had been common property for seven years. Captain Rogers told it, in 1712, in his *Cruising Voyage round the World;* in the same year Captain Cook printed it in his *Voyage to the South Sea;* and Steele filled the entire number of his *Englishman* with an account of the exile's adventures. There was no need that Defoe should take advantage of Selkirk; and although, of course, it is possible enough that he had interviews with him (it is obvious that he refers to Selkirk, in the preface, when he

ix

speaks of "a man alive, and well known, too"), there is no reason why he should not have produced *Robinson Crusoe* as it stands without ever having once seen or communicated with the old buccaneer. Defoe knew how to turn the interests of the public to his own advantage; and the interests of the public at this time were centered mainly on the exploits of famous pirates, and the chances of adventurers in far-away islands on the American and African coasts. Defoe saw in Selkirk's story a ready means of satisfying the prevailing demand, and taking the story as he found it in print, aided, it might be, by additional details furnished by Selkirk himself, he built up that wonderful romance which has ever since been regarded as the best thing of its kind in all literature. It is a pleasing fancy, no doubt, which pictures Selkirk writing out his adventures to be edited by Daniel Defoe of unenviable notoriety, but, like many more fancies, it is without foundation in fact.

While the success of *Robinson Crusoe* with the public was immediate, there is some reason to think that as a manuscript its merits were not so readily recognized. One of Defoe's earlier biographers says, indeed, that the story passed through the whole circle of the publishing trade before it found a purchaser. This is probably an exaggeration, for Defoe was too well known as a writer (he was now close on sixty) to have anything from his pen going a-begging at every book-

seller's door. Be that as it may, it is certain that the man who did venture made a very fine thing out of the enterprise. His name was Taylor, and he published, appropriately enough in this case, "at the Ship" in Paternoster Row. What he paid to Defoe has never been ascertained, but the profits of *Crusoe* accruing to himself may be estimated from the fact that, while he was a comparatively poor man when he published the book, he was reported to be "worth between forty and fifty thousand" at his death, five years later. There is no ground for believing that he ever asked Defoe to share the spoil with him, though Beattie was simple-minded enough to give him credit for such an unnecessary piece of generosity.

The original edition of *Crusoe* was in two volumes, with a third volume, which nobody has ever read, for sequel. The first volume was published on April 25, 1719, and the second followed close upon its heels. The demand was so instantaneous that a second edition—and "editions" were genuine at that time—was published only seventeen days after the first, a third edition followed twenty-five days later, and a fourth on the 8th of August. And today, with all our accumulations of books, there is still no work that is more generally read or more universally admired than this same *Robinson Crusoe*. As Johnson remarked, nobody ever laid it down without wishing it longer.

J. CUTHBERT HADDEN

# ROBINSON CRUSOE

*Illustrated by* EDWARD A. WILSON

# A Note upon the Text

THE reader of this edition will find that it contains the story as Daniel Defoe wrote it; for it follows the text as William Taylor published it, at *The Sign of the Ship* in Paternoster Row, London, on 25 April 1719. In this edition of *Robinson Crusoe* the text of the original has been carefully followed, and no attempt has been made to polish the strong unstudied diction of the author, or to improve on his homely vigorous language. In only a few instances, and those very few and unimportant, has the original text been departed from: namely, where there occur in that text (in five or six places) evident misprints, or sentences uncorrected by the author and standing meaningless or contradictory till the obvious corrections were made; and also where, in as few instances, names of places were so misspelt as to present a geographical difficulty. In the edition distributed to the members of The Limited Editions Club in 1930 (for which edition Mr. Wilson's charming illustrations were created) all of Mr. Defoe's blunders and errors were faithfully followed, including his sometimes weird syntax and spelling: the possessors of copies of that edition have a bibliographic rarity. This Heritage edition, however, is planned for ease of reading: especially by children—especially by the kind of children who will enjoy the strong flavor of Defoe's story as Defoe wrote it, in preference to the flavorless editions prepared by "children's editors." So the story as it first appeared in 1719 is reproduced here, complete.

# THE LIFE & ADVENTURES OF
# *ROBINSON CRUSOE*
## OF YORK, *MARINER*

§ *My birth and parentage. Early education. Desire to go to sea. My father's wise counsel and warnings. A mother's displeasure. I leave home. Sail from Hull to London. A great storm. My fear and repentance drowned in punch. The storm renewed. The ship springs a leak and founders. The crew saved, reach Yarmouth. Another warning despised. I travel to London.*

I WAS born in the year 1632, in the city of York, of a good family, though not of that country, my father being a foreigner of Bremen, who settled first at Hull: he got a good estate by merchandise, and, leaving off his trade, lived afterwards at York, from whence he had married my mother, whose relations were named Robinson, a very good family in that country, and from whom I was called Robinson Kreutznaer; but, by the usual corruption of words in England, we are now called, nay, we call ourselves, and write our name Crusoe, and so my companions always called me.

I had two elder brothers, one of which was lieutenant-colonel to an English regiment of foot in Flanders, formerly commanded by the famous Colonel Lockhart, and was killed at the battle near Dunkirk against the Spaniards: what became of my second brother I never knew, any more than my father or mother did know what was become of me.

Being the third son of the family, and not bred to any trade, my head began to be filled very early with rambling thoughts. My father, who was very ancient, had given me a competent share of learning, as far as house education and a country free school generally goes, and designed me for the law; but I would be satisfied with nothing but

I

going to sea, and my inclination to this led me so strongly against the will, nay, the commands of my father, and against all the entreaties and persuasions of my mother and other friends, that there seemed to be something fatal in that propension of nature tending directly to the life of misery which was to befall me.

My father, a wise and grave man, gave me serious and excellent counsel against what he foresaw was my design. He called me one morning into his chamber, where he was confined by the gout, and expostulated very warmly with me upon this subject. He asked me what reasons more than a mere wandering inclination I had for leaving my father's house and my native country, where I might be well introduced, and had a prospect of raising my fortune by application and industry, with a life of ease and pleasure. He told me it was for men of desperate fortunes on one hand, or of aspiring, superior fortunes on the other, who went abroad upon adventures, to rise by enterprise, and make themselves famous in undertakings of a nature out of the common road; that these things were all either too far above me, or too far below me; that mine was the middle state, or what might be called the upper station of low life, which he had found by long experience was the best state in the world, the most suited to human happiness, not exposed to the miseries and hardships, the labour and sufferings of the mechanic part of mankind, and not embarrassed with the pride, luxury, ambition, and envy of the upper part of mankind. He told me I might judge of the happiness of this state by this one thing—namely, that this was the state of life which all other people envied; that kings have frequently lamented the miserable consequences of being born to great things, and wish they had been placed in the middle of the two extremes,—between the mean and the great; that the wise man gave his testimony to this as the just standard of true felicity, when he prayed to have neither poverty nor riches.

He bid me observe it, and I should always find, that the calamities of life were shared among the upper and lower part of mankind; but that the middle station had the fewest disasters, and was not exposed to so many vicissitudes as the higher or lower part of mankind; nay, they were not subjected to so many distempers and uneasinesses either of body or mind, as those were who, by vicious living, luxury, and extravagances on one hand, or by hard labour, want of necessaries, and mean or insufficient diet on the other hand, bring distempers upon themselves by the natural consequences of their way of living; that the middle station of life was calculated for all kind of virtues and all kind of enjoyments; that peace and plenty were the handmaids of a middle fortune; that temperance, moderation, quietness, health, society, all agreeable diversions, and all desirable pleasures, were the blessings attending the middle station of life; that this way men went silently and smoothly through the world, and comfortably out of it, not embarrassed with the labours of the hands or of the head, not sold to the life of slavery for daily bread, or harassed with perplexed circumstances, which rob the soul of peace and the body of rest; not engaged with the passion of envy, or secret burning lust of ambition for great things; but in easy circumstances sliding gently through the world, and sensibly tasting the sweets of living, without the bitter; feeling that they are happy, and learning by every day's experience to know it more sensibly.

After this, he pressed me earnestly, and in the most affectionate manner, not to play the young man, not to precipitate myself into miseries which nature and the station of life I was born in seemed to have provided against; that I was under no necessity of seeking my bread; that he would do well for me, and endeavour to enter me fairly into the station of life which he had been just recommending to me; and that if I was not very easy and happy in the world, it must be my mere fate or fault that must hinder it, and that he should have nothing to answer for, having thus discharged his duty in warning me against measures which he knew would be to my hurt. In a word, that as he would do very kind things for me if I would stay and settle at home, as he directed, so he would not have so much hand in my misfortunes, as to give me any encouragement to go away. And, to close all, he told me I had my elder brother for an example, to whom he had used the same earnest persuasions to keep him from going into the Low Country wars, but could not prevail, his young desires prompting him to run into the army, where he was killed; and though, he said, he would not cease to pray for me, yet he would venture to say to me that, if I did take this foolish step, God would not bless me, and I would have leisure hereafter to reflect upon having neglected his counsel when there might be none to assist in my recovery.

I observed in this last part of his discourse, which was truly prophetic, though I suppose my father did not know it to be so himself, I say I observed the tears run down his face very plentifully, and especially when he spoke of my brother who was killed; and that when he spoke of my having leisure to repent, and none to assist me, he was so moved that he broke off the discourse, and told me his heart was so full he could say no more to me.

I was sincerely affected with this discourse—as indeed who could be otherwise?—and I resolved not to think of going abroad any more, but to settle at home according to my father's desire. But, alas! a few days wore it all off; and, in short, to prevent any of my father's further importunities, in a few weeks after I resolved to run quite away from him. However, I did not act so hastily neither as my first heat of resolution prompted; but I took my mother, at a time when I thought her a little pleasanter than ordinary, and told her that my thoughts were so entirely bent upon seeing the world, that I should never settle to anything with resolution enough to go through with it, and my father had better give me his consent than force me to go without it; that I was now eighteen years old, which was too late to go apprentice to a trade, or clerk to an attorney; that I was sure if I did, I should never serve out my time, and I should certainly run away from my master before my time was out, and go to sea; and if she would speak to my father to let me go one voyage abroad, if I came home again and did not like it, I would go no more, and I would promise by a double diligence to recover that time I had lost.

This put my mother into a great passion. She told me she knew it would be to no purpose to speak to my father upon any such subject; that he knew too well what was my interest to give his consent to any such thing so much for my hurt, and that she wondered how I could think of any such thing, after such a discourse as I had had with my father, and such kind and tender expressions as she knew my father had used to me; and that, in short, if I would ruin myself, there was no help for me; but I might depend I should never have their consent to it. That, for her part, she would not have so much hand in my destruction; and I should never have it to say that my mother was willing when my father was not.

Though my mother refused to move it to my father, yet, as I have heard afterwards, she reported all the discourse to him, and that my father, after showing a great concern at it, said to her with a sigh—"That boy might be happy if he would stay at home; but if he goes abroad he will be the most miserable wretch that was ever born. I can give no consent to it."

It was not till almost a year after this that I broke loose, though in the meantime I continued obstinately deaf to all proposals of settling to business, and frequently expostulating with my father and mother about their being so positively determined against what they knew my inclinations prompted me to. But being one day at Hull, where I went casually, and without any purpose of making an elopement that time; but, I say, being there, and one of my companions being going to sea to London in his father's ship, and prompting me to go with them, with the common allurement of seafaring men—namely, that it should cost me nothing for my passage—I consulted neither father nor mother any more, nor so much as sent them word of it; but, leaving them to hear of it as they might, without asking God's blessing, or my father's; without any consideration of circumstances or consequences, and in an ill hour, God knows, on the 1st of September, 1651, I went on board a ship bound for London. Never any young adventurer's misfortunes, I believe, began sooner, or continued longer than mine. The ship was no sooner gotten out of the Humber but the wind began to blow, and the waves to rise in a most frightful manner; and, as I had never been at sea before, I was most inexpressibly sick in body, and terrified in my mind. I began now seriously to reflect upon what I had done, and how justly I was overtaken by the judgment of Heaven for my wicked leaving my father's house, and abandoning my duty; all the good counsel of my parents, my father's tears and my mother's entreaties, came now fresh into my mind; and my conscience, which was not yet come to the pitch of hardness to which it has been since, reproached me with the contempt of advice, and the breach of my duty to God and my father.

All this while the storm increased, and the sea, which I had never been upon before, went very high, though nothing like what I have seen many times since; no, nor like what I saw a few days after. But it was enough to affect me then, who was but a young sailor and had never known anything of the matter. I expected every wave would have swallowed us up, and that every time the ship fell down, as I thought, in the trough or hollow of the sea, we should never rise more; and in this agony of mind I made many vows and resolutions, that if it would please God here to spare my life this one voyage, if ever I got once my foot upon dry land again, I would go directly home to my father, and never set it into a ship again while I lived; that I would take his advice, and never run myself into such miseries as these any more. Now I saw plainly the goodness of his observations about the middle station of life; how easy, how comfortably he had lived all his days, and never had been exposed to tempests at sea, or troubles on shore; and I resolved that I would, like a true repenting prodigal, go home to my father.

These wise and sober thoughts continued all the while the storm continued, and indeed some time after; but the next day the wind was abated and the sea calmer, and I began to be a little inured to it. However, I was very grave for all that day, being also a little sea-sick still; but towards night the weather cleared up, the wind was quite over, and a charming fine evening followed; the sun went down perfectly clear, and rose so the next morning; and having little or no wind, and a smooth sea, the sun shining upon it, the sight was, as I thought, the most delightful that ever I saw.

I had slept well in the night, and was now no more sea-sick but very cheerful, looking with wonder upon the sea that was so rough and terrible the day before, and could be so calm and so pleasant in so little time after. And now, lest my good resolutions should continue, my companion, who had indeed enticed me away, comes to me— "Well, Bob," says he, clapping me on the shoulder, "how do you do after it? I warrant you were frighted, wa'n't you, last night, when it blew but a capful of wind?"—"A capful, d'you call it?" said I; " 'twas a terrible storm."—"A storm, you fool you!" replies he; "do you call that a storm? Why, it was nothing at all! Give us but a good ship and sea-room, and we think nothing of such a squall of wind as that. But you're but a fresh-water sailor, Bob. Come, let us make a bowl of punch, and we'll forget all that. D'ye see what charming weather 'tis now?" To make short this sad part of my story, we went the old way of all sailors. The punch was made, and I was made drunk with it. And in that one night's wickedness I drowned all my repentance, all my reflections upon my past conduct, and all my resolutions for my future. In a word, as the sea was returned to its smoothness of surface and settled calmness by the abatement of that storm, so—the hurry of my thoughts being over, my fears and apprehensions of being swallowed up by the sea being forgotten, and the current of my former desires returned—I entirely forgot the vows and promises that I made in my distress. I found, indeed, some intervals of reflection, and the serious thoughts did, as it were, endeavour to return again sometimes; but I shook them off, and roused myself from them as it were from a distemper, and applying myself to drinking and company, soon mastered the return of those fits—for so I called them—and I had in five or six days got as complete a victory over conscience as any young fellow, that resolved not to be troubled with it, could desire. But I was to have another trial for it still; and Providence, as in such cases generally it does, resolved to leave me entirely without excuse. For if I would not take this for a deliverance, the next was to be such a one as the worst and most hardened wretch among us would confess both the danger and the mercy.

The sixth day of our being at sea we came into Yarmouth Roads; the wind having been contrary and the weather calm, we had made but little way since the storm. Here we were obliged to come to an anchor, and here we lay, the wind continuing contrary—namely, at south-west—for seven or eight days, during which time a great many ships from Newcastle came into the same roads, as the common harbour where the ships might wait for a wind for the river.

We had not, however, rid here so long, but we should have tided it up the river, but that the wind blew too fresh; and after we had lain four or five days, blew very hard. However, the roads being reckoned as good as a harbour, the anchorage good, and our ground-tackle very strong, our men were unconcerned, and not in the least apprehensive of danger, but spent the time in rest and mirth, after the manner of the sea; but the eighth day, in the morning, the wind increased, and we had all hands at work to strike our top-masts, and make everything snug and close, that the ship might ride as easy as possible. By noon the sea went very high indeed, and our ship rid forecastle in, shipped several seas, and we thought once or twice our anchor had come home, upon which our master ordered out the sheet-anchor; so that we rode with two anchors ahead, and the cables veered out to the better end.

By this time it blew a terrible storm indeed, and now I began to

8

see terror and amazement in the faces even of the seamen themselves. The master, though vigilant in the business of preserving the ship, yet, as he went in and out of his cabin by me, I could hear him softly to himself say several times, "Lord, be merciful to us; we shall be all lost, we shall be all undone," and the like. During these first hurries I was stupid, lying still in my cabin, which was in the steerage, and cannot describe my temper. I could ill reassume the first penitence, which I had so apparently trampled upon and hardened myself against. I thought the bitterness of death had been past, and that this would be nothing, too, like the first. But when the master himself came by me, as I said just now, and said we should be all lost, I was dreadfully frighted. I got up out of my cabin and looked out; but such a dismal sight I never saw. The sea went mountains high, and broke upon us every three or four minutes. When I could look about, I could see nothing but distress round us. Two ships that rid near us we found had cut their masts by the board, being deep laden; and our men cried out that a ship which rid about a mile ahead of us was foundered. Two more ships, being driven from their anchors, were run out of the roads to sea at all adventures, and that with not a mast standing. The light ships fared the best, as not so much labouring in the sea; but two or three of them drove, and came close by us, running away with only their sprit-sail out before the wind.

Towards evening the mate and boatswain begged the master of our ship to let them cut away the foremast, which he was very unwilling to; but the boatswain protesting to him that if he did not the ship would founder, he consented; and when they had cut away the foremast, the mainmast stood so loose and shook the ship so much, they were obliged to cut her away also, and make a clear deck.

Any one may judge what a condition I must be in at all this, who was but a young sailor, and who had been in such a fright before at but a little. But if I can express at this distance the thoughts I had about me at that time, I was in tenfold more horror of mind upon account of my former convictions, and the having returned from them to the resolutions I had wickedly taken at first, than I was at death itself; and these, added to the terror of the storm, put me into

9

such a condition that I can by no words describe it. But the worst was not come yet. The storm continued with such fury, that the seamen themselves acknowledged they had never known a worse. We had a good ship; but she was deep laden and wallowed in the sea, that the seamen every now and then cried out she would founder. It was my advantage in one respect that I did not know what they meant by founder till I inquired. However, the storm was so violent, that I saw what is not often seen—the master, the boatswain, and some others more sensible than the rest, at their prayers, and expecting every moment when the ship would go to the bottom. In the middle of the night, and under all the rest of our distresses, one of the men that had been down on purpose to see, cried out we had sprung a leak; another said there was four foot water in the hold.

Then all hands were called to the pump. At that very word my heart, as I thought, died within me, and I fell backwards upon the side of my bed where I sat, into the cabin. However, the men roused me, and told me that I, that was able to do nothing before, was as well able to pump as another, at which I stirred up and went to the pump, and worked very heartily. While this was doing, the master, seeing some light colliers, who, not able to ride out the storm, were obliged to slip and run away to sea, and would come near us, ordered to fire a gun as a signal of distress. I, who knew nothing what that meant, was so surprised, that I thought the ship had broke, or some dreadful thing had happened. In a word, I was so surprised, that I fell down in a swoon. As this was a time when everybody had his own life to think of, nobody minded me, or what was become of me; but another man stepped up to the pump, and thrusting me aside with his foot, let me lie, thinking I had been dead; and it was a great while before I came to myself.

We worked on; but the water increasing in the hold, it was apparent that the ship would founder; and though the storm began to abate a little, yet, as it was not possible she could swim till we might run into a port, so the master continued firing guns for help, and a light ship, who had rid it out just ahead of us, ventured a boat out to help us. It was with the utmost hazard the boat came near us; but it was impossible for us to get on board, or for the boat to lie near the ship's side, till at last, the men rowing very heartily, and venturing their lives to save ours, our men cast them a rope over the stern with a buoy to it, and then veered it out a great length, which they, after great labour and hazard, took hold of, and we hauled them close under our stern, and got all into their boat. It was to no purpose for them or us after we were in the boat to think of reaching to their own ship, so all agreed to let her drive, and only to pull her in towards shore as much as we could; and our master promised them, that if the boat was staved upon shore, he would make it good to their master; so, partly rowing and partly driving, our boat went away to the norward, sloping towards the shore almost as far as Winterton Ness.

We were not much more than a quarter of an hour out of our ship when we saw her sink, and then I understood for the first time what was meant by a ship foundering in the sea. I must acknowledge I had hardly eyes to look up when the seamen told me she was sinking; for from that moment they rather put me into the boat than that I might be said to go in. My heart was, as it were, dead within me, partly with fright, partly with horror of mind and the thought of what was yet before me.

While we were in this condition, the men yet labouring at the oar to bring the boat near the shore, we could see, when our boat, mounting the waves, we were able to see the shore, a great many people running along the shore to assist us when we should come near; but we made but slow way towards the shore, nor were we able to reach the shore, till, being past the lighthouse at Winterton, the shore falls off to the westward towards Cromer, and so the land broke off a little the violence of the wind. Here we got in, and though not without much difficulty, got all safe on shore, and walked afterwards on foot to Yarmouth, where, as unfortunate men, we were used with great humanity, as well by the magistrates of the town, who assigned us good quarters, as by particular merchants and owners of ships, and had money given us sufficient to carry us either to London or back to Hull, as we thought fit.

Had I now had the sense to have gone back to Hull, and have gone home, I had been happy, and my father, an emblem of our blessed Saviour's parable, had even killed the fatted calf for me; for, hearing the ship I went away in was cast away in Yarmouth Road, it was a great while before he had any assurance that I was not drowned.

But my ill fate pushed me on now with an obstinacy that nothing could resist; and though I had several times loud calls from my reason and my more composed judgment to go home, yet I had no power to do it. I know not what to call this, nor will I urge that it is a secret overruling decree that hurries us on to be the instruments of our own destruction, even though it be before us, and that we push upon it with our eyes open. Certainly nothing but some such decreed un-avoidable misery attending, and which it was impossible for me to escape, could have pushed me forward against the calm reasonings and persuasions of my most retired thoughts, and against two such visible instructions as I had met with in my first attempt.

My comrade, who had helped to harden me before, and who was the master's son, was now less forward than I. The first time he spoke to me after we were at Yarmouth, which was not till two or three days, for we were separated in the town to several quarters; I say, the first time he saw me, it appeared his tone was altered, and looking very melancholy, and shaking his head, asked me how I did, and telling his father who I was, and how I had come this voyage only for a trial, in order to go farther abroad. His father, turning to me with a very grave and concerned tone, "Young man," says he, "you ought never to go to sea any more; you ought to take this for a plain and visible token that you are not to be a seafaring man."—"Why, sir," said I; "will you go to sea no more?"—"That is another case," said he. "It is my calling, and therefore my duty; but as you made this voyage for a trial, you see what a taste Heaven has given you of what you are to expect if you persist. Perhaps this has all befallen us on your account, like Jonah in the ship of Tarshish. Pray," continues he, "what are you? and on what account did you go to sea?" Upon that I told him some of my story, at the end of which he burst out with a strange kind of passion, "What had I done," says he, "that such an unhappy wretch should come into my ship? I would not set my foot in the same ship with thee again for a thousand pounds." This, indeed, was, as I said, an excursion of his spirits, which were yet agitated by the sense of his loss, and was further than he could have authority to go. However, he afterwards talked very gravely to me; exhorted me to go back to my father, and not tempt Providence to my ruin; told me I might see a visible hand of Heaven against me; "And, young man," said he, "depend upon it, if you do not go back, wherever you go you will meet with nothing but disasters and disappointments, till your father's words are fulfilled upon you."

We parted soon after, for I made him little answer, and I saw him no more. Which way he went I know not. As for me, having some money in my pocket, I travelled to London by land; and there, as well as on the road, had many struggles with myself—what course of life I should take, and whether I should go home or go to sea.

As to going home, shame opposed the best motions that offered to my thoughts: and it immediately occurred to me how I should be laughed at among the neighbours, and should be ashamed to see, not my father and mother only, but even everybody else, from whence I have since often observed how incongruous and irrational the common temper of mankind is, especially of youth, to that reason which ought to guide them in such cases—namely, that they are not ashamed to sin, and yet are ashamed to repent; not ashamed of the action for which they ought justly to be esteemed fools, but are ashamed of the returning, which only can make them be esteemed wise men.

In this state of life, however, I remained some time, uncertain what measures to take and what course of life to lead. An irresistible reluctance continued to going home; and as I stayed a while, the remembrance of the distress I had been in wore off; and as that abated, the little motion I had in my desires to a return wore off with it, till at last I quite laid aside the thoughts of it, and looked out for a voyage.

That evil influence which carried me first away from my father's house, that hurried me into the wild and indigested notion of raising my fortune, and that impressed those conceits so forcibly upon me, as to make me deaf to all good advice, and to the entreaties and even command of my father—I say, the same influence, whatever it was, presented the most unfortunate of all enterprises to my view; and I went on board a vessel bound to the coast of Africa, or, as our sailors vulgarly call it, a voyage to Guinea.

§ *I make a voyage to Guinea. Am successful in a trading venture. Death of the honest captain, who had taught me mathematics and navigation. Sail again for Guinea. The ship is captured by Turkish pirates. I am in slavery at Sallee. My new master. I make my escape with the boy Xury in a long-boat.*

It was my great misfortune that in all these adventures I did not ship myself as a sailor, whereby, though I might indeed have worked a little harder than ordinary, yet at the same time I had learned the duty and office of a foremast man, and in time might have qualified myself for a mate or lieutenant, if not for a master. But as it was always my fate to choose for the worse, so I did here; for, having money in my pocket, and good clothes upon my back, I would always go

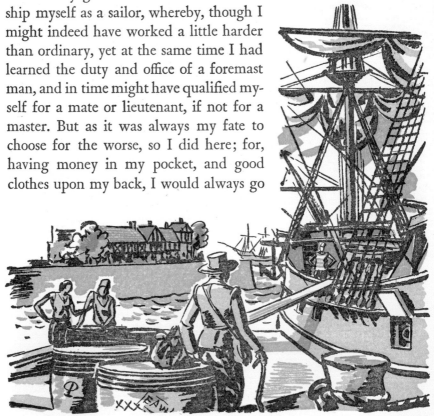

on board in the habit of a gentleman. And so I neither had any business in the ship, or learned to do any.

It was my lot first of all to fall into pretty good company in London, which does not always happen to such loose and unguided young fellows as I then was, the devil generally not omitting to lay some snare for them very early. But it was not so with me. I first fell acquainted with the master of a ship who had been on the coast of Guinea; and who, having had very good success there, was resolved to go again; and who, taking a fancy to my conversation, which was not at all disagreeable at that time, hearing me say I had a mind to see the world, told me if I would go the voyage with him I should be at no expense; I should be his messmate and his companion; and if I could carry anything with me, I should have all the advantage of it that the trade would admit, and perhaps I might meet with some encouragement.

I embraced the offer, and, entering into a strict friendship with this captain, who was an honest and plain-dealing man, I went the voyage with him, and carried a small adventure with me, which, by the disinterested honesty of my friend the captain, I increased very considerably; for I carried about £40 in such toys and trifles as the captain directed me to buy. This £40 I had mustered together by the assistance of some of my relations whom I corresponded with, and who, I believe, got my father, or at least my mother, to contribute so much as that to my first adventure.

This was the only voyage which I may say was successful in all my adventures, and which I owe to the integrity and honesty of my friend the captain, under whom also I got a competent knowledge of the mathematics and the rules of navigation, learned how to keep an account of the ship's course, take an observation, and, in short, to understand some things that were needful to be understood by a sailor. For, as he took delight to introduce me, I took delight to learn; and, in a word, this voyage made me both a sailor and a merchant; for I brought home five pounds nine ounces of gold dust for my adventure, which yielded me in London at my return almost £300, and this filled me with those aspiring thoughts which have since so completed my ruin. Yet even in this voyage I had my misfortunes too, particularly that I was continually sick, being thrown into a violent calenture by the excessive heat of the climate, our principal trading being upon the coast, from the latitude of fifteen degrees north even to the line itself.

I was now set up for a Guinea trader; and my friend, to my great misfortune, dying soon after his arrival, I resolved to go the same voyage again, and I embarked in the same vessel with one who was his mate in the former voyage, and had now got the command of the ship. This was the unhappiest voyage that ever man made; for though I did not carry quite £100 of my new-gained wealth, so that I had £200 left, and which I lodged with my friend's widow, who was very just to me, yet I fell into terrible misfortunes in this voyage; and the first was this—namely, our ship making her course towards the Canary Islands, or rather between those islands and the African shore, was surprised in the grey of the morning by a Turkish rover of Sallee, who gave chase to us with all the sail she could make. We crowded also as much canvas as our yards would spread or our masts carry to have got clear; but finding the pirate gained upon us, and would certainly come up with us in a few hours, we prepared to fight, our ship having twelve guns and the rogue eighteen. About three in the afternoon he came up with us, and bringing-to by mistake just athwart our quarter, instead of athwart our stern, as he intended, we brought eight of our guns to bear on that side, and poured in a broadside upon him, which made him sheer off again, after returning our fire and pouring in also his small shot from near two hundred men which he had on board. However, we had not a man touched, all our men keeping close. He prepared to attack us again, and we to defend ourselves; but laying us on board the next time upon our other quarter, he entered sixty men upon our decks, who immediately fell to cutting and hacking the decks and rigging. We plied them with small-shot, half-pikes, powder-chests, and such like, and cleared our deck of them twice. However, to cut short this melancholy part of our story, our ship being disabled, and three of our men killed and eight wounded, we were obliged to yield, and were carried all prisoners into Sallee, a port belonging to the Moors. The usage I had there was not so dreadful as at first I apprehended, nor was I carried up the country to the emperor's court, as the rest of our men were, but was kept by the captain of the rover as his proper prize, and made his slave, being young and nimble and fit for his business. At this surprising change of my circumstances, from a merchant to a miserable slave, I was perfectly overwhelmed; and now I looked back upon my father's prophetic discourse to me, that I should be miserable, and have none to relieve me, which I thought was now so effectually brought to pass, that it could not be worse; that now the hand of Heaven had overtaken me, and I was undone without redemption.

But, alas! this was but a taste of the misery I was to go through, as will appear in the sequel of this story.

As my new patron or master had taken me home to his house, so I was in hopes that he would take me with him when he went to sea again, believing that it would some time or other be his fate to be taken by a Spanish or Portugal man-of-war; and that then I should be set at liberty. But this hope of mine was soon taken away; for when he went to sea he left me on shore to look after his little garden, and do the common drudgery of slaves about his house; and when he came home again from his cruise, he ordered me to lie in the cabin to look after the ship.

Here I meditated nothing but my escape, and what method I might take to effect it, but found no way that had the least probability in it. Nothing presented to make the supposition of it rational; for I had nobody to communicate it to that would embark with me, no fellow-slave, no Englishman, Irishman, or Scotsman there but myself; so that for two years, though I often pleased myself with the imagination, yet I never had the least encouraging prospect of putting it in practice.

After about two years an odd circumstance presented itself, which put the old thought of making some attempt for my liberty again in my head. My patron lying at home longer than usual without fitting out his ship, which, as I heard, was for want of money, he used constantly, once or twice a week, sometimes oftener, if the weather was fair, to take the ship's pinnace, and go out into the road a-fishing; and as he always took me and a young Maresco with him to row the boat, we made him very merry, and I proved very dexterous in catching fish, insomuch that sometimes he would send me with a Moor, one of his kinsmen, and the youth—the Maresco, as they called him—to catch a dish of fish for him.

It happened one time, that going a-fishing in a stark calm morning, a fog rose so thick, that though we were not half a league from the shore we lost sight of it; and rowing we knew not whither or which way, we laboured all day and all the next night, and when the morning came we found we had pulled off to sea instead of pulling in for the shore; and that we were at least two leagues from the shore. However, we got well in again, though with a great deal of labour and some danger; for the wind began to blow pretty fresh in the morning; but particularly we were all very hungry.

But our patron, warned by this disaster, resolved to take more care of himself for the future; and having lying by him the long-boat of our English ship he had taken, he resolved he would not go a-fishing any more without a compass and some provision. So he ordered the carpenter of his ship, who also was an English slave, to build a little state-room or cabin in the middle of the long-boat, like that of a barge, with a place to stand behind it to steer and hale home the main-sheet; and room before for a hand or two to stand and work the sails. She sailed with what we call a shoulder-of-mutton sail; and the boom gibed over the top of the cabin, which lay very snug and low, and had in it room for him to lie, with a slave or two; and a table to eat on, with some small lockers to put in some bottles of such liquor as he thought fit to drink; particularly his bread, rice, and coffee.

We went frequently out with this boat a-fishing. And as I was most dexterous to catch fish for him, he never went without me. It happened that he had appointed to go out in this boat, either for pleasure or for fish, with two or three Moors of some distinction in that place and for whom he had provided extraordinarily, and had therefore sent on board the boat overnight a larger store of provisions than ordinary; and had ordered me to get ready three fuzees with powder and shot, which were on board his ship, for that they designed some sport of fowling as well as fishing.

I got all things ready as he had directed, and waited the next morning with the boat washed clean, her ancient and pendants out, and everything to accommodate his guests. When by and by my patron came on board alone, and told me his guests had put off going, upon some business that fell out, and ordered me with the man and boy as usual to go out with the boat and catch them some fish, for that his friends were to sup at his house; and commanded that as soon as I had got some fish, I should bring it home to his house; all which I prepared to do.

This moment my former notions of deliverance darted into my thoughts, for now I found I was like to have a little ship at my command; and my master being gone, I prepared to furnish myself, not for a fishing business, but for a voyage; though I knew not, neither did I so much as consider, whither I should steer; for anywhere to get out of that place was my way.

My first contrivance was to make a pretence to speak to this Moor, to get something for our subsistence on board; for I told him we must not presume to eat of our patron's bread. He said that was true; so he brought a large basket of rusk or biscuit of their kind, and three jars with fresh water into the boat. I knew where my patron's case of bottles stood, which it was evident by the make were taken out of some English prize, and I conveyed them into the boat while the Moor was on shore, as if they had been there before for our master. I conveyed also a great lump of bees'-wax into the boat, which weighed above half a hundredweight, with a parcel of twine or thread, a hatchet, a saw, and a hammer, all which were of great use to us afterwards, especially the wax to make candles. Another trick I tried upon him, which he innocently came into also. His name was Ishmael, who they call Muly or Moely; so I called to him—"Moely," said I, "our patron's guns are on board the boat; can you not get a little powder and shot? It may be we may kill some alcamies (a fowl like our curlews) for ourselves, for I know he keeps the gunner's stores in the ship." "Yes," says he, "I'll bring some." And accordingly he brought a great leather pouch, which held about a pound and a half of powder, or rather more, and another with shot, that had five or six pound, with some bullets, and put all into the boat. At the same time, I had found some powder of my master's in the great cabin, with which I filled one of the large bottles in the case, which was almost empty, pouring what was in it into another; and thus furnished with everything needful, we sailed out of the port to fish. The castle, which is at the entrance of the port, knew who we were, and took no notice of us; and we were not above a mile out of the port before we hauled in our sail, and set us down to fish. The wind blew from the north-north-east, which was contrary to my desire; for had it blown southerly, I had been sure to have made the coast of Spain, and at least reached to the Bay of Cadiz; but my resolutions were, blow which way it would, I would be gone from that horrid place where I was, and leave the rest to fate.

After we had fished some time and catched nothing—for when I had fish on my hook, I would not pull them up, that he might not see them—I said to the Moor, "This will not do; our master will not be thus served; we must stand farther off." He, thinking no harm, agreed; and being in the head of the boat, set the sails: and as I had the helm, I run the boat out near a league farther, and then brought her to, as if I would fish; when, giving the boy the helm, I stepped forward to where the Moor was, and making as if I stooped for something behind him, I took him by surprise with my arm under his legs, and tossed him clear overboard into the sea. He rose immediately, for he swam like a cork, and called to me, begged to be taken in; told me he would go all over the world with me. He swam so strong after the boat that he would have reached me very quickly, there being but little wind; upon which I stepped into the cabin, and fetching one of the fowling-pieces, I presented it at him, and told him I had done him no hurt, and if he would be quiet I would do him none. "But," said I, "you swim well enough to reach to the shore, and the sea is calm; make the best of your way to shore, and I will do you no harm, but if you come near the boat I'll shoot you through the head; for I am resolved to have my liberty." So he turned himself about and swam for the shore; and I make no doubt but he reached it with ease, for he was an excellent swimmer.

I could have been content to have taken this Moor with me and have drowned the boy, but there was no venturing to trust him. When he was gone I turned to the boy, who they called Xury, and said to him, "Xury, if you will be faithful to me, I'll make you a great man; but if you will not stroke your face to be true to me—that is, swear by Mahomet and his father's beard—I must throw you into the sea too." The boy smiled in my face, and spoke so innocently, that I could not mistrust him; and swore to be faithful to me, and go all over the world with me.

While I was in view of the Moor that was swimming, I stood out directly to sea with the boat, rather stretching to windward, that they might think me gone towards the strait's mouth (as indeed anyone that had been in their wits must have been supposed to do); for who would have supposed we were sailed on to the southward, to the truly barbarian coast, where whole nations of negroes were sure to surround us with their canoes, and destroy us; where we could never once go on shore but we should be devoured by savage beasts, or more merciless savages of human kind.

§ *We steer south and reach land. Adventure with a lion. See savages on the shore. A leopard shot. We are picked up by a Portuguese ship. The captain takes Xury. We arrive at the Brazils. I purchase a small plantation. My increasing prosperity.*

B UT as soon as it grew dusk in the evening I changed my course, and steered directly south and by east, bending my course a little toward the east, that I might keep in with the shore; and having a fair fresh gale of wind and a smooth, quiet sea, I made such sail that I believe by the next day at three o'clock in the afternoon when I first made the land, I could not be less than 150 miles south of Sallee; quite beyond the Emperor of Morocco's dominions, or, indeed, of any other king thereabouts, for we saw no people.

Yet such was the fright I had taken at the Moors, and the dreadful apprehensions I had of falling into their hands, that I would not stop, or go on shore, or come to an anchor, the wind continuing fair, till I had sailed in that manner five days; and then the wind shifting to the southward, I concluded also that if any of our vessels were in chase of me, they also would now give over. So I ventured to make to the coast, and came to an anchor in the mouth of a little river, I knew not what, or where; neither what latitude, what country, what nation, or what river. I neither saw, nor desired to see, any people; the principal thing I wanted was fresh water. We came into this creek in the evening, resolving to swim on shore as soon as it was dark, and discover the country; but as soon as it was quite dark we heard such dreadful noises of the barking, roaring, and howling of wild creatures, of we knew not what kinds, that the poor boy was ready to die with fear, and begged of me not to go on shore till day. "Well, Xury," said I, "then I won't; but it may be we may see men by day, who will be as bad to us as those lions." "Then we give them the shoot gun," says Xury, laughing; "make them run way." Such English Xury spoke by conversing among us slaves. However, I was glad to see the boy so cheerful, and I gave him a dram (out of our patron's case of bottles) to cheer him up. After all, Xury's advice was good, and I took it. We dropped our little anchor, and lay still all night—I say still, for we slept none—for in two or three hours we saw vast great creatures (we knew not what to call them) of many sorts come down to the seashore, and run into the water, wallowing and washing themselves for the pleasure of cooling themselves; and they made such hideous howlings and yellings, that I never indeed heard the like.

Xury was dreadfully frightened, and indeed so was I too, but we were both more frightened when we heard one of these mighty creatures come swimming towards our boat. We could not see him, but we might hear him by his blowing to be a monstrous, huge, and furious beast. Xury said it was a lion, and it might be so for aught I know; but poor Xury cried to me to weigh the anchor and row away. "No," says I; "Xury, we can slip our cable with the buoy to it, and go off to sea. They cannot follow us far." I had no sooner said so but I perceived the creature (whatever it was) within two oars' length, which something surprised me. However, I immediately stepped to the cabin-door, and taking up my gun, fired at him, upon which he immediately turned about and swam towards the shore again.

But it is impossible to describe the horrible noises, and hideous cries and howlings, that were raised as well upon the edge of the shore as higher within the country, upon the noise or report of the gun—a thing I have some reason to believe those creatures had never heard before. This convinced me that there was no going on shore for us in the night upon that coast; and how to venture on shore in the day was another question too, for to have fallen into the hands of any of the savages had been as bad as to have fallen into the hands of lions and tigers; at least we were equally apprehensive of the danger of it.

Be that as it would, we were obliged to go on shore somewhere or other for water, for we had not a pint left in the boat. When or where to get to it was the point. Xury said, if I would let him go on shore with one of the jars, he would find if there was any water, and bring some to me. I asked him why he would go—why I should not go and he stay in the boat? The boy answered with so much affection that made me love him ever after. Says he, "If wild mans come, they eat me; you go way." "Well, Xury," says I, "we will both go; and if the wild mans come, we will kill them. They shall eat neither of us." So I gave Xury a piece of rusk-bread to eat, and a dram out of our patron's case of bottles which I mentioned before; and we haled the boat in as near the shore as we thought was proper, and waded on shore, carrying nothing but our arms and two jars for water.

I did not care to go out of sight of the boat, fearing the coming of canoes with savages down the river; but the boy seeing a low place about a mile up the country, rambled to it; and by and by I saw him come running towards me. I thought he was pursued by some savage, or frightened with some wild beast, and I ran forward towards him to help him; but when I came nearer to him, I saw something hanging over his shoulders—which was a creature that he had shot, like a hare, but different in colour and longer legs. However, we were very glad of it, and it was very good meat; but the great joy that poor Xury came with, was to tell me he had found good water and seen no wild mans.

But we found afterwards that we need not take such pains for water, for a little higher up the creek where we were, we found the water fresh when the tide was out, which flowed but a little way up. So we filled our jars, and feasted on the hare we had killed, and prepared to go on our way, having seen no footsteps of any human creature in that part of the country.

As I had been one voyage to this coast before, I knew very well that the islands of the Canaries, and the Cape de Verd Islands also, lay not far off from the coast. But as I had no instruments to take an observation to know what latitude we were in, and did not exactly know, or at least to remember, what latitude they were in, I knew not where to look for them, or when to stand off to sea towards them; otherwise I might now easily have found some of these islands. But my hope was, that if I stood along this coast till I came to that part where the English traded, I should find some of their vessels upon their usual design of trade, that would relieve and take us in.

By the best of my calculation, that place where I now was, must be that country which, lying between the Emperor of Morocco's dominions and the negroes, lies waste and uninhabited, except by wild beasts

—the negroes having abandoned it and gone farther south, for fear of the Moors; and the Moors not thinking it worth inhabiting, by reason of its barrenness. And, indeed, both forsaking it because of the prodigious numbers of tigers, lions, leopards, and other furious creatures which harbour there; so that the Moors use it for their hunting only, where they go like an army, two or three thousand men at a time. And, indeed, for near a hundred miles together upon this coast, we saw nothing but a waste uninhabited country by day, and heard nothing but howlings and roaring of wild beasts by night.

Once or twice in the daytime, I thought I saw the Pico of Teneriffe, being the high top of the mountain Teneriffe in the Canaries; and had a great mind to venture out in hopes of reaching thither; but having tried twice, I was forced in again by contrary winds, the sea also going too high for my little vessel, so I resolved to pursue my first design and keep along the shore.

Several times I was obliged to land for fresh water after we had left this place; and once in particular, being early in the morning, we came to an anchor under a little point of land which was pretty high, and the tide beginning to flow, we lay still to go farther in. Xury, whose eyes were more about him than it seems mine were, calls softly to me and tells me that we had best go farther off the shore:—"For," says he, "look, yonder lies a dreadful monster on the side of that hillock fast asleep." I looked where he pointed, and saw a dreadful monster indeed; for it was a terrible great lion that lay on the side of the shore, under the shade of a piece of the hill, that hung as it were a little over him. "Xury," says I, "you shall go on shore and kill him." Xury looked frightened, and said, "Me kill! he eat me at one mouth"—one mouthful, he meant. However, I said no more to the boy, but bade him lie still; and I took our biggest gun, which was almost musket-bore, and loaded it with a good charge of powder and with two slugs, and laid it down; then I loaded another gun with two bullets; and the third—for we had three pieces—I loaded with five smaller bullets. I took the best aim I could with the first piece to have shot him into the head, but he lay so with his leg raised a little above his nose, that the slugs hit his leg about the knee, and broke the bone. He started up, growl-

25

ing at first; but finding his leg broke, fell down again; and then got up upon three legs, and gave the most hideous roar that ever I heard. I was a little surprised that I had not hit him on the head. However, I took up the second piece immediately; and though he began to move off, fired again, and shot him into the head, and had the pleasure to see him drop, and make but little noise, but lay struggling for life. Then Xury took heart, and would have me let him go on shore. "Well, go," said I. So the boy jumped into the water, and, taking a little gun in one hand, swam to shore with the other hand, and coming close to the creature, put the muzzle of the piece to his ear, and shot him into the head again, which dispatched him quite.

This was game indeed to us, but this was no food; and I was very sorry to lose three charges of powder and shot upon a creature that was good for nothing to us. However, Xury said he would have some of him; so he comes on board, and asked me to give him the hatchet. "For what, Xury?" said I. "Me cut off his head," said he. However, Xury could not cut off his head; but he cut off a foot and brought it with him—and it was a monstrous great one.

I bethought myself, however, that perhaps the skin of him might one way or other be of some value to us; and I resolved to take off his skin if I could. So Xury and I went to work with him; but Xury was much the better workman at it—for I knew very ill how to do it. Indeed, it took us up both the whole day; but at last we got off the hide of him, and spreading it on the top of our cabin, the sun effectually dried it in two days' time, and it afterwards served me to lie upon.

After this stop we made on to the southward continually for ten or twelve days, living very sparing on our provisions, which began to abate very much, and going no oftener into the shore than we were obliged to for fresh water. My design in this was to make the River Gambia or Senegal—that is to say, anywhere about the Cape de Verd, where I was in hopes to meet with some European ship; and if I did not, I knew not what course I had to take, but to seek for the islands or perish there among the negroes. I knew that all the ships from Europe—which sailed either to the coast of Guinea, or to Brazil, or to the East Indies—made this cape or those islands; and in a word, I put the whole of my fortune upon this single point, either that I must meet with some ship or must perish.

When I had pursued this resolution about ten days longer, as I have said, I began to see that the land was inhabited; and in two or three places, as we sailed by, we saw people stand upon the shore to look at us. We could also perceive they were quite black. I was once inclined to have gone on shore to have speech with them. But Xury was my better counsellor, and said to me, "No go, no go." However, I hauled in nearer the shore that I might talk to them, and I found they ran along the shore by me a good way.

I observed they had no weapons in their hands—except one, who had a long slender stick, which Xury said was a lance, and that they would throw them a great way with good aim. So I kept at a distance, but talked with them by signs as well as I could; and particularly made signs for something to eat. They beckoned to me to stop my boat, and they would fetch me some meat. Upon this I lowered the top of my sail and lay by; and two of them ran up into the country, and in less than half an hour came back and brought with them two pieces of dry flesh and some corn, such as is the produce of their country—but we neither knew what the one or the other was. However, we were willing to accept it, but how to come at it was our next dispute; for I was not for venturing on shore to them, and they were as much afraid of us. But they took a safe way for us all— for they brought it to the shore and laid it down, and went and stood a great way off till we fetched it on board, and then came close to us again.

We made signs of thanks to them, for we had nothing to make them amends. But an opportunity offered that very instant to oblige them wonderfully—for while we were lying by the shore, came two mighty creatures, one pursuing the other (as we took it) with great fury, towards the sea. Whether they were in sport or in rage we could not tell, any more than we could tell whether it was usual or strange; but I believe it was the latter—because in the first place, those ravenous creatures seldom appear but in the night; and, in the second place,

27

we found the people terribly frightened, especially the women. The man that had the lance or dart did not fly from them, but the rest did. However, as the two creatures ran directly into the water, they did not seem to offer to fall upon any of the negroes, but plunged themselves into the sea, and swam about as if they had come for their diversion. At last one of them began to come nearer our boat than at first I expected, but I lay ready for him; for I had loaded my gun with all possible expedition, and bade Xury load both the other. As soon as he came fairly within my reach I fired, and shot him directly into the head. Immediately he sank down into the water, but rose instantly and plunged up and down as if he was struggling for life. And so indeed he was. He immediately made to the shore; but between the wound, which was his mortal hurt, and the strangling of the water, he died just before he reached the shore.

It is impossible to express the astonishment of these poor creatures at the noise and the fire of my gun; some of them were even ready to die for fear, and fell down as dead with the very terror. But when they saw the creature dead and sunk in the water, and that I made signs to them to come to the shore, they took heart and came to the shore, and began to search for the creature. I found him by his blood staining the water; and by the help of a rope which I slung round him, and gave the negroes to haul, they dragged him on shore, and found that it was a most curious leopard, spotted and fine to an admirable degree; and the negroes help up their hands with admiration to think what it was I had killed him with.

The other creature, frightened with the flash of fire and the noise of the gun, swam on shore, and ran up directly to the mountains from whence they came, nor could I at that distance know what it was. I found quickly the negroes were for eating the flesh of this creature, so I was willing to have them take it as a favour from me; which, when I made signs to them that they might take him, they were very thankful for. Immediately they fell to work with him; and though they had no knife, yet with a sharpened piece of wood they took off his skin as readily—and much more readily than we could have done with a knife. They offered me some of the flesh, which I declined, making as if I would give it them; but made signs for the skin, which they gave me very freely, and brought me a great deal more of their provision, which, though I did not understand, yet I accepted. Then I made signs to them for some water, and held out one of my jars to them, ·turning it bottom upward, to show that it was empty, and that I wanted to have it filled. They called immediately to some of their friends; and there came two women, and brought a great vessel made of earth, and burned as I suppose in the sun. This they set down for me as before; and I sent Xury on shore with my jars, and filled them all three.

I was now furnished with roots and corn—such as it was—and water; and leaving my friendly negroes, I made forward for about eleven days more without offering to go near the shore, till I saw the land run out a great length into the sea, at about the distance of four or five leagues before me, and the sea being very calm, I kept a large offing to make this point.

At length, doubling the point at about two leagues from the land, I saw plainly land on the other side to seaward. Then I concluded, as it was most certain indeed, that this was the Cape de Verd Islands. However, they were at a great distance; and I could not well tell what I had best to do, for if I should be taken with a fresh of wind, I might neither reach one nor the other.

In this dilemma, as I was very pensive, I stepped into the cabin and sat me down, Xury having the helm, when on a sudden the boy cried out, "Master, master, a ship with a sail!" and the foolish boy was frightened out of his wits, thinking it must needs be some of his master's ships sent to pursue us, when I knew we were gotten far enough out of their reach. I jumped out of the cabin, and immediately saw not only the ship, but what she was—namely, that it was a Portuguese ship, and, as I thought, was bound to the coast of Guinea for negroes. But when I observed the course she steered I was soon convinced they were bound some other way, and did not design to come any nearer to the shore. Upon which I stretched out to sea as much as I could, resolving to speak with them if possible.

With all the sail I could make, I found I should not be able to come in their way, but that they would be gone by before I could make any signal to them. But after I had crowded to the utmost and began to despair, they, it seems, saw me by the help of their perspective-glasses, and that it was some European boat, which, as they supposed, must belong to some ship that was lost; so they shortened sail to let me come up. I was encouraged with this; and as I had my patron's ancient on board, I made a waft of it to them for a signal of distress, and fired a gun—both which they saw, for they told me they saw the smoke, though they did not hear the gun. Upon these signals they very kindly brought to, and lay by for me, and in about three hours' time I came up with them.

They asked me what I was, in Portuguese and in Spanish and in French, but I understood none of them; but at last a Scotch sailor who was on board called to me; and I answered him, and told him I was an Englishman, that I had made my escape out of slavery from the Moors at Sallee. Then they bade me come on board, and very kindly took me in and all my goods.

It was an inexpressible joy to me—that any one will believe—that I was thus delivered, as I esteemed it, from such a miserable and almost hopeless condition as I was in, and I immediately offered all I had to the captain of the ship as a return for my deliverance; but he generously told me he would take nothing from me, but that all I had should be delivered safe to me when I came to the Brazils. "For," says he, "I have saved your life on no other terms than I would be glad to be saved myself, and it may one time or other be my lot to be taken up in the same condition; besides," said he, "when I carry you to the Brazils, so great a way from your own country, if I should take from you what you have, you will be starved there, and then I only take away that life I have given. No, no, Seignor Inglese," says he, "Mr. Englishman, I will carry you thither in charity, and those things will help you to buy your subsistence there and your passage home again."

As he was charitable in his proposal, so he was just in the performance to a tittle; for he ordered the seamen that none should offer to touch anything I had. Then he took everything into his own possession, and gave me back an exact inventory of them, that I might have them, even so much as my three earthen jars.

As to my boat it was a very good one, and that he saw, and told me he would buy it of me for the ship's use, and asked me what I would

have for it? I told him he had been so generous to me in everything, that I could not offer to make any price of the boat, but left it entirely to him; upon which he told me he would give me a note of his hand to pay me eighty pieces of eight for it at Brazil, and when it came there, if anyone offered to give more he would make it up. He offered me also sixty pieces of eight more for my boy Xury; which I was loath to take: not that I was not willing to let the captain have him, but I was very loath to sell the poor boy's liberty, who had assisted me so faithfully in procuring my own. However, when I let him know my reason, he owned it to be just, and offered me this medium—that he would give the boy an obligation to set him free in ten years, if he

31

turned Christian. Upon this, and Xury saying he was willing to go to him, I let the captain have him.

We had a very good voyage to the Brazils, and arrived in the Bay de Todor los Santos, or All-Saints' Bay, in about twenty-two days after. And now I was once more delivered from the most miserable of all conditions of life; and what to do next with myself I was now to consider.

The generous treatment the captain gave me I can never enough remember. He would take nothing of me for my passage, gave me twenty ducats for the leopard's skin and forty for the lion's skin, which I had in my boat, and caused everything I had in the ship to be punctually delivered me; and what I was willing to sell he bought, such as the case of bottles, two of my guns, and a piece of the lump of bees'-wax, for I had made candles of the rest. In a word, I made about two hundred and twenty pieces of eight of all my cargo; and with this stock I went on shore in the Brazils.

I had not been long here, but being recommended to the house of a good honest man like himself, who had an "ingeino," as they call it —that is, a plantation and a sugar-house—I lived with him some time, and acquainted myself by that means with the manner of their planting and making of sugar. And seeing how well the planters lived, and how they grew rich suddenly, I resolved, if I could get license to settle there, I would turn planter among them; resolving in the meantime to find out some way to get my money which I had left in London remitted to me. To this purpose, getting a kind of a letter of naturalization, I purchased as much land that was uncured as my money would reach, and formed a plan for my plantation and settlement, and such a one as might be suitable to the stock which I proposed to myself to receive from England.

I had a neighbour—a Portuguese of Lisbon, but born of English parents—whose name was Wells, and in much such circumstances as I was. I call him my neighbour, because his plantation lay next to mine, and we went on very sociably together. My stock was but low as well as his; and we rather planted for food than anything else for about two years. However, we began to increase, and our land began to come into order; so that the third year we planted some tobacco, and made each of us a piece of ground ready for planting canes in the year to come. But we both wanted help; and now I found, more than before, I had done wrong in parting with my boy Xury.

But, alas! for me to do wrong that never did right was no great wonder. I had no remedy but to go on. I was gotten into an employment quite remote to my genius and directly contrary to the life I delighted in and for which I forsook my father's house, and broke through all his good advice; nay, I was coming into the very middle station, or upper degree of low life, which my father advised me to before, and which, if I resolved to go on with, I might as well have stayed at home, and never have fatigued myself in the world as I had done. And I used often to say to myself, I could have done this as well in England among my friends as have gone five thousand miles off to do it among strangers and savages in a wilderness, and at such a distance as never to hear from any part of the world that had the least knowledge of me.

In this manner, I used to look upon my condition with the utmost regret. I had nobody to converse with but now and then this neighbour—no work to be done but by the labour of my hands; and I used to say I lived just like a man cast away upon some desolate island that had nobody there but himself. But how just has it been, and how should all men reflect, that when they compare their present conditions with others that are worse, Heaven may oblige them to make the exchange, and be convinced of their former felicity by their experience,—I say how just has it been that the truly solitary life I reflected on, in an island of mere desolation, should be my lot, who had so often unjustly compared it with the life which I then led; in which, had I continued, I had in all probability been exceeding prosperous and rich!

I was in some degree settled in my measures for carrying on the plantation, before my kind friend, the captain of the ship that took me up at sea, went back—for the ship remained there in providing his loading and preparing for his voyage near three months—when, telling him what little stock I had left behind me in London, he gave me this friendly and sincere advice. "Seignor Inglese," says he,—for so he always called me,—"if you will give me letters, and a procuration here in form to me, with orders to the person who has your money in London, to send your effects to Lisbon to such persons as I shall direct, and in such goods as are proper for this country, I will bring you the produce of them, God willing, at my return. But since human affairs are all subject to changes and to disasters, I would have you give orders but for one hundred pounds sterling, which you say is half your stock, and yet the hazard be run for the first; so that if it come safe you may order the rest the same way, and if it miscarry you may have the other half to have recourse to for your supply."

This was so wholesome advice, and looked so friendly, that I could not but be convinced it was the best course I could take; so I accordingly prepared letters to the gentlewoman with whom I had left my money, and a procuration to the Portuguese captain, as he desired.

I wrote the English captain's widow a full account of all my adventures; my slavery, escape, and how I had met with the Portugal captain at sea, the humanity of his behaviour, and in what condition

I was now in, with all other necessary directions for my supply. And when this honest captain came to Lisbon, he found means by some of the English merchants there, to send over, not the order only, but a full account of my story, to a merchant at London, who represented it effectually to her; whereupon she not only delivered the money, but out of her own pocket sent the Portugal captain a very handsome present for his humanity and charity to me.

The merchant in London, vesting this hundred pounds in English goods such as the captain had writ for, sent them directly to him at Lisbon, and he brought them all safe to me to the Brazils; among which, without my direction—for I was too young in my business to think of them—he had taken care to have all sorts of tools, ironwork, and utensils necessary for my plantation, and which were of great use to me.

When this cargo arrived I thought my fortune made, for I was surprised with joy of it; and my good steward the captain had laid out the five pounds, which my friend had sent him for a present for himself, to purchase and bring me over a servant under bond for six years' service, and would not accept of any consideration except a little tobacco, which I would have him accept, being of my own produce.

Neither was this all. But my goods being all English manufactures, such as cloth, stuffs, bays, and things particularly valuable and desirable in the country, I found means to sell them to a very great advantage; so that I may say I had more than four times the value of my first cargo, and was now infinitely beyond my poor neighbour—I mean in the advancement of my plantation; for the first thing I did I bought me a negro slave, and an European servant also—I mean another besides that which the captain brought me from Lisbon.

But as abused prosperity is oftentimes made the very means of our greatest adversity, so was it with me. I went on the next year with great success in my plantation. I raised fifty great rolls of tobacco on my own ground, more than I had disposed of for necessaries among my neighbours; and these fifty rolls being each of above a hundred-weight were well cured and laid by against the return of the fleet from Lisbon. And now, increasing in business and in wealth, my head began to be full of projects and undertakings beyond my reach—such as are indeed often the ruin of the best heads in business.

Had I continued in the station I was now in, I had room for all the happy things to have yet befallen me for which my father so earnestly recommended a quiet, retired life, and of which he had so sensibly described the middle station of life to be full of. But other things attended me, and I was still to be the wilful agent of all my own miseries, and particularly to increase my fault and double the reflections upon myself, which in my future sorrows I should have leisure to make. All these miscarriages were procured by my apparent obstinate adhering to my foolish inclination of wandering abroad, and pursuing that inclination in contradiction to the clearest views of doing myself good in a fair and plain pursuit of those prospects and those measures of life which Nature and Providence concurred to present me with and to make my duty.

§ *My passion for wandering. Receive a tempting offer from my neighbour planters. I sail for the African coast. We are caught in a tornado. The ship strikes on a sandbank. I am cast ashore.*

As I had once done thus in my breaking away from my parents, so I could not be content now, but I must go and leave the happy view I had of being a rich and thriving man in my new plantation, only to pursue a rash and immoderate desire of rising faster than the nature of the thing admitted; and thus I cast myself down again into the deepest gulf of human misery that ever man fell into, or perhaps could be consistent with life and a state of health in the world.

To come, then, by the just degrees to the particulars of this part of my story. You may suppose that having now lived almost four years in the Brazils, and beginning to thrive and prosper very well upon my plantation, I had not only learned the language, but had contracted acquaintance and friendship among my fellow-planters, as well as among the merchants at St. Salvadore, which was our port;

and that, in my discourses among them, I had frequently given them an account of my two voyages to the coast of Guinea, the manner of trading with the negroes there, and how easy it was to purchase upon the coast for trifles—such as beads, toys, knives, scissors, hatchets, bits of glass, and the like—not only gold dust, Guinea grains, elephants' teeth, &c., but negroes for the service of the Brazils in great numbers.

They listened always very attentively to my discourses on these heads, but especially to that part which related to the buying negroes; which was a trade at that time not only not far entered into, but, as far as it was, had been carried on by the *assiento,* or permission of the Kings of Spain and Portugal, and engrossed in the public; so that few negroes were brought, and those excessively dear.

It happened, being in company with some merchants and planters of my acquaintance, and talking of those things very earnestly, three of them came to me the next morning, and told me they had been musing very much upon what I had discoursed with them of the last night, and they came to make a secret proposal to me. And after enjoining me secrecy, they told me that they had a mind to fit out a ship to go to Guinea; that they had all plantations as well as I, and were straitened for nothing so much as servants; that as it was a trade that could not be carried on, because they could not publicly sell the negroes when they came home, so they desired to make but one voyage, to bring the negroes on shore privately, and divide them among their own plantations; and in a word, the question was, whether I would go their supercargo in the ship to manage the trading part upon the coast of Guinea. And they offered me that I should have my equal share of the negroes, without providing any part of the stock.

This was a fair proposal, it must be confessed, had it been made to any one that had not had a settlement and plantation of his own to look after, which was in a fair way of coming to be very considerable, and with a good stock upon it. But for me that was thus entered and established, and had nothing to do but go on as I had begun for three or four years more, and to have sent for the other hundred pound from England, and who in that time, and with that little addition, could scarce have failed of being worth three or four thousand pounds sterling, and that increasing too,—for me to think of such a voyage was the most preposterous thing that ever man in such circumstances could be guilty of.

But I that was born to be my own destroyer, could no more resist the offer than I could restrain my first rambling designs when my father's good counsel was lost upon me. In a word, I told them I would go with all my heart if they would undertake to look after my plantation in my absence, and would dispose of it to such as I should direct if I miscarried. This they all engaged to do, and entered into writings or covenants to do so; and I made a formal will, disposing of my plantation and effects, in case of my death, making the captain of the ship that had saved my life, as before, my universal heir, but obliging him to dispose of my effects as I had directed in my will—one-half of the produce being to himself, and the other to be shipped to England. In short, I took all possible caution to preserve my effects and keep up

my plantation. Had I used half as much prudence to have looked into my own interest, and have made a judgment of what I ought to have done and not to have done, I had certainly never gone away from so prosperous an undertaking—leaving all the probable views of a thriving circumstance, and gone upon a voyage to sea, attended with all its common hazards, to say nothing of the reasons I had to expect particular misfortunes to myself.

But I was hurried on, and obeyed blindly the dictates of my fancy rather than my reason. And accordingly, the ship being fitted out and the cargo furnished, and all things done as by agreement by my partners in the voyage, I went on board in an evil hour—being the same day eight year that I went from my father and mother at Hull in order to act the rebel to their authority and the fool to my own interest.

Our ship was about 120 ton burthen; carried six guns and fourteen men, besides the master, his boy, and myself. We had on board no large cargo of goods, except of such toys as were fit for our trade with the negroes—such as beads, bits of glass, shells and odd trifles, especially little looking-glasses, knives, scissors, hatchets, and the like.

The same day I went on board we set sail, standing away to the northward upon our own coast, with design to stretch over for the African coast when they came about 10 or 12 degrees of northern latitude; which, it seems, was the manner of their course in those days. We had very good weather, only excessively hot, all the way upon our own coast, till we came the height of Cape St. Augustino; from whence, keeping farther off at sea, we lost sight of land, and steered as if we were bound for the Isle Fernand de Noronha, holding our course north-east by north, and leaving those isles on the east. In this course we passed the line in about twelve days' time; and were by our last observation in 7 degrees 22 minutes northern latitude, when a violent tornado or hurricane took us quite out of our knowledge. It began from the south-east, came about to the north-west, and then settled into the north-east; from whence it blew in such a terrible manner that for twelve days together we could do nothing but drive, and, scudding away before it, let it carry us whither ever fate and the fury of the winds directed. And during these twelve days I need not say that I expected every day to be swallowed up; nor, indeed, did any in the ship expect to save their lives.

In this distress, we had, besides the terror of the storm, one of our men died of the calenture, and one man and the boy washed overboard. About the twelfth day, the weather abating a little, the master made an observation as well as he could, and found that he was in about 11 degrees north latitude, but that he was 22 degrees of longitude difference west from Cape St. Augustino; so that he found he was gotten upon the coast of Guiana, or the north part of Brazil, beyond the River Amazones, toward that of the River Oronoque, commonly called the Great River, and began to consult with me what course he should take, for the ship was leaky and very much disabled, and he was going directly back to the coast of Brazil.

I was positively against that; and looking over the charts of the sea-coast of America with him, we concluded there was no inhabited country for us to have recourse to till we came within the circle of the Carribbe Islands, and therefore resolved to stand away for Barbadoes; which, by keeping off at sea, to avoid the indraught of the Bay or Gulf of Mexico, we might easily perform, as we hoped, in about fifteen days' sail; whereas we could not possibly make our voyage to the coast of Africa without some assistance both to our ship and to ourselves.

With this design we changed our course, and steered away northwest by west, in order to reach some of our English islands, where I hoped for relief. But our voyage was otherwise determined; for, being in the latitude of 12 degrees 18 minutes, a second storm came upon us, which carried us away with the same impetuosity westward, and drove us so out of the very way of all human commerce, that had all our lives been saved as to the sea, we were rather in danger of being devoured by savages than ever returning to our own country.

In this distress, the wind still blowing very hard, one of our men early in the morning cried out "Land!" and we had no sooner run out of the cabin to look out in hopes of seeing whereabouts in the world we were, but the ship struck upon a sand, and in a moment, her motion being so stopped, the sea broke over her in such a manner, that we expected we should all have perished immediately, and we were immediately driven into our close quarters to shelter us from the very foam and spray of the sea.

It is not easy for anyone who has not been in the like condition to describe or conceive the consternation of men in such circumstances. We knew nothing where we were, or upon what land it was we were driven, whether an island or the main, whether inhabited or not inhabited; and as the rage of the wind was still great, though rather less than at first, we could not so much as hope to have the ship hold many minutes without breaking in pieces, unless the winds by a kind of miracle should turn immediately about. In a word, we sat looking one upon another, and expecting death every moment, and every man acting accordingly as preparing for another world, for there was little or nothing more for us to do in this. That which was our present comfort, and all the comfort we had, was that, contrary to our expectation, the ship did not break yet, and that the master said the wind began to abate.

Now, though we thought that the wind did a little abate, yet the ship having thus struck upon the sand, and sticking too fast for us to expect her getting off, we were in a dreadful condition indeed, and had nothing to do but to think of saving our lives as well as we could. We had a boat at our stern just before the storm, but she was first staved by dashing against the ship's rudder, and in the next place she broke away, and either sunk or was driven off to sea; so there was no hope from her. We had another boat on board; but how to get her off into the sea was a doubtful thing. However, there was no room to debate, for we fancied the ship would break in pieces every minute, and some told us she was actually broken already.

In this distress the mate of our vessel lays hold of the boat, and with the help of the rest of the men they got her slung over the ship's side, and getting all into her, let go, and committed ourselves, being eleven in number, to God's mercy and the wild sea: for though the storm was abated considerably, yet the sea went dreadfully high upon the shore, and might well be called "den wild zee," as the Dutch call the sea in a storm.

And now our case was very dismal indeed; for we all saw plainly that the sea went so high that the boat could not live, and that we should be inevitably drowned. As to making sail, we had none; nor, if we had, could we have done anything with it: so we worked at the oar towards the land, though with heavy hearts, like men going to execution; for we all knew that when the boat came nearer the shore she would be dashed in a thousand pieces by the breach of the sea. However, we committed our souls to God in the most earnest manner, and the wind driving us towards the shore we hastened our destruction with our own hands, pulling as well as we could towards land.

What the shore was—whether rock or sand, whether steep or shoal—we knew not; the only hope that could rationally give us the least shadow of expectation was, if we might happen into some bay of gulf, or the mouth of some river, where by great chance we might have run our boat in, or got under the lee of the land, and perhaps made smooth water. But there was nothing of this appeared; but as we made nearer and nearer the shore, the land looked more frightful than the sea.

After we had rowed or rather driven about a league and a half, as we reckoned it, a raging wave, mountain-like, came rolling astern of us, and plainly bade us expect the *coup-de-grâce*. In a word, it took us with such a fury, that it overset the boat at once, and, separating us as well from the boat as from one another, gave us not time hardly to say, O God! for we were all swallowed up in a moment.

Nothing can describe the confusion of thought which I felt when

The last time of these two had well near been fatal to me; for the sea, having hurried me along as before, landed me, or rather dashed me against a piece of rock, and that with such force, as it left me senseless, and indeed helpless as to my own deliverance: for the blow taking my side and breast, beat the breath as it were quite out of my body, and had it returned again immediately, I must have been strangled in the water; but I recovered a little before the return of the waves, and seeing I should be covered again with the water, I resolved to hold fast by a piece of the rock, and so to hold my breath, if possible, till the wave went back. Now as the waves were not so high as at first, being near land, I held my hold till the wave abated, and then fetched another run, which brought me so near the shore, that the next wave, though it went over me, yet did not so swallow me up as to carry me away; and the next run I took I got to the mainland, where, to my great comfort, I clambered up the cliffs of the shore and sat me down upon the grass, free from danger, and quite out of the reach of the water.

I was now landed, and safe on shore, and began to look up and thank God that my life was saved in a case wherein there was some minutes before scarce any room to hope. I believe it is impossible to express to the life what the ecstasies and transports of the soul are when it is so saved, as I may say, out of the very grave; and I do not wonder now at that custom, namely, that when a malefactor, who has the halter about his neck, is tied up, and just going to be turned off, and has a reprieve brought to him—I say, I do not wonder that they bring a surgeon with it, to let him blood that very moment they tell him of it, that the surprise may not drive the animal spirits from the heart and overwhelm him:

"For sudden joys, like griefs, confound at first."

I walked about on the shore lifting up my hands, and my whole being, as I may say, wrapped up in the contemplation of my deliverance, making a thousand gestures and motions which I cannot describe, reflecting upon all my comrades that were drowned, and that there should not be one soul saved but myself; for, as for them, I never saw them afterwards, or any sign of them, except three of their hats, one cap, and two shoes that were not fellows.

I cast my eyes to the stranded vessel, when the breach and froth of the sea being so big, I could hardly see it, it lay so far off, and considered, "Lord, how was it possible I could get on shore?"

§ *My sad condition. First night on the island. In the morning I swim to the wreck. Construct a raft and bring ashore many useful things. View the country, and seek a proper place of habitation. The island appears barren and uninhabited by men. Other visits to the wreck. A storm blows the wreck off the land.*

AFTER I had solaced my mind with the comfortable part of my condition, I began to look round me to see what kind of place I was in, and what was next to be done, and I soon found my comforts abate, and that, in a word, I had a dreadful deliverance; for I was wet, had no clothes to shift me, nor anything either to eat or drink to comfort me, neither did I see any prospect before me but that of perishing with hunger, or being devoured by wild beasts. And that which was particularly afflicting to me was, that I had no weapon either to hunt and kill any creature for my sustenance, or to defend myself against any other creature that might desire to kill me for theirs; in a word, I had nothing about me but a knife, a tobacco-pipe, and a little tobacco in a box. This was all my provision, and this threw me into terrible agonies of mind, and for a while I ran about like a madman. Night coming upon me, I began, with a heavy heart, to consider what would be my lot if there were any ravenous beasts in that country, seeing at night they always come abroad for their prey.

All the remedy that offered to my thoughts at that time was to get up into a thick bushy tree like a fir, but thorny, which grew near me, and where I resolved to sit all night, and consider the next day what death I should die; for as yet I saw no prospect of life. I walked about a furlong from the shore to see if I could find any fresh water to drink, which I did, to my great joy, and having drunk, and put a little tobacco in my mouth to prevent hunger, I went to the tree, and getting up into it, endeavoured to place myself so as that if I should sleep I might not fall; and having cut me a short stick like a truncheon for my defence, I took up my lodging, and having been excessively fatigued, I fell fast asleep, and slept as comfortably as, I believe, few could have done in my condition, and found myself the most refreshed with it that I think I ever was on such an occasion.

When I waked it was broad day, the weather clear, and the storm abated, so that the sea did not rage and swell as before; but that which surprised me most was, that the ship was lifted off in the night from the sand where she lay by the swelling of the tide, and was driven up almost as far as the rock which I first mentioned, where I had been so bruised by the dashing me against it; this being within about a mile from the shore where I was, and the ship seeming to stand upright still, I wished myself on board, that at least I might have some necessary things for my use.

When I came down from my apartment in the tree, I looked about me again, and the first thing I found was the boat, which lay as the wind and the sea had tossed her up upon the land, about two miles on my right hand. I walked as far as I could upon the shore to have got to her, but found a neck or inlet of water between me and the boat which was about half a mile broad; so I came back for the present, being more intent upon getting at the ship, where I hoped to find something for my present subsistence.

A little after noon I found the sea very calm and the tide ebbed so far out that I could come within a quarter of a mile of the ship. And here I found a fresh renewing of my grief; for I saw evidently that if we had kept on board we had been all safe—that is to say, we had all got safe on shore, and I had not been so miserable as to be left entirely destitute of all comfort and company as I now was. This forced tears from my eyes again, but as there was little relief in that, I resolved, if possible, to get to the ship; so I pulled off my clothes, for the weather was hot to extremity, and took the water. But when I came to the ship, my difficulty was still greater to know how to get on board: for as she lay aground and high out of the water, there was nothing within my reach to lay hold of. I swam round her twice, and the second time I spied a small piece of a rope, which I wondered I did not see at first, hang down by the fore-chains so low as that with great difficulty I got hold of it, and by the help of that rope got up into the forecastle of the ship. Here I found that the ship was bulged, and had a great deal of water in her hold, but that she lay so on the side of a bank of hard sand, or rather earth, and her stern lay lifted up upon the bank, and her head low almost to the water. By this means all her quarter was free, and all that was in that part was dry; for you may be sure my first work was to search and to see what was spoiled and what was free. And first I found that all the ship's provisions were dry and untouched by the water, and being very well disposed to eat, I went to the bread-room and filled my pockets with biscuit, and eat it as I went about other things, for I had no time to lose. I also found some rum in the great cabin, of which I took a large dram, and which I had indeed need enough of to spirit me for what was before me. Now I wanted nothing but a boat to furnish myself with many things which I foresaw would be very necessary to me.

It was in vain to sit still and wish for what was not to be had, and this extremity roused my application. We had several spare yards, and two or three large spars of wood, and a spare top-mast or two in the ship. I resolved to fall to work with these, and flung as many of them overboard as I could manage of their weight, tying every one with a rope that they might not drive away. When this was done, I went down the ship's side, and pulling them to me, I tied four of them fast together at both ends as well as I could, in the form of a raft, and laying two or three short pieces of plank upon them crossway, I found I could walk upon it very well, but that it was not able to bear any great weight, the pieces being too light. So I went to work, and with the carpenter's saw I cut a spare top-mast into three lengths, and added them to my raft, with a great deal of labour and pains; but hope of furnishing myself with necessaries encouraged me to go beyond what I should have been able to have done upon another occasion.

My raft was now strong enough to bear any reasonable weight. My next care was what to load it with, and how to preserve what I laid upon it from the surf of the sea. But I was not long considering this. I first laid all the planks or boards upon it that I could get, and having considered well what I most wanted, I first got three of the seamen's chests, which I had broken open and emptied, and lowered them down upon my raft. The first of these I filled with provisions— namely, bread, rice, three Dutch cheeses, five pieces of dried goat's

49

flesh, which we lived much upon, and a little remainder of European corn which had been laid by for some fowls which we brought to sea with us; but the fowls were killed. There had been some barley and wheat together, but to my great disappointment I found afterwards that the rats had eaten or spoiled it all. As for liquors I found several cases of bottles belonging to our skipper, in which were some cordial waters, and in all about five or six gallons of rack. These I stowed by

themselves, there being no need to put them into the chest, nor no room for them. While I was doing this I found the tide began to flow, though very calm, and I had the mortification to see my coat, shirt, and waistcoat, which I had left on shore upon the sand, swim away; as for my breeches, which were only linen and open-kneed, I swam on board in them and my stockings. However, this put me upon rummaging for clothes, of which I found enough, but took no more than I wanted for present use, for I had other things which my eye was more upon—as, first, tools to work with on shore, and it was after long searching that I found out the carpenter's chest, which was indeed a very useful prize to me, and much more valuable than a ship loading of gold would have been at that time. I got it down to my raft even whole as it was, without losing time to look into it, for I knew in general what it contained.

My next care was for some ammunition and arms. There were two very good fowling-pieces in the great cabin, and two pistols; these I secured first, with some powder-horns, and a small bag of shot, and two old rusty swords. I knew there were three barrels of powder in the ship, but knew not where our gunner had stowed them; but with much search I found them, two of them dry and good, the third had taken water. Those two I got to my raft with the arms; and now I thought myself pretty well freighted, and began to think how I should get to shore with them, having neither sail, oar, nor rudder, and the least capful of wind would have overset all my navigation.

I had three encouragements—first, a smooth calm sea; second, the tide rising and setting in to the shore; third, what little wind there was blew me towards the land. And thus, having found two or three broken oars belonging to the boat, and besides the tools which were in the chest, I found two saws, an axe, and a hammer, and with this cargo I put to sea. For a mile or thereabout my raft went very well, only that I found it drive a little distant from the place where I had landed before; by which I perceived that there was some indraught of the water, and consequently I hoped to find some creek or river there, which I might make use of as a port to get to land with my cargo.

As I imagined, so it was. There appeared before me a little opening of the land, and I found a strong current of the tide set into it; so I guided my raft as well as I could to keep in the middle of the stream. But here I had like to have suffered a second shipwreck, which if I had, I think verily would have broken my heart; for, knowing nothing of the coast, my raft ran aground at one end of it upon a shoal, and not being aground at the other end, it wanted but a little that all my cargo had slipped off towards that end that was afloat, and so fallen into the water. I did my utmost, by setting my back against the chests, to keep them in their places, but could not thrust off the raft with all my strength, neither durst I stir from the posture I was in, but holding up the chests with all my might, stood in that manner near half an hour, in which time the rising of the water brought me a little more upon a level; and a little after, the water still rising, my raft floated again, and I thrust her off with the oar I had into the channel, and then driving up higher, I at length found myself in the mouth of a little river, with land on both sides, and a strong current or tide running up. I looked on both sides for a proper place to get to shore, for I was not willing to be driven too high up the river, hoping in time to see some ship at sea, and therefore resolved to place myself as near the coast as I could.

At length I spied a little cove on the right shore of the creek, to which with great pain and difficulty I guided my raft, and at last got so near as that, reaching ground with my oar, I could thrust her directly in. But here I had like to have dipped all my cargo in the sea again; for that shore lying pretty steep—that is to say, sloping—there was no place to land, but where one end of my float if it ran on shore, would lie so high, and the other sink lower as before, that it would endanger my cargo again. All that I could do was to wait till the tide was at the highest, keeping the raft with my oar like an anchor to hold the side of it fast to the shore near a flat piece of ground, which I expected the water would flow over; and so it did. As soon as I found water enough—for my raft drew about a foot of water—I thrust her on upon that flat piece of ground, and there fastened or moored her by sticking my two broken oars into the ground, one on one side near one end, and one on the other side near the other end; and thus I lay till the water ebbed away, and left my raft and all my cargo safe on shore.

My next work was to view the country, and seek a proper place for my habitation, and where to stow my goods to secure them from whatever might happen here. Where I was I yet knew not, whether on the continent or on an island, whether inhabited or not inhabited, whether in danger of wild beasts or not. There was a hill not above a mile from me, which rose up very steep and high, and which seemed to overtop some other hills which lay as in a ridge from it northward. I took out one of the fowling-pieces and one of the pistols, and a horn

of powder, and thus armed I travelled for discovery up to the top of that hill, where, after I had with great labour and difficulty got to the top, I saw my fate to my great affliction—namely, that I was in an island environed every way with the sea, no land to be seen, except some rocks which lay a great way off, and two small islands, less than this, which lay about three leagues to the west.

I found also that the island I was in was barren, and, as I saw good reason to believe, uninhabited, except by wild beasts—of whom, however, I saw none; yet I saw abundance of fowls, but knew not their kinds, neither when I killed them could I tell what was fit for food, and what not. At my coming back, I shot at a great bird which I saw sitting upon a tree on the side of a great wood. I believe it was the first gun that had been fired there since the creation of the world. I had no sooner fired, but from all the parts of the wood there arose an innumerable number of fowls of many sorts, making a confused screaming, and crying everyone according to his usual note; but not one of them of any kind that I knew. As for the creature I killed, I took it to be a kind of a hawk, its colour and beak resembling it, but had no talons or claws more than common; its flesh was carrion and fit for nothing.

Contented with this discovery, I came back to my raft, and fell to work to bring my cargo on shore, which took me up the rest of that day. And what to do with myself at night I knew not, nor indeed where to rest; for I was afraid to lie down on the ground, not knowing but some wild beast might devour me, though, as I afterwards found, there was really no need for those fears.

However, as well as I could, I barricaded myself round with the chests and boards that I had brought on shore, and made a kind of hut for that night's lodging. As for food, I yet saw not which way to supply myself, except that I had seen two or three creatures like hares run out of the wood where I shot the fowl.

I now began to consider that I might yet get a great many things out of the ship which would be useful to me, and particularly some of the rigging and sails, and such other things as might come to land; and I resolved to make another voyage on board the vessel, if possible;

and as I knew that the first storm that blew must necessarily break her all in pieces, I resolved to set all other things apart, till I got everything out of the ship that I could get. Then I called a council—that is to say, in my thoughts—whether I should take back the raft; but this appeared impracticable. So I resolved to go as before, when the tide was down; and I did so, only that I stripped before I went from my hut, having nothing on but a checkered shirt, and a pair of linen drawers, and a pair of pumps on my feet. I got on board the ship as before, and prepared a second raft; and having had experience of the first, I neither made this so unwieldy nor loaded it so hard, but yet I brought away several things very useful to me. At first, in the carpenter's stores, I found two or three bags full of nails and spikes, a great screw-jack, a dozen or two of hatchets, and, above all, that most useful thing called a grindstone. All these I secured together, with several things belonging to the gunner, particularly two or three iron crows, and two barrels of musket bullets, seven muskets, and another fowling-piece, with some small quantity of powder more, a large bag full of small shot, and a great roll of sheet lead. But this last was so heavy I could not hoist it up to get it over the ship's side. Besides these things, I took all the men's clothes that I could find, and a spare foretopsail, a hammock, and some bedding; and with this I loaded my second raft, and brought them all safe on shore, to my very great comfort.

I was under some apprehensions during my absence from the land that at least my provisions might be devoured on shore; but when I came back I found no sign of any visitor, only there sat a creature like a wild cat upon one of the chests, which, when I came towards it, ran away a little distance, and then stood still. She sat very composed and unconcerned, and looked full in my face, as if she had a mind to be acquainted with me. I presented my gun at her, but as she did not understand it, she was perfectly unconcerned at it, nor did she offer to stir away. Upon which I tossed her a bit of biscuit—though, by the way, I was not very free of it, for my store was not great. However, I spared her a bit, I say, and she went to it, smelled of it, and ate it, and looked, as pleased, for more; but I thanked her, and could spare no more. So she marched off.

Having got my second cargo on shore, though I was fain to open the barrels of powder, and bring them by parcels—for they were too heavy, being large casks—I went to work to make me a little tent with the sail and some poles which I cut for that purpose; and into this tent I brought everything that I knew would spoil either with rain or sun, and I piled all the empty chests and casks up in a circle round the tent, to fortify it from any sudden attempt either from man or beast.

When I had done this, I blocked up the door of the tent with some boards within, and an empty chest set up on end without, and spreading one of the beds upon the ground, laying my two pistols just at my head, and my gun at length by me, I went to bed for the first time, and slept very quietly all night, for I was very weary and heavy; for the night before I had slept little, and had laboured very hard all day, as well to fetch all those things from the ship as to get them on shore.

I had the biggest magazine of all kinds now that ever were laid up, I believe, for one man; but I was not satisfied still, for while the ship sat upright in that posture, I thought I ought to get everything out of her that I could; so every day at low water I went on board, and brought away some thing or other. But particularly the third time I went I brought away as much of the rigging as I could, as also all the small ropes and rope-twine I could get, with a piece of spare canvas, which was to mend the sails upon occasion, the barrel of wet gunpowder; in a word, I brought away all the sails first and last, only that I was fain to cut them in pieces, and bring as much at a time as I could, for they were no more useful to be sails, but as mere canvas only.

But that which comforted me more still was, that at last of all, after I had made five or six such voyages as these, and thought I had nothing more to expect from the ship that was worth my meddling with, I say, after all this, I found a great hogshead of bread, and three large runlets of rum or spirits, and a box of sugar, and a barrel of fine flour. This was surprising to me, because I had given over expecting any more provisions, except what was spoiled by the water. I soon emptied the hogshead of that bread, and wrapped it up parcel by parcel in pieces of the sails, which I cut out; and, in a word, I got all this safe on shore also.

The next day I made another voyage, and now having plundered the ship of what was portable and fit to hand out, I began with the cables; and cutting the great cable into pieces such as I could move, I got two cables and a hawser on shore, with all the ironwork I could get; and having cut down the sprit-sail yard, and the mizzen-yard, and everything I could to make a large raft, I loaded it with all those heavy goods, and came away. But my good luck began now to leave me; for this raft was so unwieldy and so overloaden, that after I was entered the little cove where I had landed the rest of my goods, not being able to guide it so handily as I did the other, it overset, and threw me and all my cargo into the water. As for myself it was no great harm, for I was near the shore; but as to my cargo, it was great part of it lost, especially the iron, which I expected would have been of great use to me. However, when the tide was out, I got most of the pieces of cable ashore and some of the iron, though with infinite labour: for I was fain to dip for it into the water, a work which fatigued me very much. After this I went every day on board, and brought away what I could get.

I had been now thirteen days on shore, and had been eleven times on board the ship, in which time I had brought away all that one pair of hands could well be supposed capable to bring; though I believe verily, had the calm weather held, I should have brought away the whole ship piece by piece. But preparing the twelfth time to go on board, I found the wind begin to rise. However, at low water I went on board; and though I thought I had rummaged the cabin so effectually as that nothing more could be found, yet I discovered a locker with drawers in it, in one of which I found two or three razors and one pair of large scissors, with some ten or a dozen of good knives and forks; in another I found about thirty-six pounds value in money, some European coin, some Brazil, some pieces of eight, some gold, some silver. I smiled to myself at the sight of this money. "Oh drug!" said I aloud, "what art thou good for? Thou are not worth to me, no not the taking off the ground; one of those knives is worth all this heap. I have no manner of use for thee: even remain where thou art, and go to the bottom as a creature whose life is not worth saving."

However, upon second thoughts, I took it away, and wrapping all this in a piece of canvas, I began to think of making another raft; but while I was preparing this, I found the sky overcast, and the wind began to rise, and in a quarter of an hour it blew a fresh gale from the shore. It presently occurred to me that it was in vain to pretend to make a raft with the wind off shore, and that it was my business to be gone before the tide of flood began, otherwise I might not be able to reach the shore at all. Accordingly I let myself down into the water, and swam across the channel which lay between the ship and the sand, and even that with difficulty enough, partly with the weight of the things I had about me, and partly the roughness of the water, for the wind rose very hastily, and before it was quite high water it blew a storm.

But I was gotten home to my little tent, where I lay with all my wealth about me very secure. It blew very hard all that night; and in the morning when I looked out, behold, no more ship was to be seen! I was a little surprised, but recovered myself with this satisfactory reflection, namely, that I had lost no time nor abated any diligence to get everything out of her that could be useful to me, and that indeed there was little left in her that I was able to bring away, if I had had more time.

I now gave over any more thoughts of the ship, or of anything out of her, except what might drive on shore from her wreck, as indeed divers pieces of her afterwards did; but those things were of small use to me.

§ *I fix on a spot for my tent, and proceed to fortify it. Anxiety about my powder. I see goats on the island. Hopeful thoughts.*

My thoughts were now wholly employed about securing myself against either savages, if any should appear, or wild beasts, if any were in the island; and I had many thoughts of the method how to do this, and what kind of dwelling to make, whether I should make me a cave in the earth, or a tent upon the earth. And, in short, I resolved upon both, the manner and description of which it may not be improper to give an account of.

I soon found the place I was in was not for my settlement, particularly because it was upon a low moorish ground near the sea, and, I believed, could not be wholesome, and more particularly, because there was no fresh water near it; so I resolved to find a more healthy and more convenient spot of ground.

I consulted several things in my situation which I found would be proper for me. First, health, and fresh water I just now mentioned. Secondly, shelter from the heat of the sun. Thirdly, security from ravenous creatures, whether men or beasts. Fourthly, a view to the sea, that if God sent any ship in sight I might not lose any advantage for my deliverance, of which I was not willing to banish all my expectation yet.

In search of a place proper for this, I found a little plain on the side of a rising hill, whose front towards this little plain was steep as a house-side, so that nothing could come down upon me from the top.

On the side of this rock there was a hollow place worn a little way in like the entrance or door of a cave; but there was not really any cave or way into the rock at all.

On the flat of the green, just before this hollow place, I resolved to pitch my tent. This plain was not above an hundred yards broad, and about twice as long, and lay like a green before my door, and at the end of it descended irregularly every way down into the low grounds by the sea-side. It was on the north-north-west side of the hill, so that I was sheltered from the heat every day till it came to a west and by south sun, or thereabouts, which in those countries is near the setting.

Before I set up my tent, I drew a half-circle before the hollow place, which took in about ten yards in its semi-diameter from the rock, and twenty yards in its diameter from its beginning and ending.

In this half-circle I pitched two rows of strong stakes, driving them into the ground till they stood very firm like piles, the biggest end being out of the ground about five foot and a half, and sharpened on the top. The two rows did not stand above six inches from one another.

Then I took the pieces of cable which I had cut in the ship, and laid them in rows one upon another within the circle, between these two rows of stakes, up to the top, placing other stakes in the inside, leaning against them, about two foot and a half high, like a spur to a post; and this fence was so strong that neither man nor beast could get into it or over it. This cost me a great deal of time and labour, especially to cut the piles in the woods, bring them to the place, and drive them into the earth.

The entrance into this place I made to be, not by a door, but by a short ladder to go over the top; which ladder, when I was in, I lifted over after me. And so I was completely fenced in and fortified, as I thought, from all the world, and consequently slept secure in the night, which otherwise I could not have done; though, as it appeared afterward, there was no need of all this caution from the enemies that I apprehended danger from.

Into this fence or fortress, with infinite labour, I carried all my riches, all my provisions, ammunition, and stores, of which you have the account above. And I made me a large tent, which, to preserve me from the rains that in one part of the year are very violent there, I made double—namely one smaller tent within, and one larger tent above it, and covered the uppermost with a large tarpaulin which I had saved among the sails.

And now I lay no more for a while in the bed which I had brought on shore, but in a hammock; which was indeed a very good one, and belonged to the mate of the ship.

Into this tent I brought all my provisions and everything that would spoil by the wet; and having thus enclosed all my goods I made up the entrance, which till now I had left open, and so passed and repassed, as I said, by a short ladder.

When I had done this, I began to work my way into the rock, and bringing all the earth and stones that I dug down out through my tent, I laid them up within my fence in the nature of a terrace, that so it raised the ground within about a foot and a half; and thus I made me a cave just behind my tent, which served me like a cellar to my house.

It cost me much labour and many days before all these things were brought to perfection, and therefore I must go back to some other things which took up some of my thoughts. At the same time it happened after I had laid my scheme for the setting up my tent, and making the cave, that a storm of rain falling from a thick dark cloud, a sudden flash of lightning happened, and after that a great clap of thunder, as is naturally the effect of it. I was not so much surprised with the lightning as I was with a thought which darted into my mind as swift as the lightning itself—O my powder! My very heart sank within me when I thought that at one blast all my powder might be destroyed, on which not my defence only, but the providing me food, as I thought, entirely depended. I was nothing near so anxious about my own danger, though had the powder taken fire, I had never known who had hurt me.

Such impression did this make upon me, that after the storm was over I laid aside all my works, my building and fortifying, and applied myself to make bags and boxes to separate the powder and keep it a little and a little in a parcel, in hope that whatever might come it might not all take fire at once, and to keep it so apart that it should not be possible to make one part fire another. I finished this work in about a fortnight; and I think my powder, which in all was about two hundred and forty pounds weight, was divided in not less than a hundred parcels. As to the barrel that had been wet, I did not apprehend any danger from that; so I placed it in my new cave, which in my fancy I called my kitchen, and the rest I hid up and down in holes among the rocks, so that no wet might come to it, marking very carefully where I laid it.

In the interval of time while this was doing I went out once at least every day with my gun as well to divert myself as to see if I could kill anything fit for food, and as near as I could to acquaint myself with what the island produced. The first time I went out I presently discovered that there were goats in the island—which was a great satisfaction to me; but then it was attended with this misfortune to me, namely, that they were so shy, so subtile, and so swift of foot, that it was the difficultest thing in the world to come at them. But I was not discouraged at this, not doubting but I might now and then shoot one, as it soon happened; for after I had found their haunts a little, I laid wait in this manner for them: I observed if they saw me in the valley, though they were upon the rocks, they would run away as in a terrible fright; but if they were feeding in the valleys, and I was upon the rocks, they took no notice of me; from whence I concluded that by the position of their optics their sight was so directed downward that they did not readily see objects that were above them. So afterward I took this method, I always climbed the rocks first, to get above them, and then had frequently a fair mark. The first shot I made among these creatures I killed a she-goat which had a little kid by her which she gave suck to, which grieved me heartily. But when the old one fell the kid stood stock-still by her till I came and took her up; and not only so, but when I carried the old one with me upon my shoulders, the kid followed me quite to my enclosure: upon which I laid down the dam and took the kid in my arms, and carried it over my pale, in hopes to have it bred up tame; but it would not eat, so I was forced to kill it and eat it myself. These two supplied me with flesh a great while, for I ate sparingly, and saved my provisions (my bread especially) as much as possibly I could.

Having now fixed my habitation, I found it absolutely necessary to provide a place to make a fire in, and fuel to burn; and what I did for that, as also how I enlarged my cave and what conveniences I made, I shall give a full account of in its place. But I must first give some little account of myself and of my thoughts about living, which it may well be supposed were not a few.

I had a dismal prospect of my condition; for as I was not cast away upon that island without being driven, as is said, by a violent storm quite out of the course of our intended voyage, and a great way, namely, some hundreds of leagues, out of the ordinary course of the trade of mankind, I had great reason to consider it as a determination of Heaven that in this desolate place and in this desolate manner I should end my life. The tears would run plentifully down my face when I made these reflections; and sometimes I would expostulate with myself why Providence should thus completely ruin its creatures and render them so absolutely miserable, so without help abandoned, so entirely depressed, that it could hardly be rational to be thankful for such a life.

But something always returned swift upon me to check these thoughts and to reprove me; and particularly one day, walking with my gun in my hand by the sea-side, I was very pensive upon the subject of my present condition, when reason, as it were, expostulated with me the other way, thus: Well, you are in a desolate condition it is true, but pray remember, where are the rest of you? Did you not come eleven of you into the boat—where are the ten? Why were not they saved and you lost? Why were you singled out? Is it better to be here or there?—and then I pointed to the sea. All evils are to be considered with the good that is in them, and with what worse attends them.

Then it occurred to me again how well I was furnished for my subsistence, and what would have been my case if it had not happened, which was an hundred thousand to one, that the ship floated from the place where she first struck, and was driven so near to the shore that I had time to get all these things out of her. What would have been my case if I had been forced to have lived in the condition in which I at first came on shore, without necessaries of life, or necessaries to supply and procure them? Particularly, said I aloud (though to myself), what should I have done without a gun, without ammunition; without any tools to make anything, or to work with; without clothes, bedding, a tent, or any manner of covering; and that now I had all these to a sufficient quantity, and was in a fair way to provide myself in such a manner, as to live without my gun when my ammunition was spent; so that I had a tolerable view of subsisting without any want as long as I lived: for I considered from the beginning how I would provide for the accidents that might happen, and for the time that was to come, even not only after my ammunition should be spent, but even after my health or strength should decay.

I confess I had not entertained any notion of my ammunition being destroyed at one blast—I mean my powder being blown up by lightning—and this made the thoughts of it so surprising to me when it lightened and thundered, as I observed just now.

And now being to enter into a melancholy relation of a scene of silent life, such, perhaps, as was never heard of in the world before, I shall take it from its beginning, and continue it in its order. It was, by my account, the 30th of September when, in the manner as above said, I first set foot upon this horrid island, when the sun being, to us, in its autumnal equinox, was almost just over my head; for I reckoned myself, by observation, to be in the latitude of 9 degrees 22 minutes north of the line.

§ *I resolve to keep a calendar. Secure a dog and two cats. Reflections on my condition. Begin to furnish my house. I feel the want of necessary articles. Copy of my Journal. God's goodness to me in sending seed-corn. Terrible earthquake and hurricane.*

AFTER I had been there about ten or twelve days it came into my thoughts that I should lose my reckoning of time for want of books and pen and ink, and should even forget the Sabbath days from the working days; but, to prevent this, I cut it with my knife upon a large post, in capital letters, and making it into a great cross, I set it up on the shore where I first landed—namely, I CAME ON SHORE HERE ON THE 30TH OF SEPTEMBER, 1659. Upon the sides of this square post I cut every day a notch with my knife, and every seventh notch was as long again as the rest, and every first day of the month as long again as that long one, and thus I kept my calendar, or weekly, monthly, and yearly reckoning of time.

In the next place we are to observe, that among the many things which I brought out of the ship in the several voyages which, as above mentioned, I made to it, I got several things of less value, but not all less useful to me, which I omitted setting down before; as, in particular, pens, ink, and paper, several parcels in the captain's, mate's, gunner's, and carpenter's keeping, three or four compasses, some mathematical instruments, dials, perspectives, charts, and books of navigation; all which I huddled together, whether I might want them or no. Also, I found three very good Bibles, which came to me in my cargo from England, and which I had packed up among my things; some Portuguese books also I found, and among them two or three prayer-books, and several other books; all which I carefully secured. And I must not forget that we had in the ship a dog and two cats, of whose eminent history I may have occasion to say something in its place: for I carried both the cats with me; and as for the dog, he jumped out of the ship of himself, and swam on shore to me the day after I went on shore with my first cargo, and was a trusty servant to me many years. I wanted nothing that he could fetch me, nor any company that he could make up to me; I only wanted to have him talk to me, but that would not do. As I observed before, I found pen, ink, and paper, and I husbanded them to the utmost; and I shall show that, while my ink lasted, I kept things very exact; but after that was gone I could not, for I could not make any ink by any means that I could devise.

And this put me in mind that I wanted many things, notwithstanding all that I had amassed together; and of these, this of ink was one; as also spade, pick-axe, and shovel, to dig or remove the earth; needles, pins, and thread; as for linen, I soon learned to want that without much difficulty.

This want of tools made every work I did go on heavily, and it was near a whole year before I had entirely finished my little pale or surrounded habitation. The piles or stakes, which were as heavy as I could well lift, were a long time in cutting and preparing in the woods, and more by far in bringing home; so that I spent sometimes two days in cutting and bringing home one of those posts, and a third day in driving it into the ground: for which purpose I got a heavy piece of wood at first, but at last bethought myself of one of the iron crows; which, however, though I found it, yet it made driving those posts or piles very laborious and tedious work.

But what need I have been concerned at the tediousness of anything I had to do, seeing I had time enough to do it in, nor had I any other employment, if that had been over, at least that I could foresee, except the ranging the island to seek for food, which I did more or less every day.

I now began to consider seriously my condition, and the circumstance I was reduced to, and I drew up the state of my affairs in writing, not so much to leave them to any that were to come after me, for I was like to have but few heirs, as to deliver my thoughts from daily poring upon them, and afflicting my mind; and as my reason began now to master my despondency, I began to comfort myself as well as I could, and to set the good against the evil, that I might have something to distinguish my case from worse; and I stated it very impartially, like debtor and creditor, the comforts I enjoyed against the miseries I suffered, thus:

| *EVIL* | *GOOD* |
|---|---|
| I am cast upon a horrible desolate island, void of all hope of recovery. | But I am alive, and not drowned, as all my ship's company was. |
| I am singled out and separated, as it were, from all the world, to be miserable. | But I am singled out, too, from all the ship's crew to be spared from death: and He that miraculously saved me from death can deliver me from this condition. |
| I am divided from mankind, a solitaire, one banished from human society. | But I am not starved and perishing on a barren place, affording no sustenance. |
| I have not clothes to cover me. | But am in a hot climate, where, if I had clothes, I could hardly wear them. |
| I am without any defence or means to resist any violence of man or beast. | But I am cast on an island where I see no wild beasts to hurt me, as I saw on the coast of Africa: and what if I had been shipwrecked there? |
| I have no soul to speak to, or relieve me. | But God wonderfully sent the ship in near enough to the shore, that I have gotten out so many necessary things as will either supply my wants, or enable me to supply myself even as long as I live. |

Upon the whole, here was an undoubted testimony that there was scare any condition in the world so miserable, but there was something negative or something positive to be thankful for in it; and let this stand as a direction from the experience of the most miserable of all conditions in this world, that we may always find in it something to comfort ourselves from, and to set in the description of good and evil, on the credit side of the account.

Having now brought my mind a little to relish my condition, and given over looking out to sea, to see if I could spy a ship; I say, giving over these things, I began to apply myself to accommodate my way of living, and to make things as easy to me as I could.

I have already described my habitation, which was a tent under the side of a rock, surrounded with a strong pale of posts and cables; but I might now rather call it a wall, for I raised a kind of wall up against it of turfs, about two foot thick on the outside; and after some time, I think it was a year and a half, I raised rafters from it leaning to the rock, and thatched or covered it with boughs of trees, and such things as I could get to keep out the rain, which I found at some times of the year very violent.

I have already observed how I brought all my goods into this pale, and into the cave which I had made behind me; but I must observe, too, that at first this was a confused heap of goods, which, as they lay in no order, so they took up all my place. I had no room to turn myself, so I set myself to enlarge my cave and works farther into the earth; for it was a loose sandy rock, which yielded easily to the labour I bestowed on it: and so, when I found I was pretty safe as to beasts of prey, I worked sideways to the right hand into the rock; and then, turning to the right again, worked quite out, and made me a door to come out, on the outside of my pale or fortification.

This gave me not only egress and regress, as it were, a backway to my tent and to my storehouse, but gave me room to stow my goods.

And now I began to apply myself to make such necessary things as I found I most wanted, as particularly a chair and a table; for without these I was not able to enjoy the few comforts I had in the world—I could not write or eat, or do several things with so much pleasure without a table.

So I went to work; and here I must needs observe, that as reason is the substance and original of the mathematics, so by stating and squaring everything by reason, and by making the most rational judgment of things, every man may be in time master of every mechanic art. I had never handled a tool in my life, and yet in time, by labour, application, and contrivance, I found at last that I wanted nothing but I could have made it, especially if I had had tools; however, I made abundance of things, even without tools, and some with no more tools than an adze and a hatchet, which perhaps were never made that way before, and that with infinite labour. For example, if

I wanted a board, I had no other way but to cut down a tree, set it on an edge before me, and hew it flat on either side with my axe, till I had brought it to be thin as a plank, and then dubb it smooth with my adze. It is true, by this method I could make but one board out of a whole tree, but this I had no remedy for but patience, any more than I had for the prodigious deal of time and labour which it took me up to make a plank or board. But my time or labour was little worth, and so it was as well employed one way as another.

However, I made me a table and a chair, as I observe above, in the first place, and this I did out of the short pieces of boards that I brought on my raft from the ship. But when I had wrought out some boards, as above, I made large shelves of the breadth of a foot and a half one over another, all along one side of my cave, to lay all my tools, nails, and ironwork, and, in a word, to separate everything at large in their places, that I might come easily at them. I knocked pieces into the wall of the rock to hang my guns and all things that would hang up.

So that had my cave been to be seen, it looked like a general magazine of all necessary things; and I had everything so ready at my hand that it was a great pleasure to me to see all my goods in such order, and especially to find my stock of all necessaries so great.

And now it was when I began to keep a journal of every day's employment—for indeed at first I was in too much hurry, and not only hurry as to labour, but in too much discomposure of mind—and my journal would have been full of many dull things. For example, I must have said thus: *September* 30. After I got to shore and had escaped drowning, instead of being thankful to God for my deliverance—having first vomited with the great quantity of salt water which was gotten into my stomach, and recovering myself a little—I ran about the shore, wringing my hands and beating my head and face, exclaiming at my misery, and crying out I was undone, undone! till, tired and faint, I was forced to lie down on the ground to repose, but durst not sleep for fear of being devoured.

Some days after this, and after I had been on board the ship and got all that I could out of her, yet I could not forbear getting up to the

top of a little mountain and looking out to sea in hopes of seeing a ship, then fancy at a vast distance I spied a sail, please myself with the hopes of it, and then after looking steadily till I was almost blind, lose it quite, and sit down and weep like a child, and thus increase my misery by my folly.

But having gotten over these things in some measure, and having settled my household stuff and habitation, made me a table and a chair, and all as handsome about me as I could, I began to keep my journal, of which I shall here give you the copy (though in it will be told all these particulars over again) as long as it lasted, for, having no more ink, I was forced to leave it off.

## THE JOURNAL

*September* 30, 1659. I, poor, miserable Robinson Crusoe, being shipwrecked during a dreadful storm in the offing, came on shore on this dismal unfortunate island, which I called the Island of Despair, all the rest of the ship's company being drowned, and myself almost dead.

All the rest of that day I spent in afflicting myself at the dismal circumstances I was brought to—namely, I had neither food, house, clothes, weapon, nor place to fly to, and, in despair of any relief, saw nothing but death before me—either that I should be devoured by wild beasts, murdered by savages, or starved to death for want of food. At the approach of night I slept in a tree for fear of wild creatures, but slept soundly though it rained all night.

*October* 1. In the morning I saw, to my great surprise, the ship had floated with the high tide, and was driven on shore again much nearer the island; which as it was some comfort, on one hand, for, seeing her sit upright, and not broken to pieces, I hoped, if the wind abated, I might get on board and get some food and necessaries out of her for my relief; so, on the other hand, it renewed my grief at the loss of my comrades, who, I imagined, if we had all stayed on board, might have saved the ship, or at least that they would not have been all drowned as they were; and that, had the men been saved, we might perhaps have built us a boat out of the ruins of the ship to have carried us to some other part of the world. I spent great part of this day in perplexing myself on these things; but at length, seeing the ship almost dry, I went upon the sand as near as I could, and then swam on board; this day also it continued raining, though with no wind at all.

*From the 1st of October to the 24th.* All these days entirely spent in many several voyages to get all I could out of the ship, which I brought on shore, every tide of flood, upon rafts. Much rain also in these days, though with some intervals of fair weather; but, it seems, this was the rainy season.

*October* 20. I overset my raft, and all the goods I had got upon it; but being in shoal water, and the things being chiefly heavy, I recovered many of them when the tide was out.

*October* 25. It rained all night and all day, with some gusts of wind, during which time the ship broke in pieces, the wind blowing a little harder than before, and was no more to be seen, except the wreck of her, and that only at low water. I spent this day in covering and securing the goods which I had saved, that the rain might not spoil them.

*October* 26. I walked about the shore almost all day to find out a place to fix my habitation, greatly concerned to secure myself from an attack in the night either from wild beasts or men. Towards night I fixed upon a proper place under a rock, and marked out a semicircle for my encampment, which I resolved to strengthen with a work, wall, or fortification made of double piles, lined within with cables and without with turf.

From the 26th to the 30th I worked very hard in carrying all my goods to my new habitation, though some part of the time it rained exceeding hard.

The 31st in the morning I went out into the island with my gun to seek for some food, and discover the country, when I killed a she-goat, and her kid followed me home, which I afterwards killed also, because it would not feed.

*November* 1. I set up my tent under a rock, and lay there for the first night, making it as large as I could with stakes driven in to swing my hammock upon.

*November* 2. I set up all my chests and boards, and the pieces of timber which made my rafts, and with them formed a fence round me, a little within the place I had marked out for my fortification.

*November* 3. I went out with my gun, and killed two fowls like ducks, which were very good food. In the afternoon went to work to make me a table.

*November* 4. This morning I began to order my times of work, of going out with my gun, time of sleep and time of diversion—namely, every morning I walked out with my gun for two or three hours if it did not rain, then employed myself to work till about eleven o'clock, then ate what I had to live on; and from twelve to two I lay down to sleep, the weather being excessive hot; and then in the evening to work again. The working part of this day and of the next were wholly employed in making my table; for I was yet but a very sorry workman, though time and necessity made me a complete natural mechanic soon after, as I believe it would do any one else.

*November* 5. This day went abroad with my gun and my dog, and killed a wild cat, her skin pretty soft, but her flesh good for

74

nothing. Every creature I killed I took off the skins and preserved them. Coming back by the seashore, I saw many store of sea-fowls, which I did not understand; but was surprised and almost frightened with two or three seals, which while I was gazing at, not well knowing what they were, got into the sea, and escaped me for that time.

*November* 6. After my morning walk I went to work with my table again, and finished it, though not to my liking; nor was it long before I learned to mend it.

*November* 7. Now it began to be settled fair weather. The 7th, 8th, 9th, 10th, and part of the 12th (for the 11th was Sunday), I took wholly up to make me a chair, and with much ado brought it to a tolerable shape, but never to please me; and even in the making I pulled it in pieces several times. *Note.*—I soon neglected my keeping Sundays; for, omitting my mark for them on my post, I forgot which was which.

*November* 13. This day it rained, which refreshed me exceedingly, and cooled the earth; but it was accompanied with terrible thunder and lightning, which frightened me dreadfully for fear of my powder. As soon as it was over I resolved to separate my stock of powder into as many little parcels as possible, that it might not be in danger.

*November* 14, 15, 16. These three days I spent in making little square chests or boxes, which might hold about a pound, or two at most, of powder; and so putting the powder in, I stowed it in places as secure and remote from one another as possible. On one of these three days I killed a large bird that was good to eat, but I know not what to call it.

*November* 17. This day I began to dig behind my tent into the rock, to make room for my further conveniency. *Note.*—Three things I wanted exceedingly for this work—namely, a pick-axe, a shovel, and a wheelbarrow or basket. So I desisted from my work and began to consider how to supply that want, and make me some tools. As for a pick-axe I made use of the iron crows, which were proper enough though heavy. But the next thing was a shovel or spade; this was so absolutely necessary, that indeed I could do nothing effectually without it. But what kind of one to make I knew not.

*November* 18. The next day, in searching the woods, I found a tree of that wood, or like it, which in the Brazils they call the iron tree, for its exceeding hardness. Of this, with great labour and almost spoiling my axe, I cut a piece, and brought it home too with difficulty enough, for it was exceeding heavy.

The excessive hardness of the wood, and having no other way, made me a long while upon this machine; for I worked it effectually by little and little into the form of a shovel or spade, the handle exactly shaped like ours in England, only that the broad part having no iron shod upon it at bottom, it would not last me so long. However, it served well enough for the uses which I had occasion to put it to; but never was a shovel, I believe, made after that fashion, or so long a-making.

I was still deficient, for I wanted a basket or a wheelbarrow. A basket I could not make by any means, having no such things as twigs that would bend to make wicker ware, at least none yet found out. And as to a wheelbarrow, I fancied I could make all but the wheel, but that I had no notion of, neither did I know how to go about it; besides, I had no possible way to make the iron gudgeons for the spindle or axis of the wheel to run in, so I gave it over. And so, for carrying away the earth which I dug out of the cave, I made me a thing like a hod, which the labourers carry mortar in when they serve the bricklayers.

This was not so difficult to me as the making the shovel; and yet this and the shovel, and the attempt which I made in vain to make a wheelbarrow, took me up no less than four days—I mean always excepting my morning walk with my gun, which I seldom failed, and very seldom failed also bringing home something fit to eat.

*November* 23. My other work having now stood still because of my making these tools, when they were finished I went on, and working every day as my strength and time allowed, I spent eighteen days entirely in widening and deepening my cave, that it might hold my goods commodiously.

*Note.*—During all this time I worked to make this room or cave spacious enough to accommodate me as a warehouse or magazine, a kitchen, a dining-room, and a cellar. As for my lodging, I kept to the tent, except that sometimes, in the wet season of the year, it rained so hard that I could not keep myself dry; which caused me afterwards to cover all my place within my pale with long poles in the form of rafters, leaning against the rock, and load them with flags and large leaves of trees like a thatch.

*December* 10. I began now to think my cave or vault finished, when on a sudden (it seems I hade made it too large) a great quantity of earth fell down from the top and one side, so much that, in short, it frightened me; and not without reason too, for if I had been under it, I had never wanted a grave-digger. Upon this disaster I had a great deal of work to do over again; for I had the loose earth to carry out, and, which was of more importance, I had the ceiling to prop up, so that I might be sure no more would come down.

*December* 11. This day I went to work with it accordingly, and got two shores or posts pitched upright to the top, with two pieces of boards across over each post. This I finished the next day, and setting more posts up with boards, in about a week more I had the roof secured; and the posts, standing in rows, served me for partitions to part off my house.

*December* 17. From this day to the 20th I placed shelves, and knocked up nails on the posts to hang everything up that could be hung up; and now I began to be in some order within doors.

*December* 20. Now I carried everything into the cave and began to furnish my house, and set up some pieces of boards, like a dresser, to order my victuals upon; but boards began to be very scarce with me. Also I made me another table.

*December* 24. Much rain all night and all day. No stirring out.

*December* 25. Rain all day.

*December* 26. No rain, and the earth much cooler than before and pleasanter.

*December* 27. Killed a young goat, and lamed another so that I caught it, and led it home in a string. When I had it home I bound and splintered up its leg, which was broken. *N.B.*—I took such care of it that it lived, and the leg grew well and as strong as ever; but by nursing it so long it grew tame, and fed upon the little green at my door, and would not go away. This was the first time that I entertained a thought of breeding up some tame creatures, that I might have food when my powder and shot was all spent.

*December* 28, 29, 30. Great heats and no breeze, so that there was no stirring abroad, except in the evening for food. This time I spent in putting all my things in order within doors.

*January* 1. Very hot still, but I went abroad early and late with my gun, and lay still in the middle of the day. This evening, going farther into the valleys which lay towards the centre of the island, I found there was plenty of goats, though exceeding shy and hard to come at. However, I resolved to try if I could not bring my dog to hunt them down.

*January* 2. Accordingly, the next day I went out with my dog, and set him upon the goats; but I was mistaken, for they all faced about upon the dog, and he knew his danger too well, for he would not come near them.

*January* 3. I began my fence or wall, which, being still jealous of my being attacked by somebody, I resolved to make very thick and strong.

*N.B.*—This wall being described before, I purposely omit what was said in the journal. It is sufficient to observe that I was no less time than from the 3rd of January to the 14th of April working, finishing, and perfecting this wall, though it was no more than about twenty-four yards in length, being a half circle from one place in the rock to another place about eight yards from it, the door of the cave being in the centre behind it.

All this time I worked very hard, the rains hindering me many days, nay, sometimes weeks together; but I thought I should never be perfectly secure till this wall was finished. And it is scarce credible what inexpressible labour everything was done with, especially the bringing piles out of the woods and driving them into the ground, for I made them much bigger than I need to have done.

When this wall was finished, and the outside double fenced with a turf wall raised up close to it, I persuaded myself that if any people were to come on shore there, they would not perceive anything like a habitation. And it was very well I did so, as many be observed hereafter upon a very remarkable occasion.

During this time I made my rounds in the woods for game every day when the rain admitted me, and made frequent discoveries in these walks of something or other to my advantage. Particularly I found a kind of wild pigeons, who built not as wood-pigeons, in a tree, but rather as house-pigeons in the holes of the rocks; and taking some young ones, I endeavoured to breed them up tame, and did so; but when they grew older they flew all away, which perhaps was at first for want of feeding them, for I had nothing to give them. However, I frequently found their nests, and got their young ones, which were very good meat.

And now, in the managing my household affairs, I found myself wanting in many things, which I thought at first was impossible for me to make, as indeed as to some of them it was. For instance, I could never make a cask to be hooped. I had a small runlet or two, as I observed before, but I could never arrive to the capacity of making one by them, though I spent many weeks about it. I could neither put in the heads, nor joint the staves so true to one another as to make them hold water. So I gave that also over.

In the next place, I was at a great loss for candle; so that as soon as ever it was dark, which was generally by seven o'clock, I was obliged to go to bed. I remembered the lump of bees'-wax with which I made candles in my African adventure, but I had none of that now. The only remedy I had was, that when I had killed a goat I saved the tallow; and with a little dish made of clay, which I baked in the sun, to which I added a wick of some oakum, I made me a lamp, and this gave me light, though not a clear, steady light, like a candle. In the middle of all my labours it happened that, rummaging my things, I found a little bag, which, as I hinted before, had been filled with corn for the feeding of poultry, not for this voyage, but before, as I suppose, when the ship came from Lisbon. What little remainder of corn had been in the bag was all devoured with the rats, and I saw nothing in the bag but husks and dust; and being willing to have the bag for some other use (I think it was to put powder in, when I divided it for fear of the lightning, or some such use), I shook the husks of corn out of it on one side of my fortification under the rock.

It was a little before the great rains just now mentioned that I threw this stuff away, taking no notice of anything, and not so much as remembering that I had thrown anything there, when, about a month after, or thereabout, I saw some few stalks of something green shooting out of the ground, which I fancied might be some plant I had not seen; but I was surprised and perfectly astonished when, after a longer time, I saw about ten or twelve ears come out, which were perfect green barley, of the same kind as our European, nay, as our English barley.

It is impossible to express the astonishment and confusion of my thoughts on this occasion. I had hitherto acted upon no religious foundation at all; indeed, I had very few notions of religion in my head, nor had entertained any sense of anything that had befallen me otherwise than as a chance, or, as we lightly say, what pleases God, without so much as inquiring into the end of Providence in these things, or His order in governing events in the world. But after I saw barley grow there, in a climate which I know was not proper for corn, and especially that I knew not how it came there, it startled me strangely, and I began to suggest that God had miraculously caused this grain to grow without any help of seed sown, and that it was so directed purely for my sustenance on that wild miserable place.

This touched my heart a little, and brought tears out of my eyes; and I began to bless myself that such a prodigy of nature should happen upon my account. And this was the more strange to me, because I saw near it still all along by the side of the rock some other straggling stalks, which proved to be stalks of rice, and which I knew because I had seen it grow in Africa when I was ashore there.

I not only thought these the pure productions of Providence for my support, but not doubting but that there was more in the place, I went all over that part of the island where I had been before, peering in every corner and under every rock to see for more of it; but I could not find any. At last it occurred to my thoughts that I had shaken a bag of chickens' meat out in that place, and then the wonder began to cease; and I must confess my religious thankfulness to God's providence began to abate too upon the discovering that all this was nothing but what was common; though I ought to have been as thankful for so strange and unforeseen providence as if it had been miraculous: for it was really the work of Providence as to me that should order or appoint that ten or twelve grains of corn should remain unspoiled (when the rats had destroyed all the rest), as if it had been dropped from heaven; as also that I should throw it out in that particular place, where, it being in the shade of a high rock, it sprang up immediately; whereas, if I had thrown it anywhere else at that time, it had been burned up and destroyed.

I carefully saved the ears of this corn, you may be sure, in their season, which was about the end of June; and laying up every corn, I resolved to sow them all again, hoping in time to have some quantity sufficient to supply me with bread. But it was not till the fourth year that I could allow myself the least grain of this corn to eat, and even then but sparingly, as I shall say afterwards in its order, for I lost all that I sowed the first season by not observing the proper time, for I sowed it just before the dry season, so that it never came up at all, at least not as it would have done—of which in its place.

Besides this barley, there was, as above, twenty or thirty stalks of rice, which I preserved with the same care, and whose use was of the same kind or to the same purpose—namely, to make me bread, or rather food, for I found ways to cook it up without baking, though I did that also after some time. But to return to my journal.

I worked excessively hard these three or four months to get my wall done; and the 14th of April I closed it up, contriving to go into it, not by a door, but over the wall by a ladder, that there might be no sign in the outside of my habitation.

*April* 16. I finished the ladder; so I went up with the ladder to the top, and then pulled it up after me, and let it down on the inside. This was a complete enclosure to me, for within I had room enough, and nothing could come at me from without unless it could first mount my wall.

The very next day after this wall was finished I had almost had all my labour overthrown at once, and myself killed. The case was thus: As I was busy in the inside of it, behind my tent, just in the entrance into my cave, I was terribly frightened with a most dreadful surprising thing indeed, for all on a sudden I found the earth come crumbling down from the roof of my cave and from the edge of the hill over my head, and two of the posts I had set up in the cave cracked in a frightful manner. I was heartily scared, but thought nothing of what was really the cause—only thinking that the top of my cave was falling in, as some of it had done before; and for fear I should be buried in it, I ran forward to my ladder, and not thinking myself safe there neither, I got over my wall for fear of the pieces of the hill which I expected might roll down upon me. I was no sooner stepped down upon the firm ground but I plainly saw it was a terrible earthquake, for the ground I stood on shook three times at about eight minutes' distance with three such shocks as would have overturned the strongest building that could be supposed to have stood on the earth; and a great piece of the top of a rock, which stood about half a mile from me next the sea, fell down with such a terrible noise as I never heard in all my life. I perceived also the very sea was put into violent motion by it, and I believe the shocks were stronger under the water than on the island.

I was so amazed with the thing itself—having never felt the like or discoursed with any one that had—that I was like one dead or stupefied; and the motion of the earth made my stomach sick, like one that was tossed at sea. But the noise of the falling of the rock awakened me, as it were, and rousing me from the stupefied condition I was in, filled me with horror, and I thought of nothing then but the hill falling upon my tent and all my household goods, and burying all at once; and this sunk my very soul within me a second time.

After the third shock was over, and I felt no more for some time, I began to take courage; and yet I had not heart enough to go over my wall again, for fear of being buried alive, but sat still upon the ground, greatly cast down and disconsolate, not knowing what to do. All this while I had not the least serious religious thought, nothing but the common "Lord have mercy upon me"; and when it was over, that went away too.

While I sat thus, I found the air overcast and grow cloudy, as if it would rain. Soon after that the wind rose by little and little, so that in less than half an hour it blew a most dreadful hurricane. The sea was all on a sudden covered over with foam and froth, the shore was covered with the breach of the water, the trees were torn up by the roots, and a terrible storm it was; and this held about three hours and then began to abate, and in two hours more it was calm and began to rain very hard. All this while I sat upon the ground very much terrified and dejected, when on a sudden it came into my thoughts that these winds and rain being the consequences of the earthquake, the earthquake itself was spent and over, and I might venture into my cave again. With this thought my spirits began to revive, and the rain also helping to persuade me, I went in and sat down in my tent—but the rain was so violent that my tent was ready to be beaten down with it, and I was forced to go into my cave, though very much afraid and uneasy for fear it should fall on my head.

This violent rain forced me to a new work—namely, to cut a hole through my new fortification like a sink to let the water go out, which would else have drowned my cave. After I had been in my cave some time and found still no more shocks of the earthquake follow, I began to be more composed; and now to support my spirits—which indeed wanted it very much—I went to my little store and took a small sup of rum, which however I did then and always very sparingly, knowing I could have no more when that was gone.

It continued raining all that night and great part of the next day, so that I could not stir abroad; but my mind being more composed, I began to think of what I had best do, concluding that if the island was subject to these earthquakes there would be no living for me in a cave, but I must consider of building me some little hut in an open place which I might surround with a wall as I had done here, and so make myself secure from wild beasts or men, but concluded, if I stayed where I was, I should certainly, one time or other, be buried alive.

With these thoughts I resolved to remove my tent from the place where it stood, which was just under the hanging precipice of the hill, and which, if it should be shaken again, would certainly fall upon my tent.

And I spent the two next days, being the 19th and 20th of April, in contriving where and how to remove my habitation.

The fear of being swallowed up alive made me that I never slept in quiet, and yet the apprehension of lying abroad without any fence was almost equal to it; but still when I looked about and saw how everything was put in order, how pleasantly concealed I was, and how safe from danger, it made me very loath to remove.

In the meantime it occurred to me that it would require a vast deal of time for me to do this, and that I must be contented to run the venture where I was, till I had formed a camp for myself, and had secured it so as to remove to it. So with this resolution I composed myself for a time, and resolved that I would go to work with all speed to build me a wall with piles and cables, &c., in a circle as before, and set my tent up in it when it was finished, but that I would venture to stay where I was till it was finished and fit to remove to. This was the 21st.

*April* 22. The next morning I began to consider of means to put this resolve in execution, but I was at a great loss about my tools. I had three large axes and abundance of hatchets (for we carried the hatchets for traffic with the Indians), but with much chopping and cutting knotty hard wood they were all full of notches and dull; and though I had a grindstone, I could not turn it and grind my tools too. This cost me as much thought as a statesman would have bestowed upon a grand point of politics, or a judge upon the life and death of a man. At length I contrived a wheel with a string to turn it with my foot, that I might have both my hands at liberty.—*Note.* I had never seen any such thing in England, or at least not to take notice how it was done, though since I have observed it is very common there; besides that, my grindstone was very large and heavy. This machine cost me a full week's work to bring it to perfection.

*April* 28, 29. These two whole days I took up in grinding my tools, my machine for turning my grindstone performing very well.

*April* 30. Having perceived my bread had been low a great while, now I took a survey of it and reduced myself to one biscuit-cake a day, which made my heart very heavy.

*May* 1. In the morning, looking towards the sea-side, the tide being low, I saw something lie on the shore bigger than ordinary, and it looked like a cask. When I came to it, I found a small barrel and two or three pieces of the wreck of the ship, which were driven on shore by the late hurricane; and looking towards the wreck itself, I thought it seemed to lie higher out of the water than it used to do. I examined the barrel which was driven on shore, and soon found it was a barrel of gunpowder; but it had taken water, and the powder was caked as hard as a stone. However, I rolled it farther on shore for the present, and went on upon the sands as near as I could to the wreck of the ship to look for more.

§ *The storm drives the wreck farther in-shore. I visit it daily. Find a turtle. I fall ill of fever and ague. A frightful dream. Wholesome thoughts, leading to prayer. I find a Bible.*

WHEN I came down to the ship I found it strangely removed. The forecastle, which lay before buried in sand, was heaved up at least six foot; and the stern, which was broken to pieces and parted from the rest by the force of the sea soon after I had left rummaging her, was tossed, as it were, up and cast on one side; and the sand was thrown so high on that side next her stern, that whereas there was a great place of water before, so that I could not come within a quarter of a mile of the wreck without swimming, I could now walk quite up to her when the tide was out. I was surprised with this at first, but soon concluded it must be done by the earthquake. And as by this violence the ship was more broken open than formerly, so many things came daily on shore which the sea had loosened, and which the winds and the water rolled by degrees to the land.

This wholly diverted my thoughts from the design of removing my habitation; and I busied myself mightily, that day especially, in searching whether I could make any way into the ship; but I found nothing was to be expected of that kind, for that all the inside of the ship was choked up with sand. However, as I had learned not to despair of anything, I resolved to pull everything to pieces that I could of the ship, concluding that everything I could get from her would be of some use or other to me.

*May* 3. I began with my saw, and cut a piece of a beam through, which I thought held some of the upper part or quarter-deck together; and when I had cut it through I cleared away the sand as well as I could from the side which lay highest; but the tide coming in, I was obliged to give over for that time.

*May* 4. I went a-fishing, but caught not one fish that I durst eat of, till I was weary of my sport; when just going to leave off, I caught a young dolphin. I had made me a long line of some rope yarn, but I had no hooks, yet I frequently caught fish enough, as much as I cared to eat; all which I dried in the sun, and ate them dry.

*May* 5. Worked on the wreck, cut another beam asunder, and brought three great fir planks off from the decks, which I tied together, and made swim on shore when the tide of flood came on.

*May* 6. Worked on the wreck, got several iron bolts out of her, and other pieces of ironwork, worked very hard, and came home very much tired, and had thoughts of giving it over.

*May* 7. Went to the wreck again, but with an intent not to work; but found the weight of the wreck had broken itself down, the beams being cut, that several pieces of the ship seemed to lie loose, and the inside of the hold lay so open that I could see into it, but almost full of water and sand.

*May* 8. Went to the wreck, and carried an iron crow to wrench up the deck, which lay now quite clear of the water or sand. I wrenched open two planks, and brought them on shore also with the tide. I left the iron crow in the wreck for next day.

*May* 9. Went to the wreck, and with the crow made way into the body of the wreck, and felt several casks, and loosened them with the crow, but could not break them up. I felt also the roll of English lead, and could stir it, but it was too heavy to remove.

*May* 10, 11, 12, 13, 14. Went every day to the wreck, and got a great deal of pieces of timber and boards, or planks, and two or three hundredweight of iron.

*May* 15.—I carried two hatchets to try if I could not cut a piece off of the roll of lead, by placing the edge of one hatchet and driving it with the other; but as it lay about a foot and a half in the water, I could not make any blow to drive the hatchet.

*May* 16. It had blowed hard in the night, and the wreck appeared more broken by the force of the water; but I stayed so long in the woods to get pigeons for food, that the tide prevented me going to the wreck that day.

*May* 17. I saw some pieces of the wreck blown on shore, at a great distance, near two miles off me, but resolved to see what they were, and found it was a piece of the head, but too heavy for me to bring away.

*May* 24. Every day to this day I worked on the wreck, and with hard labour I loosened some things so much with the crow, that the first blowing tide several casks floated out, and two of the seamen's chests; but the wind blowing from the shore, nothing came to land that day but pieces of timber, and a hogshead which had some Brazil pork in it, but the salt water and the sand had spoiled it.

I continued this work every day to the 15th of June, except the time necessary to get food, which I always appointed, during this part of my employment, to be when the tide was up, that I might be ready when it was ebbed out; and by this time I had gotten timber and plank and ironwork enough to have built a good boat, if I had known how; and also, I got at several times and in several pieces, near one hundredweight of the sheet lead.

*June* 16. Going down to the sea-side, I found a large tortoise or turtle. This was the first I had seen; which, it seems, was only my misfortune, not any defect of the place or scarcity; for had I happened to be on the other side of the island, I might have had hundreds of them every day, as I found afterwards; but, perhaps, had paid dear enough for them.

*June* 17. I spent in cooking the turtle. I found in her three-score eggs; and her flesh was to me at that time the most savoury and pleasant that ever I tasted in my life, having had no flesh, but of goats and fowls, since I landed in this horrid place.

*June* 18. Rained all day, and I stayed within. I thought at this time the rain felt cold, and I was something chilly, which I knew was not usual in that latitude.

*June* 19. Very ill, and shivering, as if the weather had been cold.

*June* 20. No rest all night, violent pains in my head, and feverish.

*June* 21. Very ill. Frightened almost to death with the apprehenhensions of my sad condition—to be sick and no help. Prayed to God for the first time since the storm off Hull; but scarce knew what I said, or why, my thoughts being all confused.

*June* 22. A little better, but under dreadful apprehensions of sickness.

*June* 23. Very bad again, cold and shivering, and then a violent headache.

*June* 24. Much better.

*June 25.* An ague, very violent. The fit held me seven hours, cold fit and hot, with faint sweats after it.

*June 26.* Better; and having no victuals to eat, took my gun, but found myself very weak. However, I killed a she-goat, and with much difficulty got it home, and broiled some of it and ate. I would fain have stewed it, and made some broth, but had no pot.

*June 27.* The ague again, so violent that I lay a-bed all day, and neither ate nor drank. I was ready to perish for thirst, but so weak, I had not strength to stand up or to get myself any water to drink. Prayed to God again; but was light-headed, and when I was not, I was so ignorant that I knew not what to say; only I lay and cried, "Lord, look upon me; Lord, pity me; Lord, have mercy upon me!" I suppose I did nothing else for two or three hours, till the fit wearing off I fell asleep, and did not wake till far in the night. When I waked I found myself much refreshed, but weak and exceedingly thirsty. However, as I had no water in my whole habitation, I was forced to lie till morning, and went to sleep again. In this second sleep I had this terrible dream:

I thought that I was sitting on the ground on the outside of my wall, where I sat when the storm blew after the earthquake, and that I saw a man descend from a great black cloud, in a bright flame of fire, and light upon the ground. He was all over as bright as a flame so that I could just bear to look towards him. His countenance was most inexpressibly dreadful, impossible for words to describe. When he stepped upon the ground with his feet, I thought the earth trembled, just as it had done before in the earthquake; and all the air looked, to my apprehension, as if it had been filled with flashes of fire.

He was no sooner landed upon the earth but he moved forward towards me, with a long spear or weapon in his hand, to kill me. And when he came to a rising ground at some distance, he spoke to me, or I heard a voice so terrible, that it is impossible to express the terror of it. All that I can say I understood was this, "Seeing all these things have not brought thee to repentance, now thou shalt die." At which words, I thought he lifted up the spear that was in his hand to kill me.

No one that shall ever read this account will expect that I should be able to describe the horrors of my soul at this terrible vision. I mean, that even while it was a dream, I even dreamed of those horrors. Nor is it any more possible to describe the impression that remained upon my mind, when I awaked and found it was but a dream.

I had, alas! no divine knowledge. What I had received by the good instruction of my father was then worn out by an uninterrupted series, for eight years, of seafaring wickedness, and a constant conversation with nothing but such as were like myself, wicked and profane to the last degree. I do not remember that I had in all that time one thought that so much as tended either to looking upwards toward God, or inwards towards a reflection upon my own ways. But a certain stupidity of soul, without desire of good or conscience of evil, had entirely overwhelmed me, and I was all that the most hardened, unthinking, wicked creature among our common sailors can be supposed to be, not having the least sense, either of the fear of God in danger, or of thankfulness to God in deliverances.

In the relating what is already past of my story, this will be the more easily believed, when I shall add, that through all the variety of miseries that had to this day befallen me, I never had so much as one thought of it being the hand of God, or that it was a just punishment for my sin, my rebellious behaviour against my father, or my present sins, which were great; or so much as a punishment for the general course of my wicked life. When I was on the desperate expedition on the desert shores of Africa, I never had so much as one thought of what would become of me; or one wish to God to direct me whither I should go, or to keep me from the danger which apparently surrounded me, as well from voracious creatures as cruel savages. But I was merely thoughtless of a God, or a Providence; acted like a mere brute from the principles of nature, and by the dictates of common sense only, and indeed hardly that.

When I was delivered and taken up at sea by the Portugal captain, well used, and dealt justly and honourably with, as well as charitably, I had not the least thankfulness on my thoughts. When again I was shipwrecked, ruined, and in danger of drowning on this island, I was as far from remorse, or looking on it as a judgment; I only said to myself often that I was an unfortunate dog, and born to be always miserable.

It is true, when I got on shore first here, and found all my ship's crew drowned, and myself spared, I was surprised with a kind of ecstasy and some transports of soul, which, had the grace of God assisted, might have come up to true thankfulness. But it ended where it begun, in a mere common flight of joy, or, as I may say, being glad I was alive, without the least reflection upon the distinguishing goodness of the hand which had preserved me, and had singled me out to be preserved, when all the rest were destroyed; or an inquiry why Providence had been thus merciful to me—even just the same common sort of joy which seamen generally have after they have got safe ashore from a shipwreck, and forget almost as soon as it is over; and all the rest of my life was like it.

Even when I was afterwards, on due consideration, made sensible of my condition, how I was cast on this dreadful place, out of the reach of human kind, out of all hope of relief or prospect of redemption, as soon as I saw but a prospect of living, and that I should not starve and perish for hunger, all the sense of my affliction wore off, and I begun to be very easy, applied myself to the works proper for my preservation and supply, and was far enough from being afflicted at my condition, as a judgment from heaven, or as the hand of God against me. These were thoughts which very seldom entered into my head.

The growing up of the corn, as is hinted in my journal, had at first some little influence upon me, and began to affect me with seriousness, as long as I thought it had something miraculous in it; but as soon as ever that part of the thought was removed, all the impression which was raised from it wore off also, as I have noted already.

Even the earthquake, though nothing could be more terrible in its nature, or more immediately directing to the Invisible Power which alone directs such things, yet no sooner was the first fright over, but the impression it had made went off also. I had no more sense of God or His judgments, much less of the present affliction of my circumstances being from His hand, than if I had been in the most prosperous condition of life.

But now when I began to be sick, and a leisurely view of the miseries of death came to place itself before me; when my spirits began to sink under the burden of a strong distemper, and nature was exhausted with the violence of the fever; conscience, that had slept so long, began to awake, and I began to reproach myself with my past life, in which I had so evidently, by uncommon wickedness, provoked the justice of God to lay me under uncommon strokes, and to deal with me in so vindictive a manner.

These reflections oppressed me for the second or third day of my distemper, and in the violence, as well of the fever as of the dreadful reproaches of my conscience, extorted some words from me like praying to God, though I cannot say they were either a prayer attended with desires or with hopes; it was rather the voice of mere fright and distress. My thoughts were confused, the convictions great upon my mind, and the horror of dying in such a miserable condition raised vapours into my head with the mere apprehensions; and in these hurries of my soul I know not what my tongue might express. But it was rather exclamation, such as, "Lord, what a miserable creature am I! If I should be sick, I shall certainly die for want of help, and what will become of me?" Then the tears burst out of my eyes, and I could say no more for a good while.

In this interval, the good advice of my father came to my mind, and presently his prediction, which I mentioned at the beginning of this story, namely, that if I did take this foolish step, God would not bless me, and I would have leisure hereafter to reflect upon having neglected his counsel, when there might be none to assist in my recovery. "Now," said I aloud, "my dear father's words are come to pass: God's justice has overtaken me, and I have none to help or hear me. I rejected the voice of Providence, which had mercifully put me in a posture or station of life wherein I might have been happy and easy; but I would neither see it myself nor learn to know the blessing of it from my parents. I left them to mourn over my folly, and now I am left to mourn under the consequences of it. I refused their help and assistance who would have lifted me into the world, and would have made everything easy to me; and now I have difficulties to struggle with, too great for even nature itself to support, and no assistance, no help, no comfort, no advice." Then I cried out, "Lord, be my help; for I am in great distress." This was the first prayer, if I may call it so, that I had made for many years. But I return to my journal.

*June* 28. Having been somewhat refreshed with the sleep I had had, and the fit being entirely off, I got up; and though the fright and terror of my dream was very great, yet I considered that the fit of the ague would return again the next day, and now was my time to get something to refresh and support myself when I should be ill. And the first thing I did, I filled a large square case-bottle with water, and set it upon my table, in reach of my bed; and to take off the chill or aguish disposition of the water, I put about a quarter of a pint of rum into it and mixed them together. Then I got me a piece of the goat's flesh and broiled it on the coals, but could eat very little. I walked about, but was very weak, and withal very sad and heavy-hearted in the sense of my miserable condition, dreading the return of my distemper the next day. At night I made my supper of three of the turtle's eggs, which I roasted in the ashes, and ate, as we call it, in the shell: and this was the first bit of meat I had ever asked God's blessings to, even as I could remember, in my whole life.

After I had eaten I tried to walk, but found myself so weak that I could hardly carry the gun (for I never went out without that); so I went but a little way, and sat down upon the ground, looking out upon the sea, which was just before me, and very calm and smooth. As I sat here, some such thoughts as these occurred to me:

What is this earth and sea of which I have seen so much, whence is it produced; and what am I and all the other creatures, wild and tame, human and brutal, whence are we?

Sure we are all made by some secret Power, who formed the earth and sea, the air and sky; and who is that?

Then it followed most naturally, It is God that has made it all. Well, but then it came on strangely, If God has made all these things, He guides and governs them all, and all things that concern them; for the Power that could make all things must certainly have power to guide and direct them.

If so, nothing can happen in the great circuit of His works, either without His knowledge or appointment.

And if nothing happens without His knowledge, He knows that I am here, and am in this dreadful condition; and if nothing happens without His appointment, He has appointed all this to befall me.

Nothing occurred to my thought to contradict any of these conclusions; and therefore it rested upon me with the greater force, that it must needs be that God had appointed all this to befall me; that I was brought to this miserable circumstance by His direction, He having the sole power, not of me only, but of everything that happened in the world. Immediately it followed:

Why has God done this to me? What have I done to be thus used?

My conscience presently checked me in that inquiry, as if I had blasphemed, and methought it spoke to me like a voice: Wretch! dost thou ask what thou has done? Look back upon a dreadful mis-spent life, and ask thyself what thou hast not done! Ask, Why is it that thou wert not long ago destroyed? Why wert thou not drowned in Yarmouth Roads? killed in the fight when the ship was taken by the Sallee man-of-war? devoured by the wild beasts on the coast of Africa? or, drowned here, when all the crew perished but thyself? Dost thou ask, What have I done?

I was struck dumb with these reflections, as one astonished, and had not a word to say—no, not to answer to myself; but rose up pensive and sad, walked back to my retreat, and went up over my wall, as if I had been going to bed; but my thoughts were sadly disturbed, and I had no inclination to sleep; so I sat down in my chair, and lighted my lamp, for it began to be dark. Now as the apprehension of the return of my distemper terrified me very much, it occurred to my thought that the Brazilians take no physic but their tobacco for almost all distempers; and I had a piece of a roll of tobacco in one of the chests, which was quite cured, and some also that was green and not quite cured.

I went, directed by Heaven no doubt; for in this chest I found a cure both for soul and body. I opened the chest and found what I looked for, namely, the tobacco; and as the few books I had saved lay there too, I took out one of the Bibles which I mentioned before, and which to this time I had not found leisure, or so much as inclination to look into—I say, I took it out, and brought both that and the tobacco with me to the table.

What use to make of the tobacco I knew not, as to my distemper, or whether it was good for it or no; but I tried several experiments with it, as if I was resolved it should hit one way or other. I first took a piece of a leaf and chewed it in my mouth, which indeed at first almost stupefied my brain, the tobacco being green and strong and that I had not been much used to it; then I took some and steeped it an hour or two in some rum, and resolved to take a dose of it when I lay down; and lastly I burned some upon a pan of coals, and held my nose close over the smoke of it as long as I could bear it, as well for the heat as almost for suffocation.

In the interval of this operation, I took up the Bible and began to read; but my head was too much disturbed with the tobacco to bear reading, at least that time. Only, having opened the book casually, the first words that occurred to me were these, "Call upon me in the day of trouble; I will deliver thee, and thou shalt glorify me."

The words were very apt to my case, and made some impression upon my thoughts at the time of reading them, though not so much as they did afterwards; for, as for being delivered, the word had no sound, as I may say, to me; the thing was so remote, so impossible in my apprehension of things, that I began to say as the children of Israel did, when they were promised flesh to eat, "Can God spread a table in the wilderness?" so I began to say, Can God himself deliver me from this place? and as it was not for many years that any hope appeared, this prevailed very often upon my thoughts; but, however, the words made a great impression upon me, and I mused upon them very often. It grew now late, and the tobacco had, as I said, dozed my head so much that I inclined to sleep; so I left my lamp burning in the cave lest I should want anything in the night, and went to bed; but, before I lay down, I did what I never had done in all my life—I kneeled down and prayed to God to fulfill the promise to me, that if I called upon Him in the day of trouble, He would deliver me. After my broken and imperfect prayer was over, I drank the rum in which I had steeped the tobacco, which was so strong and rank of the tobacco that indeed I could scarce get it down. Immediately upon this I went to bed. I found presently it flew up in my head violently, but I fell into a sound sleep, and waked no more till, by the sun, it must necessarily be near three o'clock in the afternoon the next day. Nay, to this hour I am partly of the opinion that I slept all the next day and night, and till almost three that day after; for otherwise I knew not how I should lose a day out of my reckoning in the days of the week, as it appeared some years after I had done. For if I had lost it by crossing and recrossing the line, I should have lost more than one day; but, certainly, I lost a day in my account, and never knew which way.

§ *I begin to recover, and feel thankful and repentant. Make a survey of the island. Find tobacco, melons, grapes, and other fruits. Build a summer bower. My daily dietary. Observe the first anniversary of my coming to the island. I learn to divide the season. My attempts at basket-making.*

B E that, however, one way or the other, when I awaked I found myself exceedingly refreshed, and my spirits lively and cheerful; when I got up I was stronger than I was the day before, and my stomach better, for I was hungry; and, in short, I had no fit the next day, but continued much altered for the better. This was the 29th.

The 30th was my well-day, of course, and I went abroad with my gun, but did not care to travel too far. I killed a sea-fowl or two, something like a brand-goose, and brought them home, but was not very forward to eat them; so I ate some more of the turtle's eggs, which were very good. This evening I renewed the medicine which I had supposed did me good the day before—namely, the tobacco steeped in rum; only I did not take so much as before, nor did I chew any of the leaf, or hold my head over the smoke. However, I was not so well the next day, which was the 1st of July, as I hoped I should have been; for I had a little spice of the cold fit, but it was not much.

*July* 2. I renewed the medicine all the three ways, and dosed myself with it as at first; and doubled the quantity which I drank.

*July* 3. I missed the fit for good and all, though I did not recover my full strength for some weeks after. While I was thus gathering strength my thoughts ran exceedingly upon this Scripture, "I will deliver thee"; and the impossibility of my deliverance lay much upon my mind in bar of my ever expecting it. But as I was discouraging myself with such thoughts it occurred to my mind that I pored so much upon my deliverance from the main affliction that I disregarded the deliverance I had received; and I was, as it were, made to ask myself such questions as these—namely, Have I not been delivered, and wonderfully too, from sickness—from the most distressed condition that could be, and that was so frightful to me? And what notice I had taken of it: Had I done my part? God had delivered me, but I had not glorified Him; that is to say, I had not owned and been thankful for that as a deliverance. And how could I expect greater deliverance?

This touched my heart very much, and immediately I kneeled down and gave God thanks aloud for my recovery from my sickness.

*July* 4. In the morning I took the Bible, and, beginning at the New Testament, I began seriously to read it, and imposed upon myself to read a while every morning and every night, not tying myself to the number of chapters, but as long as my thoughts should engage me. It was not long after I set seriously to this work, but I found my heart more deeply and sincerely affected with the wickedness of my past life. The impression of my dream revived, and the words, "All these things have not brought thee to repentance," ran seriously in my thought. I was earnestly begging of God to give me repentance, when it happened providentially the very day that, reading the Scripture, I came to these words, "He is exalted a Prince and a Saviour, to give repentance, and to give remission." I threw down the book, and with my heart as well as my hands lifted up to heaven, in a kind of ecstasy of joy, I cried out aloud, "Jesus, thou son of David, Jesus, thou exalted Prince and Saviour, give me repentance!"

This was the first time that I could say, in the true sense of the words, that I prayed in all my life; for now I prayed with a sense of my condition, and with a true Scripture view of hope founded on the encouragement of the Word of God; and from this time, I may say, I began to have hope that God would hear me.

Now I began to construe the words mentioned above, "Call on me, and I will deliver thee," in a different sense from what I had ever done before; for then I had no notion of anything being called deliverance but my being delivered from the captivity I was in: for though I was indeed at large in the place, yet the island was certainly a prison to me, and that in the worst sense in the world; but now I learned to take it in another sense. Now I looked back upon my past life with such horror, and my sins appeared so dreadful, that my soul sought nothing of God but deliverance from the load of guilt that bore down all my comfort. As for my solitary life, it was nothing; I did not so much as pray to be delivered from it, or think of it; it was all of no consideration in comparison to this. And I add this part here, to hint to whoever shall read it, that whenever they come to a true sense of things, they will find deliverance from sin a much greater blessing than deliverance from affliction.

But leaving this part, I return to my journal.

My condition began now to be, though not less miserable as to my way of living, yet much easier to my mind; and my thoughts being directed, by a constant reading the Scripture and praying to God, to things of a higher nature, I had a great deal of comfort within, which till now I knew nothing of. Also as my health and strength returned, I bestirred myself to furnish myself with everything that I wanted, and make my way of living as regular as I could.

From the 4th of July to the 14th I was chiefly employed in walking about with my gun in my hand, a little and a little at a time, as a man that was gathering up his strength after a fit of sickness; for it is hardly to be imagined how low I was, and to what weakness I was reduced. The application which I made use of was perfectly new, and perhaps what had never cured an ague before, neither can I recommend it to any one to practise, by this experiment; and though it did carry off the fit, yet it rather contributed to weakening me, for I had frequent convulsions in my nerves and limbs for some time.

I learned from it also this in particular, that being abroad in the rainy season was the most pernicious thing to my health that could be, especially in those rains which came attended with storms and hurricanes of wind; for as the rain which came in the dry season was always most accompanied with such storms, so I found that rain was much more dangerous than the rain which fell in September and October.

I had been now in this unhappy island above ten months; all possibility of deliverance from this condition seemed to be entirely taken from me, and I firmly believed that no human shape had ever set foot upon that place. Having now secured my habitation, as I thought, fully to my mind, I had a great desire to make a more perfect discovery of the island, and to see what other productions I might find which I yet knew nothing of.

It was the 15th of July that I began to take a more particular survey of the island itself. I went up the creek first, where, as I hinted, I brought my rafts on shore. I found, after I came about two miles up that the tide did not flow any higher, and that it was no more than a little brook of running water, and very fresh and good; but this being the dry season, there was hardly any water in some parts of it, at least not enough to run in any stream so as it could be perceived. On the bank of this brook I found many pleasant savannas, or meadows, plain, smooth, and covered with grass; and on the rising parts of them, next to the higher grounds, where the water, as it might be supposed, never overflowed, I found a great deal of tobacco, green, and growing to a great and very strong stalk. There were divers other plants which I had no notion of, or understanding about, and might perhaps have virtues of their own, which I could not find out.

I searched for the cassava root, which the Indians in all that climate make their bread of; but I could find none. I saw large plants of aloes, but did not then understand them. I saw several sugar canes, but wild, and, for want of cultivation, imperfect. I contented myself with these discoveries for this time, and came back musing with myself what course I might take to know the virtue and goodness of any of the fruits or plants which I should discover, but could bring it to no conclusion; for in short, I had made so little observation while I was in the Brazils, that I knew little of the plants in the field, at least very little that might serve me to any purpose now in my distress.

The next day, the 16th, I went up the same way again, and after going something farther than I had gone the day before, I found the brook, and the savannas began to cease, and the country became more woody than before. In this part I found different fruits, and, particularly, I found melons upon the ground in great abundance, and grapes upon the trees; the vines had spread indeed over the trees, and the clusters of grapes were just now in their prime, very ripe and rich. This was a surprising discovery, and I was exceedingly glad of them; but I was warned by my experience to eat sparingly of them, remembering that, when I was ashore in Barbary, the eating of grapes killed several of our Englishmen, who were slaves there, by throwing them into fluxes and fevers. But I found an excellent use for these grapes, and that was to cure or dry them in the sun, and keep them as dried grapes or raisins are kept; which I thought would be, as indeed they were, as wholesome as agreeable to eat, when no grapes might be to be had.

I spent all that evening there, and went not back to my habitation, which, by the way, was the first night, as I might say, I had lain from home. In the night I took my first contrivance, and got up into a tree, where I slept well; and the next morning proceeded upon my discovery, travelling near four miles, as I might judge by the length of the valley, keeping still due north, with a ridge of hills on the south and north side of me.

At the end of this march I came to an opening, where the country seemed to descend to the west, and a little spring of fresh water, which issued out of the side of the hill by me, ran the other way, that is due east; and the country appeared so fresh, so green, so flourishing, everything being in a constant verdure, or flourish of spring, that it looked like a planted garden.

I descended a little on the side of that delicious vale, surveying it with a secret kind of pleasure (though mixed with my other afflicting thoughts)—to think that this was all my own, that I was king and lord of all this country indefeasibly, and had a right of possession; and if I could convey it, I might have it in inheritance, as completely as any lord of a manor in England. I saw here abundance of cocoa-trees, orange, and lemon, and citron trees, but all wild, and very few bearing any fruit, at least not then. However, the green limes that I gathered were not only pleasant to eat, but very wholesome; and I mixed their juice afterwards with water, which made it very wholesome, and very cool, and refreshing.

I found now I had business enough to gather and carry home; and I resolved to lay up a store, as well of grapes as limes and lemons, to furnish myself for the wet season, which I knew was approaching.

In order to do this, I gathered a great heap of grapes in one place, and a lesser heap in another place, and a great parcel of limes and lemons in another place; and, taking a few of each with me, I travelled homeward, and resolved to come again, and bring a bag or sack, or what I could make to carry the rest home.

Accordingly, having spent three days in this journey, I came home; —so I must now call my tent and my cave. But, before I got thither the grapes were spoiled—the richness of the fruits and the weight of the juice having broken them, and bruised them, they were good for little or nothing; as to the limes, they were good, but I could bring but a few.

The next day, being the 19th, I went back, having made me two small bags to bring home my harvest. But I was surprised when, coming to my heap of grapes, which were so rich and fine when I gathered them, I found them all spread about, trod to pieces, and dragged about, some here, some there, and abundance eaten and de-voured. By this I concluded there were some wild creatures there-abouts which had done this, but what they were I knew not.

However, as I found that there was no laying them up on heaps, and no carrying them away in a sack, but that one way they would be destroyed, and the other way they would be crushed with their own weight, I took another course; for I gathered a large quantity of the grapes, and hung them up upon the out branches of the trees, that they might cure and dry in the sun; and as for the limes and lemons, I carried as many back as I could well stand under.

When I came home from this journey I contemplated with great pleasure the fruitfulness of that valley and the pleasantness of the situation, the security from storms on that side the water, and the wood, and concluded that I had pitched upon a place to fix my abode which was by far the worst part of the country. Upon the whole I began to consider of removing my habitation, and to look out for a place equally safe as where I now was situate, if possible, in that pleasant fruitful part of the island.

This thought ran long in my head, and I was exceeding fond of it for some time, the pleasantness of the place tempting me; but when I came to a nearer view of it, and to consider that I was now by the sea-side, where it was at least possible that something might happen to my advantage, and by the same ill fate that brought me hither might bring some other unhappy wretches to the same place; and though it was scarce probable that any such thing should ever happen, yet to enclose myself among the hills and woods, in the centre of the island, was to anticipate my bondage, and to render such an affair not only improbable but impossible; and that, therefore, I ought not by any means to remove.

However, I was so enamoured of this place, that I spent much of my time there for the whole remaining part of the month of July; and though, upon second thoughts, I resolved as above, not to remove, yet I built me a little kind of a bower, and surrounded it at a distance with a strong fence, being a double hedge, as high as I could reach, well staked, and filled between with brushwood; and here I lay very secure, sometimes two or three nights together, always going over it with a ladder as before; so that I fancied now I had my country house and my sea-coast house. And this work took me up to the beginning of August.

I had but newly finished my fence and begun to enjoy my labour, but the rains came on, and made me stick close to my first habitation. For though I had made me a tent like the other, with a piece of a sail, and spread it very well, yet I had not the shelter of a hill to keep me from storms, nor a cave behind me to retreat into when the rains were extraordinary.

About the beginning of August, as I said, I had finished my bower and began to enjoy myself. The 3rd of August I found the grapes I had hung up were perfectly dried, and, indeed, were excellent good raisins of the sun; so I began to take them down from the trees, and it was very happy that I did so, for the rains which followed would have spoiled them, and I had lost the best part of my winter food, for I had above two hundred large bunches of them. No sooner had I taken them all down, and carried most of them home to my cave, but it began to rain, and from hence, which was the 14th of August, it rained more or less every day till the middle of October; and sometimes so violently that I could not stir out of my cave for several days.

In this season I was much surprised with the increase of my family. I had been concerned for the loss of one of my cats, who ran away from me, or as I thought had been dead, and I heard no more tale or tidings of her till, to my astonishment, she came home about the end of August with three kittens! This was the more strange to me because, though I had killed a wild cat, as I called it, with my gun, yet I thought it was a quite different kind from our European cats; yet the young cats were the same kind of house breed like the old one; and both my cats being females, I thought it very strange. But from these three cats I afterwards came to be so pestered with cats that I was forced to kill them like vermin or wild beasts, and to drive them from my house as much as possible.

From the 14th of August to the 26th, incessant rain, so that I could not stir, and was now very careful not to be much wet. In this confinement I began to be straitened for food, but venturing out twice, I one day killed a goat, and the last day, which was the 26th, found a very large tortoise, which was a treat to me; and my food was regulated thus:—I ate a bunch of raisins for my breakfast, a piece of the goat's flesh or of the turtle for my dinner broiled—for to my great misfortune I had no vessel to boil or stew anything—and two or three of the turtle's eggs for my supper.

During this confinement in my cover by the rain I worked daily two or three hours at enlarging my cave, and by degrees worked it on towards one side till I came to the outside of the hill, and made a door or way out, which came beyond my fence or wall, and so I came in and out this way. But I was not perfectly easy at lying so open; for as I had managed myself before, I was in a perfect enclosure, whereas now I thought I lay exposed and open for anything to come in upon me. And yet I could not perceive that there was any living thing to fear, the biggest creature that I had yet seen upon the island being a goat.

*September the 30th.* I was now come to the unhappy anniversary of my landing. I cast up the notches on my post, and found I had been on shore 365 days. I kept this day as a solemn fast, setting it apart to religious exercise, prostrating myself on the ground with the most serious humiliation, confessing my sins to God, acknowledging His righteous judgments upon me, and praying to Him to have mercy on me through Jesus Christ. And having not tasted the least refreshment for twelve hours, even till the going down of the sun, I then ate a biscuit-cake and a bunch of grapes, and went to bed, finishing the day as I began it.

I had all this time observed no Sabbath-day; for as at first I had no sense of religion upon my mind, I had after some time omitted to distinguish the weeks by making a longer notch than ordinary for the Sabbath-day, and so did not really know what any of the days were. But now having cast up the days as above, I found I had been there a year, so I divided it into weeks, and set apart every seventh day for a Sabbath; though I found at the end of my account I had lost a day or two in my reckoning.

A little after this my ink began to fail me, and so I contented myself to use it more sparingly, and to write down only the most remarkable events of my life without continuing a daily memorandum of other things.

The rainy season and the dry season began now to appear regular to me; and I learned to divide them, so as to provide for them accordingly. But I bought all my experience before I had it; and this I am going to relate was one of the most discouraging experiments that I made at all. I have mentioned that I had saved the few ears of barley and rice which I had so surprisingly found springing up, as I thought, of themselves, and I believe there were about thirty stalks of rice, and about twenty of barley. And now I thought it a proper time to sow it after the rains, the sun being in its southern position going from me.

Accordingly I dug up a piece of ground as well as I could with my wooden spade, and dividing it into two parts, I sowed my grain; but as I was sowing it casually occurred to my thoughts that I would not sow it all at first, because I did not know when was the proper time for it, so I sowed about two-thirds of the seed, leaving about a handful of each.

It was a great comfort to me afterwards that I did so, for not one grain of that I sowed this time came to anything; for the dry months following, the earth having had no rain after the seed was sown, it had no moisture to assist its growth, and never came up at all till the wet season had come again, and then it grew as if it had been but newly sown.

Finding my first seed did not grow, which I easily imagined was by the drought, I sought for a moister piece of ground to make another trial in; and I dug up a piece of ground near my new bower, and sowed the rest of my seed in February, a little before the vernal equinox; and this having the rainy months of March and April to water it, sprung up very pleasantly, and yielded a good crop. But having part of the seed left only, and not daring to sow all that I had, I had but a small quantity at last, my whole crop not amounting to above half a peck of each kind.

But by this experiment I was made master of my business, and knew exactly when the proper season was to sow; and that I might expect two seed-times and two harvests every year.

While this corn was growing I made a little discovery, which was of use to me afterwards. As soon as the rains were over and the weather began to settle, which was about the month of November, I made a visit up the country to my bower, where, though I had not been some months, yet I found all things just as I left them. The circle, or double hedge, that I had made was not only firm and entire, but the stakes, which I had cut out of some trees that grew thereabouts, were all shot out and grown with long branches, as much as a willow tree usually shoots the first year after lopping its head. I could not tell what tree to call it that these stakes were cut from. I was surprised and yet very well pleased to see the young trees grow; and I pruned them, and led them up to grow as much alike as I could; and it is scarce credible how beautiful a figure they grew into in three years. So that, though the hedge made a circle of about twenty-five yards in diameter, yet the trees (for such I might now call them) soon covered it; and it was a complete shade, sufficient to lodge under all the dry season.

This made me resolve to cut some more stakes, and make me a hedge like this in a semicircle round my wall—I mean that of my first dwelling—which I did; and placing the trees or stakes in a double row, at about eight yards distance from my first fence, they grew presently, and were at first a fine cover to my habitation, and afterwards served for a defence also, as I shall observe in its order.

I found now that the seasons of the year might generally be divided, not into summer and winter, as in Europe, but into the rainy seasons and the dry seasons, which were generally thus:—

| | |
|---|---|
| Half February,<br>March,<br>Half April, | Rainy — the sun being then on or near the Equinox. |
| Half April,<br>May,<br>June,<br>July,<br>Half August, | Dry — the sun being then to the north of the Line. |
| Half August,<br>September,<br>Half October, | Rainy — the sun being then come back. |
| Half October,<br>November,<br>December,<br>January,<br>Half February, | Dry — the sun being then to the south of the Line. |

The rainy season sometimes held longer or shorter, as the winds happened to blow, but this was the general observation I made. After I had found, by experience, the ill consequence of being abroad in the rain, I took care to furnish myself with provisions beforehand, that I might not be obliged to go out; and I sat within doors as much as possible during the wet months.

In this time I found much employment (and very suitable also to the time), for I found great occasion of many things which I had no way to furnish myself with but by hard labour and constant application; particularly I tried many ways to make myself a basket, but all the twigs I could get for the purpose proved so brittle that they would do nothing. It proved of excellent advantage to me now, that when I was a boy I used to take great delight in standing at a basket-maker's in the town where my father lived to see them make their wicker-ware; and being, as boys usually are, very officious to help, and a great observer of the manner how they worked those things, and sometimes lending a hand, I had by this means full knowledge of the methods of it, that I wanted nothing but the materials, when it came into my mind that the twigs of that tree from whence I cut my stakes that grew might possibly be as tough as the sallows, and willows, and osiers in England, and I resolved to try.

Accordingly the next day I went to my country-house, as I called it, and cutting some of the smaller twigs, I found them to my purpose as much as I could desire; whereupon I came the next time prepared with a hatchet to cut down a quantity, which I soon found, for there was great plenty of them. These I set up to dry within my circle or hedge, and when they were fit for use I carried them to my cave, and here during the next season I employed myself in making, as well as I could, a great many baskets, both to carry earth, or to carry or lay up anything as I had occasion; and though I did not finish them very handsomely, yet I made them sufficiently serviceable for my purpose; and thus afterwards I took care never to be without them. And as my wicker-ware decayed I made more; especially I made strong deep baskets to place my corn in instead of sacks, when I should come to have any quantity of it.

Having mastered this difficulty, and employed a world of time about it, I bestirred myself to see if possible how to supply two wants. I had no vessels to hold anything that was liquid except two runlets, which were almost full of rum, and some glass bottles, some of the common size, and others which were case-bottles, square, for the holding of water, spirits, &c. I had not so much as a pot to boil anything, except a great kettle, which I saved out of the ship, and which was too big for such use as I designed—namely, to make broth, and stew a bit of meat by itself. The second thing I would fain have had was a tobacco-pipe, but it was impossible to me to make one; however I found a contrivance for that too at last.

I employed myself in planting my second rows of stakes or piles and in this wicker-working, all the summer or dry season, when another business took me up more time than it could be imagined I could spare.

§ *I travel across the island. Catch a parrot. Bring home a young goat. My second anniversary. Reflections upon my condition.*

I MENTIONED before that I had a great mind to see the whole island, and that I had travelled up the brook, and so on to where I built my bower, and where I had an opening quite to the sea on the other side of the island. I now resolved to travel quite across to the seashore on that side; so taking my gun, a hatchet, and my dog, and a larger quantity of powder and shot than usual, with two biscuit-cakes, and a great bunch of raisins in my pouch for my store, I began my journey. When I had passed the vale where my bower stood as above, I came within view of the sea to the west, and it being a very clear day I fairly descried land, whether an island or a continent I could not tell; but it lay very high, extending from the west to the west-south-west at a very great distance. By my guess it could not be less than fifteen or twenty leagues off.

I could not tell what part of the world this might be, otherwise than that I knew it must be part of America, and, as I concluded by all my observations, must be near the Spanish dominions; and perhaps was all inhabited by savages, where, if I should have landed, I had been in a worse condition than I was now; and therefore I acquiesced in the dispositions of Providence, which I began now to own and to believe ordered everything for the best; I say I quieted my mind with this, and left afflicting myself with fruitless wishes of being there.

Besides, after some pause upon this affair, I considered that if this land was the Spanish coast, I should certainly, one time or other, see some vessel pass or repass one way or other; but if not, then it was the savage coast between the Spanish country and Brazil, which are indeed the worst of savages, for they are cannibals, or men-eaters, and fail not to murder and devour all the human bodies that fall into their hands.

With these considerations I walked very leisurely forward. I found that side of the island where I now was much pleasanter than mine; the open or savanna fields sweet, adorned with flowers and grass, and full of very fine woods. I saw abundance of parrots, and fain I would have caught one, if possible, to have kept it to be tame, and taught it to speak to me. I did, after some painstaking, catch a young parrot, for I knocked it down with a stick, and having recovered it I brought it home; but it was some years before I could make him speak. However, at last I taught him to call me by my name very familiarly. But the accident that followed, though it be a trifle, will be very diverting in its place.

I was exceedingly diverted with this journey. I found in the low grounds hares, as I thought them to be, and foxes; but they differed greatly from all the other kinds I had met with, nor could I satisfy myself to eat them, though I killed several. But I had no need to be venturous, for I had no want of food, and of that which was very good too; especially these three sorts—namely, goats, pigeons, and turtle or tortoise, which, added to my grapes, Leadenhall Market could not have furnished a table better than I in proportion to the company. And though my case was deplorable enough, yet I had great cause for thankfulness, and that I was not driven to any extremities for food, but rather plenty, even to dainties.

I never travelled in this journey above two miles outright in a day, or thereabouts. But I took so many turns and returns to see what discoveries I could make that I came weary enough to the place where I resolved to sit down for all night; and then I either reposed myself in a tree, or surrounded myself with a row of stakes set upright in the ground, either from one tree to another, or so as no wild creature could come at me without waking me.

As soon as I came to the seashore I was surprised to see that I had taken up my lot on the worst side of the island; for here, indeed, the shore was covered with innumerable turtles, whereas on the other side I had found but three in a year and half. Here was also an infinite number of fowls of many kinds; some which I had seen, and some which I had not seen of before—and many of them very good meat—but such as I knew not the names of, except those called penguins.

I could have shot as many as I pleased, but was very sparing of my powder and shot, and therefore had more mind to kill a she-goat if I could, which I could better feed on; and though there were many goats here—more than on my side the island—yet it was with much more difficulty that I could come near them, the country being flat and even, and they saw me much sooner than when I was on the hill.

I confess this side of the country was much pleasanter than mine; but yet I had not the least inclination to remove, for as I was fixed in my habitation, it became natural to me, and I seemed all the while I was here to be as it were upon a journey, and from home. However, I travelled along the shore of the sea towards the east, I suppose about twelve miles; and then, setting up a great pole upon the shore for a mark, I concluded I would go home again, and that the next journey I took should be on the other side of the island east from my dwelling, and so round till I came to my post again: of which in its place.

I took another way to come back than that I went, thinking I could easily keep all the island so much in my view that I could not miss finding my first dwelling by viewing the country. But I found myself mistaken; for being come about two or three miles, I found myself descended into a very large valley, but so surrounded with hills, and those hills covered with wood, that I could not see which was my way by any direction but that of the sun, nor even then, unless I knew very well the position of the sun at that time of the day.

It happened, to my further misfortune, that the weather proved hazy for three or four days while I was in this valley; and not being able to see the sun, I wandered about very uncomfortably, and at last was obliged to find out the sea-side, look for my post, and come back the same way I went. And then by easy journeys I turned homeward, the weather being exceeding hot, and my gun, ammunition, hatchet, and other things very heavy.

In this journey my dog surprised a young kid, and seized upon it, and I running in to take hold of it, caught it, and saved it alive from the dog. I had a great mind to bring it home if I could; for I had often been musing whether it might not be possible to get a kid or two, and so raise a breed of tame goats, which might supply me when my powder and shot should be all spent.

I made a collar to this little creature, and with a string which I made of some rope-yarn, which I always carried about me, I led him along, though with some difficulty, till I came to my bower; and there I enclosed him and left him, for I was very impatient to be at home, from whence I had been absent above a month.

I cannot express what a satisfaction it was to me to come into my old hutch and lie down in my hammock-bed. This little wandering journey, without settled place of abode, had been so unpleasant to me, that my own house, as I called it to myself, was a perfect settlement to me compared to that; and it rendered everything about me so comfortable that I resolved I would never go a great way from it again while it should be my lot to stay on the island.

I reposed myself here a week, to rest and regale myself after my long journey; during which most of the time was taken up in the weighty affair of making a cage for my poll, who began now to be a mere domestic, and to be mighty well acquainted with me. Then I began to think of the poor kid which I had penned in within my little circle, and resolved to go and fetch it home or give it some food. Accordingly, I went, and found it where I left it; for, indeed, it could not get out, but almost starved for want of food. I went and cut boughs of trees and branches of such shrubs as I could find, and threw it over; and having fed it, I tied it as I did before, to lead it away. But it was so tame with being hungry that I had no need to have tied it, for it followed me like a dog; and as I continually fed it, the creature became so loving, so gentle, and so fond, that it became from that time one of my domestics also, and would never leave me afterwards.

The rainy season of the autumnal equinox was now come, and I kept the 30th of September in the same solemn manner as before; being the anniversary of my landing on the island, having now been there two years, and no more prospect of being delivered than the first day I came there. I spent the whole day in humble and thankful acknowledgments of the many wonderful mercies which my solitary condition was attended with, and without which it might have been infinitely more miserable. I gave humble and hearty thanks that God had been pleased to discover to me even that it was possible I might be more happy in this solitary condition than I should have been in a liberty of society and in all the pleasures of the world; that He could fully make up to me the deficiencies of my solitary state, and the want of human society, by His presence, and the communications of His grace to my soul—supporting, comforting, and encouraging me to depend upon His providence here, and hope for His eternal presence hereafter.

It was now that I began sensibly to feel how much more happy this life I now led was, with all its miserable circumstances, than the wicked, cursed, abominable life I led all the past part of my days. And now I changed both my sorrows and my joys: my very desires altered, my affections changed their gusts, and my delights were perfectly new from what they were at my first coming, or indeed for the two years past.

Before, as I walked about, either on my hunting or for viewing the country, the anguish of my soul at my condition would break out upon me on a sudden, and my very heart would die within me to think of the woods, the mountains, the deserts I was in, and how I was a prisoner locked up with the eternal bars and bolts of the ocean, in an uninhabited wilderness, without redemption. In the midst of the greatest composures of my mind, this would break out upon me like a storm, and make me wring my hands and weep like a child. Sometimes it would take me in the middle of my work; and I would immediately sit down and sigh, and look upon the ground for an hour or two together. And this was still worse to me; for if I could burst out into tears or vent myself by words it would go off, and the grief, having exhausted itself, would abate.

But now I began to exercise myself with new thoughts. I daily read the Word of God, and applied all the comforts of it to my present state. One morning, being very sad, I opened the Bible upon these words, "I will never leave thee, nor forsake thee." Immediately it occurred that these words were to me. Why else should they be directed in such a manner, just at the moment when I was mourning over my condition as one forsaken of God and man? "Well, then," said I, "if God does not forsake me, of what ill consequence can it be, or what matters it, though the world should all forsake me, seeing on the other hand if I had all the world, and should lose the favour and blessing of God, there would be no comparison in the loss?"

From this moment I began to conclude in my mind that it was possible for me to be more happy in this forsaken, solitary condition, than it was probable I should ever have been in any other particular state in the world; and with this thought I was going to give thanks to God for bringing me to this place. I know not what it was, but something shocked my mind at that thought, and I durst not speak the words. "How canst thou be such a hypocrite," said I, even audibly, "to pretend to be thankful for a condition which, however thou mayst endeavour to be contented with, thou wouldst rather pray heartily to be delivered from?" So I stopped there. But though I could not say I thanked God for being there, yet I sincerely gave thanks to God for opening my eyes, by whatever afflicting providences, to see the former condition of my life, and to mourn for my wickedness and repent. I never opened the Bible or shut it but my very soul within me blessed God for directing my friend in England, without any order of mine, to pack it up among my goods, and for assisting me afterwards to save it out of the wreck of the ship.

§ *I begin my third year on the island. The want of tools. Reap my crop of corn. I at last succeed in making tolerable earthenware vessels. How I milled and baked. I set about making a boat, but fail to get it into the water.*

THUS, and in this disposition of mind, I began my third year. And though I have not given the reader the trouble of so particular account of my works this year as the first, yet in general it may be observed that I was very seldom idle, but having regularly divided my time according to the several daily employments that were before me—such as, first, my duty to God and the reading the Scriptures, which I constantly set apart some time for thrice every day; secondly, the going abroad with my gun for food, which generally took me up three hours in every morning when it did not rain; thirdly, the ordering, curing, preserving, and cooking what I had killed or caught for my supply—these took up great part of the day. Also it is to be considered that in the middle of the day, when the sun was in the zenith, the violence of the heat was too great to stir out, so that about four hours in the evening was all the time I could be supposed to work in; with this exception, that sometimes I changed my hours of hunting and working, and went to work in the morning and abroad with my gun in the afternoon.

To this short time allowed for labour I desire may be added the exceeding laboriousness of my work—the many hours which, for want of tools, want of help, and want of skill, everything I did took up out of my time. For example, I was full two-and-forty days making me a board for a long shelf which I wanted in my cave; whereas two sawyers, with their tools and a saw-pit, would have cut six of them out of the same tree in half a day.

My case was this: It was to be a large tree which was to be cut down, because my board was to be a broad one. This tree I was three days a-cutting down, and two more cutting off the boughs, and reducing it to a log or piece of timber. With inexpressible hacking and hewing I reduced both the sides of it into chips till it begun to be light enough to move; then I turned it, and made one side of it smooth and flat as a board from end to end; then, turning that side downward, cut the other side, till I brought the plank to be about three inches thick, and smooth on both sides. Anyone may judge the labour of my hands in such a piece of work; but labour and patience carried me through that and many other things. I only observe this in particular, to show the reason why so much of my time went away with so little work—namely, that what might be a little to be done with help and tools, was a vast labour and required a prodigious time to do alone and by hand.

But notwithstanding this, with patience and labour I went through many things; and, indeed, everything that my circumstances made necessary to me to do, as will appear by what follows. I was now—in the months of November and December—expecting my crop of barley and rice. The ground I had manured or dug up for them was not great; for, as I observed, my seed of each was not above the quantity of half a peck, for I had lost one whole crop by sowing in the dry season. But now my crop promised very well, when on a sudden I found I was in danger of losing it all again by enemies of several sorts, which it was scarce possible to keep from it: as, first, the goats, and wild creatures which I called hares, who, tasting the sweetness of the blade, lay in it night and day as soon as it came up, and ate it so close that it could get no time to shoot up into stalk. This I saw no remedy for but by making an enclosure about it with a hedge, which I did with a great deal of toil, and the more because it required speed. However, as my arable land was but small, suited to my crop, I got it totally well fenced in about three weeks' time; and shooting some of the creatures in the daytime, I set my dog to guard it in the night, tying him up to a stake at the gate, where he would stand and bark all night long. So in a little time the enemies forsook the place, and the corn grew very strong and well, and began to ripen apace.

But as the beasts ruined me before while my corn was in the blade, so the birds were as likely to ruin me now when it was in the ear; for going along by the place to see how it throve, I saw my little crop surrounded with fowls of I know not how many sorts, who stood as it were watching till I should be gone. I immediately let fly among them, for I always had my gun with me. I had no sooner shot but there rose up a little cloud of fowls—which I had not seen at all—from among the corn itself.

This touched me sensibly, for I foresaw that in a few days they would devour all my hopes; that I should be starved, and never be able to raise a crop at all: and what to do I could not tell. However, I resolved not to lose my corn, if possible, though I should watch it night and day. In the first place, I went among it so see what damage was already done; and found they had spoiled a good deal of it, but that, as it was yet too green for them, the lost was not so great but that the remainder was like to be a good crop if it could be saved.

I stayed by it to load my gun; and then coming away I could easily see the thieves sitting upon all the trees about me, as if they only waited till I was gone away. And the event proved it to be so; for as I walked off as if I was gone, I was no sooner out of their sight but they dropped down one by one into the corn again. I was so provoked that I could not have patience to stay till more came on, knowing that every grain that they ate now was, as it might be said, a peck loaf to me in the consequence; but coming up to the hedge I fired again and killed three of them. This was what I wished for: so I took them up, and served them as we serve notorious thieves in England—namely, hanged them in chains for a terror to others. It is impossible to imagine almost that this should have such an effect as it had; for the fowls would not only not come at the corn, but, in short, they forsook all that part of the island, and I could never see a bird near the place as long as my scarecrows hung there.

This I was very glad of, you may be sure; and about the latter end of December, which was our second harvest of the year, I reaped my crop. I was sadly put to it for a scythe or a sickle to cut it down; and all I could do was to make one as well as I could out of one of the broad swords or cutlasses which I saved among the arms out of the ship. However, as my first crop was but small, I had no great difficulty to cut it down. In short, I reaped it my way, for I cut nothing off but the ears, and carried it away in a great basket which I had made, and so rubbed it out with my hands; and at the end of all my harvesting

I found that out of my half-peck of seed I had near two bushels of rice and above two bushels and a half of barley—that is to say, by my guess, for I had no measure at that time.

However, this was a great encouragement to me, and I foresaw that in time it would please God to supply me with bread. And yet here I was perplexed again: for I neither knew how to grind or make meal of my corn, or, indeed, how to clean it and part it; nor, if made into meal, how to make bread of it; and if how to make it, yet I knew not how to bake it. These things being added to my desire of having a good quantity of store, and to secure a constant supply, I resolved not to taste any of this crop, but to preserve it all for seed against the next season; and in the meantime to employ all my study and hours of working to accomplish this great work of providing myself with corn and bread.

It might be truly said that now I worked for my bread. It is a little wonderful, and what I believe few people have thought much upon—namely, the strange multitude of little things necessary in the providing, producing, curing, dressing, making, and finishing this one article of bread. I that was reduced to a mere state of nature found this to my daily discouragement, and was made more and more sensible of it every hour, even after I had got the first handful of seed-corn; which, as I have said, came up unexpectedly, and indeed to a surprise.

First, I had no plough to turn up the earth, no spade or shovel to dig it. Well, this I conquered by making a wooden spade, as I observed before. But this did my work in but a wooden manner; and though it cost me a great many days to make it, yet for want of iron it not only wore out the sooner, but made my work the harder, and made it be performed much worse. However, this I bore with, and was content to work it out with patience, and bear with the badness of the performance. When the corn was sowed I had no harrow, but was forced to go over it myself, and drag a great heavy bough of a tree over it, to scratch it, as it may be called, rather than rake or harrow it.

When it was growing and grown, I have observed already, how many things I wanted to fence it, secure it, mow or reap it, cure and carry it home, thrash, part it from the chaff, and save it. Then I wanted a mill to grind it, sieves to dress it, yeast and salt to make it into bread, and an oven to bake it; and yet all these things I did without, as shall be observed; and yet the corn was an inestimable comfort and advantage to me too. All this, as I said, made everything laborious and tedious to me, but that there was no help for, neither was my time so much loss to me, because, as I had divided it, a certain part of it was every day appointed to these works. And as I resolved to use none of the corn for bread till I had a greater quantity by me, I had the next six months to apply myself wholly by labour and invention to furnish myself with utensils proper for the performing all the operations necessary for the making the corn (when I had it) fit for my use.

But, first, I was to prepare more land, for I had now seed enough to sow above an acre of ground. Before I did this I had a week's work at least to make me a spade; which, when it was done, was but a sorry one indeed, and very heavy, and required double labour to work with it. However, I went through that, and sowed my seed in two large flat pieces of ground as near my house as I could find them to my mind, and fenced them in with a good hedge, the stakes of which were all cut of that wood which I had set before, and knew it would grow; so that in one year's time I knew I should have a quick or living hedge, that would want but little repair. This work was not so little as to take me up less than three months, because great part of that time was of the wet season, when I could not go abroad.

Within doors—that is, when it rained, and I could not go out—I found employment on the following occasions, always observing that all the while I was at work I diverted myself with talking to my parrot, and teaching him to speak; and I quickly learned him to know his own name and at last to speak it out pretty loud—POLL, which was the first word I ever heard spoken in the island by any mouth but my own. This, therefore, was not my work, but an assistant to my work; for now, as I said, I had a great employment upon my hands, as fol-lows—namely, I had long studied by some means or other to make myself some earthen vessels, which indeed I wanted sorely, but knew not where to come at them. However, considering the heat of the climate, I did not doubt but if I could find out any such clay, I might botch up some such pot as might, being dried in the sun, be hard enough and strong enough to bear handling, and to hold anything that was dry and required to be kept so. And as this was necessary in the preparing corn, meal, &c., which was the thing I was upon, I re-solved to make some as large as I could, and fit only to stand like jars to hold what should be put into them.

It would make the reader pity me, or rather laugh at me, to tell how many awkward ways I took to raise this paste; what odd, mis-shapen, ugly things I made; how many of them fell in, and how many fell out, the clay not being stiff enough to bear its own weight; how many cracked by the overviolent heat of the sun, being set out too hastily; and how many fell in pieces with only removing as well before as after they were dried; and, in a word, how, after having laboured hard to find the clay, to dig it, to temper it, to bring it home and work it, I could not make above two large earthen ugly things— I cannot call them jars—in about two months' labour.

However, as the sun baked these two very dry and hard, I lifted them very gently up, and set them down again in two great wicker baskets which I had made on purpose for them, that they might not break; and as between the pot and the basket there was a little room to spare, I stuffed it full of rice and barley straw. And these two pots being to stand always dry, I thought would hold my dry corn, and perhaps the meal, when the corn was bruised.

Though I miscarried so much in my design for large pots, yet I made several smaller things with better success—such as little round pots, flat dishes, pitchers, and pipkins, and any things my hand turned to; and the heat of the sun baked them strangely hard.

But all this would not answer my end, which was to get an earthen pot to hold what was liquid, and bear the fire, which none of these could do. It happened after some time, making a pretty large fire for cooking my meat, when I went to put it out after I had done with it, I found a broken piece of one of my earthenware vessels in the fire burned as hard as a stone, and red as a tile. I was agreeably surprised to see it, and said to myself that certainly they might be made to burn whole if they would burn broken.

This set me to studying how to order my fire, so as to make it burn me some pots. I had no notion of a kiln, such as the potters burn in; or of glazing them with lead, though I had some lead to do it with; but I placed three large pipkins and two or three pots in a pile, one upon another, and placed my firewood all round it, with a great heap of embers under them. I plied the fire with fresh fuel round the outside and upon the top, till I saw the pots in the inside red hot quite through, and observed that they did not crack at all. When I saw them clear red, I let them stand in that heat about five or six hours, till I found one of them, though it did not crack, did melt or run; for the sand which was mixed with the clay melted by the violence of the heat, and would have run into glass if I had gone on, so I clacked my fire gradually, till the pots began to abate of the red colour; and watching them all night that I might not let the fire abate too fast, in the morning I had three very good—I will not say handsome—pipkins and two other earthen pots as hard burned as could be desired, and one of them perfectly glazed with the running of the sand.

After this experiment I need not say that I wanted no sort of earthenware for my use; but I must needs say, as to the shapes of them, they were very indifferent, as any one may suppose, when I had no way of making them but as the children make dirt-pies, or as a woman would make pies that never learned to raise paste.

No joy at a thing of so mean a nature was ever equal to mine when I found I had made an earthen pot that would bear the fire, and I had hardly patience to stay till they were cold before I set one upon the fire again with some water in it to boil me some meat, which it did admirably well. And with a piece of a kid I made some very good broth, though I wanted oatmeal, and several other ingredients requisite to make it so good as I would have had it been.

My next concern was, to get me a stone mortar to stamp or beat some corn in; for as to the mill, there was no thought at arriving to that perfection of art with one pair of hands. To supply this want I was at a great loss; for of all trades in the world, I was as perfectly un-qualified for a stone-cutter as for any whatever; neither had I any tools to go about it with. I spent many a day to find out a great stone big enough to cut hollow, and make fit for a mortar, and could find none at all, except what was in the solid rock, and which I had no way to dig or cut out; nor, indeed, were the rocks in the island of hardness sufficient, but were all of a sandy, crumbling stone, which neither would bear the weight of a heavy pestle, nor would break the corn without filling it with sand. So after a great deal of time lost in searching for a stone, I gave it over, and resolved to look out for a great block of hard wood, which I found indeed much easier; and getting one as big as I had strength to stir, I rounded it, and formed it in the outside with my axe and hatchet, and then, with the help of fire and infinite labour, made a hollow place in it, as the Indians in Brazil make their canoes. After this I made a great heavy pestle or beater of the wood called the iron-wood, and this I prepared and laid by against I had my next crop of corn, when I proposed to myself to grind, or rather pound, my corn into meal to make my bread.

My next difficulty was to make a sieve, or search, to dress my meal, and to part it from the bran and the husk, without which I did not see it possible I could have any bread. This was a most difficult thing so much as but to think on; for to be sure I had nothing like the necessary thing to make it—I mean fine thin canvas, or stuff to search the meal through. And here I was at a full stop for many months; nor did I really know what to do. Linen I had none left, but what was mere rags. I had goats' hair, but neither knew I how to weave it or spin it; and had I known how, here were no tools to work it with. All the remedy that I found for this was, that at last I did remember I had among the seamen's clothes which were saved out of the ship some neckcloths of calico or muslin; and with some pieces of these I made three small sieves, but proper enough for the work. And thus I made shift for some years. How I did afterwards I shall show in its place.

The baking part was the next thing to be considered, and how I should make bread when I came to have corn; for, first, I had no yeast. As to that part, as there was no supplying the want, so I did not concern myself much about it; but for an oven I was indeed in great pain. At length I found out an experiment for that also, which was this—I made some earthen vessels very broad, but not deep; that is to say, about two foot diameter, and not above nine inches deep, these I burned in the fire, as I had done the other, and laid them by; and when I wanted to bake, I made a great fire upon my hearth, which I had paved with some square tiles of my own making and burning also—but I should not call them square.

When the firewood was burned pretty much into embers, or live coals, I drew them forward upon this hearth, so as to cover it all over, and there I let them lie till the earth was very hot; then sweeping away all the embers, I set down my loaf or loaves and whelming down the earthen pot upon them, drew the embers all round the outside of the pot, to keep in and add to the heat; and thus, as well as in the best oven in the world, I baked my barley loaves, and became in little time a mere pastry-cook into the bargain; for I made myself several cakes of the rice, and puddings. Indeed I made no pies, neither had I anything to put into them supposing I had, except the flesh either of fowls or goats.

It need not be wondered at if all these things took me up most part of the third year of my abode here; for it is to be observed that, in the intervals of these things, I had my new harvest and husbandry to manage; for I reaped my corn in its season, and carried it home as well as I could, and laid it up in the ear in my large baskets till I had time to rub it out, for I had no floor to thrash it on, or instrument to thrash it with.

And now indeed my stock of corn increasing, I really wanted to build my barns bigger. I wanted a place to lay it up in, for the increase of the corn now yielded me so much that I had of the barley about twenty bushels, and of the rice as much or more; insomuch that now I resolved to begin to use it freely, for my bread had been quite gone a great while. Also I resolved to see what quantity would be sufficient for me a whole year, and to sow but once a year.

Upon the whole, I found that the forty bushels of barley and rice was much more than I could consume in a year, so I resolved to sow just the same quantity every year that I sowed the last, in hopes that such a quantity would fully provide me with bread, &c.

All the while these things were doing you may be sure my thoughts ran many times upon the prospect of land which I had seen from the other side of the island; and I was not without secret wishes that I were on shore there, fancying the seeing the mainland, and thinking that in an inhabited country I might find some way or other to convey myself farther, and perhaps at last find some means of escape.

But all this while I made no allowance for the dangers of such a condition, and how I might fall into the hands of savages, and perhaps such as I might have reason to think far worse than the lions and tigers of Africa. That if I once came into their power, I should run a hazard more than a thousand to one of being killed, and perhaps of being eaten; for I had heard that the people of the Caribbean coasts were cannibals, or man-eaters; and I knew by the latitude that I could not be far off from that shore: that suppose they were not cannibals, yet that they might kill me, as many Europeans who had fallen into their hands had been served, even when they had been ten or twenty together, much more I that was but one, and could make little or no defence; all these things, I say, which I ought to have considered well of, and did cast up in my thoughts afterwards, yet took up none of my apprehensions at first; but my head ran mightily upon the thought of getting over to the shore.

Now I wished for my boy Xury and the long-boat with the shoulder-of-mutton sail, with which I sailed above a thousand miles on the coast of Africa; but this was in vain. Then I thought I would go and look at our ship's boat, which, as I have said, was blown up upon the shore a great way in the storm when we were first cast away. She lay almost where she did at first, but not quite; and was turned by the force of the waves and the winds almost bottom upward against a high ridge of beachy rough sand, but no water about her as before.

If I had had hands to have refitted her, and to have launched her into the water, the boat would have done well enough, and I might have gone back into the Brazils with her easily enough; but I might have foreseen that I could no more turn her and set her upright upon her bottom than I could remove the island. However, I went to the woods and cut levers and rollers, and brought them to the boat, resolved to try what I could do, suggesting to myself that if I could but turn her down, I might easily repair the damage she had received, and she would be a very good boat, and I might go to sea in her very easily.

I spared no pains indeed in this piece of fruitless toil, and spent, I think, three or four weeks about it. At last, finding it impossible to heave it up with my little strength, I fell to digging away the sand to undermine it, and so to make it fall down, setting pieces of wood to thrust and guide it right in the fall.

But when I had done this I was unable to stir it up again or to get under it much less to move it forward towards the water, so I was forced to give it over; and yet, though I gave over the hopes of the boat, my desire to venture over for the main increased rather than decreased as the means for it seemed impossible.

This at length put me upon thinking whether it was not possible to make myself a canoe, or periagua, such as the natives of those climates make, even without tools, or, as I might say, without hands—

namely, of the trunk of a great tree. This I not only thought possible but easy, and pleased myself extremely with the thoughts of making it, and with my having much more convenience for it than any of the negroes or Indians; but not at all considering the particular inconveniences which I lay under more than the Indians did—namely, want of hands to move it, when it was made, into the water, a difficulty much harder for me to surmount than all the consequences of want of tools could be to them. For what was it to me, that when I had chosen a vast tree in the woods, I might with much trouble cut it down, if after I might be able with my tools to hew and dub the outside into the proper shape of a boat, and burn or cut out the inside to make it hollow, so to make a boat of it,—if, after all this, I must leave it just there where I found it, and was not able to launch it into the water.

One would have thought I could not have had the least reflection upon my mind of my circumstance, while I was making this boat, but I should have immediately thought how I should get it into the sea. But my thoughts were so intent upon my voyage over the sea in it, that I never once considered how I should get it off of the land; and it was really in its own nature more easy for me to guide it over forty-five miles of sea, than about forty-five fathom of land, where it lay, to set it afloat in the water.

I went to work upon this boat the most like a fool that ever man did who had any of his senses awake. I pleased myself with the design, without determining whether I was ever able to undertake it; not but that the difficulty of launching my boat came often into my head, but I put a stop to my own inquiries into it, by this foolish answer which I gave myself, "Let's first make it; I'll warrant I'll find some way or other to get it along when 'tis done."

This was a most preposterous method; but the eagerness of my fancy prevailed, and to work I went. I felled a cedar tree—I question much whether Solomon ever had such a one for the building of the temple at Jerusalem! It was five feet ten inches diameter at the lower part next the stump, and four feet eleven inches diameter at the end of twenty-two feet, after which it lessened for a while, and then parted into branches. It was not without infinite labour that I felled this tree. I was twenty days hacking and hewing at it at the bottom. I was fourteen more getting the branches and limbs and the vast spreading head of it cut off, which I hacked and hewed through with axe and hatchet, and inexpressible labour. After this it cost me a month to shape it and dub it to a proportion, and to something like the bottom of a boat, that it might swim upright as it ought to do. It cost me near three months more to clear the inside, and work it out so as to make an exact boat of it. This I did indeed without fire, by mere mallet and chisel, and by the dint of hard labour, till I had brought it to be a very handsome periagua, and big enough to have carried six-and-twenty men, and consequently big enough to have carried me and all my cargo.

When I had gone through this work I was extremely delighted with it. The boat was really much bigger than I ever saw a canoe or periagua, that was made of one tree, in my life. Many a weary stroke it had cost, you may be sure, and there remained nothing but to get it into the water; and had I gotten it into the water, I make no question but I should have begun the maddest voyage, and the most unlikely to be performed, that ever was undertaken.

But all my devices to get it into the water failed me, though they cost me infinite labour too. It lay about one hundred yards from the water, and not more; but the first inconvenience was, it was uphill towards the creek. Well, to take away this discouragement, I resolved to dig into the surface of the earth, and so make a declivity. This I began, and it cost me a prodigious deal of pains; but who grudge pains that have their deliverance in view? But when this was worked through, and this difficulty managed, it was still much at one; for I could not more stir the canoe than I could the other boat.

Then I measured the distance of ground, and resolved to cut a dock or canal to bring the water up to the canoe, seeing I could not bring the canoe down to the water. Well, I began this work, and when I began to enter into it, and calculate how deep it was to be dug, how broad, how the stuff to be thrown out, I found, that by the number of hands I had, being none but my own, it must have been ten or twelve years before I should have gone through with it; for the shore lay high, so that at the upper end it must have been at least twenty foot deep. So at length, though with great reluctancy, I gave this attempt over also.

This grieved me heartily; and now I saw, though too late, the folly of beginning a work before we count the cost, and before we judge rightly of our own strength to go through with it.

§ *My fourth anniversary. Wise and profitable reflections. Fatal and fortunate days. My new clothing and umbrella. How five years have passed over.*

In the middle of this work I finished my fourth year in this place, and kept my anniversary with the same devotion, and with as much comfort as ever before; for by a constant study and serious application of the Word of God, and by the assistance of His grace, I gained a different knowledge from what I had before. I entertained different notions of things. I looked now upon the world as a thing remote, which I had nothing to do with, no expectation from, and indeed no desires about: in a word, I had nothing indeed to do with it, nor was ever like to have. So I thought it looked as we may perhaps look upon it hereafter—namely, as a place I had lived in, but was come out of it; and well might I say, as Father Abraham to Dives, "Between me and thee is a great gulf fixed."

In the first place, I was removed from all the wickedness of the world here; I had neither the lust of the flesh; the lust of the eye, nor the pride of life. I had nothing to covet, for I had all that I was now capable of enjoying. I was lord of the whole manor; or, if I pleased, I might call myself king or emperor over the whole country which I had possession of. There were no rivals; I had no competitor, none to dispute sovereignty or command with me. I might have raised ship-loadings of corn, but I had no use for it; so I let as little grow as I thought enough for my occasion. I had tortoise or turtles enough; but now and then one was as much as I could put to any use. I had timber enough to have built a fleet of ships. I had grapes enough to have made wine, or to have cured into raisins, to have loaded that fleet when they had been built.

But all I could make use of was all that was valuable. I had enough to eat and to supply my wants, and what was all the rest to me? If I killed more flesh than I could eat, the dog must eat it, or the vermin. If I sowed more corn than I could eat, it must be spoiled. The trees that I cut down were lying to rot on the ground; I could make no more use of them than for fuel, and that I had no occasion for but to dress my food.

In a word, the nature and experience of things dictated to me, upon just reflection, that all the good things of this world are no further good to us than they are for our use; and that whatever we may heap up indeed to give others, we enjoy just as much as we can use, and no more. The most covetous gripping miser in the world would have been cured of the vice of covetousness if he had been in my case, for I possessed infinitely more than I knew what to do with. I had no room for desire, except it was of things which I had not, and they were but trifles, though indeed of great use to me. I had as I hinted before, a parcel of money, as well gold as silver, about thirty-six pounds sterling. Alas! there the nasty, sorry, useless stuff lay; I had no manner of business for it; and I often thought with myself that I would have given a handful of it for a gross of tobacco pipes, or for a hand-mill to grind my corn; nay, I would have given it all for six-pennyworth of turnip and carrot seed out of England, or for a handful of pease and beans and a bottle of ink. As it was, I had not the least advantage by it or benefit from it, but there it lay in a drawer, and grew mouldy with the damp of the cave in the wet season; and if I had had the drawer full of diamonds it had been the same case, and they had been of no manner of value to me, because of no use.

I had now brought my state of life to be much easier in itself than it was at first, and much easier to my mind, as well as to my body. I frequently sat down to my meat with thankfulness, and admired the hand of God's providence, which had thus spread my table in the wilderness. I learned to look more upon the bright side of my condition and less upon the dark side, and to consider what I enjoyed rather than what I wanted; and this gave me sometimes such secret comforts that I cannot express them, and which I take notice of here to put those discontented people in mind of it who cannot enjoy comfortably what God has given them because they see and covet something that He has not given them. All our discontents about what we want appeared to me to spring from the want of thankfulness for what we have.

Another reflection was of great use to me, and doubtless would be so to any one that should fall into such distress as mine was, and this was, to compare my present condition with what I at first expected it should be, nay, with what it would certainly have been if the good providence of God had not wonderfully ordered the ship to be cast up nearer to the shore, where I not only could come at her, but could bring what I got out of her to the shore, for my relief and comfort; without which I had wanted for tools to work, weapons for defence, or gunpowder and shot for getting my food.

I spent whole hours, I may say whole days, in representing to myself in the most lively colours how I must have acted if I had got nothing out of the ship; how I could not have so much as got any food except fish and turtles, and that as it was long before I found any of them, I must have perished first: that I should have lived, if I had not perished, like a mere savage; that if I had killed a goat or a fowl by any contrivance, I had no way to flay or open them, or part the flesh from the skin and the bowels, or to cut it up, but must gnaw it with my teeth, and pull it with my claws like a beast.

These reflections made me very sensible of the goodness of Providence to me, and very thankful for my present condition, with all its hardships and misfortunes. And this part also I cannot but recommend to the reflection of those who are apt in their misery to say, "Is any affliction like mine?" Let them consider how much worse the cases of some people are, and their case have been if Providence had thought fit.

I had another reflection which assisted me also to comfort my mind with hopes, and this was, comparing my present condition with what

I had deserved, and had therefore reason to expect from the hand of Providence. I had lived a dreadful life, perfectly destitute of the knowledge and fear of God. I had been well instructed by father and mother, neither had they been wanting to me, in their early endeavours, to infuse a religious awe of God into my mind, a sense of my duty, and of what the nature and end of my being required of me. But, alas! falling early into the seafaring life which of all the lives is the most destitute of the fear of God, though His terrors are always before them; I say, falling early into the seafaring life, and into seafaring company, all that little sense of religion which I had entertained was laughed out of me by my messmates, by a hardened despising of dangers and the views of death, which grew habitual to me, by my long absence from all manner of opportunities to converse with anything but what was like myself, or to hear anything that was good, or tended towards it.

So void was I of everything that was good, or of the least sense of what I was, or was to be, that in the greatest deliverances I enjoyed—such as my escape from Sallee, my being taken up by the Portuguese master of the ship, my being planted so well in the Brazils, my receiving the cargo from England, and the like—I never had once the word "Thank God" so much as on my mind, or in my mouth; nor in the greatest distress had I so much as a thought to pray to Him, or so much as to say, "Lord, have mercy upon me"; no, nor to mention the name of God, unless it was to swear by and blaspheme it.

I had terrible reflections upon my mind for many months, as I have already observed, on the account of my wicked and hardened life past; and when I looked about me, and considered what particular providences had attended me since my coming into this place, and how God had dealt bountifully with me—had not only punished me less than my iniquity had deserved, but had so plentifully provided for me; this gave me great hopes that my repentance was accepted, and that God had yet mercy in store for me.

With these reflections I worked my mind up not only to resignation to the will of God in the present disposition of my circumstances, but even to a sincere thankfulness for my condition; and that I, who was yet a living man, ought not to complain, seeing I had not the due punishment of my sins; that I enjoyed so many mercies which I had no reason to have expected in that place; that I ought never more to repine at my condition, but to rejoice, and to give daily thanks for that daily bread which nothing but a crowd of wonders could have brought: that I ought to consider I had been fed even by miracle, even as great as that of feeding Elijah by ravens; nay, by a long series of miracles: and that I could hardly have named a place in the inhabitable part of the world where I could have been cast more to my advantage —a place where, as I had no society, which was my affliction on one hand, so I found no ravenous beasts, no furious wolves or tigers, to threaten my life, no venomous creatures or poisonous, which I might feed on to my hurt, no savages to murder and devour me.

In a word, as my life was a life of sorrow one way, so it was a life of mercy another; and I wanted nothing to make it a life of comfort but to be able to make my sense of God's goodness to me and care over me in this condition be my daily consolation. And after I did make a just improvement of these things, I went away and was no more sad.

I had now been here so long that many things which I brought on shore for my help were either quite gone or very much wasted and near spent.

My ink, as I observed, had been gone for some time, all but a very little, which I eked out with water a little and a little till it was so pale it scarce left any appearance of black upon the paper. As long as it lasted I made use of it to minute down the days of the month on which any remarkable thing happened to me, and first by casting up times past. I remember that there was a strange concurrence of days in the various providences which befell me, and which, if I had been superstitiously inclined to observe days as fatal or fortunate, I might have had reason to have looked upon with a great deal of curiosity.

First, I had observed that the same day that I broke away from my father and my friends, and ran away to Hull, in order to go to sea, the same day afterwards I was taken by the Sallee man-of-war, and made a slave.

The same day of the year that I escaped out of the wreck of that ship in Yarmouth Roads, that same day-year afterwards I made my escape from Sallee in the boat.

The same day of the year I was born on—namely the 30th of September—the same day I had my life so miraculously saved twenty-six years after, when I was cast on shore on this island, so that my wicked life and my solitary life began both on a day.

The next thing to my ink's being wasted was that of my bread—I mean the biscuit which I brought out of the ship. This I had husbanded to the last degree, allowing myself but one cake of bread a day for above a year, and yet I was quite without bread for near a year before I got any corn of my own; and great reason I had to be thankful that I had any at all, the getting it being, as has been already observed, next to miraculous.

My clothes began to decay too mightily. As to linen, I had had none a good while, except some checkered shirts which I found in the chests of the other seamen, and which I carefully preserved, because many times I could bear no other clothes on but a shirt: and it was a very great help to me that I had among all the men's clothes of the ship almost three dozen of shirts. There were also several thick watch-coats of the seamen's, which were left indeed, but they were too hot to wear. And though it is true that the weather was so violently hot that there was no need of clothes, yet I could not go quite naked: no, though I had been inclined to it, which I was not, nor could not abide the thoughts of it, though I was all alone.

The reason why I could not go quite naked was, I could not bear the heat of the sun so well when quite naked as with some clothes on; nay, the very heat frequently blistered my skin, whereas, with a shirt on, the air itself made some motion, and whistling under that shirt, was twofold cooler than without it. No more could I ever bring myself to go out in the heat of the sun without a cap or a hat, the heat of the sun beating with such violence as it does in that place would give me the headache presently, by darting so directly on my head without a cap or hat on, so that I could not bear it, whereas, if I put on my hat, it would presently go away.

Upon those views I began to consider about putting the few rags

I had, which I called clothes, into some order. I had worn out all the waistcoats I had, and my business was now to try if I could not make jackets out of the great watch-coats which I had by me, and with such other materials as I had; so I set to work a-tailoring, or rather indeed a-botching, for I made most piteous work of it. However, I made shift to make two or three new waistcoats, which I hoped would serve me a great while. As for breeches or drawers, I made but a very sorry shift indeed till afterwards.

I have mentioned that I saved the skins of all the creatures that I killed—I mean four-footed ones—and I had hung them up stretched out with sticks in the sun, by which means some of them were so dry and hard that they were fit for little, but others it seems were very useful. The first thing I made of these was a great cap for my head, with the hair on the outside to shoot off the rain; and this I performed so well, that after this I made me a suit of clothes wholly of these skins—that is to say, a waistcoat, and breeches open at knees, and both loose, for they were rather wanting to keep me cool than to keep me warm. I must not omit to acknowledge that they were wretchedly made; for if I was a bad carpenter, I was a worse tailor. However, they were such as I made very good shift with. And when I was abroad, if it happened to rain, the hair of my waistcoat and cap being outermost I was kept very dry.

After this I spent a great deal of time and pains to make me an umbrella. I was indeed in great want of one, and had a great mind to make one. I had seen them made in the Brazils, where they are very useful in the great heats which are there; and I felt the heats every jot as great here, and greater too, being nearer the equinox. Besides, as I was obliged to be much abroad, it was a most useful thing to me, as well for the rains as the heats. I took a world of pains at it, and was a great while before I could make anything likely to hold; nay, after I thought I had hit the way, I spoiled two or three before I made one to my mind, but at last I made one that answered indifferently well. The main difficulty I found was to make it to let down. I could make it to spread, but if it did not let down too and draw in, it was not portable for me any way but just over my head, which would not do.

However, at last, as I said, I made one to answer, and covered it with skins, the hair upwards, so that it cast off the rains like a penthouse, and kept off the sun so effectually that I could walk out in the hottest of the weather with greater advantage than I could before in the coolest; and when I had no need of it, could close it and carry it under my arm.

Thus I lived mighty comfortably, my mind being entirely composed by resigning to the will of God, and throwing myself wholly upon the disposal of His providence. This made my life better than sociable; for when I began to regret the want of conversation I would ask myself whether thus conversing mutually with my own thoughts, and, as I hope I may say, with even God himself by ejaculations, was not better than the utmost enjoyment of human society in the world.

I cannot say that after this, for five years, any extraordinary thing happened to me, but I lived on in the same course, in the same posture and place, just as before. The chief things I was employed in, besides my yearly labour of planting my barley and rice and curing my raisins, of both which I always kept up just enough to have sufficient stock of one year's provisions beforehand; I say, besides this yearly labour and my daily labour of going out with my gun, I had one labour to make me a canoe, which at last I finished; so that, by digging a canal to it of six feet wide and four feet deep, I brought it into the creek, almost half a mile. As for the first, which was so vastly big, as I made it without considering beforehand as I ought to do, how I should be able to launch it, so never being able to bring it to the water, or bring the water to it, I was obliged to let it lie where it was, as a memorandum to teach me to be wiser next time. Indeed, the next time, though I could not get a tree proper for it, and in a place where I could not get the water to it, at any less distance than as I have said, near half a mile; yet, as I saw it was practicable at last, I never gave it over; and though I was near two years about it, yet I never grudged my labour, in hopes of having a boat to go off to sea at last.

However, though my little periagua was finished, yet the size of it was not at all answerable to the design which I had in view when I made the first—I mean, of venturing over to the *terra firma,* where it was above forty miles broad. Accordingly, the smallness of my boat assisted to put an end to that design, and now I thought no more of it. But as I had a boat, my next design was to make a tour round the island; for as I had been on the other side in one place, crossing, as I have already described it, over the land, so the discoveries I made in that little journey made me very eager to see other parts of the coast; and now I had a boat, I thought of nothing but sailing round the island.

For this purpose, that I might do everything with discretion and consideration, I fitted up a little mast to my boat, and made a sail to it out of some of the pieces of the ship's sail, which lay in store, and of which I had a great stock by me.

Having fitted my mast and sail, and tried the boat, I found she would sail very well. Then I made little lockers, or boxes, at either end of my boat, to put provisions, necessaries, and ammunition, &c., into, to be kept dry either from rain or the spray of the sea; and a little long hollow place I cut in the inside of the boat, where I could lay my gun, making a flap to hang down over it to keep it dry.

I fixed my umbrella also in a step at the stern, like a mast, to stand over my head, and keep the heat of the sun off me like an awning; and thus I every now and then took a little voyage upon the sea, but never went far out, not far from the little creek. But at last, being eager to view the circumference of my little kingdom, I resolved upon my tour, and accordingly I victualled my ship for the voyage, putting in two dozen of my loaves (cakes I should rather call them) of barley bread, an earthen pot full of parched rice—a food I ate a good deal of —a little bottle of rum, half a goat, and powder and shot for killing more, and two large watch-coats of those which, as I mentioned before, I had saved out of the seamen's chests: these I took, one to lie upon, and the other to cover me in the night.

§ *I start on a voyage of discovery, and am blown out to sea. My narrow escape. An unexpected visit from Poll.*

I⟶ was the 6th of November, in the sixth year of my reign, or my captivity, which you please, that I set out on this voyage, and I found it much longer than I expected. For though the island itself was not very large, yet, when I came to the east side of it, I found a great ledge of rocks lie out above two leagues into the sea, some above water, some under it; and beyond that a shoal of sand lying dry half a league more. So that I was obliged to go a great way out to sea to double the point.

When first I discovered them I was willing to give over my enterprise and come back again, not knowing how far it might oblige me to go out to sea; and above all, doubting how I should get back again; so I came to an anchor—for I had made me a kind of an anchor with a piece of a broken grappling, which I got out of the ship.

Having secured my boat, I took my gun and went on shore, climbing up upon a hill which seemed to overlook that point, where I saw the full extent of it, and resolved to venture.

136

In my viewing the sea from that hill where I stood, I perceived a strong, and indeed a most furious current, which ran to the east, and even came close to the point. And I took the more notice of it, because I saw there might be some danger that when I came into it I might be carried out to sea by the strength of it, and not be able to make the island again. And, indeed, had I not gotten first up upon this hill, I believe it would have been so; for there was the same current on the other side the island, only that it set off at a farther distance. And I saw there was a strong eddy under the shore; so I had nothing to do but to get in out of the first current, and I should presently be in an eddy.

I lay here, however, two days, because the wind blowing pretty fresh at east-south-east, and that being just contrary to the said current, made a great breach of the sea upon the point; so that it was not safe for me to keep too close to the shore for the breach, nor to go too far off because of the stream.

The third day, in the morning, the wind having abated overnight, the sea was calm, and I ventured. But I am a warning piece again to all rash and ignorant pilots; for no sooner was I come to the point, when even I was not my boat's length from the shore, but I found myself in a great depth of water, and a current like the sluice of a mill. It carried my boat along with it with such violence that all I could do could not keep her so much as on the edge of it; but I found it hurried me farther and farther out from the eddy, which was on my left hand. There was no wind stirring to help me; and all I could do with my paddlers signified nothing. And now I began to give myself over for lost; for as the current was on both sides the island, I knew in a few leagues distance they must join again, and then I was irrecoverably gone. Nor did I see any possibility of avoiding it; so that I had no prospect before me but of perishing—not by the sea, for that was calm enough, but of starving for hunger. I had, indeed, found a tortoise on the shore as big almost as I could lift, and had tossed it into the boat; and I had a great jar of fresh water—that is to say, one of my earthen pots; but what was all this to being driven into the vast ocean, where, to be sure, there was no shore, no mainland or island for a thousand leagues at least!

And now I saw how easy it was for the providence of God to make the most miserable condition mankind could be in, worse. Now I looked back upon my desolate solitary island as the most pleasant place in the world, and all the happiness my heart could wish for was to be but there again. I stretched out my hands to it with eager wishes.

"O happy desert," said I, "I shall never see thee more! O miserable creature," said I, "whither am I going?" Then I reproached myself with my unthankful temper, and how I had repined at my solitary condition; and now what would I give to be on shore there again! Thus we never see the true state of our condition, till it is illustrated to us by its contraries; nor know how to value what we enjoy, but by the want of it. It is scarce possible to imagine the consternation I was now in, being driven from my beloved island (for so it appeared to me now to be) into the wide ocean, almost two leagues, and in the utmost despair of ever recovering it again. However, I worked hard, till indeed my strength was almost exhausted, and kept my boat as much to the northward—that is, towards the side of the current which the eddy lay on—as possibly I could; when about noon, as the sun passed the meridian, I thought I felt a little breeze of wind in my face, springing up from the south-south-east. This cheered my heart a little, and especially when in about half an hour more it blew a pretty small gentle gale. By this time I was gotten at a frightful distance from the island, and had the least cloud or hazy weather intervened, I had been undone another way too; for I had no compass on board, and should never have known how to have steered towards the island, if I had but once lost sight of it. But the weather continuing clear, I applied myself to get up my mast again, and spread my sail, standing away to the north as much as possible, to get out of the current.

Just as I had set my mast and sail, and the boat began to stretch away, I saw even by the clearness of the water some alteration of the current was near; for where the current was so strong, the water was foul; but perceiving the water clear, I found the current abate, and presently I found to the east, at about half a mile, a breach of the sea upon some rocks. These rocks, I found, caused the current to part again, and as to the main stress of it ran away more southerly, leaving the rocks to the north-east, so the other returned by the repulse of the rocks, and made a strong eddy, which ran back again to the northwest, with a very sharp stream.

They who know what it is to have a reprieve brought to them upon the ladder, or to be rescued from thieves just going to murder them, or who have been in such like extremities, may guess what my present surprise of joy was, and how gladly I put my boat into the stream of this eddy, and, the wind also freshening, how gladly I spread my sail to it, running cheerfully before the wind, and with a strong tide or eddy under foot.

This eddy carried me about a league in my way back again directly towards the island, but about two leagues more to the northward than the current which carried me away at first; so that when I came near the island, I found myself open to the northern shore of it—that is to say, the other end of the island opposite to that which I went out from.

When I had made something more than a league of way by the help of this current or eddy, I found it was spent, and served me no farther. However, I found that being between the two great currents, namely, that on the south side, which had hurried me away, and that on the north, which lay about a league on the other side: I say, between these two, in the wake of the island, I found the water at least still and running no way; and having still a breeze of wind fair for me, I kept on steering directly for the island, though not making such fresh way as I did before.

About four o'clock in the evening, being then within about a league of the island, I found the point of the rocks which occasioned this disaster stretching out, as is described before, to the southward, and casting off the current more southwardly had of course made another eddy to the north, and this I found very strong, but not directly setting the way my course lay, which was due west, but almost full north. However, having a fresh gale, I stretched across this eddy slanting north-west, and in about an hour came within about a mile of the shore, where, it being smooth water, I soon got to land.

When I was on shore, I fell on my knees and gave God thanks for my deliverance, resolving to lay aside all thoughts of my deliverance by my boat; and refreshing myself with such things as I had, I brought my boat close to the shore in a little cove that I had spied under some trees, and laid me down to sleep, being quite spent with the labour and fatigue of the voyage.

I was now at a great loss which way to get home with my boat. I had run so much hazard, and knew too much the case, to think of attempting it by the way I went out; and what might be at the other side (I mean the west side) I knew not, nor had I any mind to run any more ventures; so I only resolved in the morning to make my way westward along the shore, and to see if there was no creek where I might lay up my frigate in safety, so as to have her again if I wanted her. In about three miles or thereabouts, coasting the shore, I came to a very good inlet or bay about a mile over, which narrowed till it came to a very little rivulet or brook, where I found a very convenient harbour for my boat, and where she lay as if she had been in a little dock made on purpose for her. Here I put in, and having stowed my boat very safe, I went on shore to look about me and see where I was.

I soon found I had but a little passed by the place where I had been before, when I travelled on foot to that shore; so taking nothing out of my boat but my gun and my umbrella, for it was exceeding hot, I began my march. The way was comfortable enough after such a voyage as I had been upon, and I reached my old bower in the evening, where I found everything standing as I left it; for I always kept it in good order, being, as I said before, my country-house.

I got over the fence, and laid me down in the shade to rest my limbs, for I was very weary, and fell asleep. But judge you, if you can, that read my story, what a surprise I must be in, when I was waked out of my sleep by a voice calling me by my name several times, "Robin, Robin, Robin Crusoe; poor Robin Crusoe! Where are you, Robin Crusoe? Where are you? Where have you been?"

I was so dead asleep at first, being fatigued with rowing, or paddling, as it is called, the first part of the day, and with walking the latter part, that I did not wake thoroughly; but dozing between sleeping and waking, thought I dreamed that somebody spoke to me. But as the voice continued to repeat, "Robin Crusoe, Robin Crusoe," as last I began to wake more perfectly, and was at first dreadfully frightened, and started up in the utmost consternation. But no sooner were my eyes open, but I saw my Poll sitting on the top of the hedge, and immediately knew that it was he that spoke to me; for just in such bemoaning language I had used to talk to him, and teach him; and he had learned it so perfectly, that he would sit upon my finger, and lay his bill close to my face, and cry, "Poor Robin Crusoe, where are you? Where have you been? How come you here?" and such things as I had taught him.

However, even though I knew it was the parrot, and that indeed it could be nobody else, it was a good while before I could compose myself: first, I was amazed how the creature got thither, and then how he should just keep about the place, and nowhere else. But as I was well satisfied it could be nobody but honest Poll, I got it over; and holding out my hand, and calling him by his name Poll, the sociable creature came to me, and sat upon my thumb, as he used to do, and continued talking to me, "Poor Robin Crusoe," and "How did I come here?" and "Where had I been?" just as if he had been overjoyed to see me again; and so I carried him home along with me.

I had now had enough of rambling to sea for some time, and had enough to do for many days to sit still and reflect upon the danger I had been in. I would have been very glad to have had my boat again on my side of the island; but I knew not how it was practicable to get it about. As to the east side of the island, which I had gone round, I knew well enough there was no venturing that way; my very heart would shrink, and my very blood run chill but to think of it. And as to the other side of the island, I did not know how it might be there; but supposing the current ran with the same force against the shore at the east as it passed by it on the other, I might run the same risk of being driven down the stream, and carried by the island, as I had been before of being carried away from it; so with these thoughts I contented myself to be without any boat, though it had been the product of so many months' labour to make it; and of so many more to get it unto the sea.

In this government of my temper I remained near a year—lived a very sedate, retired life, as you may well suppose; and my thoughts being very much composed as to my condition, and fully comforted in resigning myself to the disposition of Providence, I thought I lived really very happily in all things, except that of society.

§ *My improvement in the mechanic exercises. I trap some goats. A description of my own appearance, and of my family and estates. My alarm at seeing the print of a man's foot on the shore. Look to God for deliverance. New means for defence.*

I improved myself in this time in all the mechanic exercises which my necessities put me upon applying myself to, and I believe could, upon occasion, make a very good carpenter, especially considering how few tools I had.

Besides this, I arrived at an unexpected perfection in my earthenware, and contrived well enough to make them with a wheel, which I found infinitely easier and better; because I made things round and shapeable, which before were filthy things indeed to look on. But I think I was never more vain of my own performance, or more joyful for anything I found out, than for my being able to make a tobacco-pipe. And though it was a very ugly clumsy thing when it was done, and only burned red like other earthenware, yet, as it was hard and firm, and would draw the smoke, I was exceedingly comforted with it; for I had been always used to smoke, and there were pipes on the ship, but I forgot them at first, not knowing that there was tobacco in the island; and afterwards, when I searched the ship again, I could not come at any pipes at all.

In my wicker-ware, also, I improved much, and made abundance of necessary baskets, as well as my invention showed me. Though not very handsome, yet they were such as were very handy and convenient for my laying things up in, or fetching things home in. For example, if I killed a goat abroad, I could hang it up in a tree, flay it, and dress it, and cut it in pieces, and bring it home in a basket; and the like by a turtle—I could cut it up, take out the eggs, and a piece or two of the flesh, which was enough for me, and bring them home in a basket, and leave the rest behind me. Also large deep baskets were my receivers for my corn, which I always rubbed out as soon as it was dry, and cured, and kept it in great baskets.

I began now to perceive my powder abated considerably, and this was a want which it was impossible for me to supply, and I began seriously to consider what I must do when I should have no more powder; that is to say, how I should do to kill any goat. I had, as is observed, in the third year of my being here, kept a young kid, and bred her up tame, and I was in hope of getting a he-goat, but I could not by any means bring it to pass, till my kid grew an old goat; and I could never find in my heart to kill her, till she died at last of mere age.

But being now in the eleventh year of my residence, and, as I have said, my ammunition growing low, I set myself to study some art to trap and snare the goats, to see whether I could not catch some of them alive, and particularly I wanted a she-goat great with young.

To this purpose I made snares to hamper them; and I do believe they were more than once taken in them; but my tackle was not good, for I had no wire, and I always found them broken, and my bait devoured.

At length I resolved to try a pit-fall. So I dug several large pits in the earth, in places where I had observed the goats used to feed; and over these pits I placed hurdles of my own making too, with a great weight upon them. And several times I put ears of barley, and dry rice, without setting the trap; and I could easily perceive that the goats had gone in and eaten up the corn, for I could see the mark of their feet. At length I set three traps in one night; and going the next morning, I found them all standing, and yet the bait eaten and gone. This was very discouraging. However, I altered my trap; and, not to trouble you with particulars, going one morning to see my trap, I found in one of them a large old he-goat; and in one of the other, three kids—a male and two females.

As to the old one, I knew not what to do with him; he was so fierce I durst not go into the pit to him—that is to say, to go about to bring him away alive, which was what I wanted. I could have killed him; but that was not my business, nor would it answer my end. So I even let him out, and he ran away as if he had been frightened out of his wits. But I had forgot then what I learned afterwards—that hunger will tame a lion. If I had let him stay there three or four days without food, and then have carried him some water to drink, and then a little corn, he would have been as tame as one of the kids—for they are mighty sagacious, tractable creatures where they are well used.

However, for the present I let him go, knowing no better at that time. Then I went to the three kids; and taking them one by one, I tied them with strings together, and with some difficulty brought them all home.

It was a good while before they would feed; but throwing them some sweet corn, it tempted them, and they began to be tame. And now I found that if I expected to supply myself with goat-flesh when I had no powder or shot left, breeding some up tame was my only way; when, perhaps, I might have them about my house like a flock of sheep.

But then it presently occurred to me that I must keep the tame from the wild, or else they would always run wild when they grew up. And the only way for this was to have some enclosed piece of ground, well fenced either with hedge or pale, to keep them in so effectually, that those within might not break out, or those without break in.

This was a great undertaking for one pair of hands. Yet, as I saw there was an absolute necessity for doing it, my first piece of work was to find out a proper piece of ground—namely, where there was likely to be herbage for them to eat, water for them to drink, and cover to keep them from the sun.

Those who understand such enclosures will think I had very little contrivance when I pitched upon a place very proper for all these, being a plain open piece of meadow-land or savanna (as our people call it in the western colonies), which had two or three little rills of fresh water in it, and at one end was very woody. I say they will smile at my forecast, when I shall tell them I began my enclosing of this piece of ground in such a manner that my hedge or pale must have been at least two miles about! Nor was the madness of it so great as to the compass, for if it was ten mile about, I was like to have time enough to do it in. But I did not consider that my goats would be as wild in so much compass as if they had had the whole island, and I should have so much room to chase them in that I should never catch them.

My hedge was begun and carried on, I believe, about fifty yards, when this thought occurred to me. So I presently stopped short, and for the first beginning I resolved to enclose a piece of about one hundred and fifty yards in length, and one hundred yards in breadth; which, as it would maintain as many as I should have in any reasonable time, so, as my flock increased, I could add more ground to my enclosure.

This was acting with some prudence, and I went to work with courage. I was about three months hedging in the first piece; and till I had done it, I tethered the three kids in the best part of it, and used them to feed as near me as possible, to make them familiar; and very often I would go and carry them some ears of barley, or a handful of rice, and feed them out of my hand; so that, after my enclosure was finished, and I let them loose, they would follow me up and down, bleating after me for a handful of corn.

This answered my end. And in about a year and a half I had a flock of about twelve goats—kids and all; and in two years more, I had three-and-forty—besides several that I took and killed for my food. And after that I enclosed five several pieces of ground to feed them in, with little pens to drive them into, to take them as I wanted, and gates out of one piece of ground into another.

But this is not all; for now I not only had goat's flesh to feed on when I pleased, but milk too—a thing which, indeed, in my beginning, I did not so much as think of, and which, when it came into my thoughts, was really an agreeable surprise. For now I set up my dairy, and had sometimes a gallon or two of milk in a day. And as Nature, who gives supplies of food to every creature, dictates even naturally how to make use of it; so I, that had never milked a cow, much less a goat, or seen butter or cheese made, very readily and handily, though after a great many essays and miscarriages, made me both butter and cheese at last, and never wanted it afterwards.

How mercifully can our great Creator treat His creatures, even in those conditions in which they seem to be overwhelmed in destruction! How can He sweeten the bitterest providences, and give us cause to praise Him for dungeons and prisons! What a table was here spread for me in the wilderness, where I saw nothing at first but to perish for hunger!

It would have made a Stoic smile to have seen me and my little family sit down to dinner. There was my Majesty, the prince and lord of the whole island. I had the lives of all my subjects at my absolute command—I could hang, draw, give liberty, and take it away; and no rebels among all my subjects.

Then to see how like a king I dined, too, all alone, attended by my servants. Poll, as if he had been my favourite, was the only person permitted to talk to me. My dog—who was now grown very old and crazy—sat always at my right hand; and two cats, one on one side the table and one on the other, expecting now and then a bit from my hand, as a mark of special favour.

But these were not the two cats which I brought on shore at first—for they were both of them dead, and had been interred near my habitation by my own hand; but one of them having multiplied by I know not what kind of creature, these were two which I had preserved tame, whereas the rest ran wild in the woods, and became indeed troublesome to me at last—for they would often come into my house, and plunder me too, till at last I was obliged to shoot them, and did kill a great many. At length they left me with this attendance, and in this plentiful manner I lived. Neither could I be said to want anything but society; and of that, in some time after this, I was like to have too much.

I was something impatient, as I have observed, to have the use of my boat—though very loath to run any more hazards; and therefore sometimes I sat contriving ways to get her about the island, and at other times I sat myself down contented enough without her. But I had a strange uneasiness in my mind to go down to the point of the island where, as I have said, in my last ramble, I went up the hill to see how the shore lay and how the current set, that I might see what I had to do. This inclination increased upon me every day, and at length I resolved to travel thither by land, following the edge of the shore. I did so. But had any one in England been to meet such a man as I was, it must either have frightened them, or raised a great deal of laughter. And as I frequently stood still to look at myself, I could not but smile at the notion of my traveling through Yorkshire with such an equipage and in such a dress. Be pleased to take a sketch of my figure as follows.

I had a great high shapeless cap, made of a goat's skin, with a flap hanging down behind, as well to keep the sun from me as to shoot the rain off from running into my neck—nothing being so hurtful in these climates as the rain upon the flesh under the clothes.

I had a short jacket of goat-skin, the skirts coming down to about the middle of my thighs; and a pair of open-kneed breeches of the same—the breeches were made of the skin of an old he-goat, whose hair hung down such a length on either side, that like pantaloons it reached to the middle of my legs; stockings and shoes I had none, but had made me a pair of somethings, I scarce know what to call them, like buskins, to flap over my legs and lace on either side like spatter-dashes, but of a most barbarous shape—as indeed were all the rest of my clothes.

I had on a broad belt of goat-skin dried, which I drew together with two thongs of the same, instead of buckles, and in a kind of a frog on either side of this. Instead of a sword and a dagger hung a little saw and hatchet, one on one side, one on the other. I had another belt not so broad, and fastened in the same manner, which hung over my shoulder; and at the end of it, under my left arm, hung two went up to the rock again; and then the tide of ebb being made, I plainly saw the current again as before, only that it ran farther off, being near half a league from the shore; whereas in my case it set close upon the shore, and hurried me and my canoe along with it, which at another time it would not have done.

This observation convinced me that I had nothing to do but to observe the ebbing and the flowing of the tide, and I might very easily bring my boat about the island again. But when I began to think of putting it in practice, I had such a terror upon my spirits at the remembrance of the danger I had been in, that I could not think of it again with any patience. But on the contrary, I took up another resolution, which was more safe, though more laborious; and this was, that I would build, or rather make me another periagua or canoe, and so have one for one side of the island, and one for the other.

You are to understand that now I had, as I may call it, two plantations in the island: one my little fortification or tent, with the wall about it under the rock, with the cave behind me, which by this time I had enlarged into several apartments, or caves, one within another. One of these, which was the driest and largest, and had a door out beyond my wall or fortification—that is to say beyond where my wall joined to the rock—was all filled up with the large earthen pots of which I have given an account, and with fourteen or fifteen great baskets, which would hold five or six bushels each, where I laid up my stores of provision, especially my corn, some in the ear cut off short from the straw, and the other rubbed out with my hand.

As for my wall, made, as before, with long stakes or piles, those piles grew all like trees, and were by this time grown so big, and spread so very much, that there was not the least appearance to any one's view of any habitation behind them.

Near this dwelling of mine, but a little farther within the land, and upon lower ground, lay my two pieces of corn-ground, which I kept duly cultivated and sowed, and which duly yielded me their harvest in its season; and whenever I had occasion for more corn, I had more land adjoining as fit as that.

Besides this I had my country seat, and I had now a tolerable plantation there also; for first, I had my little bower, as I called it, which I kept in repair—that is to say, I kept the hedge which circled it in constantly fitted up to its usual height, the ladder standing always in the inside. I kept the trees, which at first were no more than my stakes, but were now grown very firm and tall—I kept them always so cut that they might spread and grow thick and wild, and make the more agreeable shade, which they did effectually to my mind. In the middle of this I had my tent always standing, being a piece of a sail spread over the poles set up for that purpose, and which never wanted any repair or renewing; and under this I had made me a squab or couch, with the skins of the creatures I had killed, and with other soft things, and a blanket laid on them; such as belong to our sea-bedding, which I had saved, and a great watch-coat to cover me; and here, whenever I had occasion to be absent from my chief seat, I took up my country habitation.

Adjoining to this I had my enclosures for my cattle, that is to say, my goats; and as I had taken an inconceivable deal of pains to fence and enclose this ground, so I was so uneasy to see it kept entire, lest the goats should break through, that I never left off till with infinite labour I had stuck the outside of the hedge so full of small stakes, and so near to one another, that it was rather a pale than a hedge, and there was scarce room to put a hand through between them; which, afterwards, when those stakes grew, as they all did in the next rainy season, made the enclosure strong like a wall; indeed, stronger than any wall.

This will testify for me that I was not idle, and that I spared no pains to bring to pass whatever appeared necessary for my comfortable support; for I considered the keeping up a breed of tame creatures thus at my hand would be a living magazine of flesh, milk, butter, and cheese for me as long as I lived in the place, if it were to be forty years; and that keeping them in my reach depended entirely upon my perfecting my enclosures to such a degree that I might be sure of keeping them together; which by this method, indeed, I so effectually secured, that when these little stakes began to grow, I had planted them so very thick I was forced to pull some of them up again.

In this place, also, I had my grapes growing, which I principally depended on for my winter store of raisins; and which I never failed to preserve very carefully, as the best and most agreeable dainty of my whole diet; and, indeed, they were not agreeable only, but physical, wholesome, nourishing, and refreshing to the last degree.

As this was also about half-way between my other habitation and the place where I had laid up my boat, I generally stayed and lay here in my way thither; for I used frequently to visit my boat, and I kept all things about or belonging to her in very good order. Sometimes I went out in her to divert myself; but no more hazardous voyages would I go, nor scarce ever above a stone's cast or two from the shore, I was so apprehensive of being hurried out of my knowledge again by the currents, or winds, or any other accident. But now I come to a new scene of my life.

It happened one day about noon, going towards my boat, I was exceedingly surprised with the print of a man's naked foot on the shore, which was very plain to be seen in the sand. I stood like one thunderstruck, or as if I had seen an apparition. I listened, I looked round me; I could hear nothing, nor see anything. I went up to a rising ground to look farther. I went up the shore and down the shore; but it was all one, I could see no other impression but that one. I went to it again to see if there were any more, and to observe if it might not be my fancy; but there was no room for that, for there was exactly the very print of a foot, toes, heel, and every part of a foot;— how it came thither I knew not, nor could in the least imagine. But after innumerable fluttering thoughts, like a man perfectly confused and out of myself, I came home to my fortification, not feeling, as we say, the ground I went on, but terrified to the last degree, looking behind me at every two or three steps, mistaking every bush and tree, and fancying every stump at a distance to be a man. Nor is it possible to describe how many various shapes affrighted imagination represented things to me in; how many wild ideas were found every moment in my fancy, and what strange unaccountable whimsies came into my thoughts by the way.

When I came to my castle, for so I think I called it ever after this,

I fled into it like one pursued. Whether I went over by the ladder as first contrived, or went in at the hole in the rock which I called a door, I cannot remember; no, nor could I remember the next morning; for never frighted hare fled to cover, or fox to earth, with more terror of mind than I to this retreat.

I slept none that night. The farther I was from the occasion of my fright the greater my apprehensions were, which is something contrary to the nature of such things, and especially to the usual practice of all creatures in fear. But I was so embarrassed with my own frightful ideas of the thing, that I formed nothing but dismal imaginations to myself, even though I was now a great way off it. Sometimes I fancied it must be the devil; and reason joined in with me upon this supposition. For how should any other thing in human shape come into the place? Where was the vessel that brought them? What marks were there of any other footsteps? And how was it possible a man should come there? But, then, to think that Satan should take human shape upon him in such a place, where there could be no manner of occasion for it but to leave the print of his foot behind him, and that even for no purpose, too, for he could not be sure I should see it; this was an amusement the other way. I considered that the devil might have found out abundance of other ways to have terrified me, than this of the single print of a foot;—that, as I lived quite on the other side of the island, he would never have been so simple as to leave a mark in a place where it was ten thousand to one whether I should ever see it or not; and in the sand, too, which the first surge of the sea upon a high wind would have defaced entirely. All this seemed inconsistent with the thing itself, and with all the notions we usually entertain of the subtilty of the devil.

Abundance of such things as these assisted to argue me out of all apprehensions of its being the devil. And I presently concluded, then, that it must be some more dangerous creature—namely, that it must be some of the savages of the mainland over against me, who had wandered out to sea in their canoes, and either driven by the currents, or by contrary winds, had made the island; and had been on shore, but were gone away again to sea, being as loth, perhaps, to have stayed in this desolate island as I would have been to have had them.

While these reflections were rolling upon my mind, I was very thankful in my thoughts that I was so happy as not to be thereabouts at that time, or that they did not see my boat, by which they would have concluded that some inhabitants had been in the place, and perhaps have searched farther for me. Then terrible thoughts racked my imagination about their having found my boat, and that there were people here; and that if so, I should certainly have them come again in greater numbers and devour me; that if it should happen so that they should not find me, yet they would find my enclosure, destroy all my corn, carry away all my flock of tame goats, and I should perish at last for mere want.

Thus my fear banished all my religious hope; all that former confidence in God which was founded upon such wonderful experience as I had had of His goodness, now vanished, as if He that had fed me by miracle hitherto could not preserve by His power the provision which He had made for me by His goodness. I reproached myself with my easiness, that would not sow any more corn one year than would just serve me till the next season, as if no accident could intervene to prevent my enjoying the crop that was upon the ground; and this I thought so just a reproof, that I resolved for the future to have two or three years' corn beforehand, so that whatever might come, I might not perish for want of bread.

How strange a checker-work of providence is the life of man! and by what secret differing springs are the affections hurried about, as differing circumstances present! To-day we love what to-morrow we hate; to-day we seek what to-morrow we shun; to-day we desire what to-morrow we fear—nay, even tremble at the apprehensions of. This was exemplified in me at this time in the most lively manner imaginable: for I, whose only affliction was that I seemed banished from human society, that I was alone, circumscribed by the boundless ocean, cut off from mankind, and condemned to what I called silent life—that I was as one whom Heaven thought not worthy to be numbered among the living, or to appear among the rest of His creatures; that to have seen one of my own species would have seemed to me a raising me from death to life, and the greatest blessing that Heaven itself, next to the supreme blessing of salvation, could bestow;—I say, that I should now tremble at the very apprehensions of seeing a man, and was ready to sink into the ground at but the shadow or silent appearance of a man's having set his foot in the island.

Such is the uneven state of human life. And it afforded me a great many curious speculations afterwards, when I had a little recovered my first surprise. I considered that this was the station of life the infinitely wise and good providence of God had determined for me; that as I could not foresee what the ends of divine wisdom might be in all this, so I was not to dispute His sovereignty, who, as I was His creature, had an undoubted right by creation to govern and dispose of me absolutely as He thought fit; and who, as I was a creature who had offended Him, had likewise a judicial right to condemn me to what punishment He thought fit; and that it was my part to submit to bear His indignation, because I had sinned against Him.

I then reflected that God, who was not only righteous but omnipotent, as He had thought fit thus to punish and afflict me, so He was able to deliver me; that if He did not think fit to do it, it was my unquestioned duty to resign myself absolutely and entirely to His will; and, on the other hand, it was my duty also to hope in Him, pray to Him, and quietly to attend the dictates and directions of His daily providence.

These thoughts took me up many hours, days, nay, I may say, weeks and months; and one particular effect of my cogitations on this occasion I cannot omit—namely, one morning early, lying in my bed, and filled with thought about my danger from the appearance of savages, I found it discomposed me very much; upon which those words of the Scripture came into my thoughts, "Call upon me in the day of trouble, and I will deliver, and thou shalt glorify me."

Upon this, rising cheerfully out of my bed, my heart was not only comforted, but I was guided and encouraged to pray earnestly to God for deliverance. When I had done praying I took up my Bible, and opening it to read, the first words that presented to me were, "Wait on the Lord and be of good cheer, and He shall strengthen thy heart; wait, I say, on the Lord." It is impossible to express the comfort this gave me. In answer, I thankfully laid down the book, and was no more sad—at least, not on that occasion.

In the middle of these cogitations, apprehensions, and reflections, it came into my thought one day that all this might be a mere chimera of my own; and that this foot might be the print of my own foot when I came on shore from my boat. This cheered me up a little, too, and I began to persuade myself it was all a delusion; that it was nothing else but my own foot; and why might not I come that way from the boat as well as I was going that way to the boat? Again, I considered also that I could by no means tell for certain where I had trod and where I had not; and that if at last this was only the print of my own foot, I had played the part of those fools who strive to make stories of spectres and apparitions, and then are frighted at them more than anybody.

Now I began to take courage, and to peep abroad again; for I had not stirred out of my castle for three days and nights, so that I began to starve for provision; for I had little or nothing within doors but some barley cakes and water. Then I knew that my goats wanted to be milked, too, which usually was my evening diversion; and the poor creatures were in great pain and inconvenience for want of it; and, indeed, it almost spoiled some of them, and almost dried up their milk.

Heartening myself therefore with the belief that this was nothing but the print of one of my own feet, and so I might be truly said to start at my own shadow, I began to go abroad again, and went to my country-house to milk my flock; but to see with what fear I went forward, how often I looked behind me, how I was ready every now and then to lay down my basket and run for my life, it would have made anyone have thought I was haunted with an evil conscience, or that I had been lately most terribly frighted, and so indeed I had.

However, as I went down thus two or three days, and having seen nothing, I began to be a little bolder, and to think there was really nothing in it but my own imagination. But I could not persuade myself fully of this till I should go down to the shore again and see this print of a foot, and measure it by my own, and see if there was any similitude of fitness, that I might be assured it was my own foot. But when I came to the place, *First,* It appeared evidently to me that when I laid up my boat I could not possibly be on shore anywhere thereabouts. *Secondly,* When I came to measure the mark with my own foot, I found my foot not so large by a great deal. Both these things filled my head with new imaginations, and gave me the vapours again to the highest degree, so that I shook with cold like one in an ague. And I went home again, filled with the belief that some man or men had been on shore there; or, in short, that the island was inhabited, and I might be surprised before I was aware—and what course to take for my security I knew not.

Oh, what ridiculous resolution men take when possessed with fear! It deprives them of the use of those means which reason offers for their relief. The first thing I proposed to myself was to throw down my enclosures, and turn all my tame cattle wild into the woods, that the enemy might not find them, and then frequent the island in prospect of the same or the like booty; then to the simple thing of digging up my two corn-fields, that they might not find such a grain there, and still be prompted to frequent the island; then to demolish my bower and tent, that they might not see any vestiges of habitation, and be prompted to look farther, in order to find out the persons inhabiting.

These were the subject of the first night's cogitation, after I was come home again, while the apprehensions which had so overrun my mind were fresh upon me, and my head was full of vapours, as above. Thus fear of danger is ten thousand times more terrifying than danger itself, when apparent to the eyes; and we find the burden of anxiety greater by much than the evil which we are anxious about; and, which was worse than all this, I had not that relief in this trouble from the resignation I used to practise that I hoped to have. I looked, I thought, like Saul, who complained not only that the Philistines were upon him, but that God had forsaken him; for I did not now take due ways to compose my mind, by crying to God in my distress, and resting upon His providence, as I had done before, for my defence before, they wanted but a few piles to be driven between them that they should be thicker and stronger, and my wall would be soon finished.

So that I had now a double wall, and my outer wall was thickened with pieces of timber, old cables, and everything I could think of to make it strong; having in it seven little holes about as big as I might put my arm out at. In the inside of this I thickened my wall to about ten foot thick, with continual bringing earth out of my cave and laying it at the foot of the wall and walking upon it; and through the seven holes I contrived to plant the muskets, of which I took notice that I got seven on shore out of the ship; these, I say, I planted like my cannon, and fitted them into frames that held them like a carriage that so I could fire all the seven guns in two minutes' time. This wall I was many a weary month in finishing, and yet never thought myself safe till it was done.

When this was done I stuck all the ground without my wall, for a great way every way, as full with stakes or sticks of the osier-like wood, which I found so apt to grow, as they could well stand; insomuch that I believe I might set in near twenty thousand of them, leaving a pretty large space between them and my wall, that I might have room to see an enemy, and they might have no shelter from the young trees, if they attempted to approach my outer wall.

Thus in two years' time I had a thick grove, and in five or six years' time I had a wood before my dwelling, growing so monstrous thick and strong, that it was indeed perfectly impassable; and no men, of what kind soever, would ever imagine that there was anything beyond it, much less a habitation. As for the way which I proposed to myself to go in and out (for I left no avenue), it was by setting two ladders: one to a part of the rock which was low, and then broke in, and left room to place another ladder upon that. So, when the two ladders were taken down, no man living could come down to me without mischieving himself; and if they had come down, they were on the outside of my outer wall.

Thus I took all the measures human prudence could suggest for my own preservation; and it will be seen at length that they were not altogether without just reason, though I foresaw nothing at that time more than any mere fear suggested to me. While this was doing, I was not altogether careless of my other affairs; for I had a great concern upon me for my little herd of goats. They were not only a present supply to me upon every occasion, and began to be sufficient to me, without the expense of powder and shot, but also without the fatigue of hunting after the wild ones; and I was loath to lose the advantage of them, and to have them all to nurse up over again.

To this purpose, after long consideration, I could think of but two ways to preserve them: one was, to find another convenient place to dig a cave underground, and to drive them into it every night; and the other was, to enclose two or three little bits of land, remote from one another, and as much concealed as I could, where I might keep about half-a-dozen young goats in each place; so that, if any disaster happened to the flock in general, I might be able to raise them again with little trouble and time. And this, though it would require a great deal of time and labour, I though was the most rational design.

Accordingly, I spent some time to find out the most retired parts of the island; and I pitched upon one which was as private indeed as my heart could wish for. It was a little damp piece of ground in the middle of the hollow and thick woods where, as is observed, I almost lost myself once before, endeavouring to come back that way from the eastern part of the island. Here I found a clear piece of land—near three acres—so surrounded with woods that it was almost an enclosure by nature; at least, it did not want near so much labour to make it so as the other pieces of ground I had worked so hard at.

I immediately went to work with this piece of ground; and in less than a month's time I had so fenced it round that my flock or herd—call it which you please—who were not so wild now as at first they might be supposed to be, were well enough secured in it. So, without any further delay, I removed ten young she-goats and two he-goats to this piece; and when they were there I continued to perfect the fence till I had made it as secure as the other; which, however, I did at more leisure, and it took me up more time by a great deal.

All this labour I was at the expense of purely from my apprehensions on the account of the print of a man's foot which I had seen; for as yet I never saw any human creature come near the island, and I had now lived two years under these uneasinesses, which indeed made my life much less comfortable than it was before—as may well be imagined by any who know what it is to live in the constant snare of *the fear of man*. And this I must observe with grief, too, that the discomposure of my mind had too great impressions also upon the religious part of my thoughts; for the dread and terror of falling into the hands of savages and cannibals lay so upon my spirits that I seldom found myself in a due temper for application to my Maker— at least, not with the sedate calmness and resignation of soul which I was wont to do. I rather prayed to God as under great affliction and pressure of mind, surrounded with danger, and in expectation every night of being murdered and devoured before morning. And I must testify from my experience that a temper of peace, thankfulness, love, and affection, is much more the proper frame for prayer than that of terror and discomposure; and, that, under the dread of mischief impending, a man is no more fit for a comforting performance of the duty of praying to God than he is for repentance on a sick-bed: for these discomposures affect the mind as the others do the body: and the discomposure of the mind must necessarily be as great a disability as that of the body—and much greater, praying to God being properly an act of the mind, not of the body.

But to go on. After I had thus secured one part of my little living stock, I went about the whole island searching for another private place to make such another deposit, when, wandering more to the west point of the island than I had ever done yet, and looking out to sea, I thought I saw a boat upon the sea at a great distance. I had found a perspective-glass or two in one of the seamen's chests which I saved out of our ship; but I had it not about me, and this was so remote that I could not tell what to make of it, though I looked at it till my eyes were not able to hold to look any longer. Whether it was a boat or not I do not know; but as I descended from the hill I could see no more of it; so I gave it over—only I resolved to go no more out without a perspective-glass in my pocket.

§ *I come upon the horrible remains of a cannibal feast. My plans against the savages. A better disposition afterwards possesses me. Discover a cave or grotto, into which I remove my ammunition. My diversions and amusements. See a party of savages on the shore. Find proofs of their cannibalism.*

WHEN I was come down the hill to the end of the island—where, indeed, I had never been before—I was presently convinced that the seeing the print of a man's foot was not such a strange thing in the island as I imagined. And but that it was a special providence that I was cast upon the side of the island where the savages never came, I should easily have known that nothing was more frequent than for the canoes from the main, when they happened to be a little too far out at sea, to shoot over to that side of the island for harbour; likewise, as they often met and fought in their canoes, the victors having taken any prisoners would bring them over to the shore, where, according to their dreadful customs, being all cannibals, they would kill and eat them; of which hereafter.

When I was come down the hill to the shore, as I said above, being the south-west point of the island, I was perfectly confounded and amazed—nor is it possible for me to express the horror of my mind—at seeing the shore spread with skulls, hands, feet, and other bones of human bodies; and particularly I observed a place where there had been a fire made, and a circle dug in the earth like a cockpit, where it is supposed the savage wretches had sat down to their inhuman feastings upon the bodies of their fellow-creatures.

I was so astonished with the sight of these things that I entertained no notions of any danger to myself from it for a long while. All my apprehensions were buried in the thoughts of such a pitch of inhuman hellish brutality, and the horror of the degeneracy of human nature; which though I had heard of often, yet I never had so near a view of before. In short, I turned away my face from the horrid spectacle: my stomach grew sick, and I was just at the point of fainting, when nature discharged the disorder from my stomach; and having vomited with an uncommon violence, I was a little relieved, but could not bear to stay in the place a moment. So I gat me up the hill again with all the speed I could, and walked on towards my own habitation.

When I came a little out of that part of the island, I stood still a while as amazed; and then recovering myself, I looked up with the utmost affection of my soul, and, with a flood of tears in my eyes, gave God thanks, that had cast my first lot in a part of the world where I was distinguished from such dreadful creatures as these; and that, though I had esteemed my present condition very miserable, had yet given me so many comforts in it that I had still more to give thanks for than to complain of; and this above all, that I had, even in this miserable condition, been comforted with the knowledge of Himself and the hope of His blessing—which was a felicity more than sufficiently equivalent to all the misery which I had suffered or could suffer.

In this frame of thankfulness I went home to my castle, and began to be much easier now as to the safety of my circumstances than ever I was before; for I observed that these wretches never came to this island in search of what they could get—perhaps not seeking, not wanting, or not expecting anything here, and having often, no doubt, been up in the covered woody part of it without finding anything to their purpose. I knew I had been here now almost eighteen years, and never saw the least footsteps of human creature there before; and I might be here eighteen more, as entirely concealed as I was now, if I did not discover myself to them—which I had no manner of occasion to do, it being my only business to keep myself entirely concealed where I was, unless I found a better sort of creatures than cannibals to make myself known to.

Yet I entertained such an abhorrence of the savage wretches that I have been speaking of, and of the wretched inhuman custom of their devouring and eating one another up, that I continued pensive and sad, and kept close within my own circle for almost two years after this. When I say my own circle, I mean by it my three plantations— namely, my castle, my country seat, which I called my bower, and my enclosure in the woods. Nor did I look after this for any other use than an enclosure for my goats; for the aversion which nature gave me to these hellish wretches was such that I was as fearful of seeing them as of seeing the devil himself. Nor did I so much as go to look after my boat in all this time, but began rather to think of making me another; for I could not think of ever making any more attempts to bring the other boat round the island to me, lest I should meet with some of these creatures at sea, in which, if I had happened to have fallen into their hands, I knew what would have been my lot.

Time, however, and the satisfaction I had that I was in no danger of being discovered by these people, began to wear off my uneasiness about them; and I began to live just in the same composed manner as before—only with this difference, that I used more caution, and kept my eyes more about me than I did before, lest I should happen to be seen by any of them; and, particularly, I was more cautious of firing my gun, lest any of them being on the island should happen to hear it. And it was therefore a very good providence to me that I had furnished myself with a tame breed of goats, that I needed not hunt any more about the woods or shoot at them; and if I did catch any of them after this, it was by traps and snares, as I had done before: so that for two years after this I believe I never fired my gun once off, though I never went out without it. And, which was more, as I had saved three pistols out of the ship, I always carried them out with me—or at least two of them—sticking them in my goat-skin belt; also I furbished up one of the great cutlasses that I had out of the ship, and made me a belt to hang it on also: so that I was now a most formidable fellow to look at when I went abroad, if you add to the former description of myself the particular of two pistols, and a great broadsword hanging at my side in a belt, but without a scabbard.

Things going on thus, as I have said, for some time, I seemed, excepting these cautions, to be reduced to my former calm, sedate way of living. All these things tended to showing me more and more how far my condition was from being miserable, compared to some others; nay, to many other particulars of life which it might have pleased God to have made my lot. It put me upon reflecting how little repining there would be among mankind at any condition of life, if people would rather compare their condition with those that are worse, in order to be thankful, than be always comparing them with those which are better, to assist their murmurings and complainings.

As in my present condition there were not really many things which I wanted, so indeed I thought that the frights I had been in about these savage wretches, and the concern I had been in for my own preservation, had taken off the edge of my invention for my own conveniences; and I had dropped a good design which I had once bent my thoughts too much upon, and that was to try if I could not make some of my barley into malt, and then try to brew myself some beer. This was really a whimsical thought, and I reproved myself often for the simplicity of it; for I presently saw there would be the want of several things necessary to the making my beer that it would be impossible for me to supply. As, first, casks to preserve it in; which was a thing that, as I have observed already, I could never compass— no, though I spent, not many days, but weeks, nay months, in attempting it, but to no purpose. In the next place, I had no hops to make it keep, no yeast to make it work, no copper or kettle to make it boil. And yet all these things notwithstanding, I verily believe had not these things intervened—I mean the frights and terrors I was in about the savages—I had undertaken it, and perhaps brought it to pass too; for I seldom gave anything over without accomplishing it, when I once had it in my head enough to begin it.

But my invention now run quite another way; for night and day I could think of nothing but how I might destroy some of these monsters in their cruel, bloody entertainment, and, if possible, save the victim they should bring hither to destroy. It would take up a larger volume than this whole work is intended to be, to set down all the contrivances I hatched, or rather brooded upon in my thought, for the destroying these creatures, or at least frighting them, so as to prevent their coming hither any more. But all was abortive: nothing could be possible to take effect unless I was to be there to do it myself. And what could one man do among them when perhaps there might be twenty or thirty of them together, with their darts or their bows and arrows, with which they could shoot as true to a mark as I could with my gun?

Sometimes I contrived to dig a hole under the place where they made their fire, and put in five or six pound of gunpowder, which when they kindled their fire would consequently take fire, and blow up all that was near it. But as, in the first place, I should be very loath to waste so much powder upon them, my store being now within the quantity of one barrel, so neither could I be sure of its going off at any certain time, when it might surprise them, and at best at it would do little more than just blow the fire about their ears and fright them, but not sufficient to make them forsake the place: so I laid it aside, and then proposed that I would place myself in ambush, in some convenient place, with my three guns all double-loaded, and in the middle of their bloody ceremony, let fly at them, when I should be sure to kill or wound perhaps two or three at every shot; and then falling in upon them with my three pistols and my sword, I made no doubt but that if there was twenty I should kill them all. This fancy pleased my thoughts for some weeks, and I was so full of it that I often dreamed of it, and sometimes that I was just going to let fly at them in my sleep.

I went so far with it in my imagination, that I employed myself several days to find out proper places to put myself in ambuscade, as I said, to watch for them; and I went frequently to the place itself, which was now grown more familiar to me: and especially while my mind was thus filled with thoughts of revenge, and of a bloody putting twenty or thirty of them to the sword, as I may call it; the horror I had at the place, and at the signals of the barbarous wretches devouring one another, abated my malice.

Well, at length I found a place in the side of the hill, where I was satisfied I might securely wait till I saw any of their boats coming, and might then, even before they would be ready to come on shore, convey myself unseen into thickets of trees, in one of which there was a hollow large enough to conceal me entirely, and where I might sit and observe all their bloody doings, and take my full aim at their heads, when they were so close together as that it would be next to impossible that I should miss my shot, or that I could fail wounding three or four of them at the first shot.

In this place, then, I resolved to fix my design, and accordingly I prepared two muskets and my ordinary fowling-piece. The two muskets I loaded with a brace of slugs each, and four or five smaller bullets, about the size of pistol bullets; and the fowling-piece I loaded with near a handful of swan-shot, of the largest size; I also loaded my pistols with about four bullets each, and in this posture, well provided with ammunition for a second and third charge, I prepared myself for my expedition.

After I had thus laid the scheme of my design, and in my imagination put it in practice, I continually made my tour every morning up to the top of the hill, which was from my castle, as I called it, about three miles, or more, to see if I could observe any boats upon the sea, coming near the island, or standing over towards it. But I began to tire of this hard duty, after I had for two or three months constantly kept my watch, but come always back without any discovery, there having not in all that time been the least appearance, not only on or near the shore, but not on the whole ocean, so far as my eyes or glasses could reach every way.

As long as I kept up my daily tour to the hill to look out, so long also I kept up the vigour of my design, and my spirits seemed to be all the while in a suitable form for so outrageous an execution as the killing twenty or thirty naked savages, for an offence which I had not at all entered into a discussion of in my thoughts, any farther than my passions were at first fired by the horror I conceived at the unnatural custom of that people of the country, who it seemed had been suffered by Providence, in His wise disposition of the world, to have no other guide than that of their own abominable and vitiated passions; and consequently were left, and perhaps had been so for some ages, to act such horrid things, and receive such dreadful customs, as nothing but nature entirely abandoned of Heaven and acted by some hellish degeneracy, could have run them into. But now, when as I have said, I began to be weary of the fruitless excursion which I had made so long, and so far, every morning in vain, so my opinion of the action itself began to alter, and I began with cooler and calmer thoughts to consider what it was I was going to engage in;—what authority or call I had to pretend to be judge and executioner upon these men as criminals, whom Heaven had thought fit for so many ages to suffer unpunished, to go on, and to be, as it were, the executioners of His judgments one upon another; how far these people were offenders against me, and what right I had to engage in the quarrel of that blood, which they shed promiscuously one upon another. I debated very often with myself thus: How do I know what God himself judges in this particular case? It is certain these people do not commit this as a crime; it is not against their own consciences reproving or their light reproaching them. They do not know it to be an offence, and then commit it in defiance of divine justice, as we do in almost all the sins we commit. They think it no more a crime to kill a captive taken in war, than we do to kill an ox; nor to eat human flesh, than we do to eat mutton.

When I had considered this a little, it followed necessarily that I was certainly in the wrong in it; that these people were not murderers in the sense that I had before condemned them in my thoughts; any more than those Christians were murderers who often put to death the prisoners taken in battle; or, more frequently, upon many occasions put whole troops of men to the sword, without giving quarter, though they threw down their arms and submitted.

In the next place, it occurred to me that albeit the usage they thus gave one another was thus brutish and inhuman, yet it was really nothing to me; these people had done me no injury. That if they attempted me, or I saw it necessary for my immediate preservation to fall upon them, something might be said for it; but that I was yet out of their power, and they had really no knowledge of me, and consequently no design upon me; and therefore it could not be just for me to fall upon them. That this would justify the conduct of the Spaniards in all their barbarities practised in America, and where they destroyed millions of these people, who, however they were idolaters, and barbarians, and had several bloody and barbarous rites in their customs, such as sacrificing human bodies to their idols, were yet, as to the Spaniards, very innocent people; and that the rooting them out of the country is spoken of with the utmost abhorrence and detestation, by even the Spaniards themselves, at this time, and by all other Christian nations of Europe, as a mere butchery, a bloody and unnatural piece of cruelty, unjustifiable either to God or man; and such as for which the very name of a Spaniard is reckoned to be frightful and terrible to all people of humanity, or of Christian compassion—as if the kingdom of Spain were particularly eminent for the product of a race of men who were without principles of tenderness, or the common bowels of pity to the miserable, which is reckoned to be a mark of generous temper in the mind.

These considerations really put me to a pause, and to a kind of a full stop; and I began by little and little to be off of my design, and to conclude I had taken wrong measures in my resolutions to attack the savages; that it was not my business to meddle with them, unless they first attacked me, and this it was my business if possible to prevent; but that, if I were discovered and attacked, then I knew my duty.

On the other hand, I argued with myself, that this really was the way not to deliver myself, but entirely to ruin and destroy myself; for unless I was sure to kill every one that not only should be on shore at that time, but that should even come on shore afterwards, if but one of them escaped to tell their country-people what had happened, they would come over again by thousands to revenge the death of their fellows, and I should only bring upon myself a certain destruction, which at present I had no manner of occasion for.

Upon the whole, I concluded, that neither in principles nor in policy I ought one way or other to concern myself in this affair;—that my business was by all possible means to conceal myself from them, and not to leave the least signal to them to guess by that there were any living creatures upon the island—I mean of human shape.

Religion joined in with this prudential resolution, and I was convinced now, many ways, that I was perfectly out of my duty, when I was laying all my bloody schemes for the destruction of innocent creatures—I mean innocent as to me. As to the crimes they were guilty of towards one another, I had nothing to do with them; they were national, and I ought to leave them to the justice of God, who is the Governor of nations, and knows how by national punishments to make a just retribution for national offences, and to bring public judgments upon those who offend in a public manner, by such ways as best pleases Him.

This appeared so clear to me now, that nothing was a greater satisfaction to me than that I had not been suffered to do a thing which I now saw so much reason to believe would have been no less a sin than that of wilful murder, if I had committed it. And I give most humble thanks on my knees to God, that had thus delivered me from blood-guiltiness; beseeching Him to grant me the protection of His providence, that I might not fall into the hands of the barbarians; or that I might not lay my hands upon them, unless I had a more clear call from Heaven to do it, in defence of my own life.

In this disposition I continued for near a year after this, and so far was I from desiring an occasion for falling upon these wretches, that in all that time I never once went up the hill to see whether there were any of them in sight, or to know whether any of them had been on shore there or not, that I might not be tempted to renew any of my contrivances against them, or be provoked by any advantage which might present itself, to fall upon them; only this I did, I went and removed my boat, which I had on the other side of the island, and carried it down to the east end of the whole island, where I ran it into a little cove which I found under some high rocks, and where I knew, by reason of the currents, the savages durst not, at least would not, come with their boats upon any account whatsoever.

With my boat I carried away everything that I had left there belonging to her, though not necessary for the bare going thither—namely, a mast and sail which I had made for her, and a thing like an anchor, but indeed which could not be called either anchor or grappling—however, it was the best I could make of its kind. All these I removed, that there might not be the least shadow of any discovery, or any appearance of any boat or of any human habitation upon the island.

Besides this, I kept myself, as I said, more retired than ever, and seldom went from my cell, other than upon my constant employment —namely to milk my she-goats and manage my little flock in the wood; which, as it was quite on the other part of the island, was quite out of danger; for certain it is, that these savage people who sometimes haunted this island, never came with any thoughts of finding anything here, and consequently never wandered off from the coast. And I doubt not but they might have been several times on shore after my apprehensions of them had made me cautious as well as before; and, indeed, I looked back with some horror upon the thoughts of what my condition would have been, if I had chopped upon them, and been discovered, before that, when naked and unarmed, except with one gun, and that loaded often only with small shot. I walked everywhere peeping and peeping about the island to see what I could get;—what a surprise should I have been in, if, when I discovered the print of a man's foot, I had instead of that seen fifteen or twenty savages, and found them pursuing me, and, by the swiftness of their running, no possibility of my escaping them!

The thoughts of this sometimes sunk my very soul within me, and distressed my mind so much that I could not soon recover it, to think what I should have done, and how I not only should not have been able to resist them, but even should not have had presence of mind enough to do what I might have done; much less what now, after so much consideration and preparation, I might be able to do. Indeed, after serious thinking of these things, I should be very melancholy, and sometimes it would last a great while, but I resolved it at last all into thankfulness to that Providence which had delivered me from so many unseen dangers and had kept me from those mischiefs which I could no way have been the agent in delivering myself from, because I had not the least notion of any such thing depending, or the least supposition of it being possible.

This renewed a contemplation which often had come to my thoughts in former time, when first I began to see the merciful dispositions of Heaven in the dangers we run through in this life. How wonderfully we are delivered when we know nothing of it; how, when we are in a quandary, as we call it, a doubt or hesitation whether to go this way or that way, a secret hint shall direct us this way when we intended to go that way; nay, when sense, our own inclination, and perhaps business, has called to go the other way, yet a strange impression upon the mind, from we know not what springs, and by we know not what power, shall overrule us to go this way; and it shall afterwards appear that had we gone that way which we should have gone, and even to our imagination ought to have gone, we should have been ruined and lost. Upon these and many like reflections, I afterwards made it a certain rule with me, that whenever I found those secret hints or pressings of my mind to doing or not doing anything that presented, or to going this way or that way, I never failed to obey the secret dictate, though I knew no other reason for it than that such a pressure or such a hint hung upon my mind. I could give many examples of the success of this conduct in the course of my life, but more especially in the latter part of my inhabiting this unhappy island, besides many occasions which it is very likely I might have taken notice of if I had seen with the same eyes then that I saw with now. But it is never too late to be wise; and I cannot but advise all considering men, whose lives are attended with such extraordinary incidents as mine, or even though not so extraordinary, not to slight such secret intimations of Providence. Let them come from what invisible intelligence they will—that I shall not discuss, and perhaps cannot account for—but certainly they are a proof of the converse of spirits, and the secret communication between those embodied and those unembodied, and such a proof as can never be withstood. Of which I shall have occasion to give some very remarkable instances in the remainder of my solitary residence in this dismal place.

I believe the reader of this will not think strange if I confess that these anxieties, these constant dangers I lived in, and the concern that was now upon me, put an end to all invention and to all the contrivances that I had laid for my future accommodations and conveniences. I had the care of my safety more now upon my hands than that of my food. I cared not to drive a nail or chop a stick of wood now, for fear the noise I should make should be heard; much less would I fire a gun, for the same reason. And above all, I was intolerably uneasy at making any fire, lest the smoke, which is visible at a great distance in the day, should betray me; and for this reason I removed that part of my business which required fire, such as burning of pots and pipes, &c., into my new apartment in the woods, where, after I had been some time, I found to my unspeakable consolation a mere natural cave in the earth, which went in a vast way, and where, I dare say, no savage, had he been at the mouth of it, would be so hardy as to venture in, nor indeed would any man else; but one who, like me, wanted nothing so much as a safe retreat.

The mouth of this hollow was at the bottom of a great rock, where, by mere accident (I would say, if I did not see abundant reason to ascribe all such things now to Providence), I was cutting down some thick branches of trees to make charcoal. And before I go on I must observe the reason of my making this charcoal, which was thus:

I was afraid of making a smoke about my habitation, as I said before; and yet I could not live there without baking my bread, cooking my meat, &c. So I contrived to burn some wood here, as I had seen done in England, under turf, till it became chark, or dry coal; and then putting the fire out, I preserved the coal to carry home and perform the other services which fire was wanting for at home without danger of smoke.

But this by-the-by. While I was cutting down some wood here, I perceived that behind a very thick branch of low brushwood or underwood there was a kind of hollow place. I was curious to look into it, and getting with difficulty into the mouth of it, I found it was pretty large; that is to say, sufficient for me to stand upright in it, and perhaps another with me. But I must confess to you I made more haste out than I did in, when looking farther into the place, and which was perfectly dark, I saw two broad shining eyes of some creature, whether devil or man I knew not, which twinkled like two stars, the dim light from the cave's mouth shining directly in and making the reflection.

However, after some pause, I recovered myself, and began to call myself a thousand fools, and tell myself that he that was afraid to see the devil was not fit to live twenty years in an island all alone; and that I durst to believe there was nothing in this cave that was more frightful than myself. Upon this, plucking up my courage, I took up a great firebrand and in I rushed again, with the stick flaming in my hand. I had not gone three steps in but I was almost as much frighted as I was before; for I heard a very loud sigh, like that of a man in some pain; and it was followed by a broken noise, as if of words half expressed, and then a deep sigh again. I stepped back, and was indeed struck with such a surprise that it put me into a cold sweat; and if I had had a hat on my head, I will not answer for it that my hair might not have lifted it off! But still, plucking up my spirits as well as I could, and encouraging myself a little with considering that the power and presence of God was everywhere, and was able to protect me, upon this I stepped forward again, and by the light of the firebrand, holding it up a little over my head, I saw lying on the ground a most monstrous frightful old he-goat, just making his will, as we say, and gasping for life, and dying indeed of mere old age.

I stirred him a little to see if I could get him out, and he essayed to get up, but was not able to raise himself. And I thought with myself he might even lie there; for if he had frighted me so, he would certainly fright any of the savages, if any of them should be so hardy as to come in there while he had any life in him.

I was now recovered from my surprise, and began to look round me, when I found the cave was but very small; that is to say, it might be about twelve foot over, but in no manner of shape, either round or square, no hands having ever been employed in making it but those of mere Nature. I observed also that there was a place at the farther side of it that went in farther, but was so low that it required me to creep upon my hands and knees to go into it, and whither I went I know not. So, having no candle, I gave it over for some time, but resolved to come again the next day, provided with candles and a tinder-box, which I had made of the lock of one of the muskets, with some wildfire in the pan.

Accordingly, the next day, I came provided with six large candles of my own making—for I made very good candles now of goats tallow —and going into this low place, I was obliged to creep upon all-fours, as I have said, almost ten yards; which, by the way, I thought was a venture bold enough, considering that I knew not how far it might go, nor what was beyond it. When I was got through the strait I found the roof rose higher up—I believe near twenty foot. But never was such a glorious sight seen in the island, I dare say, as it was to look round the sides and roof of this vault or cave. The walls reflected a hundred thousand lights to me from my two candles. What it was in the rock, whether diamonds or any other precious stones, or gold, which I rather supposed it to be, I knew not.

The place I was in was a most delightful cavity or grotto of its kind as could be expected, though perfectly dark. The floor was dry and level, and had a sort of small loose gravel upon it, so that there was no nauseous or venomous creature to be seen, neither was there any damp or wet on the sides or roof. The only difficulty in it was the entrance, which, however, as it was a place of security, and such a retreat as I wanted, I thought that was a convenience, so that I was really rejoiced at the discovery, and resolved without any delay to bring some of those things which I was most anxious about to this place. Particularly, I resolved to bring hither my magazine of powder and all my spare arms—namely, two fowling-pieces, for I had three in all; and three muskets, for of them I had eight in all. So I kept at my castle only five, which stood ready mounted, like pieces of cannon, on my outmost fence, and were ready also to take out upon any expedition.

Upon this occasion of removing my ammunition, I took occasion to open the barrel of powder which I took up out of the sea, and which had been wet; and I found that the water had penetrated about three or four inches into the powder on every side, which, caking and growing hard, had preserved the inside like a kernel in a shell. So that I had near sixty pounds of very good powder in the centre of the cask, and this was an agreeable discovery to me at that time. So I carried all away thither, never keeping above two or three pound of powder with me in my castle for fear of a surprise of any kind. I also carried thither all the lead I had left, for bullets.

I fancied myself now like one of the ancient giants, which were said to live in caves and holes in the rocks, where none could come at them. For I persuaded myself, while I was here, if five hundred savages were to hunt me, they could never find me out; or if they did, they would not venture to attack me here.

The old goat, who I found expiring, died in the mouth of the cave the next day after I made this discovery; and I found it much easier to dig a great hole there, and throw him in and cover him with earth, than to drag him out. So I interred him there to prevent offence to my nose.

I was now in my twenty-third year of residence in this island, and was so naturalized to the place and to the manner of living, that could I have but enjoyed the certainty that no savages would come to the place to disturb me, I could have been content to have capitulated for spending the rest of my time there even to the last moment, till I had laid me down and died, like the old goat in the cave. I had also arrived to some little diversions and amusements, which made the time pass more pleasantly with me a great deal than it did before. At first, I had taught my Poll, as I noted before, to speak; and he did it so familiarly, and talked so articulately and plain, that it was very pleasant to me: and he lived with me no less than six-and-twenty years. How long he might live afterwards I know not; though I know they have a notion in the Brazils that they live a hundred years. Perhaps poor Poll may be alive there still, calling after Poor Robin Crusoe to this day. I wish no Englishman the ill-luck to come there and hear him; but if he did, he would certainly believe it was the devil. My dog was a very pleasant and loving companion to me for no less than sixteen years of my time, and then died of mere old age. As for my cats, they multiplied, as I have observed, to that degree that I was obliged to shoot several of them at first, to keep them from devouring me and all I had. But at length, when the two old ones I brought with me were gone, and after some time continually driving them from me, and letting them have no provision with me, they all ran wild into the woods except two or three favourites, which I kept tame, and whose young, when they had any, I always drowned. And these were part of my family. Besides these, I always kept two or three household kids about me, which I taught to feed out of my hand. And I had two more parrots which talked pretty well, and would all call Robin Crusoe, but none like my first. Nor indeed did I take the pains with any of them that I had done with him. I had also several tame sea-fowls, whose names I know not, which I caught upon the shore and cut their wings. And the little stakes which I had planted before my castle wall being now grown up to a good thick grove, these fowls all lived among these low trees, and bred there; which was very agreeable to me. So that, as I said above, I began to be very well contented with the life I led, if it might but have been secured from the dread of the savages.

But it was otherwise directed. And it may not be amiss for all people who shall meet with my story to make this just observation from it—namely, how frequently in the course of our lives the evil which in itself we seek most to shun, and which, when we are fallen into is the most dreadful to us, is oftentimes the very means or door of our deliverance, by which alone we can be raised again from the affliction we are fallen into. I could give many examples of this in the course of my unaccountable life, but in nothing was it more particularly remarkable than in the circumstances of my last years of solitary residence in this island.

It was now the month of December, as I said above, in my twenty-third year; and this being the southern solstice, for winter I cannot call it, was the particular time of my harvest, and required my being pretty much abroad in the fields: when going out pretty early in the morning, even before it was thorough daylight, I was surprised with seeing a light of some fire upon the shore, at a distance from me of about two miles, towards the end of the island, where I had observed some savages had been as before; but not on the other side; but, to my great affliction, it was on my side of the island.

I was indeed terribly surprised at the sight, and stopped short within my grove, not daring to go out lest I might be surprised; and yet I had no more peace within, from the apprehensions I had that if these savages, in rambling over the island, should find my corn standing or cut, or any of my works and improvements, they would immediately conclude that there were people in the place, and would then never give over till they had found me out. In this extremity I went back directly to my castle, pulled up the ladder after me, and made all things without look as wild and natural as I could.

Then I prepared myself within, putting myself in a posture of defence. I loaded all my cannon, as I called them—that is to say, my muskets, which were mounted upon my new fortification—and all my pistols, and resolved to defend myself to the last gasp; not forgetting seriously to commend myself to the divine protection, and earnestly to pray to God to deliver me out of the hands of the barbarians. And in this posture I continued about two hours, but began to be mighty impatient for intelligence abroad, for I had no spies to send out.

After sitting a while longer, and musing what I should do in this case, I was not able to bear sitting in ignorance any longer; so setting up my ladder to the side of the hill, where there was a flat place, as I observed before, and then pulling the ladder up after me, I set it up again, and mounted to the top of the hill, and pulling out my perspective-glass, which I had taken on purpose, I laid me down flat on my belly on the ground, and began to look for the place. I presently found there was no less than nine naked savages, sitting round a small fire they had made, not to warm them, for they had no need of that, the weather being extreme hot, but, as I supposed, to dress some of their barbarous diet of human flesh, which they had brought with them, whether alive or dead I could not know.

They had two canoes with them, which they had hauled up upon the shore; and as it was then tide of ebb, they seemed to me to wait for the return of the flood to go away again. It is not easy to imagine what confusion this might put me into, especially seeing them come on my side of the island, and so near me too; but when I observed their coming must be always with the current of the ebb, I began afterwards to be more sedate in my mind, being satisfied that I might go abroad with safety all the time of the tide of flood, if they were not on shore before. And having made this observation, I went abroad about my harvest-work with the more composure.

As I expected, so it proved; for as soon as the tide made to the westward, I saw them all take boat, and row, or paddle, as we call it, all away. I should have observed that for an hour and more before they went off they went to dancing, and I could easily discern their postures and gestures by my glasses. I could not perceive, by my nicest observation, but that they were stark naked, and had not the least covering upon them; but whether they were men or women, that I could not distinguish.

As soon as I saw them shipped and gone, I took two guns upon my shoulders, and two pistols at my girdle, and my great sword by my side without a scabbard, and with all the speed I was able to make, I went away to the hill where I had discovered the first appearance of all; and as soon as I gat thither, which was not less than two hours (for I could not go apace, being so laden with arms as I was), I perceived there had been three canoes more of savages on that place; and looking out farther, I saw they were at sea together, making over for the main.

This was a dreadful sight to me, especially when, going down to the shore, I could see the marks of horror which the dismal work they had been about had left behind it—namely, the blood, the bones, and part of the flesh of human bodies, eaten and devoured by those wretches with merriment and sport. I was so filled with indignation at the sight, that I began now to premeditate the destruction of the next that I saw there, let them be who or how many soever.

It seemed evident to me that the visits which they thus make to this island are not very frequent; for it was above fifteen months before any more of them came on shore there again;—that is to say, I never saw them, or any footsteps or signals of them, in all that time; for as to the rainy seasons, then they are sure not to come abroad, at least not so far. Yet all this while I lived uncomfortably, by reason of the constant apprehensions I was in of their coming upon me by surprise; from whence I observe that the expectation of evil is more bitter than the suffering, especially if there is no room to shake off that expectation or those apprehensions.

During all this time I was in the murdering humour, and took up most of my hours, which should have been better employed, in contriving how to circumvent and fall upon them the very next time I should see them, especially if they should be divided, as they were the last time, into two parties. Nor did I consider at all that if I killed one party—suppose ten or a dozen—I was still the next day, or week, or month, to kill another, and so another, even *ad infinitum*, till I should be at length no less a murderer than they were in being man-eaters, and perhaps much more so.

I spent my days now in great perplexity and anxiety of mind, expecting that I should one day or other fall into the hands of these merciless creatures; and if I did at any time venture abroad, it was not without looking round me with the greatest care and caution imaginable. And now I found to my great comfort how happy it was that I provided for a tame flock or herd of goats; for I durst not upon any account fire my gun, especially near that side of the island where they usually came, lest I should alarm the savages; and if they had fled from me now, I was sure to have them come back again, with perhaps two or three hundred canoes with them, in a few days, and then I knew what to expect.

However, I wore out a year and three months more before I ever saw any more of the savages, and then I found them again, as I shall soon observe. It is true they might have been there once or twice, but either they made no stay, or at least I did not hear them; but in the month of May, as near as I could calculate, and in my four-and-twentieth year, I had a very strange encounter with them, of which in its place.

The perturbation of my mind during this fifteen or sixteen months' interval was very great. I slept unquiet, dreamed always frightful dreams, and often started out of my sleep in the night. In the day great troubles overwhelmed my mind, and in the night I dreamed often of killing the savages, and of the reasons why I might justify the doing of it.

But to waive all this for a while, it was in the middle of May, on the sixteenth day, I think, as well as my poor wooden calendar would reckon; for I marked all upon the post still. I say it was the sixteenth of May, that it blew a very great storm of wind all day, with a great deal of lightning and thunder, and a very foul night it was after it. I know not what was the particular occasion of it; but as I was reading in the Bible, and taken up with very serious thoughts about my present condition, I was surprised with a noise of a gun, as I thought, fired at sea.

§ *A Spanish ship lost with all hands off the island. I go on board the wreck and obtain new supplies. Find some useless money.*

THIS was, to be sure, a surprise of a quite different nature from any I had met with before; for the notions this put into my thoughts were quite of another kind. I started up in the greatest haste imaginable, and in a trice clapped my ladder to the middle place of the rock, and pulled it after me, and mounting it the second time, got to the top of the hill, the very moment that a flash of fire bid me listen for a second gun, which accordingly in about half a minute I heard, and by the sound knew that it was from that part of the sea where I was driven down the current in my boat.

I immediately consider that this must be some ship in distress, and that they had some comrade or some other ship in company, and fired these guns for signals of distress and to obtain help. I had this presence of mind at that minute as to think that though I could not help them, it may be they might help me; so I brought together all the dry wood I could get at hand, and making a good handsome pile, I set it on fire upon the hill. The wood was dry and blazed freely, and though the wind blew very hard, yet it burned fairly out, that I was certain if there was any such thing as a ship they must needs see it: and no doubt they did, for as soon as ever my fire blazed up I heard another gun, and after that several others, all from the same quarter. I plied my fire all night long till day broke; and when it was broad day, and the air cleared up, I saw something at a great distance at sea, full east of the island, whether a sail or a hull I could not distinguish, no not with my glasses, the distance was so great, and the weather still something hazy also; at least, it was so out at sea.

I looked frequently at it all that day, and soon perceived that it did not move; so I presently concluded that it was a ship at an anchor; and being eager, you may be sure, to be satisfied, I took my gun in my hand, and ran toward the south side of the island, to the rocks where I had formerly been carried away with the current; and getting up there, the weather by this time being perfectly clear, I could plainly see, to my great sorrow, the wreck of a ship cast away in the night upon those concealed rocks which I found when I was out in my boat; and which rocks, as they checked the violence of the stream, and made a kind of counter-stream or eddy, were the occasion of my recovering from the most desperate hopeless condition that ever I had been in in all my life.

Thus, what is one man's safety is another man's destruction; for it seems these men, whoever they were, being out of their knowledge, and the rocks being wholly under water, had been driven upon them in the night, the wind blowing hard at east and east-north-east. Had they seen the island, as I must necessarily suppose they did not, they must, as I thought, have endeavoured to have saved themselves on shore by the help of their boat. But their firing of guns for help, especially when they saw, as I imagined, my fire, filled me with many thoughts. First, I imagined that upon seeing my light they might have put themselves into their boat, and have endeavoured to make the shore; but that the sea going very high, they might have been cast away. Other times I imagined that they might have lost their boat before, as might be the case many ways, as particularly by the breaking of the sea upon their ship, which many times obliges men to stave or take in pieces their boat, and sometimes to throw it overboard with their own hands. Other times I imagined they had some other ship or ships in company, who, upon the signals of distress they had made, had taken them up and carried them off. Other whiles I fancied they were all gone off to sea in their boat, and being hurried away by the current that I had been formerly in, were carried out into the great ocean, where there was nothing but misery and perishing, and that perhaps they might by this time think of starving, and of being in a condition to eat one another.

As all these were but conjectures at best, so in the condition I was in I could do no more than look on upon the misery of the poor men and pity them; which had still this good effect on my side, that it gave me more and more cause to give thanks to God, who had so happily and comfortably provided for me in my desolate condition; and that of two ships' companies who were now cast away upon this part of the world, not one life should be spared but mine. I learned here again to observe that it is very rare that the providence of God casts us into any condition of life so low, or any misery so great, but we may see something or other to be thankful for, and may see others in worse circumstances than our own.

Such certainly was the case of these men, of whom I could not so much as see room to suppose any of them were saved. Nothing could make it rational, so much as to wish or expect that they did not all perish there, except the possibility only of their being taken up by another ship in company; and this was but mere possibility indeed, for I saw not the least signal or appearance of any such thing.

I cannot explain by any possible energy of words what a strange longing or hankering of desires I felt in my soul upon this sight, breaking out sometimes thus: "Oh that there had been but one or two—nay, or but one soul saved out of this ship, to have escaped to me; that I might but have had one companion, one fellow-creature to have spoken to me, and to have conversed with!" In all the time of my solitary life I never felt so earnest, so strong a desire after the society of my fellow-creatures, or so deep a regret at the want of it.

There are some secret moving springs in the affections, which, when they are set a-going by some object in view, or be it some object, though not in view, yet rendered present to the mind by the power of imagination, that motion carries out the soul by its impetuosity to such violent eager embracings of the object, that the absence of it is insupportable.

Such were these earnest wishings that but one man had been saved! "Oh, that it had been but one!" I believe I repeated the words, "Oh, that it had been but one!" a thousand times; and the desires were so moved by it, that when I spoke the words my hands would clench together, and my fingers press the palms of my hands, that if I had had any soft thing in my hand, it would have crushed it involuntarily; and my teeth in my head would strike together, and set against one another so strong, that for some time I could not part them again.

Let the naturalists explain these things, and the reason and manner of them. All I can say to them is, to describe the fact, which was even surprising to me when I found it; though I knew not from what it should proceed. It was doubtless the effect of ardent wishes and of strong ideas formed in my mind, realizing the comfort which the conversation of one of my fellow-Christians would have been to me.

But it was not to be. Either their fate or mine, or both, forbid it; for until the last year of my being on this island, I never knew whether any were saved out of that ship or no; and had only the affliction some days after, to see the corpse of a drowned boy come on shore, at the end of the island which was next the ship-wreck. He had on no clothes, but a seaman's waistcoat, a pair of open-kneed linen drawers, and a blue linen shirt; but nothing to direct me so much as to guess what nation he was of. He had nothing in his pocket but two pieces of eight and a tobacco pipe. The last was to me of ten times more value than the first.

It was now calm, and I had a great mind to venture out in my boat to this wreck; not doubting that I might find something on board that might be useful to me. But that did not altogether press me so much as the possibility that there might be yet some living creature on board, whose life I might not only save, but might, by saving that life, comfort my own to the last degree; and this thought clung so to my heart that I could not be quiet, night nor day, but I must venture out in my boat on board this wreck; and committing the rest to God's providence, I thought the impression was so strong upon my mind that it could not be resisted, that it must come from some invisible direction, and that I should be wanting to myself if I did not go.

Under the power of this impression, I hastened back to my castle, prepared everything for my voyage, took a quantity of bread, a great pot for fresh water, a compass to steer by, a bottle of rum—for I had still a great deal of that left—a basket full of raisins. And thus loading myself with everything necessary, I went down to my boat, got the water out of her, and got her afloat, loaded all my cargo in her, and then went home again for more. My second cargo was a great bag full of rice, the umbrella to set up over my head for shade, another large pot full of fresh water, and about two dozen of my small loaves, or barley cakes, more than before, with a bottle of goat's milk, and a cheese; all which, with great labour and sweat, I brought to my boat; and praying to God to direct my voyage, I put out, and rowing or paddling the canoe along the shore, I came at last to the utmost point of the island on that side—namely, north-east. And now I was to launch out into the ocean, and either to venture or not to venture. I looked on the rapid currents which ran constantly on both sides of the island, at a distance, and which were very terrible to me, from the remembrance of the hazard I had been in before, and my heart began to fail me; for I foresaw that if I was driven into either of those cur-rents, I should be carried a vast way out to sea, and perhaps out of my reach or sight of the island again; and that then, as my boat was but small, if any little gale of wind should rise, I should be inevitably lost.

These thoughts so oppressed my mind, that I began to give over my enterprise, and having hauled my boat into a little creek on the shore, I stepped out, and sat me down upon a little rising bit of ground, very pensive and anxious, between fear and desire about my voyage;

when, as I was musing, I could perceive that the tide was turned and the flood come on, upon which my going was for so many hours impracticable. Upon this, presently it occurred to me that I should go up to the highest piece of ground I could find, and observe, if I could, how the sets of the tide or currents lay when the flood came in, that I might judge whether, if I was driven one way out, I might not expect to be driven another way home, with the same rapidness of the currents. This thought was no sooner in my head, but I cast my eye upon a little hill, which sufficiently overlooked the sea both ways, and from whence I had a clear view of the currents, or sets of the tide, and which way I was to guide myself in my return. Here I found that as the current of the ebb set out close by the south point of the island, so the current of the flood set in close by the shore of the north side, and that I had nothing to do but to keep to the north of the island in my return, and I should do well enough.

Encouraged with this observation, I resolved the next morning to set out with the first of the tide; and reposing myself for the night in the canoe, under the great watch-coat I mentioned, I launched out. I made first a little out to sea full north, till I began to feel the benefit of the current, which set eastward, and which carried me at a great rate, and yet did not so hurry me as the southern side current had done before, and so as to take from me all government of the boat; but having a strong steerage with my paddle, I went at a great rate, directly for the wreck, and in less than two hours I came up to it.

It was a dismal sight to look at. The ship, which by its building was Spanish, stuck fast, jammed in between two rocks; all the stern and quarter of her was beaten to pieces with the sea; and as her forecastle, which stuck in the rocks, had run on with great violence, her mainmast and foremast were brought by the board—that is to say, broken short off; but her boltsprit was sound, and the head and bow appeared firm. When I came close to her, a dog appeared upon her, who seeing me coming, yelped and cried; and as soon as I called him, jumped into the sea to come to me, and I took him into the boat, but found him almost dead for hunger and thirst. I gave him a cake of my bread, and he ate it like a ravenous wolf that had been starving a fortnight in the snow. I then gave the poor creature some fresh water, with which, if I would have let him, he would have burst himself.

After this I went on board; but the first sight I met with was two men drowned in the cook-room, or forecastle of the ship, with their arms fast about one another. I concluded, as is indeed probable, that when the ship struck, it being in a storm, the sea broke so·high and so continually over her, that the men were not able to bear it, and were ·strangled with the constant rushing in of the water, as much as if they had been under water. Besides the dog, there was nothing left in the ship that had life; nor any goods that I could see, but what were spoiled by the water. There were some casks of liquor—whether wine or brandy, I knew not—which lay lower in the hold, and which, the water being ebbed out, I could see; but they were too big to meddle with. I saw several chests, which I believed belonged to some of the seamen, and I got two of them into the boat, without examining what was in them.

Had the stern of the ship been fixed and the fore part broken off, I am persuaded I might have made a good voyage; for, by what I found in these two chests, I had room to suppose the ship had a great deal of wealth on board; and if I may guess by the course she steered, she must have been bound from the Buenos Ayres or the Rio de la Plata, in the south part of America, beyond the Brazils, to the Havannah, in the Gulf of Mexico, and so, perhaps, to Spain. She had, no doubt, a great treasure in her, but of no use at that time to anybody; and what became of the rest of her people I then knew not.

I found, besides these chests, a little cask full of liquor, of about twenty gallons, which I got into my boat with much difficulty. There were several muskets in the cabin, and a great powder-horn, with about four pounds of powder in it. As for the muskets, I had no occasion for them—so I left them; but took the powder-horn. I took a fire-shovel and tongs, which I wanted extremely; as also two little brass kettles, a copper pot to make chocolate, and a gridiron. And with this cargo and the dog I came away, the tide beginning to make home again. And the same evening, about an hour within night, I reached the island again, weary and fatigued to the last degree.

I reposed that night in the boat, and in the morning I resolved to harbour what I had gotten in my new cave, not to carry it home to my castle. After refreshing myself, I got all my cargo on shore, and began to examine the particulars. The cask of liquor I found to be a kind of rum, but not such as we had at the Brazils—and, in a word,

not at all good; but when I came to open the chests, I found several things of great use to me. For example, I found in one a fine case of bottles, of an extraordinary kind, and filled with cordial waters, fine, and very good; the bottles held about three pints each, and were tipped with silver: I found two pots of very good succades, or sweetmeats, so fastened also on top that the salt water had not hurt them; and two more of the same which the water had spoiled: I found some very good shirts, which were very welcome to me, and about a dozen and half of linen white handkerchiefs, and coloured neckcloths—the former were also very welcome, being exceeding refreshing to wipe my face in a hot day: besides this, when I came to the till in the chests, I found there three great bags of pieces of eight, which held out about eleven hundred pieces in all; and in one of them, wrapped up in a paper, six doubloons of gold, and some small bars or wedges of gold; I suppose they might all weigh near a pound.

The other chest I found had some clothes in it, but of little value; but by the circumstances it must have belonged to the gunner's mate, though there was no powder in it but about two pound of fine glazed powder in three small flasks, kept, I suppose, for charging their fowling-pieces on occasion. Upon the whole, I got very little by this voyage that was of any use to me: for as to the money, I had no manner of occasion for it; it was to me as the dirt under my feet; and I would have given it all for three or four pair of English shoes and stockings, which were things I greatly wanted, but had not had on my feet now for many years. I had, indeed, gotten two pair of shoes now, which I took off of the feet of the two drowned men who I saw in the wreck; and I found two pair more in one of the chests, which were very welcome to me; but they were not like our English shoes, either for ease or service, being rather what we call pumps than shoes. I found in this seaman's chest about fifty pieces of eight in royals, but no gold. I suppose this belonged to a poorer man than the other, which seemed to belong to some officer.

Well, however, I lugged this money home to my cave, and laid it up, as I had done that before which I brought from our own ship; but it was great pity, as I said, that the other part of this ship had not come to my share—for I am satisfied I might have loaded my canoe several times over with money, which, if I had ever escaped to England, would have lain here safe enough till I might have come again and fetched it.

Having now brought all my things on shore and secured them, I went back to my boat, and rowed or paddled her along the shore to her old harbour, where I laid her up, and made the best of my way to my old habitation, where I found everything safe and quiet; so I began to repose myself, live after my old fashion, and take care of my family affairs; and for a while I lived easy enough; only that I was more vigilant than I used to be, looked out oftener, and did not go abroad so much; and if at any time I did stir with any freedom, it was always to the east part of the island, where I was pretty well satisfied the savages never came, and where I could go without so many precautions, and such a load of arms and ammunition, as I always carried with me if I went the other way.

I lived in this condition near two years more. But my unlucky head, that was always to let me know it was born to make my body miserable, was all the two years filled with projects and designs how, if it were possible, I might get away from this island: for sometimes I was for making another voyage to the wreck, though my reason told me that there was nothing left there worth the hazard of my voyage; sometimes for a ramble one way, sometimes another; and I believe verily, if I had had the boat that I went from Sallee in, I should have ventured to sea, bound anywhere, I knew not whither.

I have been, in all my circumstances, a memento to those who are touched with the general plague of mankind, whence, for aught I know, one half of their miseries flow—I mean, that of not being satisfied with the station wherein God and nature hath placed them. For, not to look back upon my primitive condition, and the excellent advice of my father, the oppositon to which was, as I may call it, my *original sin*, my subsequent mistakes of the same kind had been the means of my coming into this miserable condition: for had that Providence which so happily had seated me at the Brazils as a planter, blessed me with confined desires, and I could have been contented to have gone on gradually, I might have been by this time, I mean in the time of my being in this island, one of the most considerable planters in the Brazils. Nay, I am persuaded that, by the improvements I had made in that little time I lived there, and the increase I should probably have made if I had stayed, I might have been worth a hundred thousand moidores. And what business had I to leave a settled fortune, a well-stocked plantation, improving and increasing, to turn supercargo to Guinea to fetch negroes, when patience and time would have so increased our stock at home that we could have bought them at our own door from those whose business it was to fetch them? And though it had cost us something more, yet the difference of that price was by no means worth saving at so great a hazard.

But as this is ordinarily the fate of young heads, so reflection upon the folly of it is as ordinarily the exercise of more years or of the dear-bought experience of time. And so it was with me now. And yet so deep had the mistake taken root in my temper that I could not satisfy myself in my station, but was continually poring upon the means and possibility of my escape from this place. And that I may, with the greater pleasure to the reader, bring on the remaining part of my story, it may not be improper to give some account of my first conceptions on the subject of this foolish scheme for my escape, and how and upon what foundation I acted.

I am now to be supposed retired into my castle after my late voyage to the wreck, my frigate laid up and secured under water as usual, and my condition restored to what it was before. I had more wealth, indeed, than I had before, but was not at all the richer: for I had no more use for it than the Indians of Peru had before the Spaniards came there.

It was one of the nights in the rainy season in March, the four-and-twentieth year of my first setting foot in this island of solitariness. I was lying in my bed or hammock awake, very well in health; had no pain, no distemper, no uneasiness of body, no, nor any uneasiness of mind, more than ordinary: but could by no means close my eyes; that is, so as to sleep; no, not a wink all night long: otherwise that as follows.

It is as impossible as needless to set down the innumerable crowd of thoughts that whirled through that great thoroughfare of the brain, the memory, in this night's time. I ran over the whole history of my life in miniature, or by abridgment, as I may call it, to my coming to this island, and also of the part of my life since I came to this island. In my reflections upon the state of my case since I came on shore on this island, I was comparing the happy posture of my affairs in the first years of my habitation here, compared to the life of anxiety, fear, and care which I had lived ever since I had seen the print of a foot in the sand. Not that I did not believe the savages had frequented the island even all the while, and might have been several hundreds of them at times on shore there; but I had never known it, and was incapable of any apprehensions about it. My satisfaction was perfect, though my danger was the same; and I was as happy in not knowing my danger as if I had never really been exposed to it. This furnished my thoughts with many very profitable reflections, and particularly this one: How infinitely good the Providence is which has provided, in its government of mankind, such narrow bounds to his sight and knowledge of things; and though he walks in the midst of so many thousand dangers, the sight of which, if discovered to him, would distract his mind and sink his spirits, he is kept serene and calm by having the events of things hid from his eyes, and knowing nothing of the dangers which surround him.

After these thoughts had for some time entertained me, I came to reflect seriously upon the real danger I had been in for so many years in this very island, and how I had walked about in the greatest security and with all possible tranquillity, even when perhaps nothing but a brow of a hill, a great tree, or the casual approach of night, had been between me and the worst kind of destruction; namely, that of falling into the hands of cannibals and savages, who would have seized on me with the same view as I did of a goat or a turtle, and have thought it no more a crime to kill and devour me than I did of a pigeon or a curlew. I would unjustly slander myself if I should say I was not sincerely thankful to my great Preserver, to whose singular protection I acknowledged, with great humility, that all these un-known deliverances were due, and without which I must inevitably have fallen into their merciless hands.

When these thoughts were over, my head was for some time taken up in considering the nature of these wretched creatures, I mean, the savages; and how it came to pass in the world that the wise Governor of all things should give up any of His creatures to such inhumanity, nay, to something so much below even brutality itself, as to devour its own kind.

But as this ended in some, at that time fruitless, speculations, it occurred to me to inquire what part of the world these wretches lived in; how far off the coast was from whence they came; what they ventured over so far from home for; what kind of boats they had; and why I might not order myself and my business so that I might be as able to go over thither as they were to come to me.

I never so much as troubled myself to consider what I should do with myself when I came thither, what would become of me if I fell into the hands of the savages, or how I should escape from them if they attempted me; no, nor so much as how it was possible for me to reach the coast and not be attempted by some or other of them without any possibility of delivering myself; and if I should not fall into their hands, what I should do for provision, or whither I should bend my course;—none of these thoughts, I say, so much as came in my way, but my mind was wholly bent upon the notion of my passing over in my boat to the mainland. I looked back upon my present condition as the most miserable that could possibly be: that I was not able to throw myself into anything but death that could be called worse; that if I reached the shore of the main I might perhaps meet with relief, or I might coast along, as I did on the shore of Africa, till I came to some inhabited country, and where I might find some relief; and, after all, perhaps I might fall in with some Christian ship that might take me in; and if the worse came to the worst I could but die, which would put an end to all these miseries at once. Pray note, all this was the fruit of a disturbed mind, an impatient temper, made as it were desperate by the long continuance of my troubles, and the disappointments I had met in the wreck I had been on board of, and where I had been so near the obtaining what I so earnestly longed for, namely, somebody to speak to, and to learn some knowledge from of the place where I was, and of the probable means of my deliverance: I say, I was agitated wholly by these thoughts; all my calm of mind in my resignation to Providence, and waiting the issue of the dispositions of Heaven, seemed to be suspended; and I had, as it were, no power to turn my thoughts to anything but to the project of a voyage to the main, which came upon me with such force and such an impetuosity of desire that it was not to be resisted.

§ *A strange dream. A new resolve. Another landing of the savages. I rescue a victim, and name him Friday. A description of my new servant. Remains of the cannibals' feast buried.*

WHEN this had agitated my thoughts for two hours or more with such violence that it set my very blood into a ferment, and my pulse beat as high as if I had been in a fever, merely with the extraordinary fervour of my mind about it—nature, as if I had been fatigued and exhausted with the very thought of it, threw me into a sound sleep. One would have thought I should have dreamed of it; but I did not, nor of anything relating to it. But I dreamed that as I was going out in the morning as usual from my castle, I saw upon the shore two canoes and eleven savages coming to land, and that they brought with them another savage, who they were going to kill in order to eat him; when on a sudden the savage that they were going to kill jumped away and ran for his life. And I thought in my sleep that he came running into my little thick grove before my fortification to hide himself; and that I, seeing him alone, and not perceiving that the others sought him that way, showed myself to him, and smiling upon him, encouraged him; that he kneeled down to me, seeming to pray me to assist him; upon which I showed my ladder, made him go up, and carried him into my cave, and he became my servant: and that, as soon as I had gotten this man I said to myself; Now I may certainly venture to the mainland, for this fellow will serve me as a pilot, and will tell me what to do, and whither to go for provisions, and whither not to go for fear of being devoured; what places to venture into, and what to escape.—I waked with this thought, and was under such inexpressible impressions of joy at the prospect of my escape in my dream, that the disappointments which I felt upon coming to myself and finding it was no more than a dream were equally extravagant the other way, and threw me into a very great dejection of spirit.

Upon this, however, I made this conclusion, that my only way to go about an attempt for an escape was, if possible, to get a savage into my possession, and, if possible, it should be one of their prisoners who they had condemned to be eaten and should bring thither to kill. But these thoughts still were attended with this difficulty, that it was impossible to effect this without attacking a whole caravan of them, and killing them all. And this was not only a very desperate attempt and might miscarry, but, on the other hand, I had greatly scrupled the lawfulness of it to me; and my heart trembled at the thoughts of shedding so much blood, though it was for my deliverance. I need not repeat the arguments which occurred to me against this, they being the same mentioned before. But though I had other reasons to offer now—namely, that those men were enemies to my life, and would devour me if they could; that it was self-preservation in the highest degree to deliver myself from this death of a life, and was acting in my own defence as much as if they were actually assaulting me, and the like;—I say, though these things argued for it, yet the thoughts of shedding human blood for my deliverance were very terrible to me, and such as I could by no means reconcile myself to for a great while.

However, at last, after many secret disputes with myself, and after great perplexities about it—for all these arguments one way and another struggled in my head a long time—the eager, prevailing desire of deliverance at length mastered all the rest, and I resolved, if possible, to get one of those savages into my hands, cost what it would. My next thing then was to contrive how to do it; and this, indeed, was very difficult to resolve on. But as I could pitch upon no probable means for it, so I resolved to put myself upon the watch to see them when they came on shore, and leave the rest to the event, taking such measures as the opportunity should present, let be what would be.

With these resolutions in my thoughts, I set myself upon the scout as often as possible; and indeed so often till I was heartily tired of it, for it was above a year and a half that I waited, and for great part of that time went out to the west end and to the south-west corner of the island almost every day to seek for canoes, but none appeared. This was very discouraging, and began to trouble me much; though I cannot say that it did in this case as it had done some time before that— namely, wear off the edge of my desire to the thing. But the longer it seemed to be delayed, the more eager I was for it: in a word, I was not at first so careful to shun the sight of these savages, and avoid being seen by them, as I was now eager to be upon them.

Besides, I fancied myself able to manage one, nay, two or three savages, if I had them, so as to make them entirely slaves to me, to do whatever I should direct them, and to prevent their being able at any

time to do me any hurt. It was a great while that I pleased myself with this affair; but nothing still presented. All my fancies and schemes came to nothing, for no savages came near me for a great while.

About a year and half after I had entertained these notions, and by long musing had, as it were, resolved them all into nothing for want of an occasion to put them in execution, I was surprised one morning early with seeing no less than five canoes all on shore together on my side of the island, and the people who belonged to them all landed and out of my sight! The number of them broke all my measures; for seeing so many, and knowing that they always came four or six, or sometimes more, in a boat, I could not tell what to think of it, or how to take my measures to attack twenty or thirty men single-handed; so I lay still in my castle, perplexed and discomforted. However, I put

myself into all the same postures for an attack that I had formerly provided, and was just ready for action if anything had presented. Having waited a good while, listening to hear if they made any noise, at length, being very impatient, I set my guns at the foot of my ladder, and clambered up to the top of the hill by my two stages, as usual; standing so, however, that my head did not appear above the hill, so that they could not perceive me by any means. Here I observed, by the help of my perspective-glass, that they were no less than thirty in number, that they had a fire kindled, that they had had meat dressed. How they had cooked it, that I knew not, or what it was; but they were all dancing, in I know not how many barbarous gestures and figures, their own way round the fire.

While I was thus looking on them I perceived by my perspective two miserable wretches dragged from the boats, where it seems they were laid by, and were now brought out for the slaughter. I perceived one of them immediately fell, being knocked down, I suppose, with a club or wooden sword,—for that was their way,—and two or three others were at work immediately cutting him open for their cookery, while the other victim was left standing by himself till they should be ready for him. In that very moment this poor wretch, seeing himself a little at liberty, nature inspired him with hopes of life, and he started away from them, and ran with incredible swiftness along the sands directly towards me; I mean towards that part of the coast where my habitation was.

I was dreadfully frighted, that I must acknowledge, when I perceived him to run my way; and especially when, as I thought, I saw him pursued by the whole body; and now I expected that part of my dream was coming to pass, and that he would certainly take shelter in my grove; but I could not depend by any means upon my dream for the rest of it—namely, that the other savages would not pursue him thither and find him there. However, I kept my station, and my spirits began to recover when I found that there were not above three men that followed him; and still more was I encouraged, when I found that he outstripped them exceedingly in running, and gained ground of them, so that if he could but hold it for half an hour, I saw easily he would fairly get away from them all.

There was between them and my castle the creek, which I mentioned often at the first part of my story, when I landed my cargoes out of the ship; and this I saw plainly he must necessarily swim over, or the poor wretch would be taken there. But when the savage escaping came thither, he made nothing of it, though the tide was then up, but plunging in, swam through in about thirty strokes or thereabouts, landed and ran on with exceeding strength and swiftness. When the three persons came to the creek, I found that two of them could swim, but the third could not, and that standing on the other side, he looked at the other, but went no farther; and soon after went softly back again, which, as it happened, was very well for him in the main.

I observed that the two who swam were yet more than twice as long swimming over the creek as the fellow was that fled from them. It came now very warmly upon my thoughts, and indeed irresistibly, that now was my time to get me a servant, and perhaps a companion or assistant; and that I was called plainly by Providence to save this poor creature's life. I immediately run down the ladders with all possible expedition, fetches my two guns, for they were both but at the foot of the ladders, as I observed above; and getting up again with the same haste to the top of the hill, I crossed towards the sea; and having a very short cut and all down hill, clapped myself in the way between the pursuers and the pursued; hallooing aloud to him that fled, who, looking back, was at first perhaps as much frighted at me as at them: but I beckoned with my hand to him to come back; and in the meantime I slowly advanced towards the two that followed; then rushing at once upon the foremost, I knocked him down with the stock of my piece. I was loath to fire, because I would not have the rest hear; though at that distance it would not have been easily heard, and being out of sight of the smoke too, they would not have easily known what to make of it. Having knocked this fellow down, the other who pursued with him stopped, as if he had been frighted, and I advanced apace towards him; but as I came nearer, I perceived presently he had a bow and arrow, and was fitting it to shoot at me; so I was then necessitated to shoot at him first, which I did and killed him at the first shot. The poor savage who fled, but had stopped, though he saw both his enemies fallen, and killed, as he thought, yet was so frighted with the fire and noise of my piece, that he stood stockstill, and neither came forward nor went backward, though he seemed rather inclined to fly still than to come on. I hallooed again to him, and made signs to come forward, which he easily understood, and came a little way, then stopped again, and then a little farther, and stopped again, and I could then perceive that he stood trembling, as if he had been taken prisoner, and had just been to be killed as his two enemies were. I beckoned him again to come to me, and gave him all the signs of encouragement that I could think of, and he came nearer and nearer, kneeling down every ten or twelve steps in token of acknowledgment for my saving his life. I smiled at him, and looked pleasantly, and beckoned to him to come still nearer. At length he came close to me, and then he kneeled down again, kissed the ground, and laid his head upon the ground, and taking me by the foot, set my foot upon his head: this, it seems, was in token of swearing to be my slave for ever. I took him up and made much of him, and encouraged him all I could. But there was more work to do yet; for I perceived the savage whom I knocked down was not killed, but stunned, with the blow, and began to come to himself; so I pointed to him, and showing him the savage, that he was not dead. Upon this he spoke some words to me, and though I could not understand them yet I thought they were pleasant to hear, for they were the first sound of a man's voice that I had heard, my own excepted, for above twenty-five years. But there was no time for such reflections now. The savage who was knocked down recovered himself so far as to sit up upon the ground, and I perceived that my savage began to be afraid; but when I saw that, I presented my other piece at the man, as if I would shoot him. Upon this my savage, for so I called him now, made a motion to me to lend him my sword, which hung naked in a belt by my side; so I did. He no sooner had it, but he runs to his enemy, and at one blow cuts off his head as cleverly, no executioner in Germany could have done it sooner or better; which I thought very strange for one who I had reason to believe never saw a sword in his life before, except their own wooden swords. However, it seems, as I learned afterwards, they made their wooden swords so sharp, so heavy, and the wood is so hard, that they will cut off heads even with them, ay, and arms, and that at one blow too. When he had done this, he comes laughing to me in signs of triumph, and brought me the sword again, and with abundance of gestures, which I did not understand, laid it down with the head of the savage that he had killed just before me

But that which astonished him most, was to know how I had killed the other Indian so far off. So pointing to him, he made signs to me to let him go to him; so I bade him go as well as I could. When he came to him he stood like one amazed, looking at him, turned him first on one side, then on the other, looked at the wound the bullet had made, which it seems was just in his breast, where it had made a hole, and no great quantity of blood had followed; but he had bled inwardly, for he was quite dead. He took up his bow and arrows and came back, so I turned to go away, and beckoned to him to follow me, making signs to him that more might come after them.

Upon this he signed to me that he should bury them with sand, that they might not be seen by the rest if they followed; and so I made signs again to him to do so. He fell to work, and in an instant he had scraped a hole in the sand with his hands, big enough to bury the first in, and then dragged him into it, and covered him, and did so also by the other. I believe he had buried them both in a quarter of an hour. Then calling him away I carried him, not to my castle, but quite away to my cave, on the farther part of the island. So I did not let my dream come to pass in that part; namely, that he came into my grove for shelter.

Here I gave him bread and a bunch of raisins to eat, and a draught of water, which I found he was indeed in great distress for by his running. And having refreshed him, I made signs for him to go lie down and sleep, pointing to a place where I had laid a great parcel of rice straw, and a blanket upon it, which I used to sleep upon myself sometimes; so the poor creature lay down and went to sleep.

He was a comely, handsome fellow, perfectly well made, with straight strong limbs, not too large, tall and well shaped, and as I reckon, about twenty-six years of age. He had a very good countenance, not a fierce and surly aspect; but seemed to have something very manly in his face; and yet he had all the sweetness and softness of an European in his countenance too, especially when he smiled. His hair was long and black, not curled like wool; his forehead very high and large, and a great vivacity and sparkling sharpness in his eyes. The colour of his skin was not quite black, but very tawny; and yet not of an ugly yellow nauseous tawny, as the Brazilians and Virginians, and other natives of America are; but of a bright kind of a dun olive colour, that had in it something very agreeable, though not very easy to describe. His face was round and plump; his nose small, not flat like the negroes; a very good mouth, thin lips, and his fine teeth well set, and white as ivory. After he had slumbered, rather than slept, about half an hour, he waked again, and comes out of the cave to me, for I had been milking my goats, which I had in the enclosure just by. When he espied me, he came running to me, laying himself down again upon the ground, with all the possible signs of an humble thankful disposition, making many antic gestures to show it. At last he lays his head flat upon the ground, close to my foot, and sets my other foot upon his head, as he had done before; and after this made all the signs to me of subjection, servitude, and submission imaginable, to let me know how he would serve me as long as he lived. I understood him in many things, and let him know I was very well pleased with him. In a little time I began to speak to him, and teach him to speak to me. And first, I made him know his name should be Friday, which was the day I saved his life. I called him so for the memory of the time. I likewise taught him to say Master, and then let him know that was to be my name. I likewise taught him to say Yes and No, and to know the meaning of them. I gave him some milk in an earthen pot, and let him see me drink it before him, and sop my bread in it. And I gave him a cake of bread to do the like, which he quickly complied with, and made signs that it was very good for him.

I kept there with him all that night; but as soon as it was day I beckoned to him to come with me, and let him know I would give him some clothes; at which he seemed very glad, for he was stark naked. As we went by the place where he had buried the two men he pointed exactly to the place, and showed me the marks that he had made to find them again, making signs to me that we should dig them up again and eat them! At this I appeared very angry, expressed my abhorrence of it, made as if I would vomit at the thoughts of it, and beckoned with my hand to him to come away; which he did immediately, with great submission. I then led him up to the top of the hill, to see if his enemies were gone; and, pulling out my glass, I looked and saw plainly the place where they had been, but no appearance of them or of their canoes; so that it was plain that they were gone, and had left their two comrades behind them, without any search after them.

But I was not content with this discovery; but having now more courage, and consequently more curiosity, I takes my man Friday with me, giving him the sword in his hand with the bow and arrows at his back, which I found he could use very dexterously, making him carry one gun for me, and I two for myself, and away we marched to the place where these creatures had been, for I had a mind now to get some fuller intelligence of them. When I came to the place, my very blood ran chill in my veins, and my heart sunk within me at the horror of the spectacle. Indeed it was a dreadful sight—at least it was so to me; though Friday made nothing of it. The place was covered with human bones, the ground dyed with their blood, great pieces of flesh left here and there, half-eaten, mangled and scorched; and, in short, all the tokens of the triumphant feast they had been making there, after a victory over their enemies. I saw three skulls, five hands, and the bones of three or four legs and feet, and abundance of other parts of the bodies; and Friday, by his signs, made me understand that they brought over four prisoners to feast upon; that three of them were eaten up, and that he, pointing to himself, was the fourth: That there had been a great battle between them and their next king, whose subjects it seems he had been one of; and that they had taken a great number of prisoners, all which were carried to several places by those that had taken them in the fight, in order to feast upon them, as was done here by these wretches upon those they brought hither.

I caused Friday to gather all the skulls, bones, flesh, and whatever remained, and lay them together on a heap, and make a great fire upon it, and burn them all to ashes. I found Friday had still a hankering stomach after some of the flesh, and was still a cannibal in his nature; but I discovered so much abhorrence at the very thoughts of it, and at the least appearance of it, that he durst not discover it; for I had by some means let him know that I would kill him if he offered it.

§ *I make clothes for Friday. He becomes much attached to me. My efforts to teach him. Friday's reasoning and notions of religion. Reflections on the uselessness of religious controversy.*

W̲H̲E̲N̲ we had done this, we came back to our castle, and there I fell to work for my man Friday; and first of all I gave him a pair of linen drawers, which I had out of the poor gunner's chest I mentioned, and which I found in the wreck, and which with a little alteration fitted him very well. Then I made him a jerkin of goat-skin, as well as my skill would allow, and I was now grown a tolerable good tailor; and I gave him a cap which I had made of a hare-skin, very convenient and fashionable enough; and thus he was clothed for the present tolerably well, and was mighty well pleased to see himself almost as well clothed as his master. It is true, he went awkwardly in these things at first: wearing the drawers was very awkward to him, and the sleeves of the waistcoat galled his shoulders and the inside of his arms; but a little easing them where he complained they hurt him, and using himself to them, at length he took to them very well.

The next day after I came home to my hutch with him, I began to consider where I should lodge him; and that I might do well for him, and yet be perfectly easy myself, I made a little tent for him in the vacant place between my two fortifications, in the inside of the last, and in the outside of the first. And as there was a door or entrance there into my cave, I made a formal framed door-case, and a door to it of boards, and set it up in the passage, a little within the entrance; and causing the door to open on the inside, I barred it up in the night, taking in my ladders too; so that Friday could no way come at me in the inside of my innermost wall without making so much noise in getting over, that it must needs waken me. For my first wall had now a complete roof over it of long poles covering all my tent and leaning up to the side of the hill, which was again laid cross with smaller sticks instead of laths, and then thatched over a great thickness with the rice straw, which was strong like reeds; and at the hole or place which was left to go in or out by the ladder, I had placed a kind of trap-door, which, if it had been attempted on the outside, would not have opened at all, but would have fallen down and made a great noise; and as to weapons, I took them all in to my side every night.

But I needed none of all this precaution; for never man had a more faithful, loving, sincere servant than Friday was to me; without passions, sullenness, or designs, perfectly obliged and engaged; his very affections were tied to me, like those of a child to a father, and I dare say he would have sacrificed his life for the saving mine upon any occasion whatsoever. The many testimonies he gave me of this, put it out of doubt, and soon convinced me that I needed to use no precautions as to my safety on his account.

This frequently gave me occasion to observe, and that with wonder, that however it had pleased God in His providence, and in the government of the works of His hands, to take from so great a part of the world of His creatures the best uses to which their faculties and the powers of their souls are adapted; yet that He has bestowed upon them the same powers, the same reason, the same affections, the same sentiments of kindness and obligation, the same passions and resentments of wrongs, the same sense of gratitude, sincerity, fidelity, and all the capacities of doing good and receiving good, that He has given to us; and that when He pleases to offer to them occasions of exerting these, they are as ready, nay, more ready, to apply them to the right uses for which they were bestowed than we are. And this made me very melancholy sometimes, in reflecting, as the several occasions presented, how mean a use we make of all these, even though we have these powers enlightened by the great Lamp of Instruction, the Spirit of God, and by the knowledge of His Word, added to our understanding; and why it has pleased God to hide the like saving knowledge from so many millions of souls, who, if I might judge by this poor savage, would make a much better use of it than we did.

From hence I sometimes was led too far, to invade the sovereignty of Providence, and, as it were, arraign the justice of so arbitrary a disposition of things, that should hide that light from some, and reveal it to others, and yet expect a like duty from both. But I shut it up, and checked my thoughts with this conclusion: first, That we did not know by what light and law these should be condemned; but that as God was necessarily, and by the nature of His being, infinitely holy and just, so it could not be but that if these creatures were all sentenced to absence from Himself, it was on account of sinning against that light which, as the Scripture says, was a law to themselves; and by such rules as their consciences would acknowledge to be just, though the foundation was not discovered to us. And, secondly, That still as we are all the clay in the hand of the Potter, no vessel could say to Him, Why hast Thou formed me thus?

But to return to my new companion. I was greatly delighted with him, and made it my business to teach him everything that was proper to make him useful, handy, and helpful; but especially to make him speak, and understand me when I spake: and he was the aptest scholar that ever was, and particularly was so merry, so constantly diligent, and so pleased, when he could but understand me, or make me understand him, that it was very pleasant to me to talk to him. And now my life began to be so easy, that I began to say to myself, that could I but have been safe from more savages, I cared not if I was never to remove from the place while I lived.

After I had been two or three days returned to my castle, I thought that, in order to bring Friday off from his horrid way of feeding, and from the relish of a cannibal's stomach, I ought to let him taste other flesh; so I took him out with me one morning to the woods. I went, indeed, intending to kill a kid out of my own flock, and bring him home and dress it; but, as I was going, I saw a she-goat lying down in the shade, and two young kids sitting by her. I catched hold of Friday. "Hold," says I, "stand still"; and made signs to him not to stir. Immediately I presented my piece, shot, and killed one of the kids. The poor creature, who had at a distance indeed seen me kill the savage his enemy, but did not know, or could imagine, how it was done, was sensibly surprised, trembled, and shook, and looked so amazed, that I thought he would have sunk down. He did not see the kid I had shot at, or perceive I had killed it, but ripped up his waistcoat to feel if he was not wounded, and, as I found, presently thought I was resolved to kill him; for he came and kneeled down to me, and embracing my knees, said a great many things I did not understand, but I could easily see that the meaning was to pray me not to kill him.

I soon found a way to convince him that I would do him no harm, and taking him up by the hand, laughed at him, and pointing to the kid which I had killed, beckoned to him to run and fetch it, which he did; and while he was wondering and looking to see how the creature was killed, I loaded my gun again, and by and by I saw a great fowl like a hawk sit upon a tree within shot; so to let Friday understand a little what I would do, I called him to me again, pointing at the fowl, which was indeed a parrot, though I thought it had been a hawk. I say, pointing to the parrot, and to my gun, and to the ground under the parrot, to let him see I would make it fall, I made him understand that I would shoot and kill that bird. Accordingly I fired, and bade him look, and immediately he saw the parrot fall. He stood like one frightened again, notwithstanding all I had said to him; and I found he was the more amazed because he did not see me put anything into the gun, but thought that there must be some wonderful fund of death and destruction in that thing, able to kill man, beast, bird, or anything, near or far off; and the astonishment thus created in him was such as could not wear off for a long time; and I believe, if I would have let him, he would have worshipped me and my gun! As for the gun itself, he would not so much as touch it for several days after; but would speak to it, and talk to it as if it had answered him, when he was by himself; which, as I afterwards learned of him, was to desire it not to kill him.

Well, after his astonishment was a little over at this, I pointed to him to run and fetch the bird I had shot; which he did, but stayed some time; for the parrot, not being quite dead, was fluttered a good way off from the place where she fell; however, he found her, took her up, and brought her to me; and, as I had perceived his ignorance about the gun before, I took this advantage to charge the gun again, and not let him see me do it, that I might be ready for any other mark that might present. But nothing more offered at that time; so I brought home the kid, and the same evening I took the skin off, and cut it out as well as I could; and having a pot for that purpose, I boiled or stewed some of the flesh, and made some very good broth; and after I had begun to eat some, I gave some to my man, who seemed very glad of it, and liked it very well. But that which was strangest to him was to see me eat salt with it. He made a sign to me that the salt was not good to eat, and putting a little into his own mouth he seemed to nauseate it, and would spit and sputter at it, washing his mouth with fresh water after it. On the other hand, I took some meat in my mouth without salt, and I pretended to spit and sputter for want of salt as fast as he had done at the salt. But it would not do, he would never care for salt with his meat, or in his broth; at least, not a great while, and then but a very little.

Having thus fed him with boiled meat and broth, I was resolved to feast him the next day with roasting a piece of the kid. This I did by hanging it before the fire in a string, as I had seen many people do in England, setting two poles up, one on each side the fire, and one cross on the top, and tying the string to the cross-stick, letting the meat turn continually. This Friday admired very much; but, when he came to taste the flesh, he took so many ways to tell me how well he liked it, that I could not but understand him; and at last he told me he would never eat man's flesh any more—which I was very glad to hear.

The next day I set him to work to beating some corn out, and sifting it in the manner I used to do, as I observed before; and he soon understood how to do it as well as I, especially after he had seen what the meaning of it was, and that it was to make bread of: for after that I let him see me make my bread, and bake it too, and in a little while Friday was able to do all the work for me as well as I could do it myself. I began now to consider that, having two mouths to feed instead of one, I must provide more ground for my harvest, and plant a larger quantity of corn than I used to do; so I marked out a larger piece of land and began the fence in the same manner as before; in which Friday not only worked very willingly and very hard, but did it very cheerfully. And I told him what it was for; that it was for corn to make more bread, because he was now with me, and that I might have enough for him and myself too. He appeared very sensible of that part, and let me know that he thought I had much more labour upon me on his account than I had for myself; and that he would work the harder for me, if I would tell him what to do.

This was the pleasantest year of all the life I led in this place. Friday began to talk pretty well, and understand the names of almost everything I had occasion to call for, and of every place I had to send him to, and talk a great deal to me; so that, in short, I began now to have some use for my tongue again, which indeed I had very little occasion for before—that is to say, about speech. Besides the pleasure of talking to him, I had a singular satisfaction in the fellow himself. His simple unfeigned honesty appeared to me more and more every day, and I began really to love the creature; and, on his side, I believe he loved me more than it was possible for him ever to love anything before.

I had a mind once to try if he had any hankering inclination to his own country again; and having learned him English so well that he could answer me almost any questions, I asked him whether the nation that he belonged to never conquered in battle? At which he smiled, and said, "Yes, yes; we always fight the better;" that is, he meant always get the better in fight; and so we began the following discourse:— "You always fight the better," said I; "how came you to be taken prisoner, then, Friday?"

*Friday*. My nation beat much, for all that.

*Master*. How beat; if your nation beat them, how come you to be taken?

*Friday*. They more many than my nation in the place where me was; they take one, two, three, and me. My nation over beat them in the yonder place, where me no was; there my nation take one, two, great thousand.

*Master*. But why did not your side recover you from the hands of your enemies then?

*Friday*. They run one, two, three, and me, and make go in the canoe; my nation have no canoe that time.

*Master*. Well, Friday, and what does your nation do with the men they take; do they carry them away and eat them, as these did?

*Friday*. Yes; my nation eat mans too, eat all up.

*Master*. Where do they carry them?

*Friday*. Go to other place where they think.

*Master*. Do they come hither?

*Friday*. Yes, yes, they come hither; come other else place.

*Master*. Have you been here with them?

*Friday*. Yes, I been here (points to the north-west side of the island, which it seems was their side).

By this I understood that my man Friday had formerly been among the savages who used to come on shore on the farther part of the island on the said man-eating occasions that he was now brought for. And some time after, when I took the courage to carry him to that side, being the same I formerly mentioned, he presently knew the place, and told me he was there once when they eat up twenty men, two women, and one child. He could not tell twenty in English; but he numbered them by laying so many stones on a row, and pointing to me to tell them over.

I have told this passage because it introduces what follows: that, after I had had this discourse with him, I asked him how far it was from our island to the shore, and whether the canoes were not often lost? He told me there was no danger, no canoes ever lost; but that, after a little way out to the sea, there was a current, and a wind, always one way in the morning, the other in the afternoon.

This I understood to be no more than the sets of the tide, as going out, or coming in. But I afterwards understood it was occasioned by the great draught and reflux of the mighty river Orinoco, in the mouth or the gulf of which river, as I found afterwards, our island lay; and this land which I perceived to the west and north-west was the great island of Trinidad, on the north point of the mouth of the river. I asked Friday a thousand questions about the country, the inhabitants, the sea, the coast, and what nations were near. He told me all he knew with the greatest openness imaginable. I asked him the names of the several nations of his sort of people, but could get no other name than

Caribs; from whence I easily understood that these were the Carib-
bees, which our maps place on the part of America which reaches
from the mouth of the river Orinoco to Guiana, and onwards to St.
Martha. He told me that up a great way beyond the moon, that was,
beyond the setting of the moon, which must be west from their country, there dwelt white, bearded men like me, and pointed to my great
whiskers, which I mentioned before; and that they had killed much
mans—that was his word. By all which I understood he meant the
Spaniards, whose cruelties in America had been spread over the whole
countries, and were remembered by all the nations from father to son.

I inquired if he could tell me how I might come from this island,
and get among those white men. He told me, "Yes, yes, I might go
in two canoe." I could not understand what he meant, or make him
describe to me what he meant by two canoe, till at last, with great difficulty, I found he meant it must be in a large, great boat, as big as two
canoes. This part of Friday's discourse began to relish with me very
well, and from this time I entertained some hopes that, one time or
other, I might find an opportunity to make my escape from this place,
and that this poor savage might be a means to help me to do it.

During the long time that Friday has now been with me, and that
he began to speak to me, and understand me, I was not wanting to lay
a foundation of religious knowledge in his mind. Particularly, I
asked him one time, "Who made him?" The poor creature did not
understand me at all, but thought I had asked who was his father. But
I took it by another handle, and asked him who made the sea, the
ground we walked on, and the hills and woods? He told me it was one
old Benamuckee, that lived beyond all. He could describe nothing of
this great person, but that he was very old; much older, he said than
the sea or the land, than the moon or the stars. I asked him then, "If
this old person had made all things, why did not all things worship
him?" He looked very grave, and with a perfect look of innocence
said, "All things said O to him." I asked him if the people who die in
his country went away anywhere? He said, "Yes; they all went to
Benamuckee." Then I asked him whether these they eat up went
thither too? He said, "Yes."

213

From these things I began to instruct him in the knowledge of the true God. I told him that the great Maker of all things lived up there, pointing up towards heaven; that He governs the world by the same power and providence by which He had made it; that He was omnipotent—could do everything for us, give everything to us, take everything from us: and thus, by degrees, I opened his eyes. He listened with great attention, and received with pleasure the notion of Jesus Christ being sent to redeem us; and of the manner of making our prayers to God, and His being able to hear us, even into heaven. He told me one day that if our God could hear us up beyond the sun, He must needs be a greater God than their Benamuckee, who lived but a little way off, and yet could not hear, till they went up to the great mountains where he dwelt, to speak to him. I asked him if ever he went thither to speak to him? He said, "No, they never went that were young men"; none went thither but the old men, who he called their Oowookakee—that is, as I made him explain it to me, their religious, or clergy; and that they went to say O (so he called saying prayers), and then came back and told them what Benamuckee said. By this I observed that there is priest-craft even amongst the most blinded ignorant pagans in the world; and the policy of making a secret religion, in order to preserve the veneration of the people to the clergy, is not only to be found in the Roman, but perhaps among all religions in the world, even among the most brutish and barbarous savages.

I endeavoured to clear up this fraud to my man Friday, and told him that the pretence of their old men going up to the mountains to say O to their god Benamuckee was a cheat, and their bringing word from thence what he said was much more so; that if they met with any answer, or spoke with any one there, it must be with an evil spirit. And then I entered into a long discourse with him about the devil—the original of him, his rebellion against God, his enmity to man, the reason of it, his setting himself up in the dark parts of the world to be worshipped instead of God, and as God; and the many stratagems he made use of to delude mankind to their ruin—how he had a secret access to our passions, and to our affections, to adapt his snares so to our inclinations as to cause us even to be our own tempters, and to run upon our destruction by our own choice.

I found it was not so easy to imprint right notions in his mind about the devil as it was about the being of a God. Nature assisted all my arguments to evidence to him even the necessity of a great first Cause and overruling governing Power, a secret directing Providence, and of the equity and justice of paying homage to Him that made us, and the like. But there appeared nothing of all this in the notion of an evil spirit, of his original, his being, his nature, and, above all, of his inclination to do evil, and to draw us in to do so too; and the poor creature puzzled me once in such a manner, by a question merely natural and innocent, that I scarce knew what to say to him. I had been talking a great deal to him of the power of God, His omnipotence, His dreadful aversion to sin, His being a consuming fire to the workers of iniquity; how, as He had made us all, He could destroy us and all the world in a moment; and he listened with great seriousness to me all the while.

After this I had been telling him how the devil was God's enemy in the hearts of men, and used all his malice and skill to defeat the good designs of Providence, and to ruin the kingdom of Christ in the world, and the like. "Well," says Friday; "but you say God is so strong, so great, is He not much strong, much might as the devil?" "Yes, yes," says I, "Friday, God is stronger than the devil, God is above the devil, and therefore we pray to God to tread him down under our feet, and enable us to resist his temptations, and quench his fiery darts." "But," says he again, "if God much strong, much might as the devil, why God no kill the devil, so make him no more do wicked."

I was strangely surprised at this question; and, after all, though I was now an old man, yet I was but a young doctor, and ill enough qualified for a casuist, or a solver of difficulties. And at first I could not tell what to say; so I pretended not to hear him, and asked him what he said. But he was too earnest for an answer to forget his question; so that he repeated it in the very same broken words as above. By this time I had recovered myself a little, and I said, "God will at last punish him severely; he is reserved for the judgment, and is to be cast into the bottomless pit to dwell with everlasting fire." This did not satisfy

Friday; but he returns upon me, repeating my words, " 'Reserve—at last,' me no understand. But why not kill the devil now, not kill great ago?" "You may as well ask me," said I, "why God does not kill you and me when we do wicked things here that offend Him. We are preserved to repent and be pardoned." He muses a while at this. "Well, well," says he, mighty affectionately, "that well; so you, I, devil, all wicked, all preserve, repent, God pardon all." Here I was run down again by him to the last degree; and it was a testimony to me how the mere notions of nature, though they will guide reasonable creatures to the knowledge of a God, and of a worship or homage due to the supreme being of God, as the consequence of our nature, yet nothing but divine revelation can form the knowledge of Jesus Christ, and of a redemption purchased for us, of a Mediator of the new covenant, and of an Intercessor at the footstool of God's throne;—I say, nothing but a revelation from heaven can form these in the soul; and that, therefore, the Gospel of our Lord and Saviour Jesus Christ, I mean the Word of God, and the Spirit of God, promised for the guide and sanctifier of His people, are the absolutely necessary instructors of the souls of men in the saving knowledge of God and the means of salvation.

I therefore diverted the present discourse between me and my man, rising up hastily, as upon some sudden occasion of going out; then sending him for something a good way off, I seriously prayed to God that He would enable me to instruct savingly this poor savage; assisting, by His Spirit, the heart of the poor ignorant creature to receive the light of the knowledge of God in Christ, reconciling him to Himself; and would guide me to speak so to him from the Word of God, as his conscience might be convinced, his eyes opened, and his soul saved. When he came again to me I entered into a long discourse with him upon the subject of the redemption of man by the Saviour of the world, and of the doctrine of the gospel preached from Heaven; namely, of repentance towards God and faith in our blessed Lord Jesus. I then explained to him, as well as I could, why our blessed Redeemer took not on Him the nature of angels, but the seed of Abraham, and how, for that reason, the fallen angels had no share in the redemption; that He came only to the lost sheep of the house of Israel, and the like.

I had, God knows, more sincerity than knowledge in all the methods I took for this poor creature's instruction; and must acknowledge, what I believe all that act upon the same principle will find, that, in laying things open to him, I really informed and instructed myself in many things that either I did not know or had not fully considered before, but which occurred naturally to my mind upon my searching into them for the information of this poor savage. And I had more affection in my inquiry after things upon this occasion than ever I felt before; so that whether this poor wild wretch was the better for me or no, I had great reason to be thankful that ever he came to me. My grief set lighter upon me, my habitation grew comfortable to me beyond measure; and when I reflected that in this solitary life which I had been confined to, I had not only been moved myself to look up to Heaven, and to seek to the hand that had brought me there, but was now to be made an instrument under Providence to save the life, and, for aught I know, the soul of a poor savage, and bring him to the true knowledge of religion and of the Christian doctrine, that he might know Christ Jesus, to know whom is life eternal;—I say, when I reflected upon all these things, a secret joy ran through every part of my soul; and I frequently rejoiced that ever I was brought to this place, which I had so often thought the most dreadful of all afflictions that could possibly have befallen me.

In this thankful frame I continued all the remainder of my time; and the conversation which employed the hours between Friday and me was such as made the three years which we lived there together perfectly and completely happy, if any such thing as complete happiness can be formed in a sublunary state. The savage was now a good Christian—a much better than I, though I have reason to hope, and bless God for it, that we were equally penitent, and comforted, restored penitents; we had here the Word of God to read, and no farther off from His Spirit to instruct than if we had been in England.

I always applied myself to reading the Scripture, to let him know, as well as I could, the meaning of what I read; and he, again, by his serious inquiries and questions, made me, as I said before, a much better scholar in the Scripture knowledge than I should ever have been by my own private mere reading. Another thing I cannot refrain from observing here, also from experience in this retired part of my life—namely, how infinite and inexpressible a blessing it is that the knowledge of God, and of the doctrine of salvation by Christ Jesus, is so plainly laid down in the Word of God, so easy to be received and understood, that as the bare reading the Scripture made me capable of understanding enough of my duty to carry me directly on to the

great work of sincere repentance for my sins and laying hold of a Saviour for life and salvation, to a stated reformation in practice and obedience to all God's commands, and this without any teacher or instructor (I mean human), so the same plain instruction sufficiently served to the enlightening this savage creature, and bringing him to be such a Christian as I have known few equal to him in my life.

As to all the disputes, wrangling, strife and contention which has happened in the world about religion, whether niceties in doctrines or schemes of church government, they were all perfectly useless to us, as, for aught I can yet see, they have been to all the rest in the world. We had the sure guide to heaven—namely, the Word of God; and we had, blessed be God, comfortable views of the Spirit of God, teaching and instructing us by His Word, leading us into all truth, and making us both willing and obedient to the instruction of His Word; and I cannot see the least use that the greatest knowledge of the disputed points in religion, which have made such confusions in the world, would have been to us if we could have obtained it. But I must go on with the historical part of things, and take every part in its order.

After Friday and I became more intimately acquainted, and that he could understand almost all I said to him, and speak fluently, though in broken English, to me, I acquainted him with my own story, or at least so much of it as related to my coming into the place, how I had lived there, and how long. I let him into the mystery, for such it was to him, of gunpowder and bullet, and taught him how to shoot. I gave him a knife, which he was wonderfully delighted with; and I made him a belt, with a frog hanging to it, such as in England we wear hangers in; and in the frog, instead of a hanger, I gave him a hatchet, which was not only as good a weapon in some cases, but much more useful upon other occasions.

I described to him the country of Europe, and particularly England, which I came from; how we lived, how we worshipped God, how we behaved to one another, and how we traded in ships to all parts of the world. I gave him an account of the wreck which I had been on board of, and showed him as near as I could the place where she lay; but she was all beaten in pieces before, and gone.

I showed him the ruins of our boat which we lost when we escaped, and which I could not stir with my whole strength then, but was now fallen almost all to pieces. Upon seeing this boat, Friday stood musing a great while, and said nothing. I asked him what it was he studied upon. At last says he, "Me see such boat like come to place at my nation."

I did not understand him a good while; but at last, when I had examined farther into it, I understood by him that a boat, such as that had been, came on shore upon the country where he lived; that is, as he explained it, was driven thither by stress of weather. I presently imagined that some European ship must have been cast away upon their coast, and the boat might get loose and drive ashore; but was so dull, that I never once thought of men making escape from a wreck thither, much less whence they might come; so I only inquired after a description of the boat.

§ *Friday tells me of the white mans in his country. I make a canoe. Keep another anniversary. The savages again land. We attack them and rescue a Spaniard. Friday finds his father.*

FRIDAY described the boat to me well enough; but brought me better to understand him when he added, with some warmth, "We save the white mans from drown." Then I presently asked him if there were any white mans, as he called them, in the boat. "Yes," he said; "the boat full of white mans." I asked him how many. He told upon his fingers seventeen. I asked him then what became of them. He told me, "They live, they dwell at my nation."

This put new thoughts into my head; for I presently imagined that these might be the men belonging to the ship that was cast away in sight of my island, as I now, call it; and who, after the ship was struck on the rock, and they saw her inevitably lost, had saved themselves in their boat, and were landed upon that wild shore among the savages. Upon this I inquired of him more critically what was become of them. He assured me they lived still there; that they had been there about four years; that the savages let them alone, and gave them victuals to live. I asked him how it came to pass they did not kill them and eat them. He said, "No, they make brother with them;" that is, as I understood him, a truce. And then he added, "They no eat mans but when make the war fight;" that is to say, they never eat any men but such as come to fight with them and are taken in battle.

It was after this some considerable time, that being on the top of the hill, at the east side of the island, from whence, as I have said, I had in a clear day discovered the main, or continent of America, Friday, the weather being very serene, looks very earnestly towards the mainland, and in a kind of surprise falls a-jumping and dancing, and calls out to me, for I was at some distance from him. I asked him what was the matter. "Oh, joy!" says he, "oh, glad! There see my country, there my nation!"

I observed an extraordinary sense of pleasure appeared in his face, and his eyes sparkled, and his countenance discovered a strange eagerness, as if he had a mind to be in his own country again; and this observation of mine put a great many thoughts into me, which made me at first not so easy about my new man Friday as I was before; and I made no doubt but that if Friday could get back to his own nation again, he would not only forget all his religion, but all his obligation to me; and would be forward enough to give his countrymen an account of me, and come back perhaps with a hundred or two of them, and make a feast upon me, at which he might be as merry as he used to be with those of his enemies when they were taken in war.

But I wronged the poor honest creature very much, for which I was very sorry afterwards. However, as my jealousy increased, and held me some weeks, I was a little more circumspect, and not so familiar and kind to him as before; in which I was certainly in the wrong, too, the honest grateful creature having no thought about it, but what consisted with the best principles, both as a religious Christian and as a grateful friend, as appeared afterwards to my full satisfaction.

While my jealousy of him lasted, you may be sure I was every day pumping him, to see if he would discover any of the new thoughts which I suspected were in him; but I found everything he said was so honest, and so innocent, that I could find nothing to nourish my suspicion; and, in spite of all my uneasiness, he made me at last entirely his own again; nor did he in the least perceive that I was uneasy, and therefore I could not suspect him of deceit.

One day walking up the same hill, but the weather being hazy at sea, so that we could not see the continent, I called to him, and said, "Friday, do not you wish yourself in your own country, your own nation?" "Yes," he said; "I be much O glad to be at my own nation." "What would you do there?" said I. "Would you turn wild again, eat men's flesh again, and be a savage as you were before?" He looked full of concern, and shaking his head, said, "No, no; Friday tell them to live good, tell them to pray God, tell them to eat corn-bread, cattle-flesh, milk, no eat man again." "Why then," said I to him, "they will kill you." He looked grave at that, and then said, "No, they no kill me, they willing love learn." He meant by this, they would be willing to learn. He added, they learned much of the bearded mans that come in the boat. Then I asked him if he would go back to them. He smiled at that, and told me he could not swim so far. I told him I would make a canoe for him. He told me he would go if I would go with him. "I go!" says I; "why, they will eat me if I come there." "No, no," says he; "me make they no eat you; me make them much love you." He meant he would tell them how I had killed his enemies, and saved his life, and so he would make them love me. Then he told me as well as he could how kind they were to seventeen white men, or bearded men, as he called them, who came on shore there in distress.

From this time, I confess, I had a mind to venture over, and see if I could possibly join with these bearded men, who, I made no doubt, were Spaniards or Portuguese; not doubting but, if I could, we might find some method to escape from thence, being upon the continent, and a good company together, better than I could from an island forty miles off the shore and alone without help. So, after some days, I took Friday to work again, by way of discourse, and told him I would give him a boat to go back to his own nation; and accordingly I carried him to my frigate, which lay on the other side of the island, and having cleared it of water, for I always kept it sunk in the water, I brought it out, showed it him, and we both went into it.

I found he was a most dexterous fellow at managing it, would make it go almost as swift and fast again as I could. So when he was in, I said to him, "Well now, Friday, shall we go to your nation?" He looked very dull at my saying so; which it seems was because he thought the boat too small to go so far. I told him then I had a bigger. So the next day I went to the place where the first boat lay which I had made, but which I could not get into water. He said that was big enough. But then, as I had taken no care of it, and it had lain two or three and twenty years there, the sun had split and dried it, that it was in a manner rotten. Friday told me such a boat would do very well, and would carry "much enough vittle, drink, bread;" that was his way of talking.

Upon the whole, I was by this time so fixed upon my design of going over with him to the continent, that I told him we would go and make one as big as that, and he should go home in it. He answered not one word, but looked very grave and sad. I asked him, "What was the matter with him?" He asked me again thus, "Why you angry mad with Friday, what me done?" I asked him what he meant; I told him I was not angry with him at all. "No angry! no angry!" says he, repeating the words several times; "why send Friday home away to my nation?" "Why," says I, "Friday, did you not say you wished you were there?" "Yes, yes," says he; "wish be both there—no wish Friday there, no master there." In a word, he would not think of going there without me. "I go there, Friday!" says I; "what shall I do there?" He turned very quick upon me at this. "You do great deal much good," says he; "you teach wild mans be good sober tame mans; you tell them know God, pray God, and live new life." "Alas! Friday," says I, "thou knowest not what thou sayest; I am but an ignorant man myself." "Yes, yes," says he, "you teachee me good, you teachee them good." "No, no, Friday," says I; "you shall go without me; leave me here to live by myself, as I did before." He looked confused again at that word, and running to one of the hatchets which he used to wear, he takes it up hastily, and gives it to me. "What must I do with this?" says I to him. "You take kill Friday," says he. "What must I kill you for?" said I again. He returns very quick, "What you send Friday away for?— take kill Friday, no send Friday away." This he spoke so earnestly, that I saw tears stand in his eyes. In a word, I so plainly discovered the utmost affection in him to me, and a firm resolution in him, that I told him then, and often after, that I would never send him away from me, if he was willing to stay with me.

Upon the whole, as I found by all his discourse a settled affection to me, and that nothing should part him from me, so I found all the foundation of his desire to go to his own country was laid in his ardent affection to the people and his hopes of my doing them good; a thing which, as I had no notion of myself, so I had not the least thought or intention or desire of undertaking it. But still I found a strong inclination to my attempting an escape, as above, founded on the supposition gathered from the discourse—namely, that there were seventeen bearded men there; and therefore, without any more delay, I went to work with Friday to find out a great tree proper to fell, and make a large periagua or canoe to undertake the voyage. There were trees enough in the island to have built a little fleet, not of periaguas and canoes, but even of good large vessels. But the main thing I looked at, was to get one so near the water that we might launch it when it was made, to avoid the mistake I committed at first.

At last Friday pitched upon a tree, for I found he knew much better than I what kind of wood was fittest for it; nor can I tell, to this day, what wood to call the tree we cut down, except that it was very like the tree we call fustic, or between that and the Nicaragua wood, for it was much of the same colour and smell. Friday was for burning the hollow or cavity of this tree out to make it for a boat; but I showed him how rather to cut it out with tools; which, after I had showed him how to use, he did very handily; and in about a month's hard labour, we finished it, and made it very handsome, especially when with our axes, which I showed him how to handle, we cut and hewed the outside into the true shape of a boat. After this, however, it cost us near a fortnight's time to get her along, as it were, inch by inch upon great rollers into the water. But when she was in, she would have carried twenty men with great ease.

When she was in the water, and though she was so big, it amazed me to see with what dexterity and how swift my man Friday would manage her, turn her, and paddle her along; so I asked him if he would, and if we might venture over in her. "Yes," he said; "he venture over in her very well, though great blow wind." However, I had a further design that he knew nothing of; and that was, to make a mast and sail, and to fit her with an anchor and cable. As to a mast, that was easy enough to get; so I pitched upon a straight young cedar-tree, which I found near the place, and which there was great plenty of in the island; and I set Friday to work to cut it down, and gave him directions how to shape and order it. But as to the sail, that was my particular care. I knew I had old sails, or rather pieces of old sails enough; but as I had had them now twenty-six years by me, and had not been very careful to preserve them, not imagining that I should ever have this kind of use for them, I did not doubt but they were all rotten; and, indeed, most of them were so. However, I found two pieces which appeared pretty good, and with these I went to work, and with a great deal of pains, and awkward tedious stitching (you may be sure) for want of needles, I at length made a three-cornered ugly thing, like what we call in England a shoulder-of-mutton sail, to go with a boom at bottom, and a little short sprit at the top, such as usually our ships' long-boats sail with; and such as I best knew how to manage, because it was such a one as I had to the boat in which I made my escape from Barbary, as related in the first part of my story.

I was near two months performing this last work—namely, rigging and fitting my mast and sails; for I finished them very complete, making a small stay, and sail or fore-sail to it, to assist if we should turn to windward. And, which was more than all, I fixed a rudder to the stern of her, to steer with; and though I was but a bungling shipwright, yet as I knew the usefulness, and even necessity of such a thing, I applied myself with so much pains to do it, that at last I brought it to pass, though considering the many dull contrivances I had for it that failed, I think it cost me almost as much labour as making the boat.

After all this was done, too, I had my man Friday to teach as to what belonged to the navigation of my boat; for though he knew very well how to paddle a canoe, he knew nothing what belonged to a sail and a rudder, and was the most amazed when he saw me work the boat to and again in the sea by the rudder; and how the sail jibed, and filled this way or that way, as the course we sailed changed,—I say, when he saw this he stood like one astonished and amazed. However, with a little use, I made all these things familiar to him; and he became an expert sailor, except that, as to the compass, I could make him understand very little of that. On the other hand, as there was very little cloudy weather, and seldom or never any fogs in those parts, there was the less occasion for a compass, seeing the stars were always to be seen by night and the shore by day, except in the rainy seasons, and then nobody cared to stir abroad, either by land or sea.

I was now entered on the seven-and-twentieth year of my captivity in this place; though the three last years that I had this creature with me ought rather to be left out of the account, my habitation being quite of another kind than in all the rest of the time. I kept the anniversary of my landing here with the same thankfulness to God for His mercies as at first. And if I had such cause of acknowledgment at first, I had much more so now, having such additional testimonies of the care of Providence over me, and the great hopes I had of being effectually and speedily delivered; for I had an invincible impression upon my thoughts that my deliverance was at hand, and that I should not be another year in this place. However, I went on with my husbandry, digging, planting, fencing, as usual; I gathered and cured my grapes, and did every necessary thing, as before.

The rainy season was in the meantime upon me, when I kept more within doors than at other times. So I had stowed our new vessel as secure as we could, bringing her up into the creek where, as I said, in the beginning I landed my rafts from the ship; and hauling her up to the shore at high-water mark, I made my man Friday dig a little dock, just big enough to hold her, and just deep enough to give her water enough to float in: and then, when the tide was out, we made a strong dam across the end of it, to keep the water out; and so she lay dry, as to the tide from the sea; and to keep the rain off, we laid a great many boughs of trees so thick that she was as well thatched as a house; and thus we waited for the months of November and December, in which I designed to make my adventure.

When the settled season began to come in, as the thought of my design returned with the fair weather, I was preparing daily for the voyage. And the first thing I did was to lay by a certain quantity of provisions, being the stores, for our voyage; and intended, in a week or a fortnight's time, to open the dock and launch out our boat. I was busy one morning upon something of this kind, when I called to Friday, and bid him go to the seashore and see if he could find a turtle or tortoise—a thing which we generally got once a week, for the sake of the eggs as well as the flesh. Friday had not been long gone, when he came running back, and flew over my outer wall or fence like one that felt not the ground or the steps he set his feet on; and before I had time to speak to him, he cries out to me, "O master! O master!—O sorrow!—O bad!" "What's the matter, Friday?" says I. "O—yonder—there," says he; "one, two, three canoe!—one, two, three!" By his way of speaking I concluded there were six; but on inquiry, I found it was but three. "Well, Friday," says I, "do not be frighted." So I heartened him up as well as I could. However, I saw the poor fellow was most terribly scared; for nothing ran in his head but that they were come to look for him, and would cut him in pieces and eat him; and the poor fellow trembled so, that I scare knew what to do with him. I comforted him as well as I could, and told him I was in as much danger as he, and that they would eat me as well as him: "But," says I, "Friday, we must resolve to fight them. Can you fight, Friday?" "Me shoot," says he; "but there come many great number." "No matter for that," said I again; "our guns will fright them that we do not kill;" so I asked him, "Whether, if I resolved to defend him, he would defend me, and stand by me, and do just as I bid him?" He said, "Me die, when you bid die, master." So I went and fetched a good dram of rum and gave him; for I had been so good a husband of my rum that I had a great deal left. When he had drank it, I made him take the two fowling-pieces, which we always carried, and load them with large swan-shot, as big as small pistol bullets; then I took four muskets, and loaded them with two slugs and five small bullets each; and my two pistols I loaded with a brace of bullets each; I hung my great sword as usual naked by my side, and gave Friday his hatchet.

When I had thus prepared myself, I took my perspective-glass, and went up to the side of the hill to see what I could discover. And I found quickly, by my glass, that there were one-and-twenty savages, three prisoners, and three canoes; and that their whole business seemed to be the triumphal banquet upon these three human bodies (a barbarous feast indeed), but nothing more than as I had observed was usual with them.

I observed, also, that they were landed, not where they had done when Friday made his escape, but nearer to my creek, where the shore was low, and where a thick wood came close almost down to the sea. This, with the abhorrence of the inhuman errand these wretches came about, filled me with such indignation, that I came down again to Friday and told him I was resolved to go down to them and kill them all; and asked him if he would stand by me? He was now gotten over his fright, and his spirits being a little raised with the dram I had given him, he was very cheerful, and told me, as before, "he would die, when I bid die."

In this fit of fury, I took first and divided the arms which I had charged, as before, between us. I gave Friday one pistol to stick in his girdle, and three guns upon his shoulder; and I took one pistol and the other three myself; and in this posture we marched out. I took a small bottle of rum in my pocket, and gave Friday a large bag with more powder and bullet. And as to orders, I charged him to keep close behind me, and not to stir, or shoot, or do anything till I bid him; and in the meantime not to speak a word. In this posture I fetched a compass to my right hand of near a mile, as well to get over the creek as to get into the wood; so that I might come within shot of them before I should be discovered, which I had seen by my glass it was easy to do.

While I was making this march, my former thoughts returning, I began to abate my resolution. I do not mean that I entertained any fear of their number; for as they were naked, unarmed wretches, it is certain I was superior to them—nay, though I had been alone; but it occurred to my thoughts, what call, what occasion, much less what necessity, I was in to go and dip my hands in blood, to attack people who had neither done nor intended me any wrong—who as to me were innocent; and whose barbarous customs were their own disaster, being in them a token, indeed, of God's having left them, with the other nations of that part of the world, to such stupidity and to such inhuman courses, but did not call me to take upon me to be a judge of their actions, much less an executioner of His justice: that whenever He thought fit, He would take the cause into His own hands, and by national vengeance punish them as a people for national crimes; but that, in the meantime, it was none of my business:

but it was true Friday might justify it, because he was a declared enemy, and in a state of war with those very particular people, and it was lawful for him to attack them; but I could not say the same with respect to me. These things were so warmly pressed upon my thoughts, all the way as I went, that I resolved I would only go and place myself near them, that I might observe their barbarous feast, and that I would act then as God should direct; but that unless something offered that was more a call to me than yet I knew of, I would not meddle with them.

With this resolution I entered the wood, and with all possible wariness and silence, Friday following close at my heels, I marched till I came to the skirt of the wood, on the side which was next to them; only that one corner of the wood lay between me and them. Here I called softly to Friday, and showing him a great tree, which was just at the corner of the wood, I bade him go to the tree and bring me word if he could see there plainly what they were doing. He did so, and came immediately back to me and told me they might be plainly viewed there; that they were all about their fire, eating the flesh of one of their prisoners; and that another lay bound upon the sand, a little from them, which he said they would kill next, and which fired all the very soul within me. He told me it was not one of their nation, but one of the bearded men who he had told me of, that came to their country in the boat. I was filled with horror at the very naming the white, bearded man, and going to the tree I saw plainly by my glass a white man who lay upon the beach of the sea, with his hands and his feet tied with flags, or things like rushes; and that he was a European, and had clothes on.

There was another tree, and a little thicket beyond it, about fifty yards nearer to them than the place where I was, which, by going a little way about, I saw I might come at undiscovered, and that then I should be within half shot of them; so I withheld my passion, though I was, indeed, enraged to the highest degree, and going back about twenty paces, I got behind some bushes, which held all the way till I came to the other tree; and then I came to a little rising ground, which gave me a full view of them, at the distance of about eighty yards.

I had now not a moment to lose; for nineteen of the dreadful wretches sat upon the ground, all close huddled together, and had just sent the other two to butcher the poor Christian, and bring him perhaps limb by limb to their fire, and they were stooped down to untie the bands at his feet. I turned to Friday. "Now, Friday," said I, "do as I bid thee." Friday said he would. "Then, Friday," says I, "do exactly as you see me do—fail in nothing." So I set down one of the muskets and the fowling-piece upon the ground, and Friday did the like by his; and with the other musket I took my aim at the savages, bidding him do the like. Then asking him if he was ready, he said, "Yes." "Then fire at them," said I; and the same moment I fired also.

Friday took his aim so much better than I, that on the side that he shot he killed two of them, and wounded three more; and on my side, I killed one and wounded two. They were, you may be sure, in a dreadful consternation; and all of them who were not hurt jumped up upon their feet, but did not immediately know which way to run or which way to look—for they knew not from whence their destruction came. Friday kept his eyes close upon me, that, as I had bid him, he might observe what I did. So as soon as the first shot was made, I threw down the piece and took up the fowling-piece, and Friday did the like; he sees me cock and present; he did the same again. "Are you ready, Friday?" said I. "Yes," says he. "Let fly, then," says I, "in the name of God!" and with that I fired again among the amazed wretches, and so did Friday. And as our pieces were now loaded with what I called swan-shot, or small pistol bullets, we found only two drop; but so many were wounded, that they ran about yelling and screaming, like mad creatures, all bloody and miserably wounded, most of them; whereof three more fell quickly after, though not quite dead.

"Now, Friday," says I, laying down the discharged pieces, and taking up the musket which was yet loaded, "follow me," says I; which he did, with a great deal of courage. Upon which I rushed out of the wood and showed myself, and Friday close at my foot. As soon as I perceived they saw me, I shouted as loud as I could, and bade Friday do so too; and running as fast as I could,—which, by the way, was not very fast, being laden with arms as I was,—I made directly towards the poor victim, who was, as I said, lying upon the beach or shore, between the place where they sat and the sea. The two butchers, who were just going to work with him, had left him at the surprise of our first fire, and fled in a terrible fright to the sea-side and had jumped into a canoe, and three more of the rest made the same way. I turned to Friday, and bid him step forward and fire at them. He understood me immediately, and running about forty yards to be near them, he shot at them, and I thought he had killed them all; for I saw them all fall of a heap into the boat; though I saw two of them up again quickly. However, he killed two of them, and wounded the third; so that he lay down in the bottom of the boat, as if he had been dead.

While my man Friday fired at them, I pulled out my knife and cut the flags that bound the poor victim, and loosing his hands and feet, I lifted him up, and asked him in the Portuguese tongue, "What

he was?" He answered in Latin, "Christianus;" but was so weak and faint, that he could scarce stand or speak. I took my bottle out of my pocket and gave it him, making signs that he should drink, which he did; and I gave him a piece of bread, which he ate. Then I asked him, "What countryman he was?" And he said "Espagniole;" and being a little recovered, let me know, by all the signs he could possibly make, how much he was in my debt for his deliverance. "Seignior," said I, with as much Spanish as I could make up, "we will talk afterwards, but we must fight now. If you have any strength left, take this pistol and sword and lay about you." He took them very thankfully; and no sooner had he the arms in his hands, but, as if they had put new vigour into him, he flew upon his murderers like a fury, and had cut two of them in pieces in an instant. For the truth is, as the whole was a surprise to them, so the poor creatures were so much frighted with the noise of our pieces, that they fell down for mere amazement and fear; and had no more power to attempt their own escape than their flesh had to resist our shot. And that was the case of those five that Friday shot at in the boat; for as three of them fell with the hurt they received, so the other two fell with the fright.

I kept my piece in my hand still, without firing, being willing to keep my charge ready, because I had given the Spaniard my pistol and sword. So I called to Friday, and bade him run up to the tree from whence we first fired, and fetch the arms which lay there that had been discharged—which he did with great swiftness; and then giving him my musket, I sat down myself to load all the rest again, and bade them come to me when they wanted. While I was loading these pieces, there happened a fierce engagement between the Spaniard and one of the savages, who made at him with one of their great wooden swords —the same weapon that was to have killed him before, if I had not prevented it. The Spaniard, who was as bold and as brave as could be imagined, though weak, had fought this Indian a good while, and had cut him two great wounds on his head; but the savage, being a stout lusty fellow, closing in with him, had thrown him down (being faint), and was wringing my sword out of his hand, when the Spaniard, though undermost, wisely quitting the sword, drew the pistol from his girdle, shot the savage through the body and killed him upon the spot, before I, who was running to help him, could come near him.

Friday, being now left to his liberty, pursued the flying wretches with no weapon in his hand but his hatchet; and with that he dispatched those three who, as I said before, were wounded at first and fallen, and all the rest he could come up with. And the Spaniard coming to me for a gun, I gave him one of the fowling-pieces, with which he pursued two of the savages, and wounded them both: but as he was not able to run, they both got from him into the wood, where Friday pursued them and killed one of them; but the other was too nimble for him, and though he was wounded, yet had plunged himself into the sea, and swam with all his might off to those two who were left in the canoe; which three in the canoe, with one wounded, who we know not whether he died or no, were all that escaped our hands of one-and-twenty. The account of the rest is as follows:—

3 Killed at our first shot from the tree.
2 Killed at the next shot.
2 Killed by Friday in the boat.
2 Killed by ditto, of those at first wounded.
1 Killed by ditto, in the wood.
3 Killed by the Spaniard.
4 Killed, being found dropped here and there of their
    wounds, or killed by Friday in his chase of them.
4 Escaped in the boat, whereof one wounded, if not dead.
―――
21 in all.

Those that were in the canoe worked hard to get out of gunshot; and though Friday made two or three shots at them, I did not find that he hit any of them. Friday would fain have had me take one of their canoes, and pursue them; and indeed I was very anxious about their escape, lest, carrying the news home to their people, they should come back, perhaps, with two or three hundred of their canoes, and devour us by mere multitude. So I consented to pursue them by sea, and running to one of their canoes, I jumped in, and bade Friday follow me; but when I was in the canoe I was surprised to find another poor creature lie there alive, bound hand and foot, as the Spaniard was, for the slaughter, and almost dead with fear, not knowing what the matter was; for he had not been able to look up over the side of the boat, he was tied so hard, neck and heels, and had been tied so long, that he had really but little life in him.

I immediately cut the twisted flags, or rushes, which they had bound him with, and would have helped him up; but he could not stand or speak, but groaned most piteously, believing, it seems still, that he was only unbound in order to be killed.

When Friday came to him, I bade him speak to him, and tell him of his deliverance, and pulling out my bottle, made him give the poor wretch a dram; which, with the news of his being delivered, revived him, and he sat up in the boat. But when Friday came to hear him speak, and look in his face, it would have moved anyone to tears to have seen how Friday kissed him, embraced him, hugged him, cried, laughed, hallooed, jumped about, danced, sung, then cried again, wrung his hands, beat his own face and head, and then sung and jumped about again like a distracted creature. It was a good while before I could make him speak to me, or tell me what was the matter; but when he came a little to himself, he told me that it was his father!

It is not easy for me to express how it moved me to see what ecstasy and filial affection had worked in this poor savage at the sight of his father, and of his being delivered from death; nor indeed can I describe half the extravagances of his affection after this—for he went into the boat and out of the boat a great many times. When he went in to him, he would sit down by him, open his breast, and hold his father's head close to his bosom half an hour together, to nourish it; then he took his arms and ankles, which were numbed and stiff with the binding, and chafed and rubbed them with his hands; and I perceiving what the case was, gave him some rum out of my bottle to rub them with, which did them a great deal of good.

This action put an end to our pursuit of the canoe with the other savages, who were now gotten almost out of sight. And it was happy for us that we did not; for it blew so hard within two hours after, and before they could be gotten a quarter of their way, and continued blowing so hard all night, and that from the north-west, which was against them, that I could not suppose their boat could live, or that they ever reached to their own coast.

But to return to Friday, he was so busy about his father that I could not find in my heart to take him off for some time. But after I thought he could leave him a little, I called him to me, and he came jumping and laughing and pleased to the highest extreme. Then I asked him if he had given his father any bread? He shook his head and said, "None. Ugly dog eat all up self." So I gave him a cake of bread out of a little pouch I carried on purpose; I also gave him a dram for himself, but he would not taste it, but carried it to his father. I had in my pocket also two or three bunches of my raisins, so I gave him a handful of them for his father. He had no sooner given his father these raisins but I saw him come out of the boat and run away as if he had been bewitched, he ran at such a rate—for he was the swiftest fellow of his foot that ever I saw; I say, he ran at such a rate that he was out of sight, as it were, in an instant; and though I called, and hallooed, too, after him, it was all one, away he went, and in a quarter of an hour I saw him come back again, though not so fast as he went, and as he came nearer, I found his pace was slacker because he had something in his hand.

When he came up to me, I found he had been quite home for an earthen jug or pot to bring his father some fresh water, and that he had got two more cakes or loaves of bread. The bread he gave me, but the water he carried to his father. However, as I was very thirsty too, I took a little sip of it. This water revived his father more than all the rum or spirits I had given him; for he was just fainting with thirst.

When his father had drunk, I called to him to know if there was any water left? He said "Yes;" and I bade him give it to the poor Spaniard, who was in as much want of it as his father; and I sent one of the cakes that Friday brought to the Spaniard too, who was indeed very weak, and was reposing himself upon a green place under the shade of a tree, and whose limbs were also very stiff and very much swelled with the rude bandage he had been tied with. When I saw that upon Friday's coming to him with the water, he sat up and drank, and took the bread and began to eat, I went to him and gave him a handful of raisins. He looked up in my face with all the tokens of gratitude and thankfulness that could appear in any countenance; but was so weak, notwithstanding he had so exerted himself in the fight, that he could not stand up upon his feet. He tried to do it two or three times, but was really not able, his ankles were so swelled and so painful to him; so I bade him sit still, and caused Friday to rub his ankles and bathe them with rum, as he had done his father's.

I observed the poor affectionate creature every two minutes, or perhaps less, all the while he was here, turned his head about, to see if his father was in the same place and posture as he left him sitting; and at last he found he was not to be seen; at which he started up, and without speaking a word, flew with that swiftness to him, that one could scarce perceive his feet to touch the ground as he went. But when he came, he only found he had laid himself down to ease his limbs; so Friday came back to me presently, and I then spoke to the Spaniard to let Friday help him up if he could, and lead him to the boat, and then he should carry him to our dwelling, where I would take care of him. But Friday, a lusty strong fellow, took the Spaniard quite up upon his back, and carried him away to the boat, and set him down softly upon the side or gunwale of the canoe, with his feet in the inside of it, and then lifted him quite in, and set him close to his father, and presently stepping out again, launched the boat off, and paddled it along the shore faster than I could walk, though the wind blew pretty hard too. So he brought them both safe into our creek; and leaving them in the boat, runs away to fetch the other canoe. And as he passed me I spoke to him, and asked him whither he went? He told me, "Go fetch more boat." So away he went like the wind, for sure never man or horse run like him; and he had the other canoe in the creek almost as soon as I got to it by land. So he wafted me over, and then went to help our new guests out of the boat, which he did. But they were neither of them able to walk, so that poor Friday knew not what to do.

To remedy this, I went to work in my thought, and calling to Friday to bid them sit down on the bank while he came to me, I soon made a kind of hand-barrow to lay them on, and Friday and I carried them up both together upon it between us. But when we got them to the outside of our wall or fortification, we were at a worse loss than before, for it was impossible to get them over; and I was resolved not to break it down. So I set to work again; and Friday and I, in about two hours' time, made a very handsome tent, covered with old sails, and above that with boughs of trees, being in the space without our outward fence, and between that and the grove of young wood which I had planted. And here we made them two beds of such things as I had; namely, of good rice-straw, with blankets laid upon it to lie on, and another to cover them on each bed.

§ *My island now peopled. My converse with the Spaniard. We make preparations for sending the Spaniard and Friday's father on a voyage to the mainland.*

My island was now peopled, and I thought myself very rich in subjects. And it was a merry reflection which I frequently made, how like a king I looked. First of all the whole country was my own mere property; so that I had an undoubted right of dominion. Secondly, my people were perfectly subjected; I was absolute lord and lawgiver; they all owed their lives to me, and were ready to lay down their lives, if there had been occasion of it, for me. It was remarkable, too, we had but three subjects, and they were of three different religions. My man Friday was a Protestant, his father was a Pagan and a cannibal, and the Spaniard was a Papist.

However, I allowed liberty of conscience throughout my dominions. But this is by the way.

As soon as I had secured my two weak rescued prisoners, and given them shelter and a place to rest them upon, I began to think of making some provision for them. And the first thing I did, I ordered Friday to take a yearling goat—betwixt a kid and a goat—out of my particular flock, to be killed, when I cut off the hinder quarter, and chopping it into small pieces, I set Friday to work to boiling and stewing, and made them a very good dish, I assure you, of flesh and broth, having put some barley and rice also into the broth; and as I cooked it without doors, for I made no fire within my inner wall, so I carried it all into the new tent; and having set a table there for them, I sat down and ate my own dinner also with them, and, as well as I could, cheered them and encouraged them; Friday being my interpreter, especially to his father, and indeed to the Spaniard too, for the Spaniard spoke the language of the savages pretty well.

After we had dined, or rather supped, I ordered Friday to take one of the canoes, and go and fetch our muskets and other firearms, which for want of time we had left upon the place of battle; and the next day I ordered him to go and bury the dead bodies of the savages, which lay open to the sun and would presently be offensive; and I also ordered him to bury the horrid remains of their barbarous feast, which I knew were pretty much, and which I could not think of doing myself; nay, I could not bear to see them if I went that way. All which he punctually performed, and effaced the very appearance of the savages being there; so that, when I went again, I could scarce know where it was, otherwise than by the corner of the wood pointing to the place.

I then began to enter into a little conversation with my two new subjects. And first I set Friday to inquire of his father what he thought of the escape of the savages in that canoe, and whether we might expect a return of them with a power too great for us to resist. His first opinion was, that the savages in the boat never could live out the storm which blew that night they went off, but must of necessity be drowned or driven south to those other shores where they were as sure to be devoured as they were to be drowned if they were cast away. But as to what they would do if they came safe on shore, he said he knew not; but it was his opinion that they were so dreadfully frighted with the manner of their being attacked—the noise and the fire—that he believed they would tell their people they were all killed by thunder and lightning, not by the hand of man; and that the two which appeared —namely, Friday and me—were two heavenly spirits or furies come down to destroy them, and not men with weapons. This he said he knew, because he heard them all cry out so in their language to one another; for it was impossible to them to conceive that a man could dart fire and speak thunder, and kill at a distance without lifting up the hand, as was done now. And this old savage was in the right; for, as I understood since by other hands, the savages never attempted to go over to the island afterwards; they were so terrified with the accounts given by those four men (for it seems they did escape the sea) that they believed whoever went to that enchanted island would be destroyed with fire from the gods!

This, however, I knew not, and therefore was under continual apprehensions for a good while, and kept always upon my guard, me and all my army; for as we were now four of us, I would have ventured upon a hundred of them fairly in the open field at any time.

In a little time, however, no more canoes appearing, the fear of their coming wore off, and I began to take my former thoughts of a voyage to the main into consideration, being likewise assured by Friday's father that I might depend upon good usage from their nation on his account, if I would go.

But my thoughts were a little suspended when I had a serious discourse with the Spaniard, and when I understood that there were sixteen more of his countrymen and Portuguese, who, having been cast away and made their escape to that side, lived there at peace indeed with the savages, but were very sore put to it for necessaries, and indeed for life. I asked him all the particulars of their voyage, and found they were a Spanish ship bound from the Rio de la Plata to the Havannah, being directed to leave their loading there, which was chiefly hides and silver, and to bring back what European goods they could meet with there; that they had five Portuguese seamen on board, who they took out of another wreck; that five of their own men were drowned when the first ship was lost, and that these escaped through infinite dangers and hazards, and arrived almost starved on the Cannibal coast, where they expected to have been devoured every moment.

He told me they had some arms with them, but they were perfectly useless, for that they had neither powder nor ball, the washing of the sea having spoiled all their powder but a little which they used at their first landing to provide themselves some food.

I asked him what he thought would become of them there, and if they had formed no design of making any escape? He said they had many consultations about it, but that having neither vessel nor tools to build one, nor provisions of any kind, their counsels always ended in tears and despair.

I asked him how he thought they would receive a proposal from me which might tend towards an escape? and whether, if they were all here, it might not be done? I told him with freedom I feared mostly their treachery and ill-usage of me if I put my life in their hands; for that gratitude was no inherent virtue in the nature of man; nor did men always square their dealings by the obligations they had received, so much as they did by the advantages they expected. I told him it would be very hard that I should be the instrument of their deliverance and that they should afterwards make me their prisoner in New Spain, where an Englishman was certain to be made a sacrifice, what necessity or what accident soever brought him thither; and that I had rather be delivered up to the savages and be devoured alive, than fall into the power of the Spaniards. I added, that otherwise I was persuaded, if they were all here, we might with so many hands build a bark large enough to carry us all away, either to the Brazils southward, or to the islands or Spanish coast northward; but that if in requital they should, when I had put weapons into their hands, carry me by force among their own people, I might be ill-used for my kindness to them, and make my case worse than it was before.

He answered, with a great deal of candour and ingenuity, that their condition was so miserable, and they were so sensible of it, that he believed they would abhor the thought of using any man unkindly that should contribute to their deliverance; and that if I pleased, he would go to them with the old man, and discourse with them about it, and return again, and bring me their answer, that he would make conditions with them upon their solemn oath, that they should be absolutely under my leading as their commander and captain; and that they should swear upon the holy sacraments and the gospel to be true to me, and go to such Christian country as that I should agree to, and no other; and to be directed wholly and absolutely by my orders, till they were landed safely in such country as I intended; and that he would bring a contract from them under their hands for that purpose.

Then he told me he would first swear to me himself, that he would never stir from me as long as he lived till I gave him orders; and that he would take my side to the last drop of his blood if there should happen the least breach of faith among his countrymen.

He told me they were all of them very civil, honest men, and they were under the greatest distress imaginable, having neither weapons nor clothes nor any food, but at the mercy and discretion of the savages; out of all hopes of ever returning to their own country; and that he was sure, if I would undertake their relief, they would live and die by me.

Upon these assurances, I resolved to venture to relieve them if possible, and to send the old savage and the Spaniard over to them to treat; but when we had gotten all things in a readiness to go, the Spaniard himself started an objection, which had so much prudence in it on one hand, and so much sincerity on the other hand, that I could not but be very well satisfied in it; and by his advice put off the deliverance of his comrades for at least half a year. The case was thus:—

He had been with us now about a month, during which time I had let him see in what manner I had provided, with the assistance of Providence, for my support; and he saw evidently what stock of corn and rice I had laid up, which, as it was more than sufficient for myself, so it was not sufficient, at least without good husbandry, for my family, now it was increased to number four. But much less would it be sufficient if his countrymen, who were, as he said, fourteen still alive, should come over. And least of all would it be sufficient to victual our vessel, if we should build one, for a voyage to any of the Christian colonies of America. So he told me he thought it would be more advisable to let him and the two other dig and cultivate some more land, as much as I could spare seed to sow; and that we should wait another harvest, that we might have a supply of corn for his

countrymen when they should come; for want might be a temptation
to them to disagree, or not to think themselves delivered otherwise
than out of one difficulty into another. "You know," says he, "the
children of Israel, though they rejoiced at first for their being delivered out of Egypt, yet rebelled even against God himself that delivered them, when they came to want bread in the wilderness."

His caution was so seasonable, and his advice so good, that I could
not but be very well pleased with his proposal, as well as I was satisfied with his fidelity. So we fell to digging, all four of us, as well as
the wooden tools we were furnished with permitted; and in about a
month's time, by the end of which it was seed-time, we had gotten
as much land cured and trimmed up as we sowed twenty-two bushels
of barley on and sixteen jars of rice—which was, in short, all the
seed we had to spare; nor, indeed, did we leave ourselves barely sufficient for our own food for the six months that we had to expect our
crop; that is to say reckoning from the time we set our seed aside for
sowing, for it is not to be supposed it is six months in the ground in
that country.

Having now society enough, and our number being sufficient to
put us out of fear of the savages if they had come, unless their number had been very great, we went freely all over the island wherever
we found occasion; and as here we had our escape or deliverance
upon our thoughts, it was impossible, at least for me, to have the
means of it out of mine. To this purpose I marked out several trees
which I thought fit for our work, and I set Friday and his father to
cutting them down; and then I caused the Spaniard, to whom I im-
parted my thought on that affair, to oversee and direct their work. I
showed them with what indefatigable pains I had hewed a large tree
into single planks, and I caused them to do the like, till they had made
about a dozen large planks of good oak, near two foot broad, thirty-
five foot long, and from two inches to four inches thick. What
prodigious labour it took up, any one may imagine.

At the same time I contrived to increase my little flock of tame
goats as much as I could, and to this purpose I made Friday and the
Spaniard go out one day, and myself with Friday the next day; for

we took our turns: and by this means we got above twenty young kids to breed up with the rest; for whenever we shot the dam, we saved the kids, and added them to our flock. But above all, the season for curing the grapes coming on, I caused such a prodigious quantity to be hung up in the sun, that I believe had we been at Alicant, where the raisins of the sun are cured, we could have filled sixty or eighty barrels. And these with our bread was a great part of our food; and very good living too, I assure you, for it is an exceeding nourishing food.

It was now harvest, and our crop in good order. It was not the most plentiful increase I had seen in the island, but however it was enough to answer our end; for from our twenty-two bushels of barley we brought in and thrashed out above two hundred and twenty bushels, and the like in proportion of the rice; which was store enough for our food to the next harvest, though all the sixteen Spaniards had been on shore with me; or if we had been ready for a voyage, it would very plentifully have victualled our ship to have carried us to any part of the world—that is to say, of America.

When we had thus housed and secured our magazine of corn, we fell to work to make more wicker-work, namely, great baskets in which we kept it; and the Spaniard was very handy and dexterous at this part, and often blamed me that I did not make some things for defence of this kind of work; but I saw no need of it.

And now having a full supply of food for all the guests I expected, I gave the Spaniard leave to go over to the main to see what he could do with those he had left behind him there. I gave him a strict charge in writing not to bring any man with him who would not first swear in the presence of himself and of the old savage, that he would no way injure, fight with, or attack the person he should find in the island, who was so kind to send for them in order to their deliverance; but that they would stand by and defend him against all such attempts, and wherever they went would be entirely under and subjected to his commands; and that this should be put in writing, and signed with their hands. How we were to have this done, when I knew they had neither pen or ink—that indeed was a question which we never asked.

244

Under these instructions, the Spaniard and the old savage, the father of Friday, went away in one of the canoes which they might be said to come in, or rather were brought in, when they came as prisoners to be devoured by the savages.

I gave each of them a musket with a firelock on it, and about eight charges of powder and ball, charging them to be very good husbands of both, and not to use either of them but upon urgent occasion.

This was a cheerful work, being the first measures used by me in view of my deliverance for now twenty-seven years and some days. I gave them provisions of bread and of dried grapes sufficient for themselves for many days, and sufficient for all their countrymen for about eighty days' time; and wishing them a good voyage, I see them go, agreeing with them about a signal they should hang out at their return, by which I should know them again when they came back at a distance before they came on shore.

They went away with a fair gale on the day that the moon was at full by my account, in the month of October. But as for an exact reckoning of days, after I had once lost it, I could never recover it again; nor had I kept even the number of years so punctually as to be sure that I was right, though, as it proved when I afterwards examined my account, I found I had kept a true reckoning of years.

§ *A ship appears off the island. The captain and two others landed as prisoners. We attack and overcome the mutinous crew. The ship secured.*

It was no less than eight days I waited for them, when a strange and unforeseen accident intervened, of which the like has not perhaps been heard of in history. I was fast asleep in my hutch one morning, when my man Friday came running in to me and called aloud, "Master, master, they are come, they are come!"

I jumped up, and regardless of danger, I went out as soon as I could get my clothes on, through my little grove, which by the way, was by this time grown to be a very thick wood. I say, regardless of danger, I went without my arms, which was not my custom to do; but I was surprised, when, turning my eyes to the sea, I presently saw a boat at about a league and a half's distance, standing in for the shore with a shoulder-of-mutton sail, as they call it; and the wind blowing pretty fair to bring them in; also I observed, presently, that they did not come from that side which the shore lay on, but from the southernmost end of the island. Upon this I called Friday in, and bid him lie close, for these were not the people we looked for, and that we might not know yet whether they were friends or enemies.

In the next place, I went in to fetch my perspective-glass to see what I could make of them; and having taken the ladder out, I climbed up to the top of the hill, as I used to do when I was apprehensive of anything, and to take my view the plainer without being discovered.

I had scarce set my foot on the hill, when my eye plainly discovered a ship lying at an anchor, at about two leagues and a half's distance from me south-south-east, but not above a league and a half from the shore. By my observation it appeared plainly to be an English ship, and the boat appeared to be an English long-boat.

I cannot express the confusion I was in, though the joy of seeing a ship, and one who I had reason to believe was manned by my own countrymen and consequently friends, was such as I cannot describe. But yet I had some secret doubts hung about me, I cannot tell from whence they came, bidding me keep upon my guard. In the first place, it occurred to me to consider what business an English ship could have in that part of the world, since it was not the way to or from any part of the world where the English had any traffic, and I knew there had been no storms to drive them in there as in distress; and that if they were English really, it was most probable that they were here upon no good design, and that I had better continue as I was then fall into the hands of thieves and murderers.

Let no man despise the secret hints and notices of danger, which sometimes are given him when he may think there is no possibility of its being real. That such hints and notices are given us, I believe few that have made any observations of things can deny; that they are

246

certain discoveries of an invisible world, and a converse of spirits, we cannot doubt; and if the tendency of them seems to be to warn us of danger, why should we not suppose they are from some friendly agent —whether supreme, or inferior and subordinate, is not the question; and that they are given for our good?

The present question abundantly confirms me in the justice of this reasoning; for had I not been made cautious by this secret admonition, come it from whence it will, I had been undone inevitably, and in a far worse condition than before, as you will see presently.

I had not kept myself long in this posture, but I saw the boat draw near the shore, as if they looked for a creek to thrust in at for the convenience of landing. However, as they did not come quite far enough, they did not see the little inlet where I formerly landed my rafts, but run their boat on shore upon the shore, at about half a mile from me; which was very happy for me, for otherwise they would have landed just, as I may say, at my door, and would soon have beaten me out of my castle, and perhaps have plundered me of all I had.

When they were on shore, I was fully satisfied that they were Englishmen, at least most of them. One or two I thought were Dutch; but it did not prove so. They were in all eleven men, whereof three of them I found were unarmed, and, as I thought, bound; and when the first four or five of them were jumped on shore they took these three out of the boat as prisoners. One of the three I could perceive using the most passionate gestures of entreaty, affliction, and despair, even to a kind of extravagance; the other two, I could perceive, lifted up their hands sometimes, and appeared concerned indeed, but not to such a degree as the first.

I was perfectly confounded at the sight, and knew not what the meaning of it should be. Friday called out to me in English as well as he could, "O master! you see English mans eat prisoner as well as savage mans,"—"Why," says I, "Friday, do you think they are a-going to eat them, then?"—"Yes," says Friday, "they will eat them."—"No, no," says I, "Friday; I am afraid they will murder them, indeed, but you may be sure they will not eat them."

All this while I had no thought of what the matter really was, but stood trembling with the horror of the sight, expecting every moment when the three prisoners should be killed; nay, once I saw one of the villains lift up his arm with a great cutlass, as the seamen call it, or sword, to strike one of the poor men; and I expected to see him fall every moment, at which all the blood in my body seemed to run chill in my veins.

I wished heartily now for my Spaniard, and the savage that was gone with him, or that I had any way to have come undiscovered within shot of them, that I might have rescued the three men, for I saw no firearms they had among them; but it fell out to my mind another way.

After I had observed the outrageous usage of the three men by the insolent seamen, I observed the fellows run scattering about the land, as if they wanted to see the country. I observed that the three other men had liberty to go also where they pleased; but they sat down all three upon the ground, very pensive, and looked like men in despair.

This put me in mind of the first time when I came on shore and began to look about me; how I gave myself over for lost; how wildly I looked round me; what dreadful apprehensions I had; and how I lodged in the tree all night for fear of being devoured by wild beasts.

As I knew nothing that night of the supply I was to receive by the providential driving of the ship nearer the land by the storms and tide, by which I have since been so long nourished and supported; so these three poor desolate men knew nothing how certain of deliverance and supply they were, how near it was to them, and how effectually and really they were in a condition of safety, at the same time that they thought themselves lost, and their case desperate.

So little do we see before us in the world, and so much reason have we to depend cheerfully upon the great Maker of the world, that He does not leave His creatures so absolutely destitute, but that in the worst circumstances they have always something to be thankful for, and sometimes are nearer their deliverance than they imagine;

as I did. I came as near them undiscovered as I could, and then, before any of them saw me, I called aloud to them in Spanish, "What are ye, gentlemen?"

They started up at the noise, but were ten times more confounded when they saw me, and the uncouth figure that I made. They made no answer at all, but I thought I perceived them just going to fly from me, when I spoke to them in English. "Gentlemen," said I, "do not be surprised at me; perhaps you may have a friend near you when you did not expect it."—"He must be sent directly from heaven then," said one of them very gravely to me, and pulling off his hat at the same time to me, "for our condition is past the help of man."— "All help is from heaven, sir," said I; "but can you put a stranger in the way how to help you, for you seem to me to be in some great distress? I saw you when you landed; and when you seemed to make applications to the brutes that came with you, I saw one of them lift up his sword to kill you."

The poor man, with tears running down his face, and trembling, looking like one astonished, returned, "Am I talking to God or man? Is it a real man or an angel?"—"Be in no fear about that, sir," said I; "if God had sent an angel to relieve you, He would have come better clothed, and armed after another manner than you see me in. Pray lay aside your fears; I am a man, an Englishman, and disposed to assist you, you see. I have one servant only; we have arms and ammunition; tell us freely. Can we serve you? What is your case?"

"Our case," said he, "sir, is too long to tell you while our murderers are so near; but in short, sir, I was commander of that ship; my men have mutinied against me; they have been hardly prevailed on not to murder me, and at last have set me on shore in this desolate place, with these two men with me; one my mate, the other a passenger, where we expected to perish, believing the place to be uninhabited, and know not yet what to think of it."

"Where are those brutes, your enemies?" said I; "do you know where they are gone?"—"There they lie, sir," said he, pointing to a thicket of trees. "My heart trembles for fear they have seen us and heard you speak; if they have, they will certainly murder us all."

"Have they any firearms?" said I. He answered they had only two pieces, and one which they left in the boat. "Well then," said I, "leave the rest to me; I see they are all asleep; it is an easy thing to kill them all; but shall we rather take them prisoners?" He told me there were two desperate villains among them that it was scarce safe to show any mercy to; but if they were secured, he believed all the rest would return to their duty. I asked him which they were. He told me he could not at that distance describe them; but he would obey my orders in anything I would direct. "Well," says I, "let us retreat out of their view or hearing, lest they awake, and we will resolve further;" so they willingly went back with me, till the woods covered us from them.

"Look you, sir," said I, "if I venture upon your deliverance, are you willing to make two conditions with me?" He anticipated my proposals by telling me that both he and the ship, if recovered, should be wholly directed and commanded by me in everything; and if the ship was not recovered, he would live and die with me in what part of the world soever I would send him; and the two other men said the same.

"Well," says I, "my conditions are but two. 1. That while you stay on this island with me you will not pretend to any authority here; and if I put arms into your hands, you will upon all occasions give them up to me, and do no prejudice to me or mine upon this island, and in the meantime be governed by my orders.

2. "That if the ship is, or may be recovered, you will carry me and my man to England passage free."

He gave me all the assurance that the invention and faith of man could devise, that he would comply with these most reasonable demands, and besides would owe his life to me, and acknowledge it upon all occasions as long as he lived.

"Well, then," said I, "here are three muskets for you, with powder and ball; tell me next what you think is proper to be done." He showed all the testimony of his gratitude that he was able; but offered to be wholly guided by me. I told him I thought it was hard venturing anything; but the best method I could think of was to fire upon them at once as they lay; and if any was not killed at the first volley, and offered to submit, we might save them, and so put it wholly upon God's providence to direct the shot.

He said very modestly, that he was loath to kill them if he could help it, but that those two were incorrigible villains, and had been the authors of all the mutiny in the ship, and if they escaped we should be undone still; for they would go on board and bring the whole ship's company, and destroy us all. "Well then," says I, "necessity legitimates my advice, for it is the only way to save our lives." However, seeing him still cautious of shedding blood, I told him they should go themselves, and manage as they found convenient.

In the middle of this discourse we heard some of them awake, and soon after we saw two of them on their feet. I asked him if either of them were of the men who he had said were the heads of the mutiny? He said, "No." "Well, then," said I, "you may let them escape; and Providence seems to have wakened them on purpose to save themselves. Now," says I, "if the rest escape you, it is your fault."

Animated with this, he took the musket I had given him in his hand, and a pistol in his belt, and his two comrades with him, with each man a piece in his hand. The two men who were with him, going first, made some noise, at which one of the seamen who was awake turned about, and seeing them coming, cried out to the rest. But it was too late then; for the moment he cried out, they fired—I mean the two men, the captain wisely reserving his own piece. They had so well aimed their shot at the men they knew, that one of them was killed on the spot, and the other very much wounded; but not being dead, he started up upon his feet, and called eagerly for help to the other; but the captain, stepping to him, told him it was too late to cry for help, he should call upon God to forgive his villainy, and with that word knocked him down with the stock of his musket, so that he never spoke more. There were three more in the company, and one of them was also slightly wounded. By this time I was come, and when they saw their danger, and that it was in vain to resist, they begged for mercy. The captain told them he would spare their lives, if they would give him any assurance of their abhorrence of the treachery they had been guilty of, and would swear to be faithful to him in recovering the ship, and afterwards in carrying her back to Jamaica, from whence they came. They gave him all the protestations of their sincerity that could be desired, and he was willing to believe them and spare their lives, which I was not against; only I obliged him to keep them bound hand and foot while they were upon the island.

While this was doing, I sent Friday with the captain's mate to the boat, with orders to secure her and bring away the oars and sail; which they did. And by and by, three straggling men, that were (happily for them) parted from the rest, came back upon hearing the guns fired; and seeing their captain, who before was their prisoner, now their conqueror, they submitted to be bound also, and so our victory was complete.

It now remained that the captain and I should inquire into one another's circumstances. I began first, and told him my whole history, which he heard with an attention even to amazement; and particularly at the wonderful manner of my being furnished with provisions and ammunition. And, indeed, as my story is a whole collection of wonders, it affected him deeply. But when he reflected from thence upon himself, and how I seemed to have been preserved there on purpose to save his life, the tears ran down his face, and he could not speak a word more.

After this communication was at an end I carried him and his two men into my apartment, leading them in just where I came out, namely, at the top of the house; where I refreshed them with such provisions as I had, and showed them all the contrivances I had made during my long, long inhabiting that place.

All I showed them, all I said to them, was perfectly amazing; but above all, the captain admired my fortification, and how perfectly I had concealed my retreat with a grove of trees, which, having been now planted near twenty years, and the trees growing much faster than in England, was become a little wood, and so thick, that it was unpassable in any part of it but at that one side where I had reserved my little winding passage into it. I told him this was my castle and my residence, but that I had a seat in the country, as most princes have, whither I could retreat upon occasion, and I would show him that too another time, but at present our business was to consider how to recover the ship. He agreed with me as to that, but told me he was perfectly at a loss what measures to take; for that there were still six-and-twenty hands on board, who, having entered into a cursed conspiracy, by which they had all forfeited their lives to the law, would be hardened in it now by desperation, and would carry it on, knowing that if they were reduced they should be brought to the gallows as soon as they came to England, or to any of the English colonies; and that therefore there would be no attacking them with so small a number as we were.

I mused for some time upon what he had said, and found it was a very rational conclusion; and that therefore something was to be resolved on very speedily; as well to draw the men on board into some snare for their surprise as to prevent their landing upon us and destroying us. Upon this it presently occurred to me that in a little while the ship's crew, wondering what was become of their comrades and of the boat, would certainly come on shore in their other boat to see for them, and that then perhaps they might come armed, and be too strong for us. This he allowed was rational.

Upon this I told him the first thing we had to do was to stave the boat which lay upon the beach, so that they might not carry her off; and taking everything out of her, leave her so far useless as not to be fit to swim. Accordingly we went on board, took the arms which were left on board out of her, and whatever else we found there, which was a bottle of brandy and another of rum, a few biscuit cakes, a horn of powder, and a great lump of sugar in a piece of canvas—the sugar was five or six pounds; all which was very welcome to me, especially the brandy and sugar, of which I had had none left for many years.

When we had carried all these things on shore (the oars, mast, sail, and rudder of the boat, were carried away before, as above), we knocked a great hole in her bottom, that if they had come strong enough to master us, yet they could not carry off the boat.

Indeed it was not much in my thoughts that we could be able to recover the ship; but my view was, that if they went away without the boat, I did not much question to make her fit again to carry us away to the Leeward Islands, and call upon our friends the Spaniards, in my way, for I had them still in my thoughts.

While we were thus preparing our designs, and had first by main strength heaved the boat up upon the beach, so high that the tide would not float her off at high-water mark; and besides, had broke a hole in her bottom too big to be quickly stopped, and were sat down musing what we should do; we heard the ship fire a gun, and saw her make a waft with her ancient, as a signal for the boat to come on board; but no boat stirred; and they fired several times, making other signals for the boat.

At last, when all their signals and firings proved fruitless, and they found the boat did not stir, we saw them, by the help of my glasses, hoist another boat out, and row towards the shore; and we found as they approached that there was no less than ten men in her, and that they had firearms with them.

As the ship lay almost two leagues from the shore, we had a full view of them as they came, and a plain sight of the men, even of their faces; because the tide having set them a little to the east of the other boat, they rowed up under shore to come to the same place where the other had landed, and where the boat lay.

By this means, I say, we had a full view of them, and the captain knew the persons and characters of all the men in the boat, of whom he said that there were three very honest fellows, who, he was sure, were led into this conspiracy by the rest, being overpowered and frighted.

But that as for the boatswain, who it seems was the chief officer among them, and all the rest, they were as outrageous as any of the ship's crew, and were no doubt made desperate in their new enterprise; and terribly apprehensive he was that they would be too powerful for us.

I smiled at him, and told him that men in our circumstances were past the operation of fear: that seeing almost every condition that could be was better than that which we were supposed to be in, we ought to expect that the consequence, whether death or life, would be sure to be a deliverance. I asked him what he thought of the circumstances of my life, and whether a deliverance were not worth venturing for? "And where, sir," said I, "is your belief of my being preserved here on purpose to save your life, which elevated you a little while ago? For my part," said I, "there seems to be but one thing amiss in all the prospect of it." "What's that?" says he. "Why," said I, " 'tis that, as you say, there are three or four honest fellows among them, which should be spared. Had they been all of the wicked part of the crew, I should have thought God's providence had singled them out to deliver them into your hands; for, depend upon it, every man of them that comes ashore are our own, and shall die or live as they behave to us."

As I spoke this with a raised voice and cheerful countenance, I found it greatly encouraged him; so we set vigorously to our business. We had upon the first appearance of the boat's coming from the ship considered of separating our prisoners, and had indeed secured them effectually.

Two of them, of whom the captain was less assured than ordinary, I sent with Friday, and one of the three (delivered men) to my cave, where they were remote enough, and out of danger of being heard or discovered, or of finding their way out of the woods if they could have delivered themselves. Here they left them bound, but gave them provisions, and promised them if they continued there quietly, to give them their liberty in a day or two; but that if they attempted their escape, they should be put to death without mercy. They promised faithfully to bear their confinement with patience, and were very thankful that they had such good usage as to have provisions and a light left them; for Friday gave them candles (such as we made ourselves) for their comfort; and they did not know but that he stood sentinel over them at the entrance.

The other prisoners had better usage. Two of them were kept pinioned indeed, because the captain was not free to trust them, but the other two were taken into my service upon their captain's recommendation, and upon their solemnly engaging to live and die with us. So with them and the three honest men, we were seven men, well armed; and I made no doubt we should be able to deal well enough with the ten that were a-coming, considering that the captain had said there were three or four honest men among them also.

As soon as they got to the place where their other boat lay, they run their boat into the beach, and came all on shore, haling the boat up after them; which I was glad to see, for I was afraid they would rather have left the boat at an anchor some distance from the shore, with some hands in her to guard her, and so we should not be able to seize the boat.

Being on shore, the first thing they did, they ran all to their other boat; and it was easy to see that they were under a great surprise to find her stripped, as above, of all that was in her, and a great hole in her bottom.

After they had mused a while upon this, they set up two or three great shouts, hallooing with all their might, to try if they could make their companions hear; but all was to no purpose. Then they came all close in a ring, and fired a volley of their small arms; which indeed we heard, and the echoes made the woods ring, but it was all one; those in the cave, we were sure, could not hear; and those in our keeping, though they heard it well enough yet durst give no answer to them.

They were so astonished at the surprise of this, that, as they told us afterwards, they resolved to go all on board again to their ship, and let them know there that the men were all murdered, and the long-boat staved. Accordingly, they immediately launched their boat again, and gat all of them on board.

The captain was terribly amazed, and even confounded at this, believing they would go on board the ship again, and set sail, giving their comrades up for lost, and so he should still lose the ship, which he was in hopes we should have recovered. But he was quickly as much frighted the other way.

They had not been long put off with the boat, but we perceived them all coming on shore again; but with this new measure in their conduct, which it seems they consulted together upon—namely, to leave three men in the boat, and the rest to go on shore, and go up into the country to look for their fellows.

This was a great disappointment to us; for now we were at a loss what to do: for our seizing those seven men on shore would be no advantage to us if we let the boat escape; because they would then row away to the ship, and then the rest of them would be sure to weigh and set sail, and so our recovering the ship would be lost.

However, we had no remedy but to wait and see what the issue of things might present. The seven men came on shore, and the three who remained in the boat put her off to a good distance from the shore, and came to an anchor to wait for them; so that it was impossible for us to come at them in the boat.

Those that came on shore kept close together, marching towards the top of the little hill under which my habitation lay; and we could see them plainly, though they could not preceive us. We could have been very glad they would have come nearer to us, so that we might have fired at them, or that they would have gone farther off, that we might have come abroad.

But when they were come to the brow of the hill, where they could

see a great way into the valleys and woods which lay towards the north-east part, and where the island lay lowest, they shouted and hallooed till they were weary; and not caring, it seems, to venture far from the shore, nor far from one another, they sat down together under a tree to consider of it. Had they thought fit to have gone to sleep there, as the other party of them had done, they had done the job for us; but they were too full of apprehensions of danger to venture to go to sleep, though they could not tell what the danger was they had to fear neither.

The captain made a very just proposal to me upon this consultation of theirs, namely, that perhaps they would all fire a volley again, to endeavour to make their fellows hear, and that we should all sally upon them just at the juncture when their pieces were all discharged, and they would certainly yield, and we should have them without bloodshed. I liked the proposal provided it was done while we were near enough to come up to them before they could load their pieces again.

But this event did not happen, and we lay still a long time very irresolute what course to take. At length I told them there would be nothing to be done in my opinion till night, and then, if they did not return to the boat, perhaps we might find a way to get between them and the shore, and so might use some stratagem with them in the boat to get them on shore.

We waited a great while, though very impatient for their removing; and were very uneasy when, after long consultations, we saw them start all up and march down towards the sea. It seems they had such dreadful apprehensions upon them of the danger of the place, that they resolved to go on board the ship again, give their companions over for lost, and so go on with their intended voyage with the ship.

As soon as I perceived them go towards the shore, I imagined it to be, as it really was, that they had given over their search, and were for going back again; and the captain, as soon as I told him my thoughts, was ready to sink at the apprehensions of it; but I presently thought of a stratagem to fetch them back again, and which answered my end to a tittle.

I ordered Friday and the captain's mate to go over the little creek westward, towards the place where the savages came on shore when Friday was rescued; and as soon as they came to a little rising ground, at about half a mile distance, I bade them halloo as loud as they could, and wait till they found the seamen heard them; that as soon as ever they heard the seamen answer them they should return it again; and then, keeping out of sight, take a round, always answering when the other hallooed, to draw them as far into the island, and among the woods, as possible; and then wheel about again to me by such ways as I directed them.

They were just going into the boat when Friday and the mate hallooed; and they presently heard them, and answering, run along the shore westward, towards the voice they heard, when they were presently stopped by the creek, where the water being up, they could not get over, and called for the boat to come up and set them over, as indeed I expected.

When they had set themselves over, I observed that the boat, being gone up a good way into the creek, and, as it were, in a harbour within the land, they took one of the three men out of her to go along with them, and left only two in the boat, having fastened her to the stump of a little tree on the shore.

This was what I wished for, and immediately leaving Friday and the captain's mate to their business, I took the rest with me, and crossing the creek out of their sight, we surprised the two men before they were aware; one of them lying on shore, and the other being in the boat. The fellow on shore was between sleeping and waking, and going to start up, the captain, who was foremost, ran in upon him, and knocked him down, and then called out to him in the boat to yield, or he was a dead man.

There needed very few arguments to persuade a single man to yield when he saw five men upon him, and his comrade knocked down; besides, this was, it seems, one of the three who were not so hearty in the mutiny as the rest of the crew, and therefore was easily persuaded not only to yield, but afterwards to join very sincerely with us. In the meantime Friday and the captain's mate so well managed their business with the rest, that they drew them, by hallooing and answering, from one hill to another, and from one wood to another, till they not only heartily tired them, but left them where they were very sure they could not reach back to the boat before it was dark; and indeed they were heartily tired themselves also by the time they came back to us.

We had nothing now to do but to watch for them in the dark, and to fall upon them, so as to make sure work with them.

It was several hours after Friday came back to me before they came back to their boat: and we could hear the foremost of them long before they came quite up, calling to those behind to come along; and could also hear them answer and complain how lame and tired they were, and not able to come any faster—which was very welcome news to us.

At length they came up to the boat; but 'tis impossible to express their confusion when they found the boat fast aground in the creek, the tide ebbed out, and their two men gone! We could hear them call to one another in a most lamentable manner, telling one another they were gotten into an enchanted island: that either there were inhabitants in it, and they should all be murdered; or else there were devils and spirits in it, and they should be all carried away and devoured.

They hallooed again, and called their two comrades by their names a great many times; but no answer. After some time we could see them, by the little light there was, run about wringing their hands like men in despair; and that sometimes they would go and sit down in the boat to rest themselves, then come ashore again and walk about again, and so the same thing over again.

My men would fain have me give them leave to fall upon them at once in the dark; but I was willing to take them at some advantage so to spare them, and kill as few of them as I could; and especially I was unwilling to hazard the killing any of our own men, knowing the other were very well armed. I resolved to wait to see if they did not separate; and therefore to make sure of them, I drew my ambuscade nearer, and ordered Friday and the captain to creep upon their hands and feet as close to the ground as they could, that they might not be discovered, and get as near them as they could possibly, before they offered to fire.

They had not been long in that posture but that the boatswain, who was the principal ringleader of the mutiny, and had now shown himself the most dejected and dispirited of all the rest, came walking towards them with two more of their crew. The captain was so eager, as having this principal rogue so much in his power, that he could hardly have patience to let him come so near as to be sure of him; for they only heard his tongue before. But when they came nearer, the captain and Friday starting up on their feet, let fly at them.

The boatswain was killed upon the spot, the next man was shot into the body, and fell just by him, though he did not die till an hour or two after; and the third run for it.

At the noise of the fire I immediately advanced with my whole army, which was now eight men, namely myself *generalissimo*, Friday my lieutenant-general, the captain and his two men, and the three prisoners of war, whom we had trusted with arms.

We came upon them indeed in the dark, so that they could not see our number; and I made the man we had left in the boat, who was now one of us, call to them by name, to try if I could bring them to a parley, and so might perhaps reduce them to terms; which fell out just as we desired. For indeed it was easy to think, as their condition then was, they would be very willing to capitulate. So he calls out as loud as he could to one of them, "Tom Smith, Tom Smith." Tom Smith answered immediately, "Who's that, Robinson?" for it seems he knew his voice. The other answered, "Ay, ay; for God's sake, Tom Smith, throw down your arms and yield, or you are all dead men this moment."

"Who must we yield to? where are they?" says Smith again. "Here they are," says he; "here's our captain, and fifty men with him, have been hunting you this two hours; the boatswain is killed, Will Frye is wounded, and I am a prisoner; and if you do not yield, you are all lost."

"Will they give us quarter, then," says Tom Smith, "and we will yield?" "I'll go and ask, if you promise to yield," says Robinson. So he asked the captain, and the captain then calls himself out, "You, Smith, you know my voice, if you lay down your arms immediately and submit, you shall have your lives—all but Will Atkins."

Upon this Will Atkins cried out, "For God's sake, captain, give me quarter; what have I done? They have been all as bad as I;"—which, by the way, was not true neither; for it seems this Will Atkins was the first man that laid hold of the captain when they first mutinied, and used him barbarously, in tying his hands, and giving him injurious language. However, the captain told him he must lay down his arms at discretion, and trust to the governor's mercy; by which he meant me, for they all called me governor.

In a word, they all laid down their arms, and begged their lives; and I sent the man that had parleyed with them, and two more, who bound them all; and then my great army of fifty men, which particularly with those three, were all but eight, came up and seized upon them all, and upon their boat—only that I kept myself and one more out of sight, for reasons of state.

Our next work was to repair the boat, and think of seizing the ship; and as for the captain, now he had leisure to parley with them, he expostulated with them upon the villainy of their practices with him, and at length upon the further wickedness of their design, and how certainly it must bring them to misery and distress in the end, and perhaps to the gallows.

They all appeared very penitent, and begged hard for their lives. As for that, he told them, they were none of his prisoners, but the commander of the island; that they thought they had set him on shore in a barren uninhabited island, but it had pleased God so to direct them, that the island was inhabited, and that the governor was an Englishman: that he might hang them all there if he pleased; but as he had given them all quarter, he supposed he would send them to England to be dealt with there, as justice required—except Atkins, who he was commanded by the governor to advise to prepare for death, for that he would be hanged in the morning.

Though this was all a fiction of his own, yet it had its desired effect. Atkins fell upon his knees to beg the captain to intercede with the governor for his life; and all the rest begged of him for God's sake that they might not be sent to England.

It now occurred to me that the time of our deliverance was come, and that it would be a most easy thing to bring these fellows in to be hearty in getting possession of the ship; so I retired in the dark from them, that they might not see what kind of a governor they had, and called the captain to me. When I called, as at a good distance, one of the men was ordered to speak again, and say to the captain, "Captain, the commander calls for you." And presently the captain replied, "Tell his excellency I am just a-coming." This more perfectly amazed them; and they all believed that the commander was just by with his fifty men.

Upon the captain's coming to me I told him my project for seizing the ship, which he liked of wonderfully well, and resolved to put it in execution the next morning.

But in order to execute it with more art, and secure of success, I told him we must divide the prisoners, and that he should go and take Atkins and two more of the worst of them, and send them pinioned to the cave where the others lay. This was committed to Friday and the two men who came on shore with the captain.

They conveyed them to the cave, as to a prison; and it was indeed a dismal place, especially to men in their condition.

The other I ordered to my bower, as I called it, of which I have given a full description; and as it was fenced in, and they pinioned, the place was secure enough, considering they were upon their behaviour.

To these in the morning I sent the captain, who was to enter into a parley with them; in a word, to try them, and tell me whether he thought they might be trusted or no to go on board and surprise the ship. He talked to them of the injury done him, of the condition they were brought to; and that though the governor had given them quarter for their lives as to the present action, yet that if they were sent to England they would all be hanged in chains, to be sure; but that if they would join in so just an attempt as to recover the ship, he would have the governor's engagement for their pardon.

Any one may guess how readily such a proposal would be accepted by men in their condition. They fell down on their knees to the captain, and promised, with the deepest imprecations, that they would be faithful to him to the last drop, and that they should owe their lives to him, and would go with him all over the world; that they would own him for a father to them as long as they lived.

"Well," says the captain, "I must go and tell the governor what you say, and see what I can do to bring him to consent to it." So he brought me an account of the temper he found them in, and that he verily believed they would be faithful.

However, that we might be very secure, I told him he should go back again, and choose out five of them, and tell them they might see that he did not want men, that he would take out those five to be his assistants, and that the governor would keep the other two, and the three that were sent prisoners to the castle (my cave) as hostages, for the fidelity of those five; and that if they proved unfaithful in the execution, the five hostages should be hanged in chains alive upon the shore.

This looked severe, and convinced them that the governor was in earnest. However, they had no way left them but to accept it; and it was now the business of the prisoners, as much as of the captain, to persuade the other five to do their duty.

Our strength was now thus ordered for the expedition: 1. The captain, his mate, and passenger; 2. Then the two prisoners of the first gang, to whom, having their characters from the captain, I had given their liberty, and trusted them with arms; 3. The other two who I had kept till now in my bower pinioned, but upon the captain's motion had now released; 4. These five released at last: so that they were twelve in all, besides five we kept prisoners in the cave for hostages.

I asked the captain if he was willing to venture with these hands on board the ship; for as for me and my man Friday, I did not think it was proper for us to stir, having seven men left behind, and it was employment enough for us to keep them asunder and supply them with victuals.

As to the five in the cave, I resolved to keep them fast, but Friday went in twice a day to them to supply them with necessaries; and I made the other two carry provisions to a certain distance, where Friday was to take it.

When I showed myself to the two hostages, it was with the captain, who told them I was the person the governor had ordered to look after them, and that it was the governor's pleasure they should not stir anywhere but by my direction; that if they did, they should be fetched into the castle and be laid in irons. So that as we never suffered them to see me as governor, so I now appeared as another person, and spoke of the governor, the garrison, the castle, and the like, upon all occasions.

The captain now had no difficulty before him but to furnish his two boats, stop the breach of one, and man them. He made his passenger captain of one, with four other men; and himself, and his mate and five more, went in the other. And they contrived their business very well, for they came up to the ship about midnight. As soon as they came within call of the ship, he made Robinson hail them, and tell them they had brought off the men and the boat, but that it was a long time before they had found them, and the like, holding them in a chat till they came to the ship's side; when the captain and the mate, entering first with their arms, immediately knocked down the second mate and carpenter with the butt-end of their muskets. Being very faithfully seconded by their men, they secured all the rest that were upon the main and quarter-decks, and began to fasten the hatches to keep them down who were below, when the other boat and their men, entering at the fore-chains, secured the forecastle of the ship, and the scuttle which went down into the cook-room, making three men they found there prisoners.

When this was done, and all safe upon deck, the captain ordered the mate with three men to break into the round-house where the new rebel captain lay, and having taken the alarm, was gotten up, and with two men and a boy had gotten firearms in their hands; and when the mate with a crow split open the door, the new captain and his men fired boldly among them, and wounded the mate with a musket ball, which broke his arm, and wounded two more of the men, but killed nobody.

The mate, calling for help, rushed however into the round-house, wounded as he was, and with his pistol shot the new captain through the head, the bullet entering at his mouth and came out again behind one of his ears, so that he never spoke a word; upon which the rest yielded, and the ship was taken effectually, without any more lives lost. As soon as the ship was thus secured, the captain ordered seven guns to be fired, which was the signal agreed upon with me to give me notice of his success; which, you may be sure, I was very glad to hear, having sat watching upon the shore for it till near two of the clock in the morning.

Having thus heard the signal plainly, I laid me down; and it having been a day of great fatigue to me, I slept very sound, till I was something surprised with the noise of a gun; and presently starting up, I heard a man call be by the name of "Governor, governor;" and presently I knew the captain's voice, when climbing up to the top of the hill, there he stood, and pointing to the ship he embraced me in his arms. "My dear friend and deliverer," says he, "there's your ship; for she is all yours, and so are we and all that belong to her." I cast my eyes to the ship, and there she rode within little more than half a mile of the shore; for they had weighed her anchor as soon as they were masters of her, and the weather being fair, had brought her to an anchor just against the mouth of the little creek; and the tide being up, the captain had brought the pinnace in near the place where I at first landed my rafts, and so landed just at my door.

I was at first ready to sink down with the surprise; for I saw my deliverance indeed visibly put into my hands, all things easy, and a large ship just ready to carry me away whither I pleased to go. At first, for some time, I was not able to answer him one word; but as he had taken me in his arms I held fast by him, or I should have fallen to the ground.

He perceived the surprise, and immediately pulls a bottle out of his pocket, and gave me a dram of cordial, which he had brought on purpose for me. After I had drank it, I sat down upon the ground; and though it brought me to myself, yet it was a good while before I could speak a word to him.

All this while the poor man was in as great an ecstasy as I, only not under any surprise, as I was; and he said a thousand kind tender things to me, to compose me and bring me to myself; but such was the flood of joy in my breast, that it put all my spirits into confusion. At last it broke out into tears, and in a little while after, I recovered my speech.

Then I took my turn, and embraced him as my deliverer, and we rejoiced together. I told him I looked upon him as a man sent from Heaven to deliver me, and that the whole transaction seemed to be a chain of wonders; that such things as these were the testimonies we had of a secret hand of Providence governing the world, and an evidence that the eyes of an Infinite Power could search into the remotest corner of the world, and send help to the miserable whenever He pleased.

I forgot not to lift up my heart in thankfulness to Heaven: and what heart could forbear to bless Him, who had not only in a miraculous manner provided for one in such a wilderness, and in such a desolate condition, but from whom every deliverance must always be acknowledged to proceed?

When he had talked a while the captain told me he had brought me some little refreshment, such as the ship afforded, and such as the wretches that had been so long his masters had not plundered him of. Upon this, he called aloud to the boat, and bid his men bring the things ashore that were for the governor; and indeed it was a present, as if I had been one not that was to be carried away along with them, but as if I had been to dwell upon the island still, and they were to go without me.

First he had brought me a case of bottles full of excellent cordial waters, six large bottles of Madeira wine (the bottles held two quarts apiece), two pound of excellent good tobacco, twelve good pieces of the ship's beef, and six pieces of pork, with a bag of peas, and about a hundredweight of biscuit.

He brought me also a box of sugar, a box of flour, a bag full of lemons, and two bottles of lime-juice, and abundance of other things. But besides these, and what was a thousand times more useful to me, he brought me six clean new shirts, six very good neckcloths, two pair of gloves, one pair of shoes, a hat, and one pair of stockings, and a very good suit of clothes of his own, which had been worn but very little. In a word, he clothed me from head to foot.

It was a very kind and agreeable present, as any one may imagine, to one in my circumstances. But never was anything in the world of that kind so unpleasant, awkward, and uneasy, as it was to me to wear such clothes at their first putting on.

§ *I make preparations for leaving the island. Part of the ship's crew are left behind. I bring away some relics of my long imprisonment. I arrive in England after thirty-five years' absence.*

AFTER these ceremonies were past, and after all his good things were brought into my little apartment, we began to consult what was to be done with the prisoners we had; for it was worth considering whether we might venture to take them away with us or no, especially two of them, whom we knew to be incorrigible and refractory to the last degree; and the captain said, he knew they were such rogues that there was no obliging them, and if he did carry them away it must be in irons as malefactors to be delivered over to justice at the first English colony he could come at. And I found that the captain himself was very anxious about it.

Upon this, I told him that if he desired it I durst undertake to bring the two men he spoke of to make it their own request that he should leave them upon the island. "I should be very glad of that," says the captain, "with all my heart."

"Well," says I, "I will send for them up, and talk with them for you." So I caused Friday and the two hostages—for they were now discharged, their comrades having performed their promise; I say, I caused them to go to the cave, and bring up the five men, pinioned as they were, to the bower, and keep them there till I came.

After some time I came thither dressed in my new habit; and now I was called governor again. Being all met, and the captain with me, I caused the men to be brought before me; and I told them I had

had a full account of their villainous behaviour to the captain, and how they had run away with the ship, and were preparing to commit further robberies, but that Providence had ensnared them in their own ways, and that they were fallen into the pit which they had digged for others.

I let them know that by my direction the ship had been seized, that she lay now in the road; and they might see by and by that their new captain had received the reward of his villainy, for that they might see him hanging at the yard-arm.

That as to them, I wanted to know what they had to say why I should not execute them as pirates taken in the fact, as by my commission they could not doubt I had authority to do.

One of them answered in the name of the rest, that they had nothing to say but this, that when they were taken the captain promised them their lives; and they humbly implored my mercy. But I told them I knew not what mercy to show them; for as for myself I had resolved to quit the island with all my men, and had taken passage with the captain to go for England; and as for the captain he could not carry them to England other than as prisoners in irons to be tried for mutiny and running away with the ship, the consequence of which they must needs know, would be the gallows: so that I could not tell which was best for them, unless they had a mind to take their fate in the island. If they desired that (I did not care, as I had liberty to leave it), I had some inclination to give them their lives, if they thought they could shift on shore.

They seemed very thankful for it, said they would much rather venture to stay there than to be carried to England to be hanged. So I left it on that issue.

However, the captain seemed to make some difficulty of it, as if he durst not leave them there. Upon this I seemed a little angry with the captain, and told him that they were my prisoners, not his; and that seeing I had offered them so much favour, I would be as good as my word; and that if he did not think fit to consent to it, I would set them at liberty as I found them, and if he did not like it, he might take them again if he could catch them.

Upon this they appeared very thankful, and I accordingly set them at liberty, and bade them retire into the woods to the place whence they came, and I would leave them some firearms, some ammunition, and some directions how they should live very well, if they thought fit.

Upon this I prepared to go on board the ship, but told the captain that I would stay that night to prepare my things, and desired him to go on board in the meantime and keep all right in the ship, and send the boat on shore the next day for me; ordering him in the meantime to cause the new captain, who was killed, to be hanged at the yard-arm that these men might see him.

When the captain was gone, I sent for the men up to me to my apartment, and entered seriously into discourse with them of their circumstances. I told them I thought they had made a right choice; that if the captain carried them away, they would certainly be hanged. I showed them the new captain hanging at the yard-arm of the ship, and told them they had nothing less to expect.

When they had all declared their willingness to stay, I then told them I would let them into the story of my living there, and put them into the way of making it easy to them. Accordingly I gave them the whole history of the place and of my coming to it; showed them my fortifications, the way I made my bread, planted my corn, cured my grapes; and in a word, all that was necessary to make them easy. I told them the story also of the sixteen Spaniards that were to be expected; for whom I left a letter, and made them promise to treat them in common with themselves.

I left them my firearms, namely, five muskets, three fowling-pieces, and three swords. I had above a barrel and a half of powder left; for after the first year or two I used but little and wasted none. I gave them a description of the way I managed the goats, and directions to milk and fatten them, and to make both butter and cheese.

In a word, I gave them every part of my own story. And I told them I would prevail with the captain to leave them two barrels of gunpowder more, and some garden-seeds, which I told them I would have been very glad of; also I gave them the bag of pease which the captain had brought me to eat, and bade them be sure to sow and increase them.

Having done all this I left them the next day, and went on board the ship. We prepared immediately to sail, but did not weigh that night. The next morning early two of the five men came swimming to the ship's side, and making a most lamentable complaint of the other three, begged to be taken into the ship, for God's sake, for they should be murdered, and begged the captain to take them on board though he hanged them immediately.

Upon this the captain pretended to have no power without me. But after some difficulty, and after their solemn promises of amendment, they were taken on board, and were some time after soundly whipped and pickled; after which they proved very honest and quiet fellows.

Some time after this the boat was ordered on shore, the tide being up, with the things promised to the men; to which the captain, at my intercession, caused their chests and clothes to be added; which they took, and were very thankful for. I also encouraged them, by telling them that if it lay in my way to send any vessel to take them in, I would not forget them.

When I took leave of this island I carried on board for relics the great goat-skin cap I had made, my umbrella, and my parrot; also I forgot not to take the money I formerly mentioned, which had lain by me so long useless that it was grown rusty, or tarnished, and could hardly pass for silver till it had been a little rubbed and handled; as also the money I found in the wreck of the Spanish ship.

And thus I left the island the 19th of December, as I found by the ship's account, in the year 1686, after I had been upon it eight and twenty years, two months, and nineteen days; being delivered from this second captivity the same day of the month that I first made my escape in the *Barco Longo* from among the Moors of Sallee.

In this vessel, after a long voyage, I arrived in England the 11th of June, in the year 1687, having been thirty and five years absent.

When I came to England, I was as perfect a stranger to all the world as if I had never been known there. My benefactor and faithful steward, who I had left in trust with my money, was alive, but had had great misfortunes in the world; was become a widow the second time, and very low in the world. I made her easy as to what she owed me, assuring her I would give her no trouble; but on the contrary, in gratitude to her former care and faithfulness to me, I relieved her as my little stock would afford, which at that time would indeed allow me to do but little for her; but I assured her I would never forget her former kindness to me; nor did I forget her when I had sufficient to help her, as shall be observed in its place.

§ *I visit Yorkshire, find greater part of my family dead. After-wards sail for Lisbon. Receive news about my Brazil planta-tion. The old captain's honesty and kindness. My sudden in-crease of wealth. Considerations concerning my future course.*

I WENT down afterwards into Yorkshire, but my father was dead, and my mother and all the family extinct, except that I found two sisters and two of the children of one of my brothers; and as I had been long ago given over for dead, there had been no provision made for me; so that, in a word, I found nothing to relieve or assist me; and that little money I had would not do much for me as to settling in the world.

I met with one piece of gratitude, indeed, which I did not expect; and this was, that the master of the ship, whom I had so happily de-livered, and by the same means saved the ship and cargo, having given a very handsome account to the owners of the manner how I had saved the lives of the men, and the ship, they invited me to meet them and some other merchants concerned, and all together made me a very handsome compliment upon the subject, and a present of al-most two hundred pounds sterling.

But after making several reflections upon the circumstances of my life, and how little way this would go towards settling me in the world, I resolved to go to Lisbon, and see if I might not come by some information of the state of my plantation in the Brazils, and of what was become of my partner, who I had reason to suppose had some years now given me over for dead.

With this view I took shipping for Lisbon, where I arrived in April following, my man Friday accompanying me very honestly in all these ramblings, and proving a most faithful servant upon all occasions.

When I came to Lisbon I found out by inquiry, and to my particular satisfaction, my old friend, the captain of the ship who first took me up at sea off the shore of Africa. He was now grown old and had left off the sea, having put his son, who was far from a young man, into his ship, and who still used the Brazil trade. The old man did not know me, and indeed I hardly knew him; but I soon brought him to my remembrance, and as soon brought myself to his remembrance when I told him who I was.

After some passionate expressions of the old acquaintance, I inquired, you may be sure, after my plantation and my partner. The old man told me he had not been in the Brazils for about nine years; but that he could assure me that when he came away my partner was living, but the trustees whom I had joined with him to take cognizance of my part were both dead. That, however, he believed that I would have a very good account of the improvement of the plantation: for that, upon the general belief of my being cast away and drowned, my trustees had given in the account of the produce of my part of the plantation to the procurator-fiscal, who had appropriated it, in case I never came to claim it; one third to the King, and two thirds to the monastery of St. Augustine, to be expended for the benefit of the poor, and for the conversion of the Indians to the Catholic faith; but that if I appeared, or any one for me, to claim the inheritance, it should be restored, only that the improvement or annual production being distributed to charitable uses could not be restored. But he assured me that the steward of the King's revenue (from lands) and the *proveedor,* or steward of the monastery, had taken great care all along that the incumbent, that is to say, my partner, gave every year a faithful account of the produce, of which they received duly my moiety.

I asked him if he knew to what height of improvement he had brought the plantation; and whether he thought it might be worth looking after? or whether, on my going thither, I should meet with no obstruction to my possessing my just right in the moiety?

He told me he could not tell exactly to what degree the plantation was improved, but this he knew, that my partner was grown exceeding rich upon the enjoying but one half of it; and that, to the best of his remembrance, he had heard that the King's third of my part, which was, it seems, granted away to some other monastery or religious house, amounted to above two hundred moidores a year: that as to my being restored to a quiet possession of it, there was no question to be made of that, my partner being alive to witness my title, and my name being also enrolled in the register of the country. Also, he told me that the survivors of my two trustees were very fair, honest people, and very wealthy; and he believed I would not only have their assistance for putting me in possession, but would find a very considerable sum of money in their hands for my account; being the produce of the farm while their fathers held the trust, and before it was given up as above, which, as he remembered, was for about twelve years.

I showed myself a little concerned and uneasy at this account, and inquired of the old captain how it came to pass that the trustees should thus dispose my effects when he knew that I had made my will, and had made him, the Portuguese captain, my universal heir, &c. He told me that was true; but that, as there was no proof of my being dead, he could not act as executor until some certain account should come of my death, and that, besides, he was not willing to intermeddle with a thing so remote; that it was true he had registered my will, and put in his claim; and could he have given any account of my being dead or alive, he would have acted by procuration, and taken possession of the *ingenio* (so they called the sugar-house), and had given his son, who was now at the Brazils, order to do it.

"But," says the old man, "I have one piece of news to tell you, which perhaps may not be so acceptable to you as the rest, and that is, that believing you were lost, and all the world believing so also, your partner and trustees did offer to account to me in your name for six or eight of the first years of profits, which I received; but there being at that time," says he, "great disbursements for increasing the works, building an *ingenio,* and buying slaves, it did not amount to near so much as afterwards it produced. However," says the old man, "I shall give you a true account of what I have received in all, and how I have disposed of it."

After a few days' further conference with this ancient friend, he brought me an account of the six first years' income of my plantation, signed by my partner and the merchants' trustees, being always delivered in goods, namely tobacco in roll, and sugar in chests, besides rum, molasses, &c., which is the consequence of a sugar work; and I found by this account that every year the income considerably increased, but, as above, the disbursement being large, the sum at first was small. However, the old man let me see that he was debtor to me 470 moidores of gold, besides 60 chests of sugar and 15 double rolls of tobacco, which were lost in his ship; he having been shipwrecked coming home to Lisbon about eleven years after my leaving the place.

The good man then began to complain of his misfortunes and how he had been obliged to make use of my money to recover his losses, and buy him a share in a new ship. "However, my old friend," says he, "you shall not want a supply in your necessity; and as soon as my son returns, you shall be fully satisfied."

Upon this he pulls out an old pouch, and gives me 160 Portugal moidores in gold; and giving me the writing of his title to the ship which his son was gone to the Brazils in, of which he was a quarter part owner and his son another, he puts them both into my hands for security of the rest.

I was too much moved with the honesty and kindness of the poor man to be able to bear this; and remembering what he had done for me, how he had taken me up at sea, and how generously he had used me on all occasions, and particularly how sincere a friend he was now to me, I could hardly refrain weeping at what he said to me. Therefore first I asked him if his circumstances admitted him to spare so much money at that time, and if it would not straiten him? He told me he could not say but it might straiten him a little; but, however, it was my money, and I might want it more than he.

Everything the good man said was full of affection, and I could hardly refrain from tears while he spoke. In short, I took an hundred of the moidores, and called for a pen and ink to give him a receipt for them; then I returned him the rest, and told him if ever I had possession of the plantation, I would return the other to him also, as indeed I afterwards did: and that as to the bill of sale of his part in his son's ship, I would not take it by any means; but that if I wanted the money, I found he was honest enough to pay me; and if I did not, but came to receive what he gave me reason to expect, I would never have a penny more from him.

When this was past, the old man began to ask me if he should put me into a method to make my claim to my plantation? I told him I thought to go over to it myself. He said I might do so if I pleased, but that if I did not, there were ways enough to secure my right, and immediately to appropriate the profits to my use. And as there were ships in the river of Lisbon just ready to go away to Brazil, he made me enter my name in a public register with his affidavit, affirming upon oath that I was alive, and that I was the same person who took up the land for the planting the said plantation at first.

This being regularly attested by a notary, and a procuration affixed, he directed me to send it with a letter of his writing to a merchant of his acquaintance at the place, and then proposed my staying with him till an account came of the return.

Never anything was more honourable than the proceedings upon this procuration; for in less than seven months I received a large packet from the survivors of my trustees the merchants, for whose account I went to sea, in which were the following particular letters and papers enclosed.

*First,* There was the account current of the produce of my farm or plantation from the year when their fathers had balanced with my old Portugal captain, being for six years. The balance appeared to be 1174 moidores in my favour.

*Secondly,* There was the account of four years more while they kept the effects in their hands, before the Government claimed the administration, as being the effects of a person not to be found, which they call civil death; and the balance of this, the value of the plantation increasing, amounted to as many crusadoes as made 3241 moidores.

*Thirdly,* There was the prior of the Augustine's account, who had received the profits for above fourteen years; but not being to account for what was disposed to the hospital, very honestly declared he had 872 moidores not distributed, which he acknowledged to my account; as to the King's part, that refunded nothing.

There was a letter of my partner's congratulating me very affectionately upon my being alive; giving me an account how the estate was improved, and what it produced a year, with a particular of the number of squares or acres that it contained, how planted, how many slaves there were upon it; and making two and twenty crossings for blessings, told me he had said so many Ave Marias to thank the Blessed Virgin that I was alive; inviting me very passionately to come over and take possession of my own, and in the meantime to give him orders to whom he should deliver my effects if I did not come myself; concluding with a hearty tender of his friendship and that of his family, and sent me as a present seven fine leopards' skins, which he had, it seems, received from Africa by some other ship which he had sent thither, and who, it seems, had made a better voyage than I. He sent me also five chests of excellent sweetmeats, and an hundred pieces of gold uncoined, not quite so large as moidores.

By the same fleet my two merchant trustees shipped me 1200 chests of sugar, 800 rolls of tobacco, and the rest of the whole account in gold.

I might well say now, indeed, that the latter end of Job was better than the beginning. It is impossible to express the flutterings of my very heart when I looked over these letters, and especially when I found all my wealth about me. For as the Brazil ships come all in fleets, the same ships which brought my letters brought my goods, and the effects were safe in the river before the letters came to my hand. In a word I turned pale, and grew sick; and had not the old man run and fetched me a cordial, I believe the sudden surprise of joy had overset nature and I had died upon the spot.

Nay, after that I continued very ill, and was so some hours, till a physician being sent for, and something of the real cause of my illness being known, he ordered me to be let blood, after which I had relief, and grew well; but I verily believe if it had not been eased by a vent given in that manner to the spirits, I should have died.

I was now master, all on a sudden, of above £5000 sterling in money; and had an estate, as I might well call it, in the Brazils of above £1000 a year, as sure as an estate of lands in England. And in a word, I was in a condition which I scarce knew how to understand, or how to compose myself for the enjoyment of it.

The first thing I did was to recompense my original benefactor, my good old captain, who had been first charitable to me in my distress, kind to me in my beginning, and honest to me at the end. I showed him all that was sent me; I told him that next to the providence of Heaven, which disposes all things, it was owing to him; and that it now lay on me to reward him, which I would do a hundredfold. So I first returned to him the 100 moidores I had received of him, then I sent for a notary, and caused him to draw up a general release or discharge for the 470 moidores which he had acknowledged he owed me, in the fullest and firmest manner possible: after which I caused a procuration to be drawn empowering him to be my receiver of the annual profits of my plantation, and appointing my partner to account to him, and make the returns by the usual fleets to him in my name; and a clause in the end, being a grant of 100 moidores a year to him during his life out of the effects, and 50 moidores a year to his son after him for his life. And thus I requited my old man.

I was now to consider which way to steer my course next, and what to do with the estate that Providence had thus put into my hand; and indeed I had more care upon my head now than I had in my silent state of life in the island, where I wanted nothing but what I had, and had nothing but what I wanted: whereas I had now a great charge upon me, and my business was how to secure it. I had never a cave now to hide my money in, or a place where it might lie without lock or key till it grew mouldy and tarnished before anybody would meddle with it. On the contrary I knew not where to put it, or who to trust with it. My old patron the captain, indeed, was honest, and that was the only refuge I had.

In the next place, my interest in the Brazils seemed to summon me thither; but now I could not tell how to think of going thither till I had settled my affairs, and left my effects in some safe hands behind me. At first I thought of my old friend the widow, who I knew was honest, and would be just to me; but then she was in years, and but poor, and for aught I knew might be in debt. So that, in a word, I had no way but to go back to England myself, and take my effects with me.

It was some months, however, before I resolved upon this; and therefore, as I had rewarded the old captain fully and to his satisfaction, who had been my former benefactor, so I began to think of my poor widow whose husband had been my first benefactor, and she while it was in her power my faithful steward and instructor. So the first thing I did, I got a merchant in Lisbon to write to his correspondent in London, not only to pay a bill, but to go find her out, and carry her in money an hundred pounds from me, and to talk with her, and comfort her in her poverty by telling her she should, if I lived, have a further supply. At the same time I sent my two sisters in the country each of them an hundred pounds, they being, though not in want, yet not in very good circumstances; one having been married and left a widow, and the other having a husband not so kind to her as he should be. But among all my relations or acquaintances I could not yet pitch upon one to whom I durst commit the gross of my stock, that I might go away to the Brazils and leave things safe behind me; and this greatly perplexed me.

So I resolved at last to go to England with it; where, if I arrived, I concluded I should make some acquaintance, or find some relations that would be faithful to me. And accordingly I prepared to go for England with all my wealth.

In order to prepare things for my going home, I first, the Brazil fleet being just going away, resolved to give answers suitable to the just and faithful account of things I had from thence. And, first, to the prior of St. Augustine I wrote a letter full of thanks for their just dealings, and the offer of the 872 moidores which was indisposed of; which I desired might be given, 500 to the monastery, and 372 to the poor as the prior should direct, desiring the good padre's prayers for me, and the like. I wrote next a letter of thanks to my two trustees, with all the acknowledgment that so much justice and honesty called for. As for sending them any present, they were far above having any occasion of it. Lastly, I wrote to my partner, acknowledging his industry in the improving the plantation, and his integrity in increasing the stock of the works; giving him instructions for his future government of my part, according to the powers I had left with my old patron, to whom I desired him to send whatever became due to me till he should hear from me more particularly; assuring him that it was my intention, not only to come to him, but to settle myself there for the remainder of my life. To this I added a very handsome present of some Italian silks for his wife and two daughters, for such the captain's son informed me he had; with two pieces of fine English broadcloth, the best I could get in Lisbon, five pieces of black baize, and some Flanders lace of a good value.

Having thus settled my affairs, sold my cargo, and turned all my effects into good bills of exchange, my next difficulty was which way to go to England. I had been accustomed enough to the sea, and yet I had a strange aversion to going to England by sea at that time; and though I could give no reason for it, yet the difficulty increased upon me so much that though I had once shipped my baggage in order to go, yet I altered my mind, and that not once, but two or three times.

It is true, I had been very unfortunate by sea, and this might be some of the reason; but let no man slight the strong impulses of his own thoughts in cases of such moment. Two of the ships which I had singled out to go in; I mean, more particularly singled out than any other, that is to say, so as in one of them to put my things on board, and in the other to have agreed with the captain; I say, two of these ships miscarried, namely, one was taken by the Algerines, and the other was cast away on the Start near Torbay, and all the people drowned except three: so that in either of those vessels I had been made miserable; and in which most was hard to say.

Having been thus harassed in my thoughts, my old pilot, to whom I communicated everything, pressed me earnestly not to go by sea, but either to go by land to the Groyne, and cross over the Bay of Biscay to Rochelle, from whence it was but an easy and safe journey by land to Paris, and so to Calais and Dover; or to go up to Madrid, and so all the way by land through France. In a word, I was so prepossessed against my going by sea at all, except from Calais to Dover, that I resolved to travel all the way by land; which, as I was not in haste and did not value the charge, was by much the pleasanter way. And to make it more so, my old captain brought an English gentleman, the son of a merchant in Lisbon, who was willing to travel with me; after which we picked up two more English merchants also, and two young Portuguese gentlemen, the last going to Paris only; so that we were in all six of us, and five servants; the two merchants and the two Portuguese contenting themselves with one servant between two to save the charge; and as for me, I got an English sailor to travel with me as a servant, besides my man Friday, who was too much a stranger to be capable of supplying the place of a servant on the road.

§ *I set out by land from Lisbon for England. We meet with severe weather, and are attacked by wolves. Friday's adventure with a bear. We are again attacked by wolves. I arrive safe in England. My Brazil plantation sold. I marry and try to settle in England.*

In this manner I set out from Lisbon; and our company being all very well mounted and armed, we made a little troop whereof they did me the honour to call me captain, as well because I was the oldest man as because I had two servants, and indeed was the original of the whole journey.

As I have troubled you with none of my sea journals, so I shall trouble you now with none of my land journal. But some adventures that happened to us in this tedious and difficult journey I must not omit.

When we came to Madrid, we being all of us strangers to Spain, were willing to stay some time to see the court of Spain, and to see what was worth observing; but it being the latter part of the summer we hastened away, and set out from Madrid about the middle of October. But when we came to the edge of Navarre, we were alarmed at several towns on the way with the account that so much snow was fallen on the French side of the mountains that several travellers were obliged to come back to Pampeluna, after having attempted at an extreme hazard to pass on.

When we came to Pampeluna itself we found it so indeed; and to me that had been always used to a hot climate, and indeed to countries where we could scarce bear any clothes on, the cold was insufferable. Nor, indeed, was it more painful than it was surprising to come but ten days before out of the Old Castile, where the weather was not only warm but very hot, and immediately to feel a wind from the Pyrenean mountains so very keen, so severely cold, as to be intolerable, and to endanger benumbing and perishing of our fingers and toes. Poor Friday was really frighted when he saw the mountains all covered with snow and felt cold weather, which he had never seen or felt before in his life.

To mend the matter, when we came to Pampeluna it continued snowing with so much violence and so long that the people said winter was come before its time: and the roads, which were difficult before, were now quite impassable; for, in a word, the snow lay in some places too thick for us to travel, and being not hard frozen, as is the case in northern countries, there was no going without being in danger of being buried alive every step. We stayed no less than twenty days at Pampeluna; when, seeing the winter coming on, and no likelihood of its being better, for it was the severest winter all over Europe that had been known in the memory of man, I proposed that we should all go away to Fontarabia, and there take shipping for Bordeaux, which was a very little voyage.

But while we were considering this, there came in four French gentlemen, who, having been stopped on the French side of the passes as we were on the Spanish, had found out a guide who, traversing the country near the head of Languedoc, had brought them over the mountains by such ways that they were not much incommoded with the snow; and where they met with snow in any quantity, they said it was frozen hard enough to bear them and their horses. We sent for this guide, who told us he would undertake to carry us the same way with no hazard from the snow, provided we were armed sufficiently to protect us from wild beasts; for he said upon these great snows it was frequent for some wolves to show themselves at the foot of the mountains, being made ravenous for want of food, the ground being covered with snow. We told him we were well enough prepared for such creatures, as they were, if he would ensure us from a kind of two-legged wolves, which we were told we were in most danger from, especially on the French side of the mountains. He satisfied us there was no danger of that kind in the way that we were to go: so we readily agreed to follow him; as did also twelve other gentlemen with their servants, some French, some Spanish, who, as I said, had attempted to go, and were obliged to come back again.

Accordingly, we all set out from Pampeluna with our guide, on the 15th of November. And indeed I was surprised when, instead of going forward, he came directly back with us on the same road that we came from Madrid, above twenty miles; when, being past two rivers, and come into the plain country, we found ourselves in a warm climate again, where the country was pleasant and no snow to be seen. But on a sudden, turning to the left, he approached the mountains another way; and though, it is true, the hills and precipices looked dreadful, yet he made so many tours, such meanders, and led us by such winding ways, that we were insensibly past the height of the mountains without being much encumbered with the snow. And all on a sudden he showed us the pleasant, fruitful provinces of Languedoc and Gascony, all green and flourishing; though, indeed, it was at a great distance, and we had some rough way to pass yet.

We were a little uneasy, however, when we found it snowed one whole day and a night so fast that we could not travel; but he bid us be easy, we should soon be past it all. We found, indeed, that we began to descend every day, and to come more north than before; and so, depending upon our guide we went on.

It was about two hours before night, when, our guide being something before us and not just in sight, out rushed three monstrous wolves, and after them a bear, out of a hollow way adjoining to a thick wood. Two of the wolves flew upon the guide; and had he been half a mile before us he had been devoured indeed before we could have helped him. One of them fastened upon his horse; and the other attacked the man with that violence that he had not time or not presence of mind enough to draw his pistol, but hallooed and cried out to us most lustily. My man Friday being next to me, I bid him ride up and see what was the matter. As soon as Friday came in sight of the man, he hallooed as loud as the other, "Oh, master! oh, master!" but, like a bold fellow, rode directly up to the poor man, and with his pistol shot the wolf that attacked him into the head.

It was happy for the poor man that it was my man Friday; for he having been used to that kind of creature in his country, had no fear upon him, but went close up to him, and shot him as above: whereas any of us would have fired at a farther distance, and have perhaps either missed the wolf or endangered shooting the man.

But it was enough to have terrified a bolder man than I, and indeed it alarmed all our company, when with the noise of Friday's pistol we heard on both sides the dismallest howling of wolves, and the noise redoubled by the echo of the mountains, that it was to us as if there had been a prodigious multitude of them: and perhaps indeed there was not such a few as that we had no cause of apprehensions.

However, as Friday had killed this wolf, the other that had fastened upon the horse left him immediately, and fled; having happily fastened upon his head, where the bosses of the bridle had stuck in his teeth, so that he had not done him much hurt. The man, indeed, was most hurt, for the raging creature had bit him twice, once on the arm, and the other time a little above his knee; and he was just as it were tumbling down by the disorder of his horse, when Friday came up and shot the wolf.

It is easy to suppose that at the noise of Friday's pistol we all mended our pace, and rid up as fast as the way, which was very difficult, would give us leave, to see what was the matter. As soon as we came clear of the trees, which blinded us before, we saw clearly what had been the case, and how Friday had disengaged the poor guide, though we did not presently discern what kind of creature it was he had killed.

But never was a fight managed so hardily and in such a surprising manner as that which followed between Friday and the bear, which gave us all (though at first we were surprised and afraid for him) the greatest diversion imaginable. As the bear is a heavy, clumsy creature, and does not gallop as the wolf does, who is swift and light, so he has two particular qualities, which generally are the rule of his actions. First, as to men, who are not his proper prey; I say, not his proper prey, because, though I cannot say what excessive hunger might do, which was now their case, the ground being all covered with snow; but as to men, he does not usually attempt them unless they first attack him. On the contrary, if you meet him in the woods, if you don't meddle with him he won't meddle with you. But then you must take care to be very civil to him, and give him the road; for he is a very nice gentleman, he won't go a step out of his way for a prince. Nay, if you are really afraid, your best way is to look another way and keep going on; for sometimes if you stop and stand still, and look steadily at him, he takes it for an affront. But if you throw or toss anything at him, and it hits him, though it were but a stick as big as your finger, he takes it for an affront, and sets all his other business aside to pursue his revenge; for he will have satisfaction in point of honour. That is his first quality. The next is, that if he be once affronted, he will never leave you night or day till he has his revenge, but follows at a good round rate till he overtakes you.

My man Friday had delivered our guide, and when we came up to him he was helping him off his horse—for the man was both hurt and frighted, and indeed the last more than the first—when, on a sudden, we spied the bear come out of the wood. And a vast monstrous one it was, the biggest by far that ever I saw. We were all a little surprised, when we saw him; but when Friday saw him, it was easy to see joy and courage in the fellow's countenance. "Oh! oh! oh!" says Friday, three times, pointing to him; "oh, master! you give me te leave; me shakee te hand with him; me make you good laugh."

I was surprised to see the fellow so pleased. "You fool you," says I, "he will eat you up!" "Eatee me up! eatee me up!" says Friday, twice over again; "me eatee him up; me make you good laugh. You all stay here; me show you good laugh." So down he sits, and gets his boots off in a moment, and put on a pair of pumps (as we call the flat shoes they wear, and which he had in his pocket), gives my other servant his horse, and with his gun away he flew swift like the wind.

The bear was walking softly on, and offered to meddle with no-body, till Friday, coming pretty near, calls to him, as if the bear could understand him. "Hark ye! hark ye!" says Friday; "me speakee wit you." We followed at a distance; for now, being come down on the Gascony side of the mountains, we were entered a vast great forest, where the country was plain and pretty open, though many trees in it scattered here and there.

Friday, who had, as we say, the heels of the bear, came up with him quickly, and takes up a great stone and throws at him, and hit him just on the head, but did him no more harm than if he had thrown it against a wall. But it answered Friday's end; for the rogue was so void of fear that he did it purely to make the bear follow him, and show us some laugh, as he called it. As soon as the bear felt the stone and saw him, he turns about and comes after him, taking devil-ish long strides, and shuffling along at a strange rate, so as would have put a horse to a middling gallop. Away runs Friday, and takes his course as if he run towards us for help. So we all resolved to fire at once upon the bear, and deliver my man; though I was angry at him heartily for bringing the bear back upon us when he was going about his own business another way. And especially I was angry that he had turned the bear upon us and then run away; and I called out: "You dog," said I, "is this your making us laugh? Come away, and take your horse, that we may shoot the creature." He hears me and cries out, "No shoot! no shoot! Stand still; you get much laugh." And as the nimble creature run two foot for the beast's one, he turned on a sudden on one side of us and seeing a great oak-tree fit for his purpose, he beckoned to us to follow; and doubling his pace, he gets nimbly up the tree, laying his gun down upon the ground at about five or six yards from the bottom of the tree.

The bear soon came to the tree, and we followed at a distance. The first thing he did he stopped at the gun, smelt to it, but let it lie; and up he scrambles into the tree, climbing like a cat, though so monstrously heavy. I was amazed at the folly, as I thought it, of my man, and could not for my life see anything to laugh at yet, till seeing the bear get up the tree, we all rode nearer to him.

When we came to the tree, there was Friday got out to the small end of a large limb of the tree, and the bear got about half-way to him. As soon as the bear got out to that part where the limb of the tree was weaker, "Ha," says he to us, "now you see me teachee the bear dance." So he falls a-jumping and shaking the bough, at which the bear began to totter, but stood still, and began to look behind him to see how he should get back; then, indeed, we did laugh heartily. But Friday had not done with him by a great deal. When he sees him stand still, he calls out to him again, as if he had supposed the bear could speak English, "What! you no come farther? Pray you come farther." So he left jumping and shaking the tree; and the bear, just as if he had understood what he said, did come a little farther; then he fell a jumping again, and the bear stopped again.

We thought now was a good time to knock him on the head, and I called to Friday to stand still and we would shoot the bear. But he cried out earnestly, "O pray! O pray! no shoot; me shoot by and then." He would have said by-and-by. However, to shorten the story, Friday danced so much, and the bear stood so ticklish, that we had laughing enough indeed, but still could not imagine what the fellow would do: for first we thought he depended upon shaking the bear off; and we found the bear was too cunning for that too, for he would not go out far enough to be thrown down, but clings fast with his great broad claws and feet, so that we could not imagine what would be the end of it, and where the jest would be at last.

But Friday put us out of doubt quickly; for seeing the bear cling fast to the bough, and that he would not be persuaded to come any farther, "Well, well," says Friday, "you no come farther, me go, me go, you no come to me, me go come to you." And upon this he goes out to the smallest end of the bough, where it would bend with his weight, and gently lets himself down by it, sliding down the bough, till he came near enough to jump down on his feet, and away he run to his gun, takes it up, and stands still.

"Well," said I to him, "Friday, what will you do now? Why don't you shoot him?" "No shoot," says Friday, "no yet; me shoot now, me no kill; me stay, give you one more laugh." And indeed so he did, as you will see presently: for when the bear saw his enemy gone, he comes back from the bough where he stood, but did it mighty leisurely, looking behind him every step, and coming backward till he got into the body of the tree. Then with the same hinder end foremost, he came down the tree, grasping it with his claws, and moving one foot at a time, very leisurely. At this juncture, and just before he could set his hind feet upon the ground Friday stepped up close to him, clapped the muzzle of his piece into his ear, and shot him dead as a stone.

Then the rogue turned about to see if we did not laugh, and when he saw we were pleased by our looks, he falls a-laughing himself very loud. "So we kill bear in my country," says Friday. "So you kill them!" says I. "Why, you have no guns." "No," says he; "no gun, but shoot, great much long arrow."

This was indeed a good diversion to us; but we were still in a wild place, and our guide very much hurt, and what to do we hardly knew. The howling of wolves run much in my head; and indeed, except the noise I once heard on the shore of Africa, of which I have said something already, I never heard anything that filled me with so much horror.

These things and the approach of night called us off, or else, as Friday would have had us, we should certainly have taken the skin of this monstrous creature off, which was worth saving; but we had three leagues to go, and our guide hastened us, so we left him, and went forward on our journey.

The ground was still covered with snow, though not so deep and dangerous as on the mountains; and the ravenous creatures, as we heard afterwards, were come down to the forest and plain country, pressed by hunger to seek for food; and had done a great deal of mischief in the villages, where they surprised the country people, killed a great many of their sheep and horses, and some people too.

We had one dangerous place to pass, which our guide told us, if there were any more wolves in the country, we should find them there; and this was in a small plain surrounded with woods on every side, and a long narrow defile or lane, which we were to pass to get through the wood, and then we should come to the village where we were to lodge.

It was within half an hour of sunset when we entered the first wood, and a little after sunset when we came into the plain. We met with nothing in the first wood except that in a little plain within the wood, which was not above two furlongs over, we saw five great wolves across the road, full speed one after another, as if they had been in chase of some prey, and had it in view. They took no notice of us, and were gone, and out of our sight in a few moments.

Upon this our guide, who, by the way, was a wretched faint-hearted fellow, bid us keep in a ready posture, for he believed there were more wolves a-coming.

We kept our arms ready, and our eyes about us; but we saw no more wolves till we came through that wood, which was near half a league, and entered the plain. As soon as we came into the plain we had occasion enough to look about us. The first object we met with was a dead horse—that is to say, a poor horse which the wolves had killed—and at least a dozen of them at work, we could not say eating of him, but picking of his bones rather, for they had eaten up all the flesh before.

We did not think fit to disturb them at their feast; neither did they take much notice of us. Friday would have let fly at them, but I would not suffer him by any means; for I found we were like to have more business upon our hands than we were aware of. We were not gone half over the plain but we began to hear the wolves howl in the wood on our left in a frightful manner; and presently after we saw about a hundred coming on directly towards us, all in a body, and most of them in a line as regularly as an army drawn up by experienced officers. I scarce knew in what manner to receive them; but found to draw ourselves in a close line was the only way; so we formed in a moment. But that we might not have too much interval, I ordered that only every other man should fire, and that the others who had not fired should stand ready to give them a second volley immediately if they continued to advance upon us; and that then those who had fired at first should not pretend to load their fuses again, but stand ready with every one a pistol, for we were all armed with a fusee and a pair of pistols each man; so we were by this method able to fire six volleys, half of us at a time. However, at present we had no necessity; for upon firing the first volley the enemy made a full stop, being terrified as well with the noise as with the fire. Four of them being shot into the head dropped, several others were wounded, and went bleeding off, as we could see by the snow. I found they stopped, but did not immediately retreat; whereupon remembering that I had been told that the fiercest creatures were terrified at the voice of a man, I caused all our company to halloo as loud as we could; and I found the notion not altogether mistaken, for upon our shout they began to retire and turn about. Then I ordered a second volley to be fired in their rear, which put them to the gallop, and away they went to the woods.

This gave us leisure to charge our pieces again, and that we might lose no time, we kept going; but we had but little more than loaded our fusees, and put ourselves into a readiness, when we heard a terrible noise in the same wood on our left, only that it was farther onward the same way we were to go.

The night was coming on, and the light began to be dusky, which made it worse on our side; but the noise increasing, we could easily perceive that it was the howling and yelling of those hellish creatures; and on a sudden we perceived two or three troops of wolves, one on our left, one behind us, and one or our front; so that we seemed to be surrounded with them. However, as they did not fall upon us, we kept our way forward as fast as we could make our horses go, which, the way being very rough, was only a good large trot; and in this manner we came in view of the entrance of a wood through which we were to pass at the farther side of the plain; but we were greatly surprised when, coming nearer the lane or pass, we saw a confused number of wolves standing just at the entrance.

On a sudden, at another opening of the wood, we heard the noise of a gun; and looking that way, out rushed a horse with a saddle and a bridle on him, flying like the wind, and sixteen or seventeen wolves after him, full speed; indeed, the horse had the heels of them, but as we supposed that he could not hold it at that rate, we doubted not but they would get up with him at last, and no question but they did.

But here we had a most horrible sight; for riding up to the entrance where the horse came out, we found the carcass of another horse, and of two men, devoured by the ravenous creatures; and one of the men was no doubt the same who we heard fired the gun, for there lay a gun just by him fired off; but as to the man, his head and the upper part of his body was eaten up.

This filled us with horror, and we knew not what course to take; but the creatures resolved us soon, for they gathered about us presently in hopes of prey; and I verily believe there were three hundred of them. It happened very much to our advantage that at the entrance into the wood, but a little way from it, there lay some large timber trees, which had been cut down the summer before, and I suppose lay there for carriage. I drew my little troop in among those trees, and placing ourselves in a line behind one long tree, I advised them all to light, and keeping that tree before us for a breastwork, to stand in a triangle, or three fronts, enclosing our horses in the centre.

We did so, and it was well we did; for never was a more furious charge than the creatures made upon us in the place. They came on us with a growling kind of a noise, and mounted the piece of timber, which, as I said, was our breastwork, as if they were only rushing upon their prey; and this fury of theirs, it seems, was principally occasioned by their seeing our horses behind us, which was the prey they aimed at. I order our men to fire as before, every other man; and they took their aim so sure, that indeed they killed several of the wolves at the first volley; but there was a necessity to keep a continual firing, for they came on like devils, those behind pushing on those before.

When we had fired our second volley of our fusees, we thought they stopped a little, and I hoped they would have gone off; but it was but a moment, for others came forward again: so we fired two volleys of our pistols, and I believe in these four firings we had killed seventeen or eighteen of them, and lamed twice as many; yet they came on again.

I was loath to spend our last shot too hastily; so I called my servant —not my man Friday, for he was better employed; for, with the greatest dexterity imaginable, he had charged my fusee and his own while we were engaged; but, as I said, I called my other man, and giving him a horn of powder, I bade him lay a train all along the piece of timber, and let it be a large train. He did so, and had but just time to get away when the wolves came up to it, and some were got up upon it; when I, snapping an uncharged pistol, close to the powder, set it on fire. Those that were upon the timber were scorched with it, and six or seven of them fell, or rather jumped in among us, with the force and fright of the fire. We despatched these in an instant, and the rest were so frighted with the light, which the night, for it was now very near dark, made more terrible, that they drew back a little.

Upon which I ordered our last pistol to be fired off in one volley, and after that we gave a shout. Upon this the wolves turned tail, and we sallied immediately upon near twenty lame ones, who we found struggling on the ground, and fell a-cutting them with our swords; which answered our expectation, for the crying and howling they made was better understood by their fellows, so that they all fled and left us.

We had, first and last, killed about threescore of them; and had it been daylight, we had killed many more. The field of battle being thus cleared, we made forward again; for we had still near a league to go. We heard the ravenous creatures howl and yell in the woods, as we went, several times, and sometimes we fancied we saw some of them; but the snow dazzling our eyes, we were not certain; so in about an hour more we came to the town where we were to lodge, which we found in a terrible fright, and all in arms; for it seems that, the night before, the wolves and some bears had broken into the village in the night, and put them in a terrible fright, and they were obliged to keep guard night and day, but especially in the night, to preserve their cattle, and indeed their people.

The next morning our guide was so ill, and his limbs swelled with the rankling of his two wounds, that he could go no farther; so we were obliged to take a new guide there, and go to Toulouse, where we found a warm climate, a fruitful, pleasant country, and no snow, no wolves, or anything like them. But when we told our story at Toulouse, they told us it was nothing but what was ordinary in the great forest at the foot of the mountains, especially when the snow lay on the ground. But they inquired much what kind of a guide we had gotten that would venture to bring us that way in such a severe season; and told us it was surprising we were not all devoured. When we told them how we placed ourselves, and the horses in the middle, they blamed us exceedingly, and told us it was fifty to one but we had been all destroyed: for it was the sight of the horses which made the wolves so furious, seeing their prey; and at other times they are really afraid of a gun; but being excessively hungry, and raging on that account, the eagerness to come at the horses had made them senseless of danger; and that if we had not by the continued fire, and at last by the stratagem of the train of powder, mastered them, it had been great odds but that we had been torn to pieces; whereas had we been content to have sat still on horseback, and fired as horsemen, they would not have taken the horses for so much their own, when men were on their backs, as otherwise: and withal they told, that at last, if we had stood all together, and left our horses, they would have been so eager to have devoured them, that we might have come off safe, especially having our firearms in our hands, and being so many in number.

For my part I was never so sensible of danger in my life; for seeing above three hundred devils come roaring and openmouthed to devour us, and having nothing to shelter us or retreat to, I gave myself over for lost; and as it was, I believe I shall never care to cross those mountains again. I think I would much rather go a thousand leagues by sea, though I were sure to meet with a storm once a week.

I have nothing uncommon to take notice of in my passage through France, nothing but what other travellers have given an account of with much more advantage than I can. I travelled from Toulouse to Paris, and without any considerable stay, came to Calais, and landed safe at Dover, the 14th of January, after having had a severe cold season to travel in.

I was now come to the centre of my travels, and had in a little time all my new discovered estate safe about me, the bills of exchange which I brought with me having been very currently paid.

My principal guide and privy counsellor was my good ancient widow, who, in gratitude for the money I had sent her, thought no pains too much or care too great to employ for me: and I trusted her so entirely with everything that I was perfectly easy as to the security of my effects; and indeed I was very happy from my beginning, and now to the end, in the unspotted integrity of this good gentlewoman. So I resolved to stay at home, and if I could find means for it, to dispose of my plantation.

To this purpose I wrote to my old friend at Lisbon; who in return gave me notice that he could easily dispose of it there, but that if I thought fit to give him leave to offer it in my name to the two merchants, the survivors of my trustees, who lived in the Brazils, who must fully understand the value of it, who lived just upon the spot, and who I knew were very rich, so that he believed they would be fond of buying it, he did not doubt but I should make 4000 to 5000 pieces of eight the more for it.

Accordingly I agreed, gave him order to offer it to them, and he did so; and in about eight months more, the ship being then returned, he sent me an account that they had accepted the offer, and had remitted 33,000 pieces of eight to a correspondent of theirs at Lisbon to pay for it.

In return, I signed the instrument of sale in the form which they sent from Lisbon, and sent it to my old man, who sent me bills of exchange for 32,800 pieces of eight to me for the estate; reserving the payment of 100 moidores a year to him, the old man, during his life, and 50 moidores afterwards to his son for his life, which I had promised them, which the plantation was to make good as a rent-charge. And thus I have given the first part of a life of fortune and adventure, a life of Providence's checker-work, and of a variety which the world will seldom be able to show the like of. Beginning foolishly, but closing much more happily than any part of it ever gave me leave so much as to hope for.

Any one would think that in this state of complicated good fortune I was past running any more hazards; and so indeed I had been, if other circumstances had concurred; but I was inured to a wandering life, had no family, not many relations, nor, however rich, had I contracted much acquaintance; and though I had sold my estate in the Brazils, yet I could not keep the country out of my head, and had a great mind to be upon the wing again; especially I could not resist the strong inclination I had to see my island, and to know if the poor Spaniards were in being there, and how the rogues I had left there had used them.

My true friend the widow earnestly dissuaded me from it, and so far prevailed with me that for almost seven years she prevented my running abroad; during which time I took my two nephews, the children of one of my brothers, into my care. The eldest having something of his own, I bred up as a gentleman, and gave him a settlement of some addition to his estate after my decease. The other I put out to a captain of a ship; and after five years, finding him a sensible, bold, enterprising young fellow, I put him into a good ship, and sent him to sea. And this young fellow afterwards drew me in, as old as I was, to further adventures myself.

In the meantime, I in part settled myself here; for, first of all, I married, and that not either to my disadvantage or dissatisfaction, and had three children, two sons and one daughter. But my wife dying, and my nephew coming home with good success from a voyage to Spain, my inclination to go abroad and his importunity prevailed, and engaged me to go in his ship as a private trader to the East Indies. This was in the year 1694.

In this voyage I visited my new colony in the island, saw my successors the Spaniards, had the whole story of their lives, and of the villains I left there; how at first they insulted the poor Spaniards; how they afterwards agreed, disagreed, united, separated; and how at last the Spaniards were obliged to use violence with them; how they were subjected to the Spaniards; how honestly the Spaniards used them: a history, if it were entered into, as full of variety and wonderful accidents as my own part, particularly also as to their battles with the Caribbeans, who landed several times upon the island; and as to the improvement they made upon the island itself; and how five of them made an attempt upon the mainland, and brought away eleven men and five women prisoners, by which, at my coming, I found about twenty young children on the island.

Here I stayed about twenty days, left them supplies of all necessary things, and particularly of arms, powder, shot, clothes, tools, and two workmen, which I brought from England with me; namely, a carpenter and a smith.

Besides this, I shared the island into parts with them, reserved to myself the property of the whole, but gave them such parts respectively as they agreed on; and having settled all things with them, and engaged them not to leave the place, I left them there.

From thence I touched at the Brazils, from whence I sent a bark, which I bought there, with more people to the island; and in it, besides other supplies, I sent seven women, being such as I found proper for service, or for wives to such as would take them. As to the Englishmen, I promised them to send them some women from England, with a good cargo of necessaries, if they would apply themselves to planting; which I afterwards performed. And the fellows proved very honest and diligent after they were mastered, and had their properties set apart for them. I sent them also from the Brazils five cows, three of them being big with calf, some sheep, and some hogs; which, when I came again, were considerably increased.